To Rick

AZTEC
Love Song

HARZ MAY '11

MARTY ROSS

Weathervane Press

Weathervane Press

Published in 2009 by Weathervane Press
92 Lime Grove, Newark, Notts NG24 4AH
www.weathervanepress.co.uk

ISBN 978 09562193 2 9

Cover background image by Witr
www.dreamstime.com

Printed in the United Kingdom
by Lightning Source UK Ltd.

"If I hide my face for sorrow, there is cause enough... and if I cover it for secret sin, what mortal might not do the same?"
-- Nathaniel Hawthorne, *The Minister's Black Veil*

One

"Okay, so I'm a murderer - deal with it," I declared, through sheer force of stare, to the blue-rinsed old bag eyeballing my unfamiliar presence across the bus's aisle. Murderer-*ess*... I corrected myself, relishing that snaky hiss at the end.

Not that I *was* a murderess, I conceded as the old woman turned away. Not thereabouts, anyway, not yet - although the bloodshed was already so firmly planned, so inescapable for the bleeder in question, that I might as well have been wearing my victim's skin for a pashmina.

With the rain outside ceaseless and the bus's heater cranked high, I had to keep wiping condensation from the window to get any sense of where we were. My latest wipe, as the bus dipped down a hill, revealed neatly-trimmed bushes bordering spacious gardens and spick-and-span housefronts, the whole scene so familiar that it was like seeing a ghost solidify in a haunted mirror. I was back in Newton Mearns and my stop was near. With a tremor in my hand as I tinged the bell, I got off.

A short walk through a narrow lane brought me to the sprawl of houses below Mearns Castle. Hood and umbrella raised, I wandered a roundabout route uphill. There were even more houses thereabouts than I remembered, spots which had been fields when I was a kid now buried under tastefully grand housing developments, a couple of them with *his* name attached to a board in front. I went nowhere near his house itself; I had to renew acquaintance with my own first.

I emerged at the suburb's upper limit, facing a stretch of fields into which the builders hadn't yet sunk their diggers. I continued uphill on the road bordering those fields, a few saturated cows shlurping their hooves through a boggy hollow, the last surviving farmhouse clenching a lonely gloom behind the windows in its whitewashed façade.

I soon reached the hill's summit, the houses on my near side giving way first to the drive of the castle and then to the secondary school, the extra wing of concrete block architecture this had gained since my days there blocking the castle from view. You, or your ghost, called to me from the puddled emptiness of the playground. Not just yet, my love - I told you, and walked on.

Crossing the road, passing the fenced-in sports pitches which had eaten up another field, I continued along the narrower road bisecting the farmland beyond. Soon I saw our house and its outbuildings, sprouting like a clump of mushrooms at the far end of an untidy field. Turning the next corner, confronting the clubhouse of the golf course which had claimed the fields that once faced our house, I proceeded along the narrowing road, the old house looking so like itself that it might have been a few hours - the length of a school day, maybe - since I stood before it last. And yet, as I drew closer, it revealed itself as ravaged by the actual time gone by.

On the ground floor, the door and windows were boarded up, those upper windows that weren't boarded naked of glass, the interiors utterly black beneath the flaking red paint of the gabling. Checking no club-swinger on the golf course was ogling me, I waded through the overgrown grass to the wreck of the cowshed adjoining the house's far end. This, doorless, had been left wide open to the suburb's tame line in graffiti artists: 'JAMIE-D' spray-painted in red on one wall, 'DAN MASSIVE' on another, the concrete floor littered with crumbled-off stonework, rags of old silage bags, sweet wrappers and shattered beer and vodka bottles.

The inner doorway, connecting this shed to the kitchen of the house, stood doorless, a careful ascent of the single glass-littered step taking me into the ruin time and other factors had made of my childhood home, much of the built-in furniture still standing but ripped apart, graffiti-streaked, mouldering. The carpets had been torn about where not hacked away entirely, exposing gaps in the floorboards beneath, some of these yielding watery hints of the long-flooded cellar below. The faded wallpaper hung shredded where not sagged, the floor scattered with shattered glass, with broken-off ends of the furnishings, with rat-droppings and fragments of ceiling.

After stuffing my smaller rucksack, the one I would need for my escape, into the cupboard beneath the sink, I ventured through to the little hallway at the far end of the ground floor. The stairs climbing from that hall had lost all but a pole or two of their banister, the still-carpeted steps heaped with yet more broken glass and collapsed plaster. I risked the ascent, steeled for every step to snap under me.

If everywhere below lay in a riot of odds and ends, upstairs the dereliction bore an austere calm, the bedrooms empty of all but the remaining boards on their windows, the faint clingings of pattern to their wallpaper, and - of course - the stir and reaching forth of memories, crowding thicker upon me in this calm than in the chaos below.

I entered *your* room. This was the darkest, hollowest room of all, featureless save for the bulging of ivy through the single broken window on the back wall, the pale light from the yard making the leaves gleam like the claw of some outsized lizard scaling the outside wall.

I closed my eyes, breathed you in, sifted your scent past the rotting of wood and stone. I sank to my knees. There was broken glass amid the carpet's fibre; I felt it bite through my tights to the flesh and bone of my knees; I wept.

I crawled, huddled, into the darkest corner of the room, sobbed your name again and again. The stench of all that had happened fattened in my nostrils, dragged tighter the walls, forced fuller in my heart that scream which, soon, was going to set bleeding an eardrum or two, eardrums just for starters.

Outside, I caught the thwack of a golf club on the course opposite. I wondered if it was his. That would have been sweet: his nibs swaggering about in his Slazenger V-neck, smug and secure and set for, oh, such a fall, so close to where I sat, every tear I shed digging deeper the pit in which I'd soon see him buried.

Two

I found the coffee-shop easily enough, tucked in among the other neat little shops clustered halfway down the Mearns Road, the names of most of them changed since I had been there last, their essential nature altered not one jot: a hairdressers salon, a chemists, a dry-cleaning shop, a newsagents with a tiny post office desk wedged amid the chocolate bars and childrens comics.

"Abigail & Amelia's", the coffee shop was named, after my landlady-to-be and that other lady of significant interest. Stepping into it, peeling off my hood and folding and shaking my umbrella, I instantly identified that latter ladyship, for all the years that had gone by and the brevity of my previous sightings of her. That look of ageing, careworn glamour, combined with a tersely bossy attitude to the younger women around her, matched the more recent photos I'd seen, the stories I'd been told.

As I stepped to the counter, she masked her scowl with a smile. She had just begun to tell me to take a seat and that a waitress would be across when I politely interrupted, asking if Abby was in.

She frowned slightly. But before I had begun to clarify, I saw realisation ease her features.

"Oh," she said, "You'll be...."

"Melinda," I replied. "Melinda Carido."

"Yes, yes, she mentioned you were.. - Is it today you're - ..?"

"I *did* say tomorrow. But I caught sight of this beautiful weather and thought I'd get here early, maybe do a spot of sunbathing on that balcony of hers."

"Well," she belatedly smiled, her voice purest Newton Mearns: the gravelly pie and beans of the urban Glasgow accent

4

refined into spun glass and icing sugar, "I'm afraid it's not looking the day for that. This won't be what you're used to in... Where was it?"

"Mexico," I said. "Sounds like she's told you all about me."

"No, no, not... not... well, em, yes, a little. I'm-"

"Amelia. Amelia Hutcher."

"Yes, um, Abby... Abigail's partner... business that is, eh..." She blushed. "She... she's just popped up to Mearns Cross on an errand. Why don't you take a seat, have a little something to warm yourself up?"

"You've tempted me into it," I said, seating myself at the one small table which wasn't already commandeered by plumy-voiced local ladies. Amelia dispatched one of the waitresses and I ordered a pot of Lapsang Souchong, plus a home-baked scone with jam and cream. While enjoying these, I took further note of Her Ladyship as she presided over her chintzy little fiefdom. I'll make a boneyard, an abattoir, of your cosy kingdom, I thought, sipping my smoky brew while she corrected the symmetry of a display of fondant fancies.

I was almost finished when the bell above the door tinkled, Abby entering on the heel of a rainy gust, tearing a headscarf from her short black hair and smiling at the trade the *dreich* weather had washed in. She had reached the counter and begun a report on the success of her errand before noticing me. Her words shrivelled, that businesslike smile shallowing, and then deepening beyond any kind of smile at all.

She sat opposite me, reached across to clasp my hands. I slid them off the table-top, for decorum's sake. She sighed, shaking slightly.

"I thought..." she murmured, "...you said tomorrow...."

"I like to surprise you," I said. "And I know you like being surprised."

She glanced about, then leaned further across the table, dropping her voice to a whisper.

"I like *you*..." she said. "However and whenever."

I settled further back in my chair.

"Here I am. Not with my luggage. I'll fetch that tomorrow.

5

But here's the part of me that counts. Ready to move in, soon as you're finished here."

"I'll take you now."

"Mind your language. We're in Newton Mearns, don't forget."

"Home, I mean."

"I thought this place opened until half four."

"This place can get along without me. Amelia runs a tight ship."

"So I've seen."

"I sometimes feel a wee touch redundant when she's in full steam behind the counter. Come on. I want to see you settled."

I told her to wait while I crossed to the counter, catching her colleague's eye and pulling out my purse to settle the bill.

" All okay?" Amelia asked, tapping at the cash register.

"Lovely."

"The Lapsang's an acquired taste."

"Just the thing for a *dreich* day."

"I'm sure."

"Bit of smoke on the breath."

"Mm."

"Oh, one thing...."

"Yes?"

I slid one of my little posters from my bag.

"I wondered if I could charm you into putting one of my posters in your window?"

She took the sheet, studied it.

"Oh yes," she said, with a hint of genuine interest. "Abigail mentioned. You're a drama teacher?"

"Yeah. Starting classes, d'you see, over at Crookfur Pavilion. One for the younger kids, another for teenagers. I've talked the council into some support, so obviously I'm keen to make a success of it."

"Yes..." she said. "Gives the young ones something to do, I suppose. Yes, yes, of course we'll put it up."

I thanked her, collected my change and moved towards the door, Abby opening it as I approached. As she did so, Amelia's son, soaked through, crossed the threshold, blowing wet hair out of his eyes with an upward puff of breath. And everything that came later took on its full weight of inevitability.

He had a younger kid with him, a girl: his niece, I presumed. She glowered at myself, the coffee shop and the world in general from beneath a streaming hood and a tangle of saturated brown hair. The boy himself, or young man rather, had faced the rain without hood or raincoat, his flimsy combat jacket hanging open on a soaked white T-shirt, the fringe of his untidy black hair half-plastered across his brow. The greenish blue of his eyes fixed on me, resisting the little girl's attempts to drag him onward.

I had stopped too, only vaguely aware of Abby waiting for me beyond the young man's shoulder. An awkward smile twitched the remnants of baby fat around his slender cheekbones. I could have eaten him whole.

It wasn't the appropriate spot, however: not amid the fondant fancies and toasted croissants and geriatric chatter about that morning's cover story in the Daily Mail. So I stepped onward and he allowed himself to be dragged aside.

I faced Abby. Her rain-spotted features had lost their smile. I stepped by her, raising my umbrella to shield us both as she guided me towards her car, parked opposite. Just as the door closed at my back, I caught the beginnings of a diatribe from the boy's mother about his not having dressed for the rain.

"A looker, isn't he?" Abby said as we settled into the car.

"Hmm?" I replied.

"Luke. Amelia's son."

"Well..." I shrugged, "...their kind of money, I'm sure they can afford bone structure."

"Their kind of money... tell me about it," she said, starting the engine and pulling away from the kerb. "Her highness is trying to buy me out. Buy me out of *my* coffee shop, the place I built out of nothing, long before she swanned along with her bail-out cash and the high and mighty manner that's never let me forget the favour. Now she's up for buying me out entirely. Says the place needs a rethink, a shift upmarket, whatever other fancy ideas that husband of hers has been muttering across the pillow. And apparently I'm not cut out for keeping pace with their innovations. Christ - that family! Like a 'Good Housekeeping' version of the Borgias.... Sorry." She took my hand. "You don't want to hear about my headaches."

"If we're going to be flatmates, I doubt there'll be much escape from them."

She squeezed my hand tighter.

"I'll try not to be a pain," she said.

"You cry out your sob stories any time," I said, "This shoulder of mine'll soak up anything you throw at it."

"I've cried enough lately," she said. "You're my shot at smiling for a change."

I squeezed her hand back. Soon, I reckoned, I wouldn't have to fake my own smile.

Three

'Broomcliffe' was the name of the block of flats, Abby's apartment located on the top floor of what was the only tallish building thereabouts, even the neighbouring blocks no more than three storeys high, the presence of flats at all an exception rather than the rule amid yet more houses and villas and bungalows.

"Pardon the 60's architecture," said Abby as we pulled up in the car park. "Or maybe you shouldn't. Not with everything else around here faking being older and quainter than it is."

"You sound at home here," I ventured.

"Nothing brought me here, and nothing's keeping me here, but that damned café. Maybe I should take Amelia up on her offer, move back into the city, someplace with a more happening culture than dinner dances at the golf club. Somewhere a girl not completely mummified could feel at home."

"This is *my* home, as of today," I said. "You could try feeling at home with me."

She drew a deep breath, then slid off her seatbelt and clamped a hand upon my lap.

"Oh Mel," she said, "Right now, I feel more at home here than I have in a long time. And, hey, we're still in the car park."

"So why don't you take me up and make me comfortable?"

Her flat was what I expected: a little untidy but moderately stylish, a Picasso from one of his more genteel periods on the wall above the fireplace; a bunch of middlebrow French movies on a DVD rack of varnished wood; pine floorboards, a little scuffed. Beyond the living room was a balcony. I stepped onto it, the partition of blue glass beneath the rail on which I leaned very 1960's indeed.

Below, rooftops and neatly-manicured gardens extended into grey distance, the rain washing the pastel shades to a pallid vagueness. Abby looped her arms about me from behind, kissing my neck and nuzzling my ear.

"You're going to get even wetter than you are already," she said. "Come on in. Get those wet things off. Have a bath."

"This place is so beautiful," I murmured. "In the rain, especially."

"Newton Mearns?" she giggled. "Oh yeah. Who needs Venice or the Alhambra?"

"You've lived here too long to realise. Haven't wandered, like I have, in the wilder places of the world."

"Chance would be a fine thing."

"I've wandered enough of them, and long enough, to see the beauty in the calm of a place like this."

"It's felt too calm to me for too long. C'mon, let's make it a wee bit wilder at least."

I turned to her, all smiles.

"I'm all yours," I said.

"You don't really want to curl up all alone in the spare room, do you?" she said, leading me inside and beginning to undress me.

"I thought that was what was on offer."

"Only because I didn't want to seem too pushy. I know this is all new to you, this kind of relationship...."

"Yeah. Just an innocent who strayed into an unfamiliar bar one day, incautious about whose smile she returned. Please be patient with my learning curve."

"With that and every other curve," she smiled.

I began an unfastening of her clothes. "Let me show you how quickly I get a grasp on things," I told her.

Four

The next evening, we collected my stuff from the tenement on the south side of Glasgow and I moved in properly, putting the stuff into the spare room, just to keep my options open and Abby on the right sort of tenterhooks. Within a week, I had begun my drama classes. Attendance was patchy at first, healthier with the younger kids than with the older, but these sweet little suburbanites were easier to deal with than the kids in some of the shitholes where I'd previously taught and turn-out rapidly increased. Things had only been up and running for a couple of weeks when Luke showed up in the pavilion out by the Crookfur playing fields.

He was there, however, only to escort that niece of his to my junior class. Glimpsing them amid the bustle of what was mostly mothers dropping off their kids, I hastened across, the boy looking eager to dump the little girl and get away.

"Hi there," I said, "And this is...?"

"Emily," Luke said on her behalf, Emily staring up at me with a guardedness to make me think, for neither the first nor the last time, of a small wild animal. "She wants to join your class. - Don't you?"

He gave her a nudge. She glowered at him, then looked back up at me, giving the tiniest nod.

"Anyhow, um...." the boy said, "...my Mum... Emmy's gran... she'll pick her up afterwards."

"Yes," I said, "I know your Mum. I've met you too, haven't I? Just for a moment?"

"Yeah," he said. "You're... you've moved in with Abby."

"Yes," I replied, relishing his inability to meet my eye. "Practically family. - Come on, Emily. If your brother wants to join in, I have a young adults class. He's a wee bit tall for this one."

"I could always crouch," he said, reconnecting with my gaze.

"You're welcome to try. We could treat it as a drama exercise."

"No thanks," he said. "I've had enough drama in real life recently without looking for it in a class."

"You don't say."

"Anyway, um, my Mum'll pick her up." He was already heading for the door. He cast a glance back my way before slipping out into the still-bright evening.

I looked to the girl, but Emily had wandered past me, plonking herself on one of the chairs against the far wall. And she clung to that end of the room for much of the class, only grudgingly taking part in the games and improvisations, reluctant to seek a partner when she did so.

There was only one moment when she truly became engaged. I had arranged the group in a circle for 'Instant Impro': two kids at a time in the circle's centre, improvising to a scenario I set them, with one of the kids then replaced by another from the circle, at which point I would change the scenario. I called Emily in to replace one of two boys improvising an argument in a sweet-shop over gooey gobstoppers, a twinge of humour on my part making me prompt her with the words "Okay, Emily, you're the world's most evil Grandad. Show us how nasty and horrible you can be."

She stared at me for a second, then stepped into the circle, turning her stare upon the scrawny boy with whom she was to perform. At that point she stopped and did nothing for a moment, the kids around her giggling, her partner yearning for a cue. Finally, he took matters into his own hands, playing himself in the role of a wee boy chirpy to the point of bumptiousness. "Sit yourself down, Gran'pa," he smirked. "Before your teeth fall out!"

"Look-" said Emily, her tone cutting short the general laughter, "- Look what you've done."

She stepped closer to the boy, no attempt made at a child's conventional parody of a grandfatherly stance. "Fooling around, thinking you're smart and clever, dragging this family through the dirt. What do you have to say for yourself? Huh?!"

The boy, unprepared for this lurch into psychodrama, had precisely nothing to say. "Run out of pretty tunes, have we?" she pressed. "You run about like a pervert, a madman, a criminal, and you expect me to get you out of trouble, yet again? It'd make more sense to bury you and tramp the earth flat."

The boy flashed a smile my way, imploring me to rescue him. A conscientious drama teacher would, of course, have done just that. But conscientious is the last thing I'd claim to be and, besides, I was learning something, which is what a good class ought to be all about.

"Is that the best you can do?" said Emily, giving him a shove. "Smile like a stupid kid? Shame this family and think you can grin your way out of it? You're not a child anymore and I'm sick and tired of your boyish charm and the trouble it causes. Sick and - tired!"

At this, she threw herself at the boy, bringing low his greater stature under a bombardment of blows from her tiny but drum-tight fists. "Emily!" I cried, bolting into the circle, grabbing her around the waist and whirling her back with such speed that her feet left the ground. The boy dropped onto his backside and burst into tears, blood sputtering from his nostrils and lips.

I carried Emily out of the circle before risking setting her down. But in releasing her, I found myself confronted by the sweet, rather shy slip of a girl who had dithered over playing the game minutes before.

"It was just acting," she said.

"A wee bit too realistic, maybe," I said.

"I wanted to do it like how it is," she timidly protested. "I've...."

"Yes?" I asked.

"I've seen how it is," I made out past the racket the the boy was making as he choked and snorted and wept his way up onto his knees.

Had we been alone, I would have pressed her further but

her acting partner was demanding my attention, so I let the matter rest while I helped him up, tipping his head back and pressing a clump of paper handkerchief to his nose. I escorted him to the kitchen leading off from the main hall, calling over my shoulder that the other kids should have a second crack at the chasing game we had played earlier. As I bathed his nose, however, my glancings back towards the hall showed the kids hovering just beyond the kitchen doorway, looking on with pallid concern. I couldn't spot Emily.

Letting the boy sit on his own in the kitchen, I returned to the hall and did my best at making something productive out of the class's remaining fifteen minutes. Emily, I noticed, had retreated to her chair by the wall.

I had, of course, a job on my hands explaining a bloody nose to a suburban parent. The boy's mother - who had looked rigid with anxiety delivering the kid in the first place - took the news as if I was reporting his being ravaged by a werewolf. A flush of tears and a smothering embrace of the boy, who seemed keen to let the blow to his pride be forgotten, was followed by an attempt to confront Emily, who she spotted still on that chair at the hall's far side. I discouraged her long enough for her son to win her over with his demands to be taken home before things got *"toooo embaaaarassin', Mummmm-!"*

"That whole family!" the mother discreetly snarled as she left, "swan around the Mearns like royalty. Except I've heard a whisper or two there's nastier things in their closet than madam there."

Soon all the other children had been collected, leaving the madam in question my sole companion.

"Your grandmother's coming for you, I think," I said to her.

"S'ppose," she murmured.

"Should be here any minute."

"Mm."

"You sorry?"

Her gaze tilted up to take in my approach.

"Sorry?"

"For bouncing poor Josh's head around the room like that."

14

She gave a humourless smile.

"I was just playing around."

"You play a tough game."

"I've seen worse."

"So you implied."

"What's... 'implied'?"

"Well it...."

There was the sound of a car drawing to a stop just outside, headlights raking the hall's interior. The girl looked past me, sliding off her chair.

"That's them," she said. "Gran and Gran'pa."

"Your Gran'pa too?" I looked towards the door.

"His car."

I heard a door opening and closing, followed by a clack of heels on the tarmac by the foot of the steps outside. I waited for the sound of a more masculine footstep, hate shivering within me like a cornered animal. But that sound did not come.

Meanwhile, the high-heeled tread climbed the steps, this swiftly followed by the appearance of Amelia in the doorway.

"Sorry I'm late," she gasped. "Everyone else away?"

"It's okay," I said. "Emily and I have been having a chat."

"Oh dear... Emily, why don't you go and wait in the car with Gran'pa? Go on!"

Emily darted past us. As I stepped closer to the doorway, I could see the car below, side-on to the building: a large black Mercedes, the angle at which it sat, purring, preventing me from seeing more than a darkly-coated shoulder past the driving seat window.

I turned to Amelia, told her what had happened without making too big a deal of it. But what I said was enough to send her wandering into the centre of the floor as if I had heaped all the worries of the world between her shoulder-blades. She stopped at a point where a few spots of blood could be seen on the floor.

"She's not had the easiest of times, Emily," she said. "Her parents divorced just last year, and it wasn't... well, it wasn't a very civilised affair."

"Violent?" I asked.

15

It was hard to tell whether the sharpness with which she looked round at me suggested defensiveness, or merely outrage, towards my suggestion.

"I'm sorry," I said. "I'm prying. I just thought...."

"Well," she replied, "I suppose there's violence and... violence. I'm sorry, anyway. You won't...?"

"Throw her out? Not for a first offence. And she did play her role rather powerfully. I don't want to wholly discourage a sense of realism in the performances here."

"It's all very difficult," she said, "Laura... our daughter, Emily's mother... she has a good job, but it's very demanding, scarcely ideal for a single parent. Other than financially. So the rest of the family has to play its part. And, well, I've got the coffee shop and my husband...! Which leaves poor Luke taking care of her more often than not. And that's hardly ideal, for either of them."

"Luke seems a considerate kid. Which isn't the rule with young men his age."

"Luke?" She faced me, the sheen of tears in her eyes unmistakeable. "Oh, Luke's an angel. Except...."

"Except?"

"Well, he's had his troubles too. I don't suppose he's signed up for that other drama class of yours, the one for the older kids?"

"Too much drama in his real life, or so he told me."

I caught her wincing. "A future as a performer," she said, "was just the thing he had his eye on up until a few months ago."

"Really?"

"Now, however, I'm not sure his eye is on anything at all. Other than dragging himself from one end of the day to the other with the minimum of strain on his attention. Would you... would you do me a favour? Please?"

"Name it."

She stepped closer, clasped both my hands.

"Next time he brings Emily around, I'd appreciate it if you'd make a serious attempt at persuading him to join your classes. He had, I mean he *has*, so much talent and I can't bear to think of it just... He needs some outlet for it, something more in his life than babysitting."

"We'll work on him from both ends, shall we?" I suggested. "And see if we can't win him over somewhere in the middle."

A smile flickered about her lips, lightening the burden of wrinkle and pallor upon what must once have been a real glamour girl's puss. It was gone a second later.

"I'm sorry," she said, letting my hands go. "I haven't the right to tangle you in the problems of our family."

"Well, I'm new here, remember. Keen to make friends. Friends help one another out."

The smile crept back towards her features, only to be smacked down by the blast of a car horn. She flinched.

"My husband..." she said. "Patience not one of his virtues, - I do beg your pardon. Oh, could you tell Abigail... Never mind. I'll see her tomorrow."

She hurried down the steps. I watched from the threshold as she crossed to the car, the fumes from the exhaust tinted red, like dragon breath, by the tail lights. I had come there steeled for a stealthy game, yet as the car - *his* car - began pulling away, I found myself hurrying down the steps, doing all I could to catch up with the vehicle short of an outright sprint, the edges of my gaze scanning the tarmac for some weapon - a rock, maybe - I could shove through the window at his side, cutting him dead without further ado.

But nothing came to hand and the car was already speeding out onto the Ayr Road, without my having so much as glimpsed his face. The instant I abandoned the chase, tears stabbed through me.

Returning to the flat, I found Abby doing her tapestry in front of some documentary about Bach on the Arts channel. As she looked round at me, tears surprised me all over again. She rose, embraced me, thinking it was comfort I was after. I dragged her to her bedroom.

Afterwards, we lay knotted around one another and I told her about my evening, focusing on the hints I had been given about young Luke's recent history.

17

"Luke?" she responded. "Oh yeah, poor kid. Raised to be the Golden Boy, practically booked into Gordonstoun the day he first said 'Da-Da'. Shuttled around one fancy private school after another, in the hope that one of them would spark the passion for scholarship his folks were forking up all that money to subsidise. But instead he just messed with drink, drugs, failed exams, got himself expelled, took some fearsome tellings-off from his father and did it all over again at the next school.

"Then, just this last year, he suddenly seemed to have found his calling. His most recent school made a big deal of performing arts and - guess what? - suddenly young Luke was enthused by the old nine-to-four. Even started a band with one of the other kids. Looked like he might go so far as to take his exams seriously, have a crack at some high-grade university. Then something went wrong."

"What?"

"Not sure. I'm stuck with Lady Amelia day-in, day-out, but she's never given me anything beyond the vaguest hint. Some serious family embarrassment, obviously. Anyhow, he got expelled again without sitting those exams. A 'gap year' is how his mother likes to refer to his current scholastic limbo. Ha! Some gap. - Any more wine going? Thanks.... And so he sits around the house, looks after his sister's kid, stirs his father's temper, tugs his mother's heartstrings, ponders his future. Keeps quiet about the conclusions he comes to. Shame. He *is* a looker, isn't he?"

"Yes," I said, "That for starters."

Five

In fact, it was before he next delivered Emily to the drama class that I met Luke again. And this time it was chance rather than calculation which drove our paths together: fate, perhaps, if I was fishing around for a justification, which I wasn't and amn't.

I was picking up some groceries at the Mearns Cross Shopping Centre. With no classes that evening, I had offered to cook Abby and myself one of the recipes I'd picked up in Mexico: whichever one, basically, the local Asda could stretch to in terms of ingredients. This supermarket, dominating one end of the shopping centre, had supplanted the William Low supermarket of my girlhood, most of the other shops having changed hands, likewise, without the essential layout of the place having changed at all: a single storey and a single broad aisle with shops along both sides but the supermarket the only reasonably large one among them.

Large though it was, I was forced to compromise on a couple of ingredients and so it was in a mood of mild grievance against culinary provincialism that I hefted my bags from the supermarket, only to have my mood lightened by a glimpse, on passing the newsagents, of Luke at the shop's far end, browsing the magazines.

As I stepped into the shop, passing a heated conversation between the woman at the till and an elderly gent regarding dog waste round the back of the public library, I noticed my quarry discreetly pulling a complimentary CD off the cover of one of the music magazines. He had angled his body towards the back wall of the shop while he did this and it was only now that he turned and caught sight of me. The soft pink of those plush young features paled and he seemed to shrink in an instant from young manhood to cowed childhood. I stepped up to him, his hand shielding the pocket of his combat jacket into which the CD had been stuffed.

I looked at the magazine he had just replaced, "BBC Music..." I noted, "Classical? The youth of today is full of surprises. What are they giving away this month? - Tchaikovsky. A little passionate for the i-Pod generation, no?"

He sighed, dropped his gaze, moved to draw the CD from his pocket. "Don't you dare," I said. His hand froze. "What are you trying to do?" I went on. "Get yourself marked as a thief with me right next to you? I've a reputation to uphold as a responsible teacher. If you're stealing that thing, I suggest you get on with it and get out of here. - I'll buy an Aero and distract the shopkeeper."

I did just that and followed him out. He waited for me beyond the shop doorway, watching me now with a wary smile. I took a bite of my Aero and as he opened his mouth to say something, I broke off another lump, popping it between his lips. "Green inside," I said. "Just like you. C'mon."

The most significant change to the lay-out of the shopping centre was the café that had been set up in the little indoor square at the far end of the centre from the supermarket, the wooden tables enclosed by a Toytown fence swaddled in plastic greenery. A sign told us to wait to be seated, but I waltzed past it and took a seat in the centre of the tables, indicating that Luke should sit opposite me.

I said nothing to him while we awaited a waitress, enjoying his visible straining after the beginnings of conversation. But our order was taken quickly, after which I asked him to 'hand it over'. With a glance past either shoulder, he pulled out the CD, passing it to me. I gave it a glance.

"*'Francesca da Rimini'*.... Oh look, there they are on the cover, Dante's lovers swirling around one another in the pit of Hell. You know the piece?"

"Never heard of it. Not really into that classical shit."

"Then why risk six months in Barlinnie over it?"

"Barlinnie might be less boring than this place."

"Your ass is too cute for prison. Take it from me."

Again, he looked shunted to the edge of his comfort zone, although not completely displeased by the experience.

"Anyhow," I continued, "What's so boring about the lap of luxury which is Newton Mearns?"

"You should try being on the dole in it."

"Unemployed? Gee, I thought you were dogging off school."

"No," he said, abruptly serious. "School's over for me. For good."

"Really? That boring, too?"

"It was. But that's not why I'm out of it."

"You didn't nick an apple from teacher's desk, did you?"

"It was a private school. The staff expected fancier bribes than that."

"What did they expect from you that they didn't get?"

"I think they got more than they were asking for."

"Such as?"

"You're nosy. If you don't mind my saying."

"I'm a teacher. I take an interest in the development of the young. Even when it doesn't pay well."

"Well, I'm a lost cause. If I were you, I'd stand clear and let me become just another adult, soon as I can."

"Hell being young, huh?"

"Certainly doesn't live up to the adverts."

"Did you see *my* advert? For that drama class I run for kids - sorry, young adults - just your age?"

"I knew you'd get round to that."

"You did?"

"Word's reached you from my Mum, has it? By way of Abby?"

"Word about what?"

"About the shining career I had ahead of me in showbiz, until recently that is."

"What deprived Scottish culture of those riches?"

"What's that term they use in showbiz?" he asked. "Oh yeah... 'creative differences'."

Our coffee and paninis arrived. He busied himself stuffing his pretty mouth.

"With who?" I belatedly asked.

"Mm?" he replied.

"Who did you have differences with?"

He chewed, swallowed.

"The world, more or less."

"Oh, you angry boy. You need taking in hand."

"I'm not angry. Not now. Hey... I stroll around here, shoplifting, a nice lady comes along, buys me lunch. Like you say, it's the lap of luxury. - Oh, you *are* picking up the bill, aren't you?"

"Make you a deal. I'll buy lunch if you come to one of my classes. And I don't just mean to hand your niece over."

"I'm retired from the stage."

"It's not the stage. Just a class. More freedom to fool around."

"I've retired from classes, too. And maybe from fooling around as well."

"You fooled around with Tchaikovsky there."

"That was a whim."

"Come to my class, on a whim."

"You can't have whims in advance. If I have that particular whim on the night in question, you might see me. Otherwise, don't hold all the other kiddies up waiting."

"That's a hell of a wall you're building around you."

"Not sure it's high enough yet."

"So long as you don't forget to put in the odd door or window."

"I'm looking out at you, amn't I?"

"Then you'll know I'm nothing to be scared of."

"I'm not scared."

"Prove it."

"I'll prove it right now."

"I don't have a class on right now."

"I'll prove it all the same. You gonna get this bill?"

Six

I rejoined him at the far side of the Toytown fence.

"I don't care for that smile, young man," I told him, although I liked it very much. "You look like you're up to no good."

"Me? I'm an angel. Too much of a one not to repay you for lunch."

"Repay me how?"

"I'll shoplift something for you."

"What?"

"Go on. I've got seriously good at it over the last few months. Anything you want you can have, from anywhere in this whole centre."

"You're asking me to solicit a crime."

"You helped me get away with my last one."

"We all have our whims, maybe."

"Have one now. Bet I can steal anything you want."

"I'll play along, if you play along with me. And come to my class."

"Maybe I will."

"Promise."

He shrugged.

"Okay."

"Then take one of these bags and come with me."

I curled my freed arm around his and steered him towards a small but classy boutique. "You'll need to act like my boyfriend," I murmured in his ear, "So we don't attract suspicion."

"Won't I -..." he began and then stopped.

"Don't you look a bit young for me, you mean?" I said. "Hey - don't knock the older woman till you've tried her. Now

23

stand here while I browse."

Letting go his arm and leaving my shopping bags at his feet, I started rifling through the rails. I kept glancing over at him and could see, as he shuffled from foot to foot, that the bravado with which he'd made his offer was a fragile thing. The kid was living from moment to moment and struggling to make the moments add up. Which left him ripe for the picking. I motioned him over. The girl behind the counter kept reading her Heat magazine and blowing gum-bubbles, her colleague busy stapling a poster of some anorexic in a baby-doll dress to the wall by the entrance to the changing rooms.

As Luke drew near, I pulled a sapphire-blue evening gown off one of the rails, holding it in front of me. "Think you can fit this in your pocket?" I asked.

His face puckered with concentration as he shook his head, scanning the rails about me. "Something simpler," he mumbled. "Easier to hide."

His eyes fixed on one rail in particular. I smiled as I followed his stare. Replacing the dress, I stepped to that corner where the lingerie hung, lifting a bra on its plastic hanger from the display. "How about this?" I asked as he drew near.

"Awkward shape" he muttered. "For concealment, y'know."

Smiling, I replaced the bra and picked off their hook a very classy pair of panties in semi-transparent pink lace. "What d'you think, darling?" I asked, holding them up and play-acting the devoted other half. "Are they me?"

He looked from me to the till, and then from me to the other assistant, before taking them off me. "No, not quite," he said, speaking louder, after which he dropped his voice to its lowest note yet. "Why don't you give me a hand? Find something else. Take it to the counter. Ask a question or two. If you can get both those girls involved, it'll be a real help."

"You're the professional."

"Just an amateur, but I know what I'm doing," he replied, replacing the panties on their rack and smiling at the assistant at the back of the shop, who had glanced our way. "Now... if you could give me a little kiss, maybe... it might, you know, make

24

her over there a bit more uncomfortable about being so nosy. Just a, like, a peck, you know."

Seizing the back of his neck with both hands, I drew him into a serious mangling of lips, relishing the shudder that racked him from his scalp to the tail of his spine. Then I let him go. "I don't do pecks," I told him.

After another little browse, I lifted off a sweater dress, carrying it to the till. "Hi," I said, "The wool in this dress, I can't see from the label, do you know if it's organic?"

"Organic?" the girl responded, looking as if I'd asked whether or not the fabric was Martian.

"Yeah, you know," I said, "Sometimes there's toxins in the sheep-dip. I have very sensitive skin and sometimes there's a reaction. Toxoplasmosis, it's called. So I can only wear organic fabrics. And I wondered...."

"Sweetheart!" Luke called. I looked around. He was edging towards the door, carrying my shopping bags. "I'm just gonna load the car. See you out there."

"Sure," I replied, before turning to the other shop assistant and asking, "Do you know anything about it?"

"S-sorry...?" the girl asked, her eyes only reluctantly shifting from a glance at Luke's back.

"Toxoplasmosis," I told her as she approached. "I need to know if this dress is organic."

"Organic?" she said. "I thought you only got that with food."

"So you don't stock any organic clothes?"

"I didn't know there was any such thing."

"Nowadays, they hardly stock anything else at Harvey Nick's down in London. Check the fashion page of your magazine there. - Oh, you don't mind putting this back on the rack, do you?"

Leaving the dress on the counter, I walked out. Luke was nowhere to be seen, either in the shop or the aisle outside. Recalling his parting words, I exited into the car park at the rear of the shopping centre.

"Excuse me, sir!" I called to Luke, who came into view just ahead of me. He turned. "Do you mind if I check your bags, sir?" I asked, catching up with him. "I suspect you may be in possession of stolen goods."

He held out my shopping bags. "You're welcome to check," he said.

I took the bags from him, setting them down on the pavement and making a cursory check of the uppermost groceries. "Gee, I must have been wrong," I said. "Terribly sorry, sir."

"You're not wrong," he responded, "Just too ladylike to dig as deep as you should have done."

Looking around to check we were not being watched, he reached under the waistband of his jeans, just by the crotch, and pulled out the slender lacy crumple he had stuffed there. "Sorry about the crumpling," he said. "Needs must."

I took them from him, fingering them across the palm of my hand. "Well, at least they're warm," I said.

A harassed mother with a couple of screeching toddlers came trundling a shopping trolley through the doors at our back. I closed my hand around the panties and told Luke to follow me with the bags.

I led him around the corner to a more secluded spot in the shadow of a couple of giant wheelie bins. No sooner were we there than I reached up under my skirt and stripped down the black cotton panties I was wearing, stepping my booted feet out of them and then pulling on the stolen pair with matching swiftness, taking a moment to straighten their fit through the fabric of my skirt.

"Mmm...." I said to Luke, just short of his eyes rolling from his skull, "...a wee bit tight. But nothing wrong with a little extra emphasis down there. Here, you can keep these. I'm going up in the world, obviously."

I passed the black panties into his hand and picked up my shopping bags, walking away towards the main road. "Now keep your part of the bargain," I called over my shoulder, "And come to my class, Tuesday night."

I continued on without waiting for his answer. I knew it already.

Seven

And sure enough, the following Tuesday, five minutes into the class, Luke slid his gorgeousness into the hall, settling at the back of the group. As I encouraged them all to split into smaller groups for the evening's first exercise, I noted that he knew and was friendly with some of the other kids. At one point, however, his growing enthusiasm for the drama game I had set them saw him stumbling against a boy in the neighbouring group, this a tall and surly kid called Stu who I'd sussed was only there to humour his sweet little charmer of a girlfriend, Molly.

Instantly contact had been made, Stu was shoving Luke away so violently both of them almost lost their footing, this followed by a tirade from Stu about "Smart-arse fuckin' private school cunts, clear out of fuckin' order! Ponce back to your fuckin' prep and rugger before a fuckin' humble bastard lays you flat!"

Both myself and Molly intervened, she bringing her boyfriend to heel with a shove of her own and a demand that he "Stop throwing himself around like a bloody hoodie and get the hang of hanging out in a friendly bloody drama class!" I, meanwhile, faced Luke, who showed little sign of seeking to get his own back, for all the sharpness of stare he cast past me to Stu.

I turned to Stu and made clear the unacceptability of that order of crap in my class: "I'm so in the mood to chuck you out for good, as of now."

"No, please," Molly said, "He's acted like a prick and knows it. - You know it, don't you? - He knows it." Stu shifted uneasily within his unpleasant skin. "Give him a second chance," she went on. "And I'll make sure he behaves."

"That true, Stuart?" I asked.

"Yeah," he summoned the eloquence to tell me.

"Okay," I said, turning to take in the whole class, "Let's all be in this together, folks! Friends, comrades, collaborators, *comancheros*, fellow artists, call it what you will. Now, let's make a fresh start on this exercise."

As I stepped back towards the centre of the room, I double-checked the respective stances of Stu and Luke: the former being bustled by his girlfriend back into the position he had occupied before the altercation, Luke hovering on the spot to which he had been pushed, at first continuing to stare at Stu, but then turning my way and flashing me an almost conspiratorial smile, before returning to his group and taking command of their improvisation.

And from that point on, he was brilliant. In impro after impro, he began by outclassing the others in wit and imagination, after which his flair began to infect those with whom he collaborated, so that soon kids whose performing experience didn't extend beyond the school panto or hamming it up for one another's mobile phones were swaggering through their scenes like hotshots from the Actors Studio.

Afterwards, the collective buzz was so strong that it took a while to evict the kids so I could lock up. And Luke was the last to go. I postponed any private word while packing my bag, content to feel him hovering behind me, impatient for my attention. I must have extended his agony a minute or two too long, for just as I was zipping the bag, I heard a sharp couple of clicks and the lights went off, stranding us amid bands of pale blue moonlight, his shadow stretched among these, falling across the table at which I stood. The shadow swelled as he stepped towards me.

"You were right and I was wrong," I heard him say. "It *was* a good idea me coming here. You're a good teacher."

"Thanks," I said, without turning.

"Way good. How did you get on with the other half of our deal? Huh? They still a snug fit? You wearing them now?"

I felt his hand caress my backside, which was clad in tight jeans. I turned, slapping him so hard he stumbled sideways and almost fell, the crack of the blow ringing around the hall. I caught the gleam of childish tears in his eyes. After a second he turned and walked to the door. I slung my bag over my shoulder and followed.

"You're damn right I was right," I called down from the top of the steps outside. He looked up at me. I leaned on the rail, smiled. "You belong here. You're good. Very good. And you better come to the next one, or I'll smack you harder still." I descended the steps. "Oh, and I'm not wearing panties tonight," I told him. "These jeans are a little tight for them. And just because I hit you, doesn't mean I'm totally averse to tender attention. Just ask next time. And then who knows?"

Face brightening, he made the first twitch of a fresh move. I arrested him with the press of a finger upon his chest.

"Off you go, little boy," I said. "Catch up on your beauty sleep. Just don't overdo it and rob us of breath completely."

He nodded. "See you next lesson," he said, walking off across the car park, keeping his eyes on me until he had gone some distance. Belatedly facing forward, he continued for only a couple of steps before stopping. Then he began striding back towards me.

"My Dad's car," he explained, hurrying past me. "Outside the country club. Don't want him to see me walking away from here. He's not the kind of Dad who'd be happy about his son and heir poncing round a drama class. No offence. See you!"

He sprinted off across the playing fields, heading for the gate at their far end. I walked in the direction he had initially taken, approaching the new-ish country club at the car park's far end, its swimming pool brightly illuminated behind tall windows. And there, parked almost at the doorway, was the black Mercedes which had collected Emily and her grandmother the other night. And all the horror which had brought me there seemed to coil around me, dragging me across the doorstep of the club.

Eight

I had joined the club a couple of weeks before; it was a convenient place to unwind after a class and had all the mod cons for keeping in trim, which I considered crucial to my battle plan. Indeed, the thought of a swim and a steam that very night had seen me put my bathing suit in my bag.

I wandered to the exercise room, where an assortment of variously plump and haggard suburbanites were sweating away at the bikes and treadmills, but not so many of them as to make it difficult to scan every face within seconds. Of course, I had seen my quarry - as an adult - only in photographs, buried in a couple of group shots Abby had shown me, as well as in pictures in his company's brochures and on its website; a good looking man, not in his son's class, but gilded by the kind of success that can set the most ordinary features glinting with charm and confidence. But those features were not to be seen in the exercise room.

He was predictably absent from the ladies hairdressing salon and similarly absent from the bar and restaurant. I turned towards the women's changing room, supposing that if I didn't find him by the pool - and I almost hoped I wouldn't, so suddenly unprepared did I feel for a direct encounter - I could at least have a swim to relax myself.

Stepping onto the poolside, I found the place empty of all but a few isolated bathers, none of them the one I sought. To hell with him, I told myself, plunging into the deep end.

It was pleasant to lose myself in those light blue depths. Not for the first time, I closed my eyes and tried to imagine what it might be like to drown in darker, colder waters. And, again not for the first time, I imagined your ghost floating there alongside me.

30

As I began to run out of air and swam reluctantly for the surface I saw, past the water's ripple, a tall figure strolling by the pool's near side, the greying blonde hair and the confident stride of the tall, supple body in its tight blue trunks leaving me certain I had found him whom I both dreaded and needed to find.

I broke the surface, watching as the figure, already by the pool's far corner, pulled open the door of the steam room and disappeared inside. I fixed the breath firmer in my chest and dragged myself from the water.

Pulling open the glass door, fighting my way past the billowing of the hot, moist air within, I struggled to adjust my eyes from the brightness of the pool area to the dimness of the small and narrow steam room, tiny blue and golden bulbs set into the ceiling reflecting their light off walls decorated with a mosaic of small blue tiles into which an image of a semi-abstract golden fish had been worked, petite fangs hinted at in its gaping mouth.

Just below this image ran a bench of wooden slats which then extended, forming an L-shape, along the narrower far wall. Upon this latter extent sat a great fat man in outsized, almost knee-length bathing shorts, his bald head and the sags of flesh about his chest and belly sweat-glazed and bobbing as he strained after breath.

"Yeah..." he was saying, "...Yeah, I... I know how... how hard you bounce the ball, you -...." He looked up, saw me, fell silent.

"I play the game like the game needs playing," a more composed voice purred from the end of the bench nearest me. "No crime in that."

It was my quarry who had spoken. He sat within inches of me, his back against the tail of that golden fish, his face turned away from me in the steamy half-light. I saw where Luke had inherited his profile.

I stepped by him, settling a short way further along that same bench. I rested the back of my head against the wall and closed my eyes, not daring yet to look him in the face. And in the blackness behind my closed lids, I saw *you*... your white limbs and ribs spiralling, sinking, through black waters, cold as the steam room was hot.

"Awwwfff..." the plump man wheezed, "I'm beaten."

I opened my eyes, looked to him as he began urging his body off the bench.

"You look it," said Luke's father.

"Nothing beats you, of course," the fat man countered, waddling his hairy-backed form towards the door, "You flash bastard."

"Nothing anybody's come up with yet, anyhow," came the response. Still I did not, could not, look that way.

The other man opened the door. Cold air cut through the heat. Then the door closed, sealing us in together. Fat beads of moisture bled down the condensation misting door and tiles, dripping from the ceiling and landing on my skin with startling coolness. Again, I closed my eyes, thought of Mum and Dad and *you*....

"You okay?"

I opened my eyes. Slowly I turned my head. Close as he was, and seen now face to face, his features remained half-obscured. But there was no mistaking what a looker he remained after all these years, his the brand of handsomeness that can be shored up indefinitely by life's more concrete successes.

"What did you say?" I asked.

"I wondered if you were okay."

"Okay?"

"You jumped a little there."

"Oh, I... I dropped off for a second. Bad dream."

"You look too good to be having those."

"Do I?"

"If you don't mind my saying."

"If I *do* mind, it's too late to get you to unsay it."

"Confidentially," he said, "I've lived my life on the assumption that the only way worth looking is forward."

"Forward's how you strike me."

"Nothing wrong with a strong first impression. Haven't seen you here before."

"Maybe you've not been looking hard enough."

"Oh, my eyes are always open."

"Like a shark's?"

"Like a one man welcoming committee. Welcome."

He held out his hand. I didn't shake it.

"Rick Hutcher," he told me. "If you've moved into the area, chances are you've moved into a place I put up."

"You're a builder?"

He smiled, not wholly amused. "Glorified," he said. "Hutcher Homes. Our developments are all over the place. You must have seen them."

"I think I have. You're the people saving the community from being overwhelmed by all those nasty open fields."

"We're hardly talking Alpine meadows. What's the odd scrap of grass if it makes way for nice homes in a nice area for, on the whole, nice people?"

"Let's just be careful the Mearns doesn't drown in 'nice'."

"You either don't know the Mearns, or you know it ever-so-slightly too well."

"Oh, I'm a stranger here. As you've probably guessed."

"Then suddenly the place has more to be said for it than 'nice'."

"You think so?"

"I told you. I keep my eyes wide open. It's the secret of my success."

"Careful success doesn't go to your head."

"Oh, I'm careful. Don't you worry."

He tilted his head back against the wall, the fingers of his right hand absent-mindedly raking the pale fur crowning his chest. That middle-aged body looked like it had been worked hard in the gym next door.

"Phewww..." I sighed, taking hold of the cleavage of my bathing suit and tugging it back and forth, fanning the body within. "Hot in here."

"Not *too* hot, I hope?"

"You hang around in a steam room," I said, "You've got to expect to get a little sticky."

"You must wish we were Scandinavians. You wouldn't

have to wear that suit."

"Or you those trunks."

His asymmetric smile betrayed how wrong-footed he was.

"Alas," he said, "It *is* Newton Mearns."

"It's also near closing time. And all but empty out there. I bet we have this place to ourselves for the twenty minutes left."

"You're a bold young lady."

"How bold are you?"

"Bold, I suppose, by standards round here. But then, you're not from around here. So I might struggle to keep up."

"Looks like it. I worked a couple of seasons in an Austrian ski resort. Thereabouts, they think it's the most innocent thing in the world to strip off in a steam room. Whether it's male, female or mixed."

"What did you work as? A sexy chalet maid?"

"I was training to be a *masseuse*."

"Oh really?"

"Really. People didn't wear trunks for that either. So you can understand how straight-laced I find this place."

"There's a little more give in my lacing than you might think."

"Prove it."

"Eh?"

"Get your trunks off and lie down there. I'll show you my skills. My massage skills, that is."

He stared at me, torn between a businessman's wariness over any deal that wasn't in writing and an after-hours keenness for just such a gamble. Slowly he stood, glancing to the door, the condensation on the glass thicker than ever but showing no hint of anyone approaching. He faced me again, fixing his thumbs in the waistband of his trunks but hesitating over doing anything more.

My own bathing suit was a two-piece, the upper half a tight-clinging vest top with bikini bottoms below. With a casual tug, I pulled the top half over my head, arching my back to make sure he got a good look at all I wanted him to see.

"C'mon," I said.

He pushed down his trunks. "I hope you're not going to

34

get me into trouble," he said. The half-light wrapped much of what he had to show in shadow, but I could tell he was as well-maintained there as elsewhere; half-roused, indeed, by the proceedings so far.

"Go on, lie down," I told him, indicating the stretch of bench on which his plump friend had sat minutes before. He stepped by me, more confidence in his movements now he was naked. He lay on his front, undulating his buttocks a little, settling himself as comfortably as possible.

"Don't get stuck in those slats," I said, standing.

"You're certainly a breath of fresh air in these parts," he mused.

"Well, close your eyes and relax," I said, hitching my fingers in my bikini bottoms, "And let's see how fresh we can get with one another."

"You'll find me putty in your hands," he replied.

"Just let me get these bottoms off first," I said, as soon as his eyes were closed. But instead, I was pulling my top back on. "Oh yeah," I said, picking up his trunks from the floor, "Nice to be naked."

I thought, stepping backwards towards the door, of how you would have appreciated seeing him laid out like that: his pale-arsed hunkiness and his perfect helplessness, like a chicken on a spit. I pushed open the door and strode out to the poolside, catching his yelp of surprise and indignation as the door swung closed. I tossed his trunks into the pool and went to get changed.

Nine

Emboldened, I was at their house before he was. It wasn't a long walk from Crookfur, although I got briefly lost amid the sameness of the suburban streets. Then, rounding what looked like another unrewarding corner, I found the place looming before me, white walled and brightly lit against the damp blue shadows. At first I supposed the house's seeming so much larger was down to my having been so much smaller when last I saw it. But I soon realised that the building must have been substantially extended at its far side, to the point where I wondered if the house next door hadn't been demolished to accommodate this.

Skirting around the house on the opposite pavement, I saw that the narrow footpath behind the tall wooden fence of the back garden still stood. I scurried along this then, fixing fingers and feet amid the fence's slightly warped slats, dragged myself upward and over it, dropping on the other side.

Raising myself, I crossed the small orchard at the foot of the garden. Advancing to the wicker screen separating this area from the garden's upper end, I crept around its corner, bringing the rear of the house into view. The house had been extended in this direction too, the modest conservatory I remembered replaced by a glass-fronted extension built the length of the house's ground floor. The lights within were on, showing the extension furnished with Sunday supplement good taste. Emily sat at a desk at one end, playing a game on a computer, her feet dangling above the floor. Luke was slumped on a couch, listening to music through earphones, his face towards me but buried in a Japanese Manga paperback.

A good half hour went by, my furtive share in their calm finally interrupted by the sound of a car approaching at the house's far side, its wheels scrunching up the driveway. I tensed, anticipating the King's furious return to his castle. Luke lowered his book and pulled out one of his earphones, turning first towards the extension's inner door and then to his niece, calling something that had her glancing around and muttering before she returned to the more interesting goings-on on the computer.

A figure appeared in the inner doorway, but rather than being the father this was a young woman in a pinstripe business suit, short skirt and killer heels. She mouthed a 'Hello' to Luke, who responded with a vague wave, then crossed to Emily, embracing her from behind.

Emily seemed less than enthused by the interruption and it was only after a caress of her hair, a kiss to the top of her head and a gentle nudge that the girl was persuaded to start switching off the computer. Amelia stepped through the doorway, carrying Emily's coat and glancing at her watch. A conversation began between Amelia and the woman I assumed was her daughter Laura, their expressions signalling a rapid shortening of tempers on both sides. Luke shoved his earphone back in, Emily hopping down from the seat and tugging on her coat.

It was just as the quarrelling voices rose to the point where I could make out, through the glass, their resonance if not their sense, that I heard a second car approach, the sleek roar of its engine unmistakable. I heard it stop and its door slam, followed by the opening and still louder slamming of the house's front door, this causing Amelia to pause halfway through the point she was making. She looked towards the inner doorway, calling. Her daughter began bustling Emily in that direction.

Before they reached it, the man of the house had materialised, fully dressed but with the scars of his recent humiliation still there for me, at least, to detect in the set of his features. He brightened slightly on seeing his daughter and grandchild, giving the latter a fond rub on the top of her head and the former a tight hug.

His wife intervened, prompting what soon became a three-way argument, the two women the heartiest combatants. Luke rose, kissed his niece, then stepped to the glass doors facing onto the lawn, picking something off a hook on the wall and then sliding one of the doors open just enough to permit his slipping out into the night. He closed the door at his back and wandered my way.

I drew back into deeper shadow as he approached the near end of the wickerwork screen. Passing it, he veered towards a small stone building in the garden's bottom corner, the obscurity thereabouts making it hard for me to see if it was merely a glorified garden shed or something more elaborate. He unlocked the door, shuddering its rusty hinges open with his shoulder and then disappearing within.

A dusty amberish light came on behind a window adjoining that door, Luke appearing behind the unwashed glass, fumbling among a jumble of indistinct objects by the foot of the window-frame. Something was knocked over, suffering a muffled smash on the floor, Luke voicing a similarly muffled curse before re-emerging, reaching back to switch off the light and tug the door closed.

He stepped to a small ornamental pond just in front of the hut, sitting on one of the wrought-iron chairs spaced irregularly around it, his back to me. I caught the red spark of a cigarette lighter and then the moonlit waft of a little cloud of smoke, its odour amusingly transgressive. I forgave him the suburban triviality of his vice.

He only managed a few prolonged inhalations before the sound of the extension door being slid open disturbed us both. Luke tossed his roll-up into the pond, wafting with his hand the smoke around his head. We both looked round to see his sister manoeuvring those spiky heels across the lawn.

"Luke -... Luke, sweet, where are you?" she called, gleaming in the moonlight with hard-ass class, from the sleek black bob of her hair to her halo of expensive perfume, older than Luke by what I took to be the better part of a decade, in command of life in a way I supposed her baby brother stood little chance of ever matching.

"Oh there you are," she said, stepping close by me and approaching the pond. "What you doing out here? Trying to

38

catch a goldfish? - Oh..." She sniffed. "I get you. Gimme a puff. I could use a little narcosis."

"The goldfish got there ahead of you."

"Oh you didn't, did you?" She leaned over the back of his seat, wrapping her arms around him. "My wee angel scared he'd be sent to bed without his supper?"

He reached back and stroked her arm.

"I've wound up Mum and Dad enough for one lifetime, don't you think?" I heard him say. "Happy leaving the aggro to you this evening."

"How generous of you," she said, pulling another chair up close to his. "When they have so much of it to hand out." She sat, her chair angled in such a way that she could settle her legs across Luke's lap.

"You want a down-to-earth cigarette?" she asked, pulling out a packet and a lighter. "Guaranteed to give you cancer, rescuing you from the Hell of human existence well ahead of time."

"Thanks, but my life's way too full of joy at the delights existence offers."

"Yeah, I see it in your face. Anyhow, you get an earful of my evening's share of parental affection?"

"Mum's lecture on motherhood?"

"All that nudging and coughing up to get me into, then through, law school and now I'm just kick-starting a career, I'm taking all this shit off her, just 'cause it demands more flexible hours than a bloody ten-to-four coffee shop. You don't get far in criminal law clocking off at six on the dot. Em's been okay, hasn't she?"

"Em's been fine."

"It's her future I'm slaving my arse off to subsidise. And the fall-out from the divorce hasn't exactly left me flush. Lawyer's fees! Anyhow, what's *she* got to moan about? It's you shouldering the bulk of the hassle. Never think I don't appreciate it."

She swung her legs off his lap, stood, seized him in an embrace that must have squeezed the breath from the poor kid, then tilted his head upward for a kiss on the forehead. "A

39

bloody angel, baby brother," she told him, caressing his face, "That's what you are. Why the fuck didn't I marry someone like you?"

"Because it would have been illegal."

"Worse than that, Luke. I wouldn't have been worthy of you."

"You say that? After everything?"

"After everything? Yes I do. Because one thing that you did wrong, very wrong, does not amount to any kind of '*everything*'. It's done, Luke, those who love you have seen the matter settled. For good."

"Good, sis?"

"As good as we could manage. You weren't the only one to blame..."

"Don't we both know it."

"Don't make a rod of it for your back or mine. Or anyone else's. It's done. Buried. We're all sorry and we've all moved on. All except you. Take *your* turn, Luke. Try living again. It's not as scary as you might think."

"Maybe I've made a start already."

"Oh yeah?"

"I joined a drama class."

"What?" she giggled. "The one Em goes to? Method acting with the tiny tots, are you?"

"They have another class, for those of us too old to be patronised about going there."

"Well, that's good, Luke. That's great. All that talent... it's time you stopped bottling it up and waiting for it to go flat."

"There's more than my talent getting stimulated at that place."

"You don't say."

"I just did. So long as it's strictly between you and me."

"Strictly between you and me, spill the beans. What drama have you got yourself caught up in?"

"Maybe it's love. - Don't look so frightened, sis."

"Love?"

"Maybe I'm kidding myself. All the same, day-dreams make a nice change from nightmares."

40

"Go for it, Luke. You're overdue for love. Just... just be careful."

"Careful, sis?"

"With that heart of yours."

"Meaning?"

"You know how easily...."

"What?"

"Your heart's not exactly comfortable being kicked around, is it?"

"That's why I'm keeping a tight hold on it this time."

"So long as no one gets hurt, yourself first and foremost."

"I'm taking so much care, sis, I'm barely drawing breath in the other person's presence."

"Christ, Luke..." she sighed, "You're still just a kid. A sweet, floundering, fabulous, heart-rending kid. So much time ahead of you for toughening up that delicate wee ticker and finding it a home."

"Who knows better than you how *in*delicate this heart of mine can be?"

"I know that compared with the villainy I'm used to, day-in, day-out, you err on the side of innocence." She turned her back on him, smoking her cigarette as she faced the pond's dark waters. "Take it from me, Luke... Jesus, the workload there is in human bestiality and human scheming."

"If anyone can stamp them out and make this world a paradise, it's you, Sis."

She faced him. "Even I'm not that ambitious. But I'll do my best. Listen... I have to get Em home before Mum's high horse puts her head through the ceiling. And I have a father who burned to death his own wife and kid to deal with in the morning. Here..." From her classy handbag, she drew a classy purse and from that pulled what looked like several tenners, pressing them into Luke's hands. "Don't fritter it away throwing marijuana at the goldfish. Ask your sweetheart out. Get as much love as your deserve, Luke. And not a jot less."

She kissed his forehead, then started back towards the house. Luke watched her go. I watched Luke, as he returned his attention to the dark waters of the pond, hardly moving for long minutes.

Eventually, his mother called, asking if he was coming in. Without answering, he rose and turned, facing in my direction with a shadow-faced intensity that made me wonder if he hadn't spotted me. Then a glint of moonlight along one side of his face revealed it as soaked in tears. He turned and walked to the house.

Ten

I remained among those bushes for the remainder of the night. Even after the daughter's car had driven away and the extension's lights had been switched off, I lingered, seating myself upon the moist earth at the wicker screen's corner, watching lights go on and off behind the closed curtains of the rooms upstairs. The house settled into darkness and still I stared at it, as if demanding of its silence an answer to what I was doing there. The night grew colder, damper, lonelier and thus I felt steadily more at home in it.

I must have slipped briefly into sleep an hour or so later, for I woke with a start, my disorientated glancings around coming to rest on one of the smaller upstairs windows, where a light had come on behind the curtains. I guessed it was Luke's window, picturing him sleepless within, his mind worrying away - I flattered myself - at some unrequited thought I had put there.

A light rain began drumming the leaves. I wondered if it wasn't time I left. Lowering my gaze as I began to think of levering myself up from the ground, I caught sight of a black boot upon the grass to one side of me.

I looked up the black-trousered leg to which the boot was attached, weighty, husky breathings rasping out just above. The figure to whom boot, leg and breaths belonged loomed over me, its sole movement the slight rise and fall those breathings induced in a chest thickly garbed in black. It was the sight of the face above which arrested my own breath, for the mask it wore made me wonder if one of the Aztec Gods hadn't pursued me from Mexico.

The mask, certainly, seemed to combine human and animal qualities, the lower half dominated by a squat proboscis like that of some outsized insect, the eyes above great gleaming circles, yet with some glint of a more human gaze behind. It was only as I glimpsed a blink in that gaze-within-a-gaze that I fully wakened to the fact that I was looking at a figure disguised by a gas mask from the First or Second World War.

I began to rise.The figure backed away, swivelling towards the bottom end of the garden. I launched myself after it, grabbing a black cotton sleeve. The figure spun about, tore its arm free, pushing me back with its gloved hands. As it turned to hurry on, I made a second charge, this time slamming myself against its back, sending it stumbling over the edge of the little pond, its legs splashing down into the knee-deep water. I seized the nozzle of the mask, intending to wrench it off. But the figure grabbed the forelegs of one of the wrought iron chairs at the pond's edge, swinging it round and thumping the metal into my knee.

As I stumbled back, agonised, the figure dragged itself from the water and advanced on me, holding that same chair like a weapon, swinging it back and forth so I could hear its weight scythe the air. I limped my retreat until I had almost backed into the wickerwork screen. The figure hurled the chair my way.

I ducked, and only just low enough, for I felt the metal bulk brush my curls and uppermost ear as it flew past, smacking into the screen and buckling the frail structure. The masked figure made a fresh turn for the rear of the garden and I made a fresh pursuit, this time throwing myself at full length, wrapping my arms around its calves, bringing it crashing down just short of the pond, its flailing arm knocking another chair noisily into the water.

No sooner was the figure down than it had swivelled on the ground, torn a foot free and smacked the sole of its boot into my face, knocking me aside. Thrown onto my back, feeling the other leg wriggle free, the next thing I knew my assailant was towering above me again. It grabbed me, wrenching me to my feet, hurrying me a few steps across the grass and then throwing me once more onto my back, my shoulder blades suffering a hard impact upon the paving stones at the edge of the pond, the

44

back of my head suffering a dip into a nothingness that I knew must have the pond's dark waters just below.

The figure dropped, kneeling astride my chest, clamping a leathery hand across the lower half of my face, pushing my head down, down, against my attempts to resist. Already I could feel the dangling curls at the back of my head growing thick and heavy with the moss and silty water amid which they had sunk, the water's tiny ripplings and the harsh breathings through the nozzle of the mask an inadequate soundtrack for what I realised might be the drama of my own death, the eyeholes in the mask now black as the water in which I was about to drown.

I had just reached up to make a second attempt at clawing off, or at least dragging askew, that mask when light fell sharply across it from the side, reflecting off the glass eyeholes in such a way as to set my plight starkly mirrored upon them. But then the masked face was turning away towards the house and an instant later I was released, the figure rising swiftly and abandoning me. As I squirmed up to a sitting position, I caught sight of Hutcher darting into view behind the extension's glass, clad in dressing gown and pyjamas. I looked round to see the masked figure already clambering over the rear fence and dropping on the other side. As Hutcher bellowed through the glass, I made my own sprint for the fence, keeping my head low.

My foot kicked at some object in the grass. It fluttered like a broken-winged bird. I grabbed it, feeling paper in my hand but having to hurry on without a proper look. Rolling it in a tube and stuffing an end in my jacket pocket, I climbed the fence more clumsily than my assailant, but got to its summit, in my panic, almost as swiftly, risking a glance back to see Amelia, in her nightgown, hurrying into the extension, her husband unlocking one of the glass doors and sliding it open.

I dropped into the narrow lane on the other side and hurried on, my predecessor vanished. From the far side of the fence, I heard Hutcher cry across the garden's length: "Last time, you bastard! Last time!" I also caught his wife's harsh whisper that he should be quiet: "The neighbours, Rick! The neighbours!"

I put several streets between myself and them before

pausing, by the light of a sluggish dawn, to inspect the object I had picked up and which I supposed my fellow intruder had dropped. It was an old American comic, 'Superboy' writ large on the cover above an image of the boy himself bursting through a wall to save the world. I opened the comic and what met me within were not the expected super-heroics and word balloons but rather a few stapled-in sheets filled with darker, blurrier illustrations.

I had to shift beneath a street lamp before I could make these out as black and white photographs printed out by the smudgiest of domestic ink jet printers - two or three of them to each of the six pages stapled between Superboy's covers - several of the shots so vaguely focused that I had virtually to press my face to the paper to confirm them as close-ups of portions of a naked human body twisted in what I thought at first were obscenely sexual postures, only to realise I was looking at shots of injuries taken while the blood was still thick and black upon them: images of limbs twisted and broken; of a mouth splayed like the sorest wound of all, an idiot grin bloodily slobbering around broken teeth; of a single eye staring up past drying trickles from a bleeding scalp. A hint of bloodily-matted body hair here and there suggested a male body but I could not be sure of its sex, or if it was several injured bodies that were depicted, that isolated mouth and eye all the face on show.

It was only the last of these inner pages which provided a respite from the mutilations, this blank of photo but scribbled across in marker pen with the words: *SUPER AT SHATTERING BONES - AS CERTAIN OF US KNOW ONLY 2 WELL!!! (You read it here FIRST....!!!!!)*

I rolled the 'comic' up and carried it home.

Eleven

I crept into the flat at Broomcliff, assuming Abby would be long asleep. Stepping into the darkened living room to pour myself the nightcap I had more than earned, I was startled by the clicking on of a lamp by the wall at my back, this accompanied by the words "So you're alive."

I turned. Abby sat at one end of the couch, a shawl drawn around her white satin nightgown, legs clad in purple bedsocks drawn up beneath her. She had helped herself to a drink, or several of them, already: a crystal tumbler sat, all but emptied, next to a similarly drained bottle of sherry.

"Yes," I acknowledged. "A bit wet, but alive."

"A bit?" she said. "Half-drowned, that's how you look."

"Thanks. It's this season's hot look."

"Is it? I might try it myself if I weren't feeling so secure in your love right now."

"Let's get some sleep. I'll reassure you of it in the morning."

"It *is* the morning."

"The other end of the morning."

"I'm not sure I'm in the mood to sleep, even now."

"Well, if that amount of sherry won't do the trick, what will?"

"Can't you guess?"

"Not without some sleep. Sorry."

"Don't you have more to be sorry about than that?"

"Such as?"

"Such as my having to sit here, clean through the night, thinking the worst about you?"

"The worst?"

"About why you hadn't come home, wondering what sort

47

of hole you'd fallen into where your mobile couldn't even get a signal."

"Well, you know what the Mearns is like," I said, pouring my own drink, "I got kidnapped by brigands, dragged to an orgy and had to fuck my way out."

"That was one of the things I was worried you might be doing," she said. "Fucking your way out of something."

"In the Mearns? Chance would be a... Well, where I wonder would one go to fuck one's way *into* such a thing?"

"If you're beautiful enough, and charming enough, and bold enough, I don't doubt something can be sniffed out."

"Abby, if you're drunk enough and tired enough and paranoid enough, you can worry yourself into believing any old nonsense. It's still nonsense."

"Of course I worry," she said, crossing to me on unsteady feet. "I love you. If you can't deal with that, then we have a problem."

"I can deal with it. It's the 24 hour surveillance I'm less than keen on."

"I'm sorry," she said, licking her finger-tip and using it to wipe what must have been some mud from my face. "It's hard when you care for someone like I care for you, when you're stark awake and eaten alive with it. I haven't had anyone to care for like this for so long. And so I get... scared. I mean... there's a lot about you to scare a girl."

I caught her caressing hand by the wrist, arresting it.

"Such as?"

"Such as you giving away so little about who you are, where you've come from, why the hell you've tangled yourself up with me."

"I tangled myself there for fun," I said. "So long as it *is* fun, I'm happy to stay tangled."

"Just *fun*?" she frowned.

"What else in life ought one to waste one's time taking seriously?"

"I've got a few too many laughter lines to go wasting my time, Mel, even on fun. I want... I need... something more to cling to. And instead, the more I reach out to you, the more my hands fill with... well, I don't know what some of it amounts to. A few hours back, I wandered into the spare room. Killing time, you know?"

"Into *my* room?" I let go her hand.

"It's my flat. Nothing in it should be out of bounds to me, surely?"

"Even in love, there have to be some boundaries."

"I have my boundaries too, you know. If something freaks me out seriously, that's a boundary crossed. Come on. - *Please?*"

She seized my hand, urging me along the hallway to the spare room. As she opened the door and switched on the light, I tugged my hand free. "Show me," I said.

She moved to the wardrobe. I wondered if this was the moment to kill her. Opening the wardrobe doors, she knelt down, which would have been all the more convenient.

From beneath the jumble of shoes, books, bags and other oddments with which I had stuffed the lower portion of the wardrobe, she tugged out the smallest of my suitcases, provoking from me a breath of laughter, of relief should this prove the worst thing she had uncovered. Hearing me, she looked round.

"It's - what? - just a joke?" she asked. "I hope it is." She clicked open the case's battered fastenings. "Is it... is it okay to... to touch these things?"

"Of course it's not."

"No?" Her hands flinched, her expression ridiculously concerned, doubtless from her having touched the contents already.

"They're my private things."

"I mean... Christ, I mean: is it witchcraft?"

I laughed out loud.

"Is it?" she pressed.

I dropped to one knee next to her, lifting out the skull, with its covering mosaic of tiny tiles of gold and purple. She drew back, as if fearful the uneven teeth might take a bite out of her.

"Is *this* what you're frightened of? My casting Aztec

curses on the good folk of Newton Mearns? With a plastic skull? Abby, these are just souvenirs..." I popped the 'skull' back in the case, lifting out the stuffed jaguar paw. "Tat for the tourists. Not an authentic Aztec heirloom among them. You knew I'd lived in Mexico. Is it a huge surprise I've hung on to a few mementoes? Sweetheart, you've been phoning the tarot lines a little too often."

"Yeah," she said, "But what does *this* have to do with Mexico?"

She reached into the case, tugging on the loose end of its lining and drawing out from underneath the brochure I had concealed there.

"This is last year's shareholders report for Amelia's husband's firm," she said. "You see? 'Hutcher Houses: Where Aspirations Find A Home.' And there's the man himself, King Rick, smiling all over the inside cover."

"So?" I asked.

"This... stuffed away in here... what's this to do with you?"

"I don't know what you're getting at."

"The Hutchers! Did you know about them, have an interest in them, before you came here and hooked up with his wife's part-... My God... Did that have anything... anything?!... to do with you attaching yourself to me?"

"You're getting more and more paranoid, Abby. It must be sleep deprivation. C'mon, let's get to bed."

Holding the jaguar paw by the wooden handle attached to the end that had been severed from the rest of the beast, I caressed the curved backs of the lengthy claws against her cheeks. She swiped the paw aside.

"Answer me!" she said.

I gently removed the brochure from her hands.

"When I first thought of moving here, I reckoned I might be able to buy myself a flat. So I researched the property situation. That was one of umpteen brochures I got hold of. Don't know what it was doing there. Must have slipped behind the lining and got forgotten about while I was chucking all the others out."

50

"I... I don't know if I... believe you, trust you, I... I don't know if I understand."

"The last thing I'm here for, Abby, is to be understood. What a killer that can be. Of romance, I mean. Of love and fascination and...."

I had curled the jaguar's claws around the left shoulder strap of her nightgown, giving the lace playful tugs. Now a hard pull tore the strap away at its front end, the fabric below slipping off her breast. She attempted to raise the flap. A swipe from the claw scratched the back of her hand, forcing her to let the damage remain. I began stroking the sheerest points of the claws around the soft, pale, slightly sagged flesh of her tit. She winced, her nipple stiffening.

"...sheer sweet violent sensation," I concluded.

"I... I'm not sure I'm in the mood right now," she replied, fixing her hand atop the spotted paw.

"I'll put you in the mood," I told her.

She pushed the paw aside, stood, turned away. I hooked the claws in her nightgown's lower folds, a wrench with it dragging the whole garment down below Abby's knees. Naked but for white cotton pants and those purple bedsocks, she jerked around and stumbled back, tripping over the gown's crumple and falling onto her side. I scuttled after her, tearing the gown clear of her feet and hooking the claws in the waistband of her pants, yanking them down with a brusqueness that left shallow, thinly-bleeding scratches the length of her left thigh. I planted myself atop her.

"Never you mind what I'm doing here," I told her. "Here I am and that's that. Here with you. Which is a decent deal for both of us. Too good a deal, I'd say, for us to be undermining it with some silly Q & A. Accept things as they are and I'll get on with showing you all the more interesting things we can do with our time. I'll start right now, shall I?"

"I... I just..." she murmured, "...just want to be... you know... loved."

"Then shut the fuck up and let's get through to your bed. Meanwhile, stop messing with my stuff. Or I really will put an Aztec curse on you."

"I'm... I'm cursed already, Mel. I've told you the shit luck I've had finding love. The ways I've hurt myself between getting hurt by others. How close I've let myself get to... to surrender. Absolute surrender. Christ, the mistakes I've made, and nearly made, the violence I've felt, towards myself most of all.... That first night, with us, the night you... well it was you seduced me, wasn't it, the more I think of it... I lay awake, watching you sleep, and thought... here's my last roll of the dice, last... whatever. Has to be. I can't get hurt any more. Better to not... not hurt at all."

She shut her eyes on thickening tears.

"Then let's roll that dice," I told her, seized by a certain tenderness towards the poor lonely cow, even as the thought of killing her, too, took on a weightier rooting in my mind.

Twelve

The larger dice, rolled already, rapidly turned up the score I was after. Luke went so far as to show up on time for the following week's class, taking part in a session based around scenes from "A Midsummer Night's Dream".

Molly, who had arrived without the shove-happy Stu, paired up with Luke for the scene of love-under-a-spell between Lysander and Helena, and both got so rapidly into the groove of the thing, especially when I got them to put aside their photocopied texts and improvise in contemporary speech, that the effect, there in that hall with its flat electric lighting and blank furnishings, was quite magic, the pitch of Molly's performance swiftly rising to meet that of Luke, until their enacted flirtation struck all of us, I think, as blurring the line between performance and reality.

When, at the end, they caught one another in an unprompted kiss, a giggle ran around the onlookers, gaining volume and knowingness as the embrace lengthened. I managed a smile, albeit to hide a pang of jealousy. As they finally broke apart, their own giggling seemed a less credible piece of acting than what had gone before.

My jealousy was compounded when, at the end of the class, I tried to weave my way towards Luke, only to see him and Molly wandering out into the night, chatting and giggling to one another, his hand conspicuous against the small of her back as he steered her onwards. And then they were gone.

I felt ludicrously close to weeping as the door closed at the back of the last of the kids. I zipped up my bag, switched off the lights and locked up, exiting through the back door, the better to snatch a breath of fresh air on the playing fields before starting home.

No one else was about. The tall trees lining the far end of the field rustled in the breeze, a silvery-blue moon above them. I recalled the moment this whole scheme had first occurred to me, as I sat at the foot of a faraway pyramid, staring at that same white orb above what, there, was the edge of jungle. Every rustle of those distant leaves had seemed pregnant with Aztec gods, greedy for rebirth in the veins of even an exile passing through. Now, back home, I wondered if I oughtn't to catch a bus to some fresh exile, forget the whole plan while the blood lay unspilled, find some easier reason for existing. But even here, the Aztec gods that were my love and anger had too strong a grip on my innards for any other option to be viable. I turned away, heading for the main road.

It was as I was skirting the pavilion that I became aware of muffled mutterings and sighings and laughter from the top of the short grassy slope on my right, this crowned with a cluster of tall Scots pines. The loudest note of laughter yet was instantly recognisable. I started up the slope, creeping between the broad trunks until I saw, within the shadows of the dense bushes to the rear of the trees, Luke and Molly lying at full length in the grass, lips locked in a kiss, her short denim skirt discarded by her feet, her hand steering his under the waistband of her white panties, which had some doubtless amusing slogan printed across them that I couldn't read from my distance. She drew her head back from their kiss.

"Nice," she told him. "Feels nice. Nice for you?"

"Yeah," he nodded, uncertainly.

"Yeah... oh yeah...." she echoed, her guiding hand rubbing his back and forth behind the thin cotton of the panties, "That's a sensitive hand you've got there, sweet thing. More sensitive than... oh, never mind."

She pulled his hand from her underwear, then lifted her behind and bent her knees upward, sliding off the panties and kicking them clear. She caught hold of his hand again, placing it across the little crumple of pinkish flesh a spread of her thighs exposed more fully.

"In... inside...." she was telling him. "Go on, Luke. You... you've never...?" She pressed his hand tighter. "Oh yeah...

54

yeah... You know... what you're doing... Oh wow, you... you got me so turned on tonight... my leading man, my.... Oh... Luke...."

They kissed again. His hand worked at her, stirring sighs and sobs until, abruptly, she pulled the hand away and pushed him back, wriggling herself to a sitting position. "Go on," she told him, "On your knees. Now. Quick!"

He complied, while she tugged his jacket and the T-shirt beneath over his head, exposing the sleek pallor of his torso. "Oh, abso-fuckin'-lutely," she declared, sliding her hand up his taut belly and hairless chest, "You're it, totally. One hundred per fuckin' cent...."

She unfastened his belt and jeans, shoving them halfway down his thighs, exposing his slender rump and freeing the erect strain of his penis. She looked on it for a second with the fondness otherwise reserved in girls that age for bunny rabbits and Shetland ponies, then cupped her hand around it. He suffered a violent shudder.

"Oh yeah," she said, "The real fuckin' deal, that's you. Don't be scared. I'll show you. It's so fuckin' easy."

She dipped her head, her experience in such matters plain to see in her unrushed rhythm, his lack of anything other than fantasised preparation signalled by his not knowing where to put his hands, and by the tremors that set him swaying on his knees like the whitest birch-trunk in a stiff breeze.

Enough was enough. I stepped from the shadows. Molly saw me first, wriggling to her feet so swiftly it looked for a second as if she might take her mouthful with her.

"We... we were just...." she muttered, looking around for, and then grabbing, her panties and skirt, an awkward attempt at a smile struggling across her lips. "...Extra rehearsal... you know...?" She turned and ran, attempting to step into the discarded clothing as she went, managing this, too, with what looked like practised skill.

Luke had remained as he was. It was only now, as I stepped before him, that full awareness of the indelicacy of his situation crept across features half-dopey with pleasure. He looked up at me, blushed, dipped his eyes and began to rise, catching hold of the crumple of jeans and boxer shorts around his knees.

"Just a minute," I said. He froze, every inch of him shrivelling with a childish shame, save those grown-up inches still stubbornly pointing my way. "Don't think I'm not impressed," I told him. "You and your cute little co-star really took your parts to heart tonight, obviously. But you ought to be careful someone less open-minded than me doesn't catch you at it. Don't you dare saddle me with a reputation for tempting young minds towards wicked behaviour."

He made a fresh move towards a raising of his shorts and trousers.

"Wait," I said. Again, he froze. "First rule of being a naughty boy: get rid of the evidence."

I raised my foot, the toe of my right boot jabbing his penis, urging it completely upright. I pressed the sole against his cock's underside, rubbing the organ's upper surface against his belly. For a few seconds, his mouth gaped, this followed by his severest shudder yet, a lurch of semen spattering the folds of my skirt, the space between the nipples of his hairless chest and, in its dying drops, the tan leather of my boot.

I lowered my foot. He sagged so severely that one of his hands had to grab the thorny bushes alongside him to hold his body upright.

"Okay," I said. "You can get dressed."

He looked up at me with the eyes of a beaten animal, making no move to comply. I picked up the combined crumple of his jacket and T-shirt, pulling free the latter and sliding it over his head. He let go the bush and raised his arms, letting me pull the shirt onto them. As soon as I had tugged and smoothed it down his torso, he dragged up and fastened his trousers, reaching across the grass for his combat jacket.

I had stepped back. Grabbing the bush again, he drew himself upright on legs unsteady as an old man's, his gaze lowered. A moment passed and then he tilted his head my way, still not looking up, muttered "Thanks," and then "Sorry", and walked away, rapidly gaining a young man's pace.

Thirteen

I had barely turned from the sight of his silhouette merging with the shadows across the car park's near end when a scuffling sound, accompanied by cries and grunts, drew my attention back that way, where I spotted a tight knot of darkness, multiple-limbed, by the all but empty car park's far end. In particular, I caught a wounded yelp in what instantly resonated with me as being Luke's voice.

I hurried that way, breaking into a run. By the time I had reached the car park's tarmac, the murky huddle had taken on the more definite contours of a group of four boys circling another, prone, figure, the foremost grunts among those upright unmistakably issuing from Stu, Luke's sparring partner from the previous week. "Mess with mah fuckin' burd, ya posh cunt?" he snarled as he kicked his victim's midsection. "Try it again and I'll leave you with fuck all to shove her way!"

"Heyyy!" I yelled, summoning all the ferocity of tone I knew myself to possess. "Get the fuck out of here or it's the fuckin' polis!"

They were sweet little suburban thugs: their circle instantaneously split apart as they hastened one another towards the exit onto the street, only young Stuart having the nerve to glare over his shoulder before following the others.

I ran to Luke, who lay curled on his side, unmoving. I dropped to one knee and gave a delicate shake to his uppermost shoulder. Barely had I touched him than he reared up, a swing of his arm knocking me onto my backside as he swivelled a bloodied face my way, his features rigid with defensive fury. Then he saw who it was that had touched him and ferocity was replaced by embarrassment scarcely less hostile. He pushed himself up onto his feet and almost immediately crumpled back onto his knees, clutching his side and spitting a bloody froth.

Rising, I settled a hand at each of his shoulders. He made a feeble attempt at shrugging me off; this time I held firm. "Screw the nut, Prince Charming," I told him. "You're obviously not so well-loved in this world you can afford to cold-shoulder someone risking her own ass to help. Now come with me and let's get you cleaned up."

He sighed, spat a little more blood and then let me help him rise, another twinge in his ribs seeing him sag against me for much of our short journey back towards the pavilion. I steered him through the main hall - leaving its light off so we wouldn't attract attention or interruption - and into one of the two tiny changing rooms in the short back corridor. Clicking on the light, I eased him into a seat on the bench running along one wall, then began running hot water into the little sink on the facing wall.

"You seem on your way to a serious reputation, kiddo," I said, "with the girlies *and* their boyfriends."

He shrugged, which plainly hurt. "Like I care."

"I'd care, if I were you, about having my beautiful body bounced around like that."

"Yeah," he said, recapturing some of his unbruised swagger, "I've already caught your show of appreciation for it."

"Then you shouldn't be shy about showing me it again," I said, turning off the tap.

He frowned, the frown hurting his bruised, bloodied, grit-spotted and thick-lipped features.

"Come on," I insisted, "Come over and let's get a look at the damage. - Come on!"

He rose, stepped across. I put a finger under his chin, tilting his head, examining a bruised cheek and the beginnings of a black eye on one side, the cut and swelling to his lower lip on the other, a deep scratch to the eyebrow above. "Don't worry," I mused, "You're still handsome. Halfway to rugged, suddenly."

I tore a paper towel from the holder above the sink, crumpling an end and dipping it in the sinkful of warm water, dabbing it at his cut brow. He winced, tried to draw his head back. I wrapped my other hand around the back of his neck, holding him where I wanted him, and started stroking blood and dirt from his lip, by which point he had grown more tolerant of my attentions.

"Okay," I said, taking a step back, "You'd better get that jacket and T-shirt off."

Again, a frowning. Again it hurt, releasing a thin dribble of blood from the wound above his eye. "Huh?" was the best he could say.

"Let's see the damage. Those ribs of yours seemed to be taking a lot of the punishment. Go on. You're not afraid, are you?"

"Afraid?"

"Of me. I've seen so much more of you than your cute little belly button, after all."

He pulled off his jacket and dragged the T-shirt over his head as swiftly as a succession of twinges and winces would allow. That luscious upper half of his, so porcelain-perfect a few minutes ago, now stood revealed as bruised down both sides, worse on the left than the right, the damage around his ribs shading from grey to greyish blue, crimson and purple to the sickliest yellow. I almost shrieked my outrage at this desecration, almost sprinted the suburb's streets to thump matching bruises through the small and ugly souls responsible.

Instead, I stepped close and ran the sheerest tips of my fingers up the ribs on that left side. He trembled and almost jumped at my touch. I looked him hard in the eye.

"You're the most beautiful thing in the world," I sighed. "And it's a crime to treat you as anything less."

"Is that how you're treating me?" he countered.

"You think maybe I'm a wee bit forward? Indelicate? You're just going to have to come to terms with that."

I caught hold of his belt, began unfastening it. He pushed me back.

"What the fuck are you playing at?" he asked.

"What?" I responded. "You think I'm maybe not playing fair? Trying to lay bare that sweet bod of yours and keeping my own all covered up? Okay, let's even the score."

I pulled my black sweater over my head, tossed it aside, unhooked my bra, hurled that the same way. As breath made a belated drop into his lungs, he lurched forward, clumsily setting a hand on each of my breasts. I reached sidelong, collected a handful of water from the sink, sloshing it across his face. He stepped back, shaking his head.

"You're jumping a round of the game, eager beaver," I said, sitting on the bench and unzipping my boots before sitting back and extending a foot. "Here," I told him, "Get these off me."

He sank to one knee, slid off one boot and then the other. I peeled off the socks I had on beneath, tossing them in his face before standing and swiftly unzipping and wriggling off my skirt, leaving myself clad only in tights and black panties. He reached for the waistband of the tights, began pulling it down. I slapped his hands aside.

"No," I declared. "I'm the teacher here. I say who gets naked first. And I say it's you, pretty boy."

He stood, stepped back, kicked off his baseball boots, showing distinct promise in next getting rid of his sweaty-looking sports socks. He then pushed down jeans and boxers in a single movement, stepping swiftly clear of their crumple. He was not erect, this understandable after that eruption I had forced upon him so recently, but that sweet slender dangle of his was already accumulating fresh substance. I moved close again, cupping it and the balls behind with my hand. He made a fresh reach for my tights and panties.

"Not yet," I told him, gripping the shaft itself, its softness rising and setting firm: just the thing for my dragging him with me as I collected my keys and then led him out of the changing room, along the short corridor and through the main hall to the back door, which looked onto the playing fields rather than the car park. The doors were automatic, folding apart when their sensor was activated. I turned my key in the lock alongside and they flapped open, draping a chilly night breeze around us. We shivered together and he pulsed fatter in my hand.

"Now," I whispered, "We're going to sprint up into those trees where you played your little boy games with Molly and if

60

someone sees us, they see us and fuck them. Because, you and me, we're going to be an outrage against this place. Aren't we? Huh?" He gave a shallow nod. "Then follow me!"

I let go his cock, stripped off my tights and panties, cast them in his face and then sprinted ahead of him into the night.

We dashed along the side of the building, onto the grass, past the little fenced-in infants play area and then up amid the pines. I heard a car pulling out of the country club's car park, stereo thumping. Other cars swished by on the main road beyond. At the road's far side, the windows of suburban villas glowed in warm, sedate hues and I could almost make out the babble and drone of all the TV sets housed within.

Yet the silence and shadow in which we ran, in which he caught me and fought me around to face him, in which I pushed him to the ground and sat astride him, murdered it all, slaughtered the normality, if the normality had only known. I caught hold of his cock, worked it within me, riding that stupid, beauteous kid as if raping the whole suburb. He clawed and clutched at my thighs but lay essentially helpless and swiftly came, the sputter of his juice within me warm and sweet. I tilted my head towards the cold stars and knew what was to come had just been inscribed there in bone-white letters.

I sagged atop him, then slid away and wandered back to the pavilion, caring less than ever if anyone spotted me, letting him follow as fast or slow as he liked. I was halfway there when he rushed past me, boyishly shy, giggling his panic. I followed him inside at my own pace.

Still naked, I stood by a window in the corridor outside the changing rooms, leaning on the sill, surveying the car park and those villas across the road, my own reflection, ghost-pale, afloat between myself and them, half-frightening me with its silver-blue serenity.

"You..." I heard the kid say, reappearing at my side. As he fumbled after his next word, I glanced around. He had dressed. "...You're everything, every fuckin'... I mean -...." He laid a hand on my arm. "I want to give my life to you. I don't know what the fuck that means. I mean it, anyway. You... you're the most.... I need to see you again. Like, like this, I mean, I... A

61

miracle, you are. Like... like lightning clean through me. I....
Look. I'm shaking." He withdrew his hand.

"Feeling's mutual, Luke," I said. "Feel for yourself."

I caught his hand, drove it between my legs, where my
cunt still lay hot and damp.

"But you run along, meanwhile," I continued, slipping his
hand away, "You're just a kid, after all. Don't be out too late."

He nodded, smiled. His face still hurt. He hurried past me.
I watched him cross the car park, glancing a couple of times
over his shoulder. I masturbated myself, swiftly, deftly, over the
thought of all I had planned for him. My burning brow clunked
the cold glass as I came. Then I went into the changing room
and sat down and wept.

Fourteen

When I got back, Abby - sat, God bless her, on the couch in her Snoopy nightie chewing muesli - asked how I had got on. I told her the class had been stimulating and left it at that. Half an hour later, as I sat alongside her, showered and changed into my own nightie, Abby's hand creeping onto my half-naked thigh, the doorbell went and Abby, cursing, rose to answer it.

I had just switched from the dreary Discovery channel documentary Abby had been watching to a film about brain-sucking aliens when I caught the voice of Luke's mother, atonal with distress, from the hallway. Half a moment later, Amelia was pushing into the living room.

"Do you know what's happened to Luke?" she asked.

"Luke?" I responded.

"He's come home looking like - "

"Looking like a bloody rugby team's used him for the ball." This was the father's voice, the sentence begun in the hall, the man himself only stepping into view in time to pronounce the last couple of words, his commanding voice dropping an octave in consequence of his having seen me there.

"Rick, um, maybe we're intruding...." muttered Amelia, noting that myself and Abby were in our night-things.

"What the hell," he snapped, eyes not leaving me, "We're all friends here, surely?"

"It's Luke," Amelia said. "He's been attacked. His face... he didn't show up like that at the class, surely? Did he go to the class?"

I nodded. "He went to the class."

"Not like that?!"

"No. He was his usual good-looking self."

"Well, then... I don't know. He wouldn't say anything to

us, just raced right up to his bedroom, slammed the door. We thought you might know something."

"In case there should be any charges needing pressed," her husband butted-in.

"I do know what you're talking about," I said.

"Oh yes?" the father frowned.

"He'd just left my class, heading across the car park, when I caught sight of him being attacked."

"Oh God," Amelia muttered.

"I scared them off, but not quite fast enough, obviously."

"Who was it?" the father demanded.

I shrugged. "It was dark. I didn't get a good look. And I've not been around long enough to be an expert on the local tearaways. I took Luke in, sorted him out as best I could. Sent him on his way."

"And you... you didn't ... didn't think to... to phone us, warn us...?" Amelia said.

"He's a big kid. A young man, indeed. I figured he could do his own crime reporting."

"He wouldn't confide in us," his father all-but-snarled, "if a snake bit him."

"We've had..." Amelia sighed, "...so much trouble with him. I thought those drama classes might at least...."

"He's excelling at those drama classes," I said, just as Abby returned to the room, tightening her dressing gown and tossing a towelling robe across to me. "He has talent."

His father snorted. "Oh, he has talent, alright."

I stood, drew the robe about me without bothering to fasten it.

"I'd have faith in him if I were you. He has quite a future, pointed in the right direction."

"Look," said Amelia, "I'm sorry about butting in on you like this, but we got such a shock. - Abby, you should have seen him. His beautiful face...."

"And you're saying you can't help us identify the thugs responsible?" her husband interjected.

"I told you. I can't. Sorry."

"Nor help us find out why it happened?"

"Ask your son. Show him a little patience. He might respond, sooner or later."

"I don't need to be told how to handle my own son," he glowered.

"Rick!" his wife protested.

"We're wasting our time here," he said. "At least as much as Luke is wasting his time at those poncified drama classes."

"You should pop along to one of them," I suggested. "Join in, even. You might surprise yourself. Talent's supposed to run in families, isn't it?"

"If only one had some control over the forms it takes. Come on, Amy, let's go." He strode for the door.

"I'll see you out," I said.

"I *am* sorry," Amelia reiterated as I ushered her back into the hallway. "It's just... *this*... after all the... all the other things...."

"Other things?" I asked.

She caught my arm, looked me in the eye, then looked round at Abby, who retreated further into the living room. Amelia faced me again.

"This isn't, you see...." she whispered, "...the first time there's been... *violence*...."

"Amy!" her husband bellowed from the flat's doorway. Her grasp on my arm tightened and then let me go. She hurried after his bark. I glanced to Abby, who was lighting a cigarette, eyes awkwardly downcast. She turned away, headed back towards the couch.

I followed Amelia. Her husband had stepped onto the stairwell landing, holding open the door of the flat. As Amelia crossed the threshold, she called back to Abby some triviality about arrangements for the shop the next day. Her husband gave a sigh deeper than the stairwell and Amelia, flinching, hurried out without waiting for Abby's reply, Hutcher following close behind.

I was just easing the door closed when it flew open, knocking me backward. Luke's father lunged into view, kicking the door shut with his heel, then grabbing both my arms and pinning me against the wall of the hallway.

"What's your game?" he asked in the harshest of whispers. "Who are you? What do you want?"

"Rick...?" Amelia called from the stairwell.

"Mel, you okay?" Abby called from the living room.

"I'll find out," he hissed, before turning away, letting himself out and slamming the door at his back. I heard him calling down to his wife about having found the missing glove in his pocket.

I stepped back into the living room, where Abby had resumed her seat on the couch, switching the Discovery Channel on again.

"Violence?" I asked her.

"I don't know anything more than you," she said. "But I reckon it's a hell of a skeleton, even for the size of a Hutcher closet."

Fifteen

The next morning, Abby had barely gone to work when there came a knock on the door, disturbing me while I ran myself a bath. Tugging my robe about my nightgown, I advanced in ill-temper to answer it, my mood lightening as I opened the door.

Luke stood there in his usual uniform of jeans, T-shirt and combat jacket, every item, as well as every hair on his gorgeous head, utterly soaked, the bunch of unwrapped flowers in his hand sagged and dripping. He half-raised them, glanced down, noticed their saturated wilting and then shoved them behind his back.

"It's raining," he explained. "I got a bit wet."

"Then you'd better come in and get a bit dry."

"Oh, I brought you..." he began, drawing the flowers from behind his back. "I picked them down by the burn."

"Looks like you picked them out of the burn," I said, taking them off him and hurling them over my shoulder before closing the door. "Now get those clothes off and let's get you dried."

He stripped without hesitation, the previous night's injuries somewhat paled but still livid, his cock healthier than ever in its swift stir.

"I didn't sleep last night," he said, "And not 'cause of some sore ribs. The ache was to see you, be with you, let you know what I feel for you. I'm showing you right now."

"Then maybe I should show you," I said, stripping off the little I was wearing, "how mutual that feeling is."

Afterwards, with the extent of our feelings demonstrated, we sank together into the brimming heat of the bath, me relaxing into his embrace from behind, the wrap of his arms around me feeling very manly.

"You know your folks popped round here last night?" I said.

"Yeah.... - You didn't...?"

"Tell them you fucked your drama teacher till she begged for mercy? I skipped that part."

"Many thanks."

"They seem awfully worried about their baby boy."

"That's why he's keeping any feelings or experiences he might have well clear of their smothering hands."

"These hands of mine are a little gentler, no? Feel free to lay in them anything you want to share."

"I already have."

"There's more to you, surely, than all I've got a hold on already?"

"Not a lot more worth bothering yourself about."

"What tragic resignation in one so young."

"Yeah, well, resignation's been the only response to life that's made sense to me recently."

"Why?"

"Never mind why."

"Maybe I do mind. Maybe I'm going to mind whether you let me or not."

"What matters is I'm all of a sudden toying with the idea of opting back into life. But let's keep it between ourselves for the time being, okay?"

"Between ourselves, I caught a little whisper about trouble at that school of yours."

"What are you? A private detective?"

"Very private. Able to keep a secret. They chucked you out, I heard."

"They weren't the first."

"Why should the whisper I heard about that be all mixed up in my head with another whisper from your Mum, last night? The whisper of a single word."

"What word?"

" 'Violence'."

"That's mothers for you. Always out to put the most

68

generous spin on what their kids get up to."

"What *did* you get up to?"

"You're starting to sound like a mother yourself."

"I'm hardly acting like one this morning, am I?"

"What did I get up to? I started a band, tried to."

"And, what? You got into an argument over a middle eight and someone poked you in the eye with a drumstick?"

"There are more serious things than that to fight about. More serious weapons to grab hold of."

"Such as?"

"The weapon doesn't really matter, I suppose. It's the anger at the back of it that makes the difference."

"What were you angry about?"

"The crap coming the other way."

"What crap?"

"Let's just say, it came my way and I fought it, hard as it deserved."

"Did you win the fight?"

A terse little breath tickled my shoulder, suggesting a bitter smirk.

"You've seen what I'm like in a fight. A bit of a girl."

"Not from where I'm sitting, you're not."

"Thanks. I could do with having a fan."

"But not a *confidante*?"

"Some things a boy needs more than others. A present worth living in's more important than a past worth talking about. Fuck the past. Dig a grave for it, dump it in. Free yourself to build a future over the bloody thing."

"A past you won't face up to is a pretty unstable foundation."

"I have faced it!" he declared, shoving me forward as he fought his way out of the bath. "Again and again and again, till I'm sick of its ugly mug. The last thing I'm looking for, here with you, is you shoving it between us when, Christ!, you're as beautiful to me as it's... well, never mind how it is - WAS! All that's been is been and gone. Dead. And I don't want what's dead coming back and back till... well, never mind."

He faced me from the bathroom doorway, clumps of soap-suds clinging about his pinky nakedness.

"You can have the whole of who I am, here and now," he said, "But the past, my past, is..."

"Dead?"

"I like it that way. The only thing I like more is standing here watching your tits bob on the top of that water."

"They're feeling a little unloved right now, baby boy. Get back in here and keep them warm."

He had just begun to step forward, the smile returning to his face, when we both caught the sound of a key turning in the flat's front door. He swivelled, stupefied, towards the bathroom's open doorway while I made my own leap from the bath, dragging him aside even as the flat's door could be heard clicking open.

Running, naked, into the living room, I saw the door into the hallway hanging half-ajar, permitting a clear view through to me as soon as the front door should finish its inward swing. I grabbed Luke's discarded clothes and flowers, hurling them behind the couch. Even so, I still had a sports sock in my hand when I caught sight of Abby stepping through the door. I clutched the sock behind my back.

Abby stared at me with bafflement and growing amusement, one hand pulling a wet scarf off her head, the other holding a partially folded and rain-beaded tartan golf umbrella.

"I'm in the bath," I said.

"You *were*, obviously. Now you're dripping all over my floor. Mightn't a towel be a good idea?"

"I thought you were a burglar," I countered.

"All the more reason to grab a towel, surely? Unless you were anticipating a sexy burglar."

"Surely a sexy landlady isn't too troubled seeing me like this?"

"No. In fact, she's suddenly not so sure she needs those Mogadon she popped home for."

"Mogadon? Let me guess: another tough morning with your business partner?"

"What do you think? King Richard popped his head around the door to help Amelia bully me over their so-brilliant business plans. By the time he fucked off back to his cement mixers, I felt like he'd rattled my head around in one of them. Hence the need for something to sooth the pain before I start beating my head off the rock cakes. Maybe I've found something better than anything in the medicine cabinet. Look at you..." she sighed, stepping closer, "...like Venus, fresh from the shell."

Her fingers flicked a bunching of suds from my left nipple. The hand in which I did not hold the incriminating sock brushed her touch aside.

"Sorry, Abby," I told her, "Sometimes a girl's in the mood for a quickie and sometimes she's not."

"Does it have to be a quickie?" she asked, hand drifting back towards my tit. "I could join you in that bath. For a slow soak."

"From the sound of things, it might be dangerous to take your eyes off the shop for too long, surely?" I suggested, taking gentle but firm hold of that hand.

"Fuck the shop. That's the thought you put in my mind, beautiful. I'll sell up to the Hutchers, just like they're harassing me to do. We'll be free, then. We can turn the rest of our lives into the longest, sweetest quickie the world's ever known."

"Fine," I said. "Soon as I'm in the mood. I'm not right now."

Her face, which had flirted a moment before with naked devotion, now hardened and aged, long-familiar with disappointment.

"What's wrong?" she asked. "Even stood there like that, you can't summon a response better than 'piss off'?"

"I'm not your fucking concubine, Abby," I said. "I have moments when I'm yours and moments when I'm mine and nobody else's. Deal with it. It's called being in a grown-up relationship."

She tugged her hand from my grasp.

"You're sure that's what we have?" she queried. "When one minute you're ravishing me and the next you're standing naked in front of me, saying '*What? Sex?*' - and at no moment are you letting me halfway close to whatever's in that beautiful

71

head of yours? And now, these last few days, it's like you're looking clean through me, like I was some dull grey ghost and you had more solid things on your mind. Am I paranoid, or isn't that so?"

"If I'm so private with my thoughts, or you're so paranoid, what is there I can say that you'll believe?"

She reached behind me, catching both my wrists in a tight grasp as she pulled me against her, Luke's sock still dangling, unseen, from my hand.

"Love me," she said, "I know love when I feel it. When I feel it, I'll believe you."

"I'm an old-fashioned girl, Abby," I quietly insisted. "You can't squeeze love out of me like sauce from a bottle."

She pushed me back from her, so violently I almost fell. She looked down at herself, brushed off a clump of soap-suds which had shifted from my front to hers.

"I told myself I'd never... never again..." she muttered to herself, before looking up at me. "Anyway," she continued in a firmer tone, "If it's not love that's brought you to my door, then what is it?"

She didn't wait for the reply I was not about to give, striding to the bathroom and rattling her precious Mogadon out of the medicine cabinet while I tossed Luke's sock behind the couch and backed towards the bathroom door.

"You and the Hutchers -- Christ, why don't you all go fuck yourselves?!" snapped Abby, casting me the briefest of sidelong glances as she strode back across the living room, slamming the front door behind her as she left.

I sagged against the door-frame. Abby ought to have been no more to me than a means to an end, a bolthole in the Mearns and a route to information on the Hutchers; all the same, it was a crying shame to see any poor cow fucked around in this world; I could have wept if the fucker, this time round, wasn't me myself.

"We're lucky she didn't need a piss," I said, swivelling into the bathroom.

At first, I thought Luke had disappeared, the surface of the bath water unbroken by his beauty. It was only as I stepped

72

closer that I saw him lying, wholly submerged, at the bottom of the tub, his face staring blind, unblinking, up through the soapy water, slightly bloated and yielding not a bubble of breath.

My own breath froze within me. I dropped to my knees at the side of the tub, tried to summon the courage to drag him to the surface. But his beauty seemed abruptly too perfect for touching: like *yours*, floating in that place in my mind where you can never be rescued.

It was as I averted my misting gaze that a single tiny bubble popped on the surface, catching the corner of my eye. I looked round as a rush of water and a howl of wet hair and flesh erupted next to me, Luke spewing water and then gulping sufficient breath to accommodate a husky gust of laughter.

I drew back, rose to my feet, let him laugh and cough the hilarity out of his quaking form, then slapped him so hard the blow almost scooped him from the tub. As his head swayed back towards proper alignment with his neck and shoulders, I clamped my hand across his face, driving his upper half back under the water until it hit the base of the tub, his lower half spasming above the water's surface, legs kicking soapy spray the height of the tiled walls. I held him down murderously long, wanting this play-actor to feel the reality of drowning - until I realised that drowning him was what I was actually doing. I let him go, stepping back as he erupted from the water a second time, no laughter now as he spewed and sputtered his way back to breathing oxygen.

I threw myself onto my knees, seizing the hair at the back of his head and pulling him into a kiss that all but bit the breath back out of him, clinging there till I felt him begin to flail with a fresh drowning, at which point I let him go again. His real drowning could wait a while longer.

Sixteen

It was plain we needed some more private spot for our assignations. And so, the following morning, as drizzle washed the suburb's colours paler, I made my way up towards the primary school at Kirkhill, arriving just as the first bell of the morning ceased ringing and the yummy mummies retreated, climbing into their mighty 4 x 4's for the short trip to a morning spent in front of the TV chat shows or swanking it up in the coffee shops and local boutiques.

Passing the tall metal fence, I glanced through at the adjoining summit of the grassy embankment overlooking the 1960's concrete box school buildings. It was on that embankment that my twelve year old self had first surrendered to a male embrace, and to matching stirrings of my own, hot and innocent as the blades of grass beneath us. Those and all my other fun and games therein hadn't felt like much at the time; yet my years there now shone like a paradise from which the stricter demands of secondary school had been experienced as a sort of Fall, a life that had been a bright game becoming, almost overnight, a tramp round a prison yard. Although your death, just ahead of that transition, undoubtedly tainted my general impression of the great ice-cream-and-jelly party we call life.

All the grown-ups had gone from the school gates by the time I reached them, all of them except Luke, if his youthfulness could be counted under that heading. He stood in the shelter of a tall, broad sycamore, a look on his face grey as the rain brightening as he caught sight of me. I took his hand and drew him onward at my side.

I led him up the narrow road and narrower footpath which wound clear of even the most extensive of the newer housing developments, so that soon we stood between meagre scraps of farmland and the outer corner of the golf course. And the old house, my house, *our* house, loomed just ahead.

Luke's step slowed as he saw where I was, by this time, almost dragging him. "You have to see this," I told him.

I steered him through the ruin of the cowshed and up the step into what remained of the kitchen. Broken glass crunched beneath our feet, rain-drips filtering through innumerable cracks in the ceiling. I felt my grasp of Luke's hand tighten until it risked snapping his bones. Oh Luke... I almost wished you could have dragged me away, saved me from my vow. Yet that hand of mine was already locking all the exits.

"Weird old place...." Luke muttered.

"You haven't been here before?"

"Barely noticed it before. You can hardly see it from outside, all that ivy stuff all over it. I think maybe -..."

"Yes?"

"Oh, this was ages ago. A couple of guys I knew at school said they brought their girlfriends to some old place for... well, you know. I think they got a bit of a fright."

"A fright how?"

"Frightened themselves, I bet. Hearing things. Like it was haunted, you know."

"I wouldn't be surprised if it is."

"What?"

"A family lived here, Luke. Before your time. Things went badly for them. Very badly."

"Badly how?" He stopped walking, his grip on my hand refusing to let me walk any further without him.

"Those that survived had to leave. Those that didn't... well, some tragedies are guaranteed to leave ghosts behind."

"What sort of tragedy was it?"

I looked round at him, smiled.

"I don't know the whole story," I said. "I'm a newcomer hereabouts, remember?"

"You know more than me. And I've lived here all my life. How come?"

"Maybe I overhead some rumour in your Mum's coffee shop. You can imagine how those blue rinses might gossip about a family gone bad. Or maybe... maybe I'm just sensitive to spirits in the air. In a place like this, certainly."

He pulled his hand free of mine.

"Ask the spirits for me: what the fuck's going on here?"

I smiled, started toying with his belt.

"The spirits say: strip off and stop asking questions."

He pushed me back.

"No, come on," he retorted. "Let's go somewhere else. Somewhere that doesn't give me the creeps."

"Do *I* give you the creeps, Luke?"

"I didn't say that."

"But I do, all of a sudden, don't I?"

"Maybe... I mean... I don't know...."

"What are you scared of? Being naked in front of the grown-up lady? Too late. She's already mistress of every pore on your pretty hide. So let her get her hands on it now."

"It... it's cold... damp...."

"So you suffer a little shiver or two. I can make you shiver worse than any draught. Don't we both know it?"

"There..." he glanced around, "...there's broken glass everywhere."

"So you get a teeny weeny cut or two. I'll kiss them better."

"Can't we just...?"

"Just what?"

"You know, sit and... talk for a while?"

"Like a real boy- and girlfriend, you mean?"

"Maybe we can give that a shot."

"Maybe that's not what I want."

"Maybe my cock's all you want."

"It'll do for starters."

"It's what comes after you've got me wondering about."

"The less shy you are about taking your clothes off, the sooner we'll get to that point."

He gave a dissatisfied snort, then swiftly stripped off with the sullen application of a schoolboy executing a punishment exercise under his headmistress's eye, shivering as the damp breeze through the broken and unboarded windows at the back of the house pinched his bared skin, the pale perfection of his

76

form more dazzling than ever against that rot and ruination.

Fully naked, he suffered his severest shudder yet. I took a step towards him. He took a step back, yelping as his bare foot pressed one of the sharp scraps littering the place. Spasming into a clumsy hop, he twisted upward his left footsole, trying to pluck a grey fragment from a dark ooze of blood at his heel. I couldn't suppress a laugh at his discomfort, at his cock's floppy dance as he hopped. I pushed him over.

He landed on his back across one of the most sharply-littered stretches of ragged carpet. Crying out, he wriggled and leapt back to his feet, running past me, so that I could see how many beads of glass and grit and other fragments had stuck in his skin, from his bottom to the base of his neck. In the doorway to the rear of the kitchen, he turned, facing me with the look of a rabbit in a tautening snare. I smiled fondly and stepped after him.

He looked sidelong, across the little hallway on whose threshold he stood and towards the back door. But then he glanced down at his nakedness before looking to his discarded clothes, myself now between him and them.

"What are you trying to do to me?" he asked.

"Don't worry, little boy," I told him, "A game's all it is. Now, do you have the nerve to play?"

Childish anxiety fought upon his features with adult excitement, the latter finally coming to the fore. He turned and dashed into the hall. I hurried after him, saw him running upstairs, slipping a couple of times on the debris heaping the steps, this throwing him forward into a swift crawl. I ascended after him, unrushed.

By the time I reached the landing above, he had slipped from sight. I scanned the doorways of the darkened rooms, venturing first into the largest, once Mum and Dad's, its boarded up darkness and blankness of furnishing instantly dampening my delight in the game, memories crowding upon me until I almost heard Mum's sobbings, felt Dad clutching me for support.

I reeled away to what had once been my bedroom, finding it likewise empty of my quarry. I burrowed my face against the wallpaper's rotting ponies, weeping seizing me, a weeping and a wonderment at the action I had trapped myself in, the actions which yet lay ahead. "Luke...?" the innocent child in me sobbed, aching to set us both free. I stepped from that room, crossing to the landing's far side, to the room which had been yours.

As I stepped through into a darkness deeper than that of any other room in the house, deeper but tinted a dark olive shade by the seepage of daylight past the ivy choking the broken window at the room's far end, I discerned a low weeping and saw, in the obscurity below the window, a huddle of naked beauty, its head dipped low and hair in an untidy flop as it rocked on its knees and picked at the pale arch of its back.

And although common sense told me it was Luke, there hovered around that form the possibility of its head rising to reveal *your* features, the figure standing and unfurling *your* nakedness, still more radiant than his. "Luke...?" I murmured, unsure which of the two of you I most wanted to answer.

The face swivelled my way and I saw that it was - of course it was - Luke's, tears glinting upon it.

"Did I hurt you?" I asked.

"What do you think?" he all but whimpered.

"Lie down," I said, approaching.

"Oh yeah," he replied. "With all this jaggedy shit sticking out of my back. Bright fuckin' idea."

"Lie on your front," I said. "And let me see what I can do for you."

"We've seen already what you can do. Seen enough, maybe?"

"No," I replied. "Not nearly enough."

Grabbing the hair at the back of his head, I hurled him flat on his front, the floorboards rattling. As he struggled to rise, I sat astride his thighs, pressing my hand against the glass fragments embedded in the small of his back. He yelped and lay flat.

"You have to trust me, Luke," I said. "Trust is everything when two people are as close as we're set to be. Do I hurt you? Well and good. There's more to being naked together than just taking your clothes off."

I plucked aside the largest of the tiny shards fixed in the skin of his buttocks. A budding of blood, tiny, rose at the spot the shard had been.

"I may be a monster from outer space, by Newton Mearns standards, but there are planets I can take you -..." I drew out another shard, flicked it aside; he whimpered, "...-strange and wondrous planets, if you only have the guts for the flight. A wee bit rough and dirty down on their surface, earthy. Not a place a good little suburban boy, faithful son and heir, future leading light of the golf club, overall bloodless ponce, would ever want to go. Much too fiery and radioactive. But what about you, Luke? You monster enough to join me there? To strip off a layer of human skin, if needs be? Huh, Luke?"

By this point, I had picked, brushed, flicked aside the worst fragments from their sticking places in his skin. At my every touch, he had shuddered, venting pained sighs, more tiny buds and trickles of blood coursing from the minute wounds until a threadwork of crimson trickles spread across his skin. I began kissing his cuts, lapping at their overflow. He gave a series of shallower, less pained flinchings. The blood's mild saltiness blended the sour with the almost-sweet, even as the thought of all I was doing threatened my throat with gagging.

There was a good deal of grit and other particles mixed with the blood, forcing me to spit aside each mouthful rather than attempt swallowing it. "Are you hard?" I asked him.

"Mmm," he mumbled.

"Then take hold of yourself, get yourself off. I'll take care of the rest. I'll take care of you."

He wriggled a hand beneath his lower belly and soon slow undulations were working their way through his buttocks and the small of his back. I resumed my kissing and licking, pulling off my raincoat and sweater and bra, rubbing my tits against him. He came, before long, with a spasm and a sob. I raised my head, strands of blood dangling from my lip, my lower curls matted with the clotting damp, my breasts lacquered with crimson.

I wiped my mouth with my wrist, then ran off, retching. At the far side of the landing, I plunged into the shadows of my old room, huddling in its far corner. I closed my eyes as tears welled and in the darkness behind the lids, I saw the dead eyes of my childhood dolls ranged around me, staring accusingly; I wondered if their accusation was that I wasn't bloodthirsty enough.

I opened my eyes. Sunlight flowed into the room, the dolls and cuddly toys, the frisky ponies patterning the wallpaper, all basking in the warmth and brightness. Below, in the kitchen, I could hear Mum scraping at some crusted pot, singing along to the radio. Outside, in the yard behind the house, Dad was footering with the tractor's engine, rousing it to oily snorts without ever quite getting it to tick over properly. A nearby cow hooted her derision. I could smell the turned and turning earth.

And *you*... I could hear you at the landing's other end, plucking chords from your guitar, muttering some song you were making up and would never write down, some song of love unrequited or requited the wrong way, which is how the best songs always go. I called to you, silently but with all my heart. I heard your thumb thwack a wrong note, then the guitar was clunked down and you were stepping through, moaning about my needfulness.

You loomed in my doorway, leaning on the jamb, a tower of strength in your white T shirt, your cut-off jeans, your precocious height - yet a delicate, fragile thing, too, in a world I knew, even then, to be largely composed of jagged obstacles, violent gestures. You stepped towards me, blind to how soon the earth would give beneath your feet.

I opened my eyes. Luke stood in the doorway. He had dressed himself. The rain fell heavier than ever outside, dripping its drips through the building's thousand cracks.

"You okay?" he asked.

"Me?" I crossed my arms across my breasts.

"I couldn't find you," he said, stepping across the room. "Thought you'd run away."

"Where would I run?"

"You look beautiful." He held my sweater and bra. He tossed them to the floor at one side of me.

"I hurt you," I said.

"That's okay."

"Is it?"

"It was kind of sweet... once I got used to it. People hurt one another all the time. I suppose sometimes it can even be a sign of...."

"Of?"

"Of love. Don't you think?" He stood above me. It was hard to see his features in the gloom.

"You're kind of young for a philosopher," I suggested, pulling on my bra.

"I'm growing all the time. Through experience, mostly."

I reached up, took his hand, drew him onto one knee at my side.

"Experience can be a bruising, bitter thing," I said. "Believe me."

"Bitter can be sweet," he suggested. "That's why they call it bitter-sweet."

"You've got a smart little arse. But that's not why I'm calling you 'smart-arse'. Here, do me up." I twisted away from him, so he could get at the catch of my bra.

"I need," he said, fumbling around, "maybe a wee bit more experience with *this* kind of thing."

No sooner had he fixed the catch than I turned sharply, locking my grasp about his chin and cheeks.

"You don't know what experience is," I said. "Not yet."

"I'm waiting for you to show me."

I pushed him from me, sent him stumbling back as I rose to my feet.

"Some things can't be shown. They can only be lived. They can't be play-acted. You have to know them from their dead centre, no way out till the worst has been known. The family who lived here... that's what they lived through. The whole small, immense world of suburban cruelty closed over them, a tidal wave, right out of a clear blue sky. It drowned them, but still had the meanness to keep them bobbing around a while. The heaviest heart can take an age to sink. What game could I pervert you with that would give you the tiniest taste of pain like that?"

"You..." he began, "...you knew them?"

"I know how they - *felt*!"

I gave his chest a harder push still. I'm not sure what I was doing. Feeling rather than thinking: a little mad with it. But certainly I didn't have anything worse in mind than his falling over his own feet, nicely prone for some fresh indecency that would come to me in a moment.

But I'd failed to take into account the gnaw of time into the fabric of the place, his clumping backward steps provoking the briefest, sorest creak from the bare floorboards before that whole section of floor snapped beneath him, sending him plunging through the jagged hole amid an uprush of yellow dust.

So thick was this dust that I lost sight of him, the cry he released too swiftly choked for it to help me locate him. I rushed forward, my smarting eyes only clearing on the sight of the floor's rough-edged gap a fraction of a second before I would have stumbled through. It was a second further before I noticed two hands clinging to the hole's edge.

As the dust began clearing, I saw Luke hanging by the slender purchase of those hands on the splintered edge, his legs swinging beneath him, his dust-masked face looking up at me with red-rimmed eyes, those and his mouth wide with awareness of the drop below. I could see that fragments of collapsed ceiling had smashed through the kitchen floor, so that he was threatened not with a drop of a single storey, but with a further plunge into the cellar beneath.

And I thought, as he looked to me for rescue: how perfect for the place itself to claim him, to gulp him down like some sea-bed crustacean chomping a passing minnow. But was it, I wondered, enough: had I, myself, gulped enough vengeance yet? Had I yet coupled long enough, fierce enough, with this passion of mine?

I extended a hand. One of Luke's own hands slipped, yellow with dust, red with bleeding, from the ragged wood. It flapped to his side, far below. I saw mortal dread quicken in his boyish features, further scraps of ceiling raining around him, rattling on the floor of the kitchen, splashing into the damp of the cellar. A push on his single clinging hand was all that was required. I made the move my passion demanded.

Seventeen

The weekend brought a fleeting spot of brighter weather, in time for the fete held that Saturday at Crookfur Playing Fields, this a fundraiser for the local Rotary Club's efforts on behalf of children in parts of the world sadly lacking suburbia's comforts and self-congratulatory knees-ups.

I myself had nothing to do with the shindig's organisation - although the pavilion used for my drama classes had been commandeered for the dual function of refreshments hall and second hand bookstall - but I wandered along for the hell of it, browsing the stalls by the edge of the playing fields and spectating on the various sporting events involving kids from the local schools.

I was just turning from one of the food stalls, a home-made onion bhajee in my hand, when I spotted Luke's father and sister leading Emily between them, the kid dressed in shorts and a T-shirt with a large number 17 pinned to it. Discreetly following them as they made their way to the point where the next race was to start, I saw Hutcher senior dispensing what looked like pointers towards athletic victory, each marked with the jab of a thumb. Even on the starting line, as Emily set her potato on her tablespoon, he was looming at the poor kid's shoulder, pointing along the track and proffering guidance.

The starting whistle was, in fact, delayed by several seconds while Laura extracted her father from the line of nervy kiddywinks. And when the signal shrilled to commence the egg and spoon race, he stood still for the briefest instant before striding through the crowd to keep pace with the front runners, yelling encouragement to his granddaughter, a fisted hand giving the air emphatic punches. Emily struggled to remain near the forefront, the potato wobbling ever more precariously before tumbling from her spoon halfway along.

As Emily reached down to recapture her 'egg' and then reset it on her spoon, Hutcher senior's imprecations reached a new cheek-reddening pitch. Laura caught up with him, dividing her attention between a gentler encouragement for her daughter and an attempt at lowering her father's volume. As Emily strove to regain her previous pace, stuck amid the most sluggish third of the competitors, Hutcher marched forward again, only slightly less emphatic than before in tone and gesture.

I stepped into his path. He bumped against me. I gave him a moment to take on board the full discomfort of seeing me there. And then I spoke.

"Don't worry," I said, "Nowadays egg and spoon racing isn't the only career option open to a girl."

He did not reply. Laura caught up with him again, her attention still on her daughter.

"Oh... well," she was saying, "Just remember, Dad, it's the taking part." She noticed me. "Hi..." she said, uncertain.

"Hello," I replied.

"Laura," said her father, "This is Miss Carido. Or is it *Ms.*? Emily's drama teacher. Oh, Luke's too."

Laura's guarded smile broadened. "Hi," she repeated, extending her hand, "Nice to meet you. Heard good things about you."

"Glad to hear it," I replied. "Is Luke around?"

"I could tell you more about the whereabouts of Lord Lucan than those of my son," Hutcher gruffed.

"Emily's not one to be voluble about anything," Laura said, "Least of all about any class she attends, but she's strung together several words of enthusiasm for your classes. - Oh, look... Well, at least she's not last. Come on, Dad...."

Laura hurried forward, applause sounding from further up the track. "With you in a sec," said her father. She glanced over her shoulder, surprised by his sudden lack of interest in the end of the race, but then continued on. Hutcher faced me again.

"Making yourself at home in our little community, I see," he said.

"Feel like a native already."

"Oh, you're still not quite like anything I'm used to."

"Well we've barely had a chance to get acquainted."

"Too much of a chance, I think."

"Or too little?"

"I wouldn't dismiss out of hand any suggestion made by an attractive woman," he said. "As well you know. I'd just make sure my wallet was out of her reach. My wallet and my balls."

"You think I'm bothered about either of those?"

"I don't know what it is you're after," he said. "But I reckon I ought to be careful with you all the same."

"An excess of caution can take the fun out of life."

"It's my life. I've never let anyone dictate to me what I do with it."

"No. You strike me as the kind of man who'd rather do the dictating."

"You read me right. So don't think you can mess with me twice and get away with it."

"Is that a challenge?"

"You're not up to the challenge I could give you, not now I know what I'm dealing with."

"*Do* you know?"

"I know enough to be going on with. And, if you don't mind, I'll get on now and catch up with my family."

"Until the next time, then," I ventured as he strode by me.

"Don't go tempting more trouble than you can handle," he snorted over his shoulder.

I watched him hasten to the finishing line, where he caught up with Laura and Emily, the latter receiving a motherly arm around her shoulders, her scowl for the spoon and potato still in her hand suggesting precious little enthusiasm for the contest in the first place. Her grandfather launched into what looked like a series of coaching tips for her next crack at egg-and-spoon supremacy, this received with a deepening of her scowl.

I turned away, stepping inside the pavilion and seeking out the cake and coffee stall Abby and Amelia had set up. Amelia greeted me with a smile as I reported her daughter's Dunkirk spirit; Abby was less enthused by my presence.

I bought a *Café Vienna* and a banana cream muffin and wove my way to the sole empty table in the small seating area between the stalls, this ordinarily the room in which my drama classes were held. I had barely sat down when I noted Laura's appearance at her mother's stall, followed by her making her way across to me, cup in hand.

"Hi again," she said, "Mind if I...?"

"Please," I said, indicating the empty seat facing mine.

"Don't mean to disturb you, but I... well, I... I wanted to ask you about... well, frankly, about Luke."

"Oh yes?"

"Hasn't put in an appearance, has he?"

"Not that I've seen."

"I thought he might wander along. Been out of sight for the last few days, sound of things."

"Well, he hasn't crossed my path."

"You've probably seen more of him than we have, recently. Your drama classes seem to have given him the first outside interest he's had in a long while."

"The interest is mutual."

"Sorry?"

"He has a genuine talent. It would be nice to feel I could help him make something of it."

"You know..." she faltered, giving her coffee a languorous stir, "...about Luke's problems?"

"No," I said, "Not really."

"Not really?"

"I have caught the odd hint."

She sighed, glanced at her mother's stall, checking business there was still brisk. "I care so much for that stupid kid. We've always been close. And he's a very easy person to love. Except..."

"Go on."

"We're not all so selfless and kind and sensitive in this world. If you are, let's face it, someone sooner or later takes it as a licence to... to fool about, whether behind your back or bang in front of you, kicking your heart around 'cause it falls

86

within easy reach. Taking advantage, provoking you. For whatever reason. Luke... that last school he was at... well, he suffered, I think, several varieties of hassle, not least from some of the friends, the so-called friends, he made there. Fancy private schools... that degree of privilege can do strange things to young minds. He had... Look, I'm telling you this 'cause I know you've made a difference to him, 'cause I think the more you know, the more you'll understand and the more you understand, the more you might be able to reach to things in him that need reaching, that need bringing out of hiding."

"Things such as what?"

She paused, bit her lip. I could see the lawyer in her striving for the upper hand over the sister, trying to evaluate my trustworthiness from a cooler distance.

"There was a...." she finally resumed, "...thing... with him and... and another kid there, a... an intense kind of thing."

"Intense how?"

"A... a friendship. But more than that. They started a band. Like Lennon and McCartney, you know. Sonny and Cher. Only not quite so harmonious. This kid... well, it got out of hand. There was... listen, the last thing I want to do is give the wrong idea. Luke's a good kid with a great future. If he can only stir himself to it. But...."

"Yes?"

"Mum and Dad, you see, they barely acknowledge its having happened. Luke himself even more so. So I suppose I've been floundering around for someone to talk it over with."

"Here I am."

"There was... well, it got physical at the end. The aggro, I mean."

"Aggro?"

"Violence. Of... of more than one sort. But what it led to was expulsion."

"Whose violence?"

"I'm not going to sit here and say Luke was entirely innocent. I'm a lawyer. I know no one's ever... ever totally innocent in matters like these. But... but listen, all Luke needs is a fresh start, a shot at showing what's best in him. He has so much talent. If he could get into a drama school, something like that... if you could steer him where he needs steering, not give up on him even when... *if*.... Look, a little faith, that's all he needs.."

"I'm on it already," I said. "Don't you worry."

"I hear he even has a romance going."

"A romance?" I sipped my coffee.

"I assumed it was maybe with some cute little actress in your class."

"We have a few of those. Though what they do in their own time is up to them."

"He certainly sounded smitten. Heaven knows he's fanciable."

"Isn't he just?"

These were a couple of words too many. I saw the lawyer in her fasten on my slip.

"Tell me more about this violence," I asked, trying to shift the subject sideways. But I could see she had retreated from her position of candour: far enough back to be distracted by the sight of her father, Emily in hand, as he made his way towards us. Both he and Emily looked distinctly rained upon.

Laura faced me again as they drew near. "You and I," she said, suddenly formal, "Maybe need to find a quieter spot. For a more confidential chat. First opportunity that presents itself."

"I'll be around," I replied.

"It's raining," said her father, standing over us. "And Emily has cold feet over the hundred metre dash."

"I'll come last and get all muddy," said Emily, already mud-spattered.

"That's okay, sweetheart," said Laura, rising and drawing out a handkerchief to wipe muddy drops from her daughter's face. "You can sit here instead and have a hot chocolate."

"Here," I said, rising, "You can have my seat."

"You're in on the plot, are you?" muttered her grandfather.

"What plot would this be?" I queried.

"To sap the sporting fibre from the next generation of Hutchers. I thought you'd be more in favour of little girls

88

playing games."

"I am," I told him. "So long as they've a shot at winning."

I continued onward, passing Abby and Amelia's stall with a friendly smile; Amelia returned it but Abby did not. I made a tactical retreat towards the door, only to be caught by the wrist a few steps on and dragged around to face Abby's stare.

"Are you going to ignore me the livelong day?" she asked in the severest of whispers.

"You have a stall to run," I replied. "And I'm enjoying the *fete*. Where's the problem for either of us?"

Her grasp shifted to a gentler, twin-handed clasp of my hand.

"Please, Mel, I'm sorry," she said. "But... but honestly... what's this thing on your mind that keeps pushing me further and further aside? What is it that keeps you disappearing from the flat longer and longer each day? Till all hours of the night? Last night, for example?"

"Oh, you know the Mearns," I explained. "Chock-a-block with stimulating distractions."

"Depends, I suppose, on the kind of stimulation you're talking about."

"Maybe I've got a season ticket to the opera house."

"Newton Mearns doesn't have one. Most of the entertainment hereabouts is behind closed doors. You... you haven't found yourself a closed door to go behind, have you?"

"You maybe should take a break from your stall, Abby," I suggested, freeing my hand from her grasp. "I think you've inhaled too many fumes off the coffee."

"I can smell someone else on you, I'm sure of that," she said, voice shrinking to a quieter whisper still.

"It's my perfume. It's called 'Get-A-Life'."

"I thought I *had* got hold of one. Only now it's trying to slip through my fingers."

"Maybe it's within its rights," I said, turning away. I caught a sigh from her halfway to a sob.

Eighteen

I was moving back towards a view of the track, where an older group of kids were racing through the intensifying rain, when I felt a hand from amid the thinning crowd caress my backside. No sooner had I flinched than a crotch replaced the hand, pressing upon me while the hand and its fellow slid around my waist.

"Your beauty's blocking my view, Miss Carido," Luke said, lips close at my ear. "I may have to give you a shove."

I shoved his hands aside, took a small step forward. "Where have you been hiding yourself?" I asked, without looking round.

"Anywhere I was out of my family's line of view," he said, stepping alongside me, faking an interest in the race.

"They speak highly of you," I responded.

"That's sweet, but I'm not feeling like a son or brother today. More like a rootless creature of the woods, keen to pounce on your fuckable arse."

"Not here, darling," I murmured. "You'll distract the front runners."

"I didn't mean right here. Not enough space for stripping you naked and laying you flat."

"Temper your language, young man. This *fete* is being organised by the Rotary Club."

"Well, why don't we rotate our asses round to... - Shit. My Dad."

I followed the tilt of his attention towards the door of the pavilion, where his father had just stepped into view and was glancing up at the rainclouds, plainly of a mind to see if he couldn't have the Heavens demolished and replaced with a better lot. Lowering his eyes, he fastened them on the spot where I stood. I looked around to catch Luke's response. But Luke was not there.

I turned back towards his father. He had started stepping towards me. I turned away along the side of the track, doing my best to lose myself to his view amid a crowd the rain was rapidly dispersing.

I had not gone far before I caught sight of Luke, who had just rounded the near end of the track and now risked a glance back my way, pouting a little kiss and indicating with a nod of his head the line of trees marking the rear perimeter of the playing field. Then he looked past me, prior to both quickening his pace and weaving a more obfuscatory path among the other bystanders.

I too looked back, spotting his father still stepping my way. He seemed on the verge of giving me some wave or other gesture that would make it difficult for me to walk on without looking blatantly shifty, when an elderly couple in matching waxed jackets stepped from among the onlookers, the man distracting Hutcher with a handshake and some cheery prattle, complete with pointings towards the overcast sky. I hurried on.

I had again lost sight of Luke. Proceeding around the track's far side, I looked towards the trees but could see no trace of him among them. I paused to watch the runners making heavy work of their latest lap, then turned and, checking Hutcher was still distracted, wandered towards the trees. Reaching them, I made a discreet disappearance amid the narrow but dense band of foliage.

The ground there dipped slightly and I had barely crunched and slid my booted feet a couple of steps amid the fallen twigs, mouldering leaves and discarded sweet wrappers and crisp packets carpeting the dip when Luke's hand, still rough with lacerations from his indoor cliffhanging a few days before, fastened itself across my mouth, his other hand reaching round my waist from behind, its fingers delving up under the hem of my skirt, tugging at the crotch of my tights until the thin fabric ripped. He dragged the crotch of my panties to one side, a fingertip seeking out my most naked spot and teasing it pinker still. He bit into the lobe of my ear, shifting his silencing hand from my mouth to my breast. I was conquered: swifter than ever.

He whirled me around, cast me back against a rough-barked tree, fixing a hungry kiss upon me from which I had to struggle clear to draw breath.

"You're a disgrace to the neighbourhood," I whispered, easing him back slightly with a teasing push on his chest. "Assaulting your teacher while she's trying to watch the 400 metres."

"I nearly got my neck broke the other day," he said striving to press closer than ever, "When I survived, I promised myself two things: I'd say a big thank you to the woman who saved me, and that I'd pass up no chance in the life she'd handed back to me."

I introduced a little tenderness into the matter, caressing the rain-spotted beauty of his face, gladder than ever of my decision to prioritise love over death, for the time being anyway.

"Oh, Luke," I sighed, "Let's really set light to this damp, dull corner of the world. If we fuck hard enough, right here, right now, maybe we can set these trees burning, see the good folk scatter in a panic from their sports day, maybe roast a few Rotarians to ash and black bone. Let's go for it, Luke. Let's burn the Mearns down. Let's be the fiercest crime this place ever saw."

I kissed at his lip until the kiss became a bite, his blood welling hot and sweet at the tip of my tongue. Below, I fought to unfasten his cock. He fumbled his way back under my skirt. Nearby, I could hear cheers as the kids neared their finishing line.

I almost had his rigid flesh in my hand when I felt his rippings at my tights freeze and withdraw, his kiss dragging itself clear of mine, at cost of a harsher tear to his bloodied lip. I looked up. He was staring past me and the tree trunk. I heard a crackling in the undergrowth from that direction. I twisted my head around to look that way, steeled to confront his father and to turn the screw in his coffin lid by its next couple of twists.

It was not, however, Rick Hutcher who stood facing us amid the foliage's rainy drips but Abby, her expression's depth of devastation more naked than any amount of fucking in the dirt could ever have made us. I became aware of how much of Luke's blood had dribbled from my own lip. I licked it away.

Abby turned, hurried off, fighting past the branches, snagging herself and having to rip herself free. I wriggled clear of Luke and darted after her, worried momentarily about the screwing down of my own coffin lid.

Nineteen

By the time I caught up with Abby, she was in the car park, opening the door of her car. I stepped alongside her, pushing the door closed with a jab of my hand that almost clipped off a couple of her fingers. Rather than look round at me, she stared at the shut door and then opened it again. Again, I pushed it shut.

Another second passed before she faced me. "Haven't you got more important things to be getting on with?" she asked.

"Not right now," I replied. "He's a kid. He's got erections to spare."

"You're damn right he's a kid. My friend and partner's kid. What the fuck are you doing with him?"

"It's self-explanatory, surely?"

"Not all of it. Not by any means. Who the fuck are you? And what game are you playing? With him *and* me?"

"Where's the harm in a game or two?"

"The harm? The harm? Here's the harm...!" A slender fist punched the centre of her chest. "Christ Almighty, Mel, I... Jesus, I... I fucking loved you. And you... were you faking it with me, all the way through? Why, Melinda? For the bed and board, the passport to suburban comfort, the... My God-!" Those saturated features took on the sharpness of sudden realisation.

"Listen, Abby," I said, "Why don't we go somewhere private and -..."

"That family..." she interrupted, "...that brochure from Rick's business, those questions you kept asking... You came here with something in your head about the Hutchers, didn't you? Is that... is that what I was your passport to? Is that what I was there for? To get you in close -..."

"Abby, listen…"

"You listen! - Close enough for that luscious cunt of yours to latch onto junior's unemployed prick and then - Hey! - 'settle for the sidelines, Abby, the serious fucking's about to begin'."

Her voice, bitter but discreet at first, was creeping towards sufficient volume to draw the attention of others in the car park. I spotted Hutcher, Laura and little Emily among them. Abby, noting the fix of my gaze in their direction, glanced that way too. When she returned her attention to me, a smile was seeping into her features.

"They, I suppose, don't know what you're getting up to with Golden Boy?" she asked. "Maybe they should be told before you commit any further outrage among the local shrubberies."

"Abby…" I began, catching her arm. She shrugged my grasp aside.

"Don't fret," she said. "I'm not quite ready to be the ludicrous figure I'd cast in an eye or two hereabouts: the dyke who couldn't keep her true love off the cock of some overgrown schoolboy. No, Mel, I'll lick this wound myself for a wee while. Which doesn't mean you're getting away with it. I'll make sure of that. Meanwhile, find yourself another flophouse!"

She reopened the car door. I caught her arm once again. She pulled the arm up and free with a force that smacked the back of her hand into my face, knocking me off my feet. I found myself on my back, splayed across several puddles. Abby loomed above me, looking half shocked and half triumphant, glancing from side to side in a first hint of embarrassment at her own vehemence.

"Don't - !" she said. "Just - just… don't! I… Enough, you know? Enough's enough! Enough!"

She climbed into her car, screeching away while I was still rising, spattering me with the spray the wheels threw up. I succumbed to my own twinge of suburban embarrassment, standing there half-soaked as Abby's car sped out onto the road. Hearing steps approaching, I only reluctantly looked around and then wished I had walked swiftly in the opposite direction for it was Hutcher who was drawing near, complete with a grin that all but applauded the spectacle and tossed me a tip.

"You look in need of a lift home," he said.

"No thanks," I replied. "I'll walk."

"You ought to consider giving the male sex another shot," he suggested. "We're a bit less butch, maybe, when it comes to throwing our punches."

"But they get thrown all the same, don't they?" I retorted. "And it's the lower blows that do the real harm. Don't you think?"

I walked away. As far as my own blows were concerned, the next few would have to be deft and below the radar. Or that was the plan, anyway.

Twenty

I slowed the pace of my stride as I neared the tower block at Broomcliffe. Abby's car sat outside. I looked to the top floor, where I could see the balcony door hanging open. Instinctively, I checked the pavement below was bare of any fallen body, then let myself in, taking the stairs rather than the lift, this providing me with a little more time for strategy.

I entered the flat. I thought of calling her name, but did not. The place was silent, save for rainy drippings reaching me through the open door of the balcony, a couple of rooms away. I made a swift turn for my room. The door was closed. A corner of paper stuck out beneath the door's foot.

I shoved the door open. The draught from its inward passage worked a momentary whirlwind amid the chaos of scattered papers, clothes, nick-nacks and of every other damn thing I had brought to the place. One sheet of paper fluttered against my toe. I picked it up.

It was a page I had torn from a library book a year before in Mexico City, the page filled by a photograph of an Aztec mask, the fixed howl of blue and black mosaics photographed against a white background. Upon that background, just the other day, I had sketched, or doodled at best, and only from memory, the naked miracle of Luke's form as it reclined upon the floor of my other, older bedroom. I had tactfully left the body headless, but such tact would have been a joke to Abby in the light of all she'd seen that day. I cast the page back to the floor and hurried from the room, guilt and anger in their own whirl within me, anger - of course - whirling uppermost.

I entered the living room, at the far end of which the balcony door yawned on the damp grey afternoon, the moistened light shining across the orderly furnishings and fixing my eye to the coffee table and the sheet of paper set dead centre on the dark mirror of its surface. I picked it up. Read it.

Enough's enough. I'm going. You? Should take you with me. All the way. But enough's enough. Listen world: she tore my heart in two. So lonely I've been, so long. All that crap off the Hutchers on top of it. I'd have grasped at anything, anyone that made me feel loved, needed. Any damned thing. Stupid cow. Instead, I opened my door to a meaner deal still than I was taking off my so-called partners. Well, now I know the whole story. About her AND the Hutchers. Christ, what I know. A whole mountain of small and nasty things and at least one major betrayal. And a big, heartless nothing beyond them all. So what's the point? Time to say cheerio to all that crap. Here I go. Into the big O of nOthing. An O like a scream. Silent scream, like in a painting. O my emptied heart. O.

I looked towards the balcony door. I stepped through, walked to its waist-high glass partition. Poised on the metal rail at its top was a glass tumbler, whatever reddish liquid lay within much diluted by the rain. I looked over the rail, down at the pavement and car park far below, their tarmac itself a dark mirror with the rain's sheen. Still no body met my eye. I caught a couple of the softest footfalls at my back, then felt a hand sliding between my shoulder blades.

It paused a second before pushing and then push it did, knocking me against the rail. As my hand flailed, it knocked the glass off the rail. I saw the tumbler spin ahead of me and then down, spewing its liquid, taking its time over hitting the tarmac. Landing, the tiny vessel made an impressive shattering, shards flying the width of the pavement and across the edge of the car park, startling an elderly woman in a transparent rain hood and eggshell blue coat who was unloading bagfuls of groceries from the boot of her car.

She glanced up and it was only then that I fully became aware of my remaining on the balcony, my hands grasping the metal rail so tightly the bones felt as if they might splinter from the tension, the pushing hand now gone from my back. I turned, still dizzy, to be met by a bat-swarm of slaps about my face and body, the mind driving them too distraught to focus any single blow sufficiently to induce anything more than a tragicomic parody of pain. Abby swivelled away from her assault as abruptly as she had begun it. I took a second glance down and saw the old woman still staring up our way.

I stepped cautiously after Abby, who had lurched back into the living room, slumping in a chair at the table where her note lay. She sat side-on to me, her head pointedly turned away as it balanced on the fist above a bent elbow. Her other hand reached for the note, drew it towards her, then pushed it aside.

"What the fuck d'you write at a moment like this?" she asked the far wall. "How the fuck d'you fix it all on a single page, so the world might understand? I'm past caring if it understands."

"A suicide note?" I asked, stepping out of the rain.

"For the half minute it took to write it was," she said. "Then you came in and I thought - what the fuck, I'll kill her instead."

She turned her head my way. Her face was leeched of colour, the eyes red.

"I mean it," she said. "The violence to do it was in me, just for a moment. Christ, it would have been lovely to see your head smack that pavement." Her head dipped and she sobbed, striking a note that sounded like it wheezed through a gash in her ribs. "I didn't mean that. Lovely... that's one of umpteen words that doesn't do justice to the first time I saw you naked, the first time you laid me just as bare, curling your nakedness against mine, so warm in the night. Here's the solution, I thought.... To all the coldnesses of the world. Except it was only one coldness more, wasn't it, luring me into its grip, like hypothermia, which I've heard makes you sweat buckets even as it lays you dead.

"Why did you kill me, Melinda? Push me from that height? The worst thing is... it wasn't murder, was it? It didn't have that much calculation, that much care, behind it. You were climbing towards something else entirely, the heat of that kid's gonads, maybe, and knocked me down with a side-swipe of your elbow, a flick of your heel. Didn't you care? Ever? About all you meant to me? Who are you? What is it you came here for? Why isn't it me?"

"I do care," I told her. "You're confusing fucking in the dirt with caring. And not caring. Anyway, things here, for me, don't begin and end with caring."

"With what, then? What's this fixation with the Hutchers? And how does that fit in with all the Aztec stuff?"

"Why don't we go for a drive?" I suggested.

Twenty One

It wasn't a long journey but seemed, as surely as in the old days, like the crossing of a borderline between two utterly dissimilar countries, suburbia giving way to the skewed, skeletal fencings, the wind-denuded fields, the isolated huddlings of mud-spattered livestock, which together defined the farmland beyond the Mearns, past even the spot where our old house stood. Abby kept casting me quizzical glances as she drove: folk rarely exited the Mearns in this direction unless they had cows to feed or amorous designs on the sheep. I directed her onwards.

"Here," I said, indicating a thin gravelled track leading off from the increasingly narrow road. I had to indicate it a second time before she took the hint, her little car making hard work of the shift to a surface designed for no vehicle less hardy than a tractor. The track, hemmed in at either side by a shred of fence, ascended a slope with outcrops of bare rock and thorny bushes near its top. Near that summit, the gravel of the track gave way to muddy tractor ruts amid which the car slid like an ox on an ice rink.

"Keep going," I told her. "Live dangerously. I can recommend it."

She forced the car on. Soon we were at the top of the slope, the tractor ruts having shallowed into nothing, the fencing at either side of us sagged out of existence some way back. Still I signalled the car forward, telling Abby we would see what we had come to see in another moment.

And, sure enough, as we bridged the summit and began bumping down the stubbly grass on its other side, there came into view, past the raindrops on the windscreen, the short downward slope overlooking the more sudden drop formed by the steep circular hollow just beyond, this filled at its foot, as ever, with the blackest imaginable water. Abby braked, wary of the slope's slipperiness, the car sliding awkwardly forward and to the side before stopping.

We sat without speaking, the rain drumming the car's roof and drowning the view through the windscreen now the wipers were switched off. "Why?" Abby finally said, not looking round but sliding her hand atop mine.

I drew my hand free, releasing my seat-belt and opening the door. "Get out and I'll tell you," I said.

The afternoon was slumping towards a bedraggled twilight, the landscape stripped of colour. Pummeled by the rain and chilly wind, I stepped to the edge of the drop to the gust-whipped waters. The turf and rock there were steep and slippery; one was taking one's life in one's hands. Below, the water lapped rocks black as scabs ringing a poisoned mouth; a supermarket trolley, upturned and rusting, languished on the far bank. Abby stepped alongside me, her sturdy golfing umbrella straining in the wind.

"Can't you hear it?" I asked. "The laughter of children?"

Hanging onto the umbrella's fluttering tartan fabric with one hand, she cast me a bewildered frown.

"Not here and now, maybe," I continued. "The odd ghostly echo, I mean. Echoes of a day... well, long gone. Brighter than today. Height of summer. The kids off school, having a whale of a time. The innocent pleasures of youth, huh? These kids weren't so young. Teenagers. Old enough to know better. Except kids, maybe, don't know any higher value than the game that gets the biggest laughs. The laughs that day were at one particular kid's expense. Yes, that's right. One of those echoes is of a kid screaming, not laughing."

I looked from the black waters to Abby's face. Poor thing, she understood me less than ever.

"A kid drowned here, a long while back. Down there in those black depths. It was Rick Hutcher who put him there."

The muscles of Abby's face were set so tight against the wind that no obvious shift in her expression was visible. Yet I detected a widening of her eyes, a deepening of the dark circles at their centre.

"He doesn't advertise that fact, does he, in his glossy

brochures?" I went on. "He committed a murder right here and was never caught, strolled away, laughing still, got on with that brilliant career of his, raised kids of his own, sharked his superiority around the fishtank of the Mearns, few guessing the innocent guts he had bubbling away in his belly."

"*You* know," she said. "How come?"

I looked back down at the waters.

"I met the parents," I told her. "The parents of the boy who drowned. This was... years later. In Mexico. They'd sold up here. Broken-hearted. Unavenged. No one hereabouts took their allegations seriously. Hutcher's father being almost as powerful as Hutcher himself grew up to be. They died, the parents. Soon after telling me their story. The... the father shot himself. The mother, she... well, she just shrivelled up with sorrow until one day she blew away in a cloud of dust. Them going like that set me thinking about how overdue justice was. And I was in need, maybe, of a mission in life. So here I came, to investigate, to get as close as I could to the Hutchers, which you've seen me do."

"With what in mind?"

"Like I told you. Justice."

"What kind of justice?"

"I haven't yet got close enough to decide."

"How much closer is it possible to get?"

"I'll tell you when I get there."

"And I'm supposed to stand by and let you get on with it? Even though it's my friends you're stalking?"

"You haven't sounded so friendly towards them of late, not with the Hutchers set on kicking you out of your own business."

"All the same... I can at least understand what's going on *there*."

"What do you think's going on *here* beyond an appeal to your sense of justice?"

"And I'm supposed to believe all you've told me?"

"You don't believe someone like Hutcher could be responsible for someone's death, two or three deaths maybe?"

"He's not a man I'd trust within six feet of my ass, figuratively or otherwise, but I've never known him accused of anything more than a ruthless business sense. You're the one who's come out of nowhere, telling wild stories, asking for them to be taken on trust. And though I trusted you once, Mel, I'm not sure I have it in me to trust you now. Maybe you're the one whose cupboard should be checked for skeletons. Who are you?"

A gust of wind caught the inside of her umbrella, almost lifting her off her feet, swaying her sideways above the drop to the pool. I reached forward, seizing the umbrella's wooden shaft, steadying her even as the spokes and fabric flipped inside out. She looked at me as if uncertain whether I had meant to give her or the wind a helping hand.

She tugged herself and the umbrella clear of me, stumbling back up the slope as she struggled to pull the umbrella right way round. I took another look at the waters below, then started back towards the car, reaching it ahead of her.

"What are you doing?" she asked, reaching the open door of the driving seat to find me already behind the wheel.

"Get in the passenger seat," I told her. "It's going to be hard turning this thing back towards the road. I used to drive a 4 x 4 on jungle tracks back in Mexico. I know what I'm doing. Trust me." She looked as if she didn't. "Here, give me that...."

I pulled the umbrella from her hands just as she finished folding it. I stuffed it in the narrow gap between the inner side of my seat and the gear stick.

"Go on," I said. "Get in. We'll go home and dry out and talk things over. Come on! It needs talking over, doesn't it?"

She stared at me a little longer and then moved to the other side of the car, climbing into the passenger seat. I closed my door. She had left the key in the ignition. As she closed her door, I started the engine. Her arm, stretching across me, fixed its hand across the hand of mine which had just done this.

"Hold on," she frowned. "Didn't you say you'd never driven a car?"

"Then or now, I was lying," I replied. "Let's see where the truth lies."

Knocking her hand aside, I sent the car into an onward lurch down the slope. "Mel - !" Abby yelped. Throwing my own door open again, as route of escape, I saw her drag on her seat belt and smiled at her failure to appreciate how certain her death was.

Twenty Two

I drove over the edge of the drop. Abby yelped down a breath, choking off any other sound she might make. In the silence which followed, we watched the car tip forward, its windscreen filling with the black water's choppy surface. I felt a terror of my own - Heaven knows, this idea was only cementing itself in my head even as I executed it - but there was exhilaration mixed there too: after all, if I should die down in those depths, wouldn't that bind us together, I thought - you and I - closer than anything I might accomplish alive?

I was mesmerised a second too long by those bottomless thoughts, for as I twisted round to make my intended leap clear, my door swung shut in my face. I reached to tug it open, even as the water thundered around us, its pressure sealing my exit while I was thrown side-on, bruisingly hard, against the wheel, the upper corner of my head thumping the windscreen.

Enveloped in silt-swirling blackness, we dropped with a dreamlike slowness towards the bed of the pool. Water, mercilessly cold, began spurting across our legs from under the dashboard, my startled breaths vaporous, ghostly, in the near-total dark that had enveloped the car's interior.

The front of the car hit the muddy bottom, the impact throwing up an ash-grey cloud of silt. The car began tilting from its face-down position, but only slightly before its underside clanked against the steep slope of rock at the pool's side, this fixing the vehicle in its upended position, leaving us still facing the bottom of the pool.

But not for long, in my case. I yanked the lever to lower flat the back of my seat, which in our new position meant tilting it upward. I began scrambling up it in the direction of the back seat and rear windows, dragging the folded golf umbrella up with me, wriggling my legs clear of the trough of icy, cowshit-smelling water which had already filled the area between the front seats and the dashboard, water now leaking around the doors and numerous other weaknesses in the car's thin shell, so that I struggled through criss-crossing cascades of the reeking liquid, the metal and glass of the vehicle voicing a whole scale of groans, like a gored whale.

Abby groaned, too. She must have been shaken unconscious in her seat-belt, for it was only now that I heard her moving about, fumbling with the belt but failing to unfasten it. There followed a brief pause in which I heard her breathe the words "*God help us....*", as if she had just realised what that blackness outside the windows amounted to. The next thing I knew, her hand had latched on the flesh of my leg between boot and skirt.

I looked down. Her face was tilted towards me, bone-white and wide-eyed. "*What...? - What...?!*" she muttered. The window at her side gave a shrill creak and she glanced that way. I wrenched my leg free, grabbing the handle on the inside of the backseat door directly above me, using it to drag myself further up.

"Melinda!" she cried and I felt her fumbling for fresh purchase upon me. I jabbed the wooden point of the umbrella into her eye. She yelped, let go. I hauled myself onward, up to the level of the back seat, setting my knees upon the now-horizontal back of Abby's seat. She began a fresh struggling with her seat belt, punching its catch.

I began thumping the umbrella's bulky wooden handle into the centre of the window at the left end of the back seat. The glass gave a muffled sob at each impact but yielded no crack. I pounded harder.

Beneath me, Abby's moans swelled into a wailing, this followed by the click of her seat belt releasing and a fuller rustle and splash of movement. I swung the umbrella shoulder-strainingly hard and this time, as the handle hit the pane, a web of slender, shallow cracks spun itself across the centre of the glass. I gave the cracked area a still harder thump.

"*Wh... what... Melinda? No... no.. - Melinda!*" I heard

Abby yelp, but paid her no heed, more concerned with the first oozings and spurtings of dark water through the cracks. But then she came floundering up at my back, perching her own knees alongside mine on the seat back and wrapping her arms around me, trying to wrestle the umbrella from my grasp.

I attempted to shove her aside with my elbow and hip. She was so precariously positioned on the seat back that it did not take much shoving before she dropped into the watery pit where the front seats had been, landing against the steering wheel and jabbing a drowned bleat from the horn. Yet, in falling, her momentum had torn the umbrella from my hands. It splashed down next to her.

I was considering climbing down to regain it when the cracking glass squealed, followed by an inward explosion of the pane, a rush of chilly water washing me off the seat. I splashed down atop Abby. She yowled, at least one of her bones audibly cracking. As the reeking flood engulfed us, I downed a lungful of air.

I struggled upward, swimming for the gap where the window had been, all but blind amid the density of the silt. I had just felt my way past the back of the passenger seat when I felt Abby's arms and fingernails close around me again. I twisted about, confronting a looming of white face through the water's darkness, the chilled, contorted features scarcely recognisable past the oily oozings from her jabbed and now-sightless eye, the other eye glaring wide enough for two.

I tried to push free. She clawed at my face. As we fought, my left hand, flailing backward, met with a shard of the window's glass tumbling slowly through the dense liquid. I swung it at Abby, slicing its edge across her face. Blood billowed from the cut, blacker than octopus ink, blinding her good eye, her grip loosened sufficiently for me to shove her back, resuming my swim for the broken window.

Although all of the glass had given way save for a few small shards around the edges, the gap opened was a tight fit and I had to wriggle through, catching skin and clothes several times and having to rip them free. I had got all but my legs through when I felt them seized, looking back to see a bloated jellyfish, which minutes before had been Abby, tentacled there. It was easy enough to drag a leg clear; I kicked my boot into her face and she sank once more. I finished wriggling free.

I had barely escaped the car when, unsettled perhaps by my own strugglings, it toppled forward, the back end which had previously lain uppermost tilting with a metallic groan. As it did so, Abby's face, horribly itself again, loomed and tilted within the frame of the window I had escaped. The whiteness and blackness of her wounded features fixed their blind gaze my way as the car swung upside down, dropping towards a landing on its roof, the toppling sucking her deeper into the car's interior. As she slid from sight, she threw wide her mouth, venting dark bubbles, mixed in with which I was certain I could hear a watery scream.

The upside-down car thumped to rest, sending up a cloud of silt and dead vegetation, this so thick that the vehicle disappeared in its midst, only that string of bloody bubbles escaping. I turned, resumed my swim for the surface with the cramped pang of breath left me. And then something else caught me from behind, its arms soft, white, undulating.

I twisted around. It was *you*... you as you must have looked that day you drowned. You hung before me, caught amid the black weeds of the submerged slope, white and naked and horribly young, as if not a day had gone by. Your hands reached for me, boneless, your whitened eyes and fish-gnawed lips grateful for the rescue they thought I brought, your beauty, from the watery rill of your hair to the playful bob of your sex, undiminished.

But no; it was not gratitude you faced me with but joy: a deforming joy that melted your features even as I looked upon them, a joy at my crimes in your name, crimes that suddenly churned my belly faster than that reek of slurry in the water.

You touched me again. I fought clear. Again you caught me; again I fought, breath spilling from my lungs and bubbling up in front of me. And through those bubbles, I saw it was not *you* hanging there, but only some man-sized crumple of white polythene which someone had fly-tipped in the pool and which had got itself snarled in the coarse vegetation. *You*... you floated in my mind and nowhere else.

I hurled myself at the surface. My head erupted into the rainy air, sobbing and howling down oxygen. I swam to the rocks at the water's edge, clambering up among them.

I sat there a while, staring at the pool's rain-pocked, wind-chopped surface, waiting for the water to drown the echo of Abby's scream. But I doubt it has to this day.

I clawed my way to the field above, following the puddled wheel-ruts of Abby's car, shivering as if her ghost kept jabbing me in the back, and then wandered, dripping, along the road until a curve on it brought me out above a view of the Mearns's neat and tidy expanse.

I heard a greasy rattling behind me. I turned. Past the far side of the road, a tractor was approaching the hedge dividing the road from the field beyond. I crossed the road. The tractor stopped. The driver leaned out of his cab. I thought I could see a twinge of fear on his face at the figure I presented: all mud and wet hair, a Siren slithered inland in search of human blood. He looked like old farm-stock: clearer-eyed, I suspected, than all those suburbanites down below.

Twenty Three

It was, of all people, Rick Hutcher who came to rescue me from the dismal taste in television of the farmer's family. The police, after a brief interview, had moved on to the pool, content to leave me, showered and changed into jeans and woolen sweater a couple of sizes too large, to be looked after by the farmer and his wife, she a dour woman scaled to the clothes I had slipped into.

Neither farmer nor wife said anything much, flitting in and out of the shadows of their great dusty house while keeping a watchful eye on me, as if fearful I might indeed be some monster from the pool's depths which had assumed human form. Whenever a police vehicle flashed by, I caught them flinching as if suppressing the urge to fling open a window and call for help.

But their two kids - a boy of about ten so plump his Pop could have made a pretty penny on him had he only come equipped with snout and curly tail, plus a waif of a five or six year old girl who looked more like the ghost of a child than the thing itself - seemed content with my company, trundling their toys around my thick-socked feet as I slumped on their couch, enlisting me as audience for their channel-hopping through television's cheesier delights.

Finally their mother dragged an ironing board into the room's rear corner and tersely demanded a switch to 'Strictly Come Dancing'. The son glumly complied and for what must have been a quarter of an hour, but felt like a night and a half, we watched spangled smilers flaunting their non-entity in steadily less interesting circles.

The knock on the door came as a mutual relief, the farmer's wife virtually running to answer it. I made a point of not looking round from a flaccid rumba, readying myself, as much as I could, for some cop with a headful of questions imposing himself between me and the TV set.

But the murmuring voice I caught from the hallway was immediately recognisable and I tensed, still not looking round, with a quite different order of wariness. Abruptly he was there in front of me, sinking to one knee. His expression dislocated my sense of reality still further, so solemnly friendly and supportive did he look.

"You okay?" Hutcher asked. "I mean... well, obviously not, but... Anyway, I came to take you... home. Home with us." His hand patted mine where they lay on my lap. "We can pick up some of your things, whatever you need, from the... from the flat. And then... You ready to go?"

I nodded. He rose, took my right hand in a warm clasp while I shivered myself up from the couch. "Here," he said, pulling off his raincoat and draping it around my shoulders, keeping his arm there as he steered me to the door, where the farmer and his wife stood, the latter yelling at her kids to turn the TV down. Hutcher thanked them; the farmer accepted this with the most minimal nod.

Hutcher's Mercedes was parked outside. "My wife, Amelia, she..." he began, helping me into the car, "...well, we just have to pick her up first. She's just up the road. She wanted... needed... to see. And the police wanted someone there who... well, you know. There has to be a... an identification."

He drove a short distance along the country roads. It was dark now, his headlights illuminating the jagged hedgerows against the surrounding blackness. We turned up the same track Abby and I had taken, a cluster of lights, many of them flashing blue, crowning the summit of the slope.

We did not go far up the slope before Hutcher stopped. I looked at him, his profile fixed ahead and caged in shadow. A favourite spot? - I felt like asking him.

"I... I'll just go and get Amy," he said, climbing out. I climbed out too. "You can wait here if you like," he suggested. I drew his coat tighter about me and wandered up the slope ahead

110

of him.

I could hear him following, could catch, above the grindings and clankings of whatever was being done at the top of the slope, a strain in his breath which the slope's mild gradient could scarcely justify in a man so fit. I increased my pace, making as much torture for him as I could out of the short walk.

We were not halfway there when a figure appeared out of the darkness just ahead. It was Amelia, her arms wrapped about herself, her face catching the glow of the headlights at our back and shining like the skull of some forlorn spectre, her tear-reddened eyes fixing a discomfited and discomfiting focus upon me.

She stopped just short of me, a shudder convulsing her. "They dragged her out of there," she said, her voice barely audible. "I saw."

"Alright," interjected her husband, sliding that protective arm around me once again, "I said to Melinda we'd take her to the flat, let her pick up what she needs, then take her to our place. For the night."

"Oh yes. Of course," she murmured. "Our place."

"Well then, let's make a move before the police start getting all officious."

He began guiding me back towards his car. Amelia followed close behind; I couldn't see her, but that red-rimmed gaze felt almost tangible at my back.

Hutcher was just opening the passenger seat door for me when a call from slightly further up the slope saw us all turning that way, taking in the approach of a woman in early middle age with short but thickly curled red hair, sleek spectacles and a lumpish anorak worn over a pinstriped business suit, a pair of mud-clotted wellingtons completing the ensemble, a male constable in uniform at her side.

"Just a moment there, Ms... Carido, isn't it?" she said. "I'm sorry but we need to have a word. Detective Sergeant Galbraith." She held out her hand. I shook it. It felt like a copper's hand: a cold claw faking *bonhomie*.

"Hello," I replied. "What word is it you need to have?"

"We'll need a statement from you, at the very least. It would be useful if you could come with us to the station for that."

"Yes," I replied. "Of course. I just need to... to the flat... our... our flat, to... to go, to... to get some of my own clothes."

"Oh yes," she said. "The flat you shared with the deceased."

"I rented a room off her."

"Well, I'm sure we can clarify that and a few other matters besides. Constable McLain here will get the car. We'll give you a lift."

"*We're* giving her a lift."

It was Hutcher who interrupted.

"I think it's best if we..." the D.S began to retort.

"She's not under arrest, is she?" he queried.

"Of course not."

"Then she can choose her means of transport, surely?" he said, before turning to me. "We'll take you to the flat and then to the station. And I'll see if my daughter can't meet us there. My daughter- " he informed the policewoman, "- is a lawyer. A damn good lawyer."

"I've crossed her path, Mr. Hutcher," the D.S acknowledged with a sharp little smile. "Just, please, tell her not to complain about the station coffee this time. It came across as a wee bit snooty last time she did it."

"She knows her stuff, on all kinds of fronts. We'll see you there, in as much or as little time as it takes. Come on, Melinda. - Amy?"

He encouraged me into the passenger seat, leaving his wife to clamber in the back, then reversed away with a crunch of gears sufficiently impatient to remind me - if reminder were needed - that this was the scene of his crime as much as of mine.

Twenty Four

"Okay - cut to the chase," Hutcher snapped as we sped along the country lanes. He made frequent glancings in his rear view mirror; the wing mirror on my side revealed a police car keeping pace with us. "Was it suicide?"

"Suicide?" I asked.

"Did you know about last year? Did she tell you?"

"Tell...?"

"Abby! Did she tell you about the previous girl? Christ, what a surprise she didn't! - Eh, Amy?"

"What... what girl?"

"You're not the first cute little dyke she kicked off her sensible shoes over. Nor the first to trample her heart in return. Nor even the first to suffer the blow-back."

"I don't know what you're talking about."

"Last year! Her and.... What was the cutesie in the blonde bob called? Amy?" His wife mumbled something from the back seat. "What was that?" he barked. "Sally," Amelia repeated, marginally louder.

"Sally, that's it," he said. "You didn't know?"

"Know what?"

"Well, she was cute enough. Not as cute as you, maybe, but who is? Anyway, they had a falling out at a party, so Abby drives herself and blondie home, the latter snoring her pretty little drunken head off. Abby drives into the garage, shuts the door, rigs a tube from the exhaust through the car window, the girlfriend's window, mind you. Then she snuggles in alongside her, switches on the ignition. This attempt at a *liebestod* comes a cropper when some old biddy taking her poodle for its last crap of the night taps on the garage door, complaining about the smell, then raises the alarm. Turns out Abby hadn't locked the door. 'A cry for help', one might assume. Anyway, they were both saved, even if the relationship wasn't. Sufficient word got round for it to warrant a paragraph or two in the local paper. - You didn't know any of this?"

"A year ago, it was?" I replied. "I was in Mexico."

"She didn't mention anything to you?"

"No. Maybe she assumed it would be a turn-off."

"What happened with the two of you back there?" Now it was Amelia who spoke, her voice suddenly sharp and commanding. "Was it... was it anything like that? Like that with Sally, last year?"

"She's had... she had... a lot on her mind, certainly...." I said.

"With you?" Hutcher snorted. "I'll bet."

"Not just with me."

"With what, then?" Amelia asked.

"She was... well, there's no point hiding it...."

"Hiding what?"

"...she was worried you were trying to take the shop off her."

"God...." Amelia sighed.

"It preyed on her mind and then, well, I came along, piling a lot more stress there besides. You saw how she reacted this afternoon at the *fete*. It... it wasn't the first time she'd been... well, rough with me. I followed her back to the flat, where... well, she had a shot at pushing me over the balcony."

"Who could blame her?"

"Rick!" Amelia chided.

"Some old woman below saw us," I continued. "Abby calmed down a bit after that. Told me to come with her while we drove up to that... that pool. She knew the spot, I didn't. Said she wanted to make things up with me. I wasn't sure, but I... I wanted to believe her. So we parked up there, just above the pool. Our attempt at making-up didn't get very far, not with the mood she was in. She was so angry...."

"Angry at what?" Amelia asked.

"I'd been unfaithful."

"You don't say," Hutcher sneered.

114

"Well, yes, she was angry about that, but all that other stuff about the shop got dragged in too. The gist being that she felt she'd been fucked about too much by everything and everyone. Felt it was time she took control. She was so... so fired up, you know? Crazed, you might say."

"I know her temper, certainly," Amelia conceded.

"She hit me, still harder than you saw her do. And then... well, next thing I knew the car was rolling, straight for that drop. So fast it rolled. Did she do it deliberately? I don't know. I... I suppose she must have taken the hand-brake off at least. I mean, I've never driven a car, I don't know how the stupid things work. She even seemed... oh, I don't know...."

"What?" Amelia pressed.

"To drive straight for the edge. But it all happened so fast...."

"Abby...." Amelia murmured, "Abby, you stupid cow...."

"Then we were in the water, and I was fighting my way out, as quick as I could. I don't know what happened to Abby. I do now, obviously. I left her there... Jesus."

I dipped my head, cradled my face in my hand, made a discreet weeping sound that would, I reckon, have wrung the heart of an S.S Kommandant. But when, after a long moment, Hutcher spoke again, his tone remained brisk, sceptical.

"Is that the way it actually happened? And no bullshit?"

I faced him. My eyes had worked up a genuine sheen of tears.

"You're not sure about believing me?" I said. "Then maybe you'll believe Abby."

"What?" Amelia asked, a leap in her tone suggesting she thought I was proposing something paranormal.

"She left a note," I said. "A suicide note. And she gave us all a mention."

Twenty Five

We swerved into the car park of the flats at Broomcliffe; both Hutchers accompanied me into the building. We all silently noted that pursuing police car pulling to a stop at the far side of the road.

My own key had been lost in the pool's silty waters, but Amelia had called at the coffee shop for the spare which Abby kept there. The flat door opened with a click like a drip on a mortuary slab, the interior onto which it yielded rainy-dark and feeling damp - as if the shadows were mud seeped from the depths of the pool that had left the place ownerless.

At my back, one of the Hutchers switched on the hallway light. I strode to the living room, where Abby's suicide note still lay. I slipped it off the table, pressed it upon Amelia.

"Read it," I told her and her husband. "You decide what to do with it. I'm just not sure it's the best thing for her memory for the police to read it."

Amelia began reading. I said I was going to shower and change. Amelia gave a pained sigh. Hutcher tugged the note from her hand.

The mere lip service Abby and I had paid to my occupying the spare room meant most of my clothes were in the main bedroom. Stepping into it, I saw the duvet still rumpled down on the unmade bed, Abby having had to head off early for the *fete* and myself having been impatient as ever of domestic chores that morning. I recalled waking there at six to feel her curled against my back as I lay on my side, her uppermost arm draped around my belly. The warmth and pulse of her so close against me had wakened my usual 6 am thoughts of the life I might lead were I to make that warmth my cause, as opposed to murder and all its complications.

Half an hour later, I had watched my lover through half-shut eyes, pretending to be asleep, as she slipped her exquisite middle-aged nakedness into plain white panties and bra, pulling on tights and making that familiar little bend at the knees as she drew the fabric taut. The furthest thing from my mind as I lay there was that before the afternoon was out I should have killed her; whatever the opposite of murder might be, there my most recent fancies in that bed had lain.

I collected some clothes and hurried to the bathroom. On my way there, I heard the Hutchers arguing in whispers in the living room.

"Well, if the poor cow killed herself," Hutcher was saying, "then that's a crying shame, but it was her own choice. And now the business is yours, ours, for the taking, albeit - Heaven knows! - not the way we wanted. So the last thing we need is our plans being overshadowed by some sleazy scandal, or posthumous innuendo, such as does nobody and nothing any good, least of all Abby's memory. You heard Melinda - she's in no hurry to blacken Abby's name, whatever she might have been put through."

"I don't trust her, Rick," Amelia replied. "Melinda, I mean."

"I'm not sure I do, but I trust my instincts where her type's concerned. She's a tease, Amy, nothing more nor less, a hot-to-trot little prick- and clit-tease who got out of her depth with Abby. If you'll pardon the pun. Well, I know that sort…"

"I'll bet you do!"

"I know it and I can deal with it. Let's just keep her close and sweet till this mess is cleaned up. Do we really want the police making an issue of any strong-arm tactics we might have attempted with Abby over the shop?"

"Rick - my God, if that that had any part…."

"Abby's decisions were her own. There's no justice in any of the rest of us taking the blame for them. Let's just keep our heads and make sure Abby rests in peace with the minimum of hassle. Which is the best thing we can do for her right now."

"Oh, you're such a sentimental soul, aren't you?"

"You know me better than that, Amy. But you also know

how expert I am about keeping what's mine clear of the shit and shiny clean."

"Oh yes, Rick, I've always known."

"What?"

"Never mind. Never mind!"

The conversation fizzled out and I continued towards the shower, wasting no further time in stripping off those farm-wife's garments and stepping under a shower switched to its steamiest heat. I did my best to scour the pool's stink from skin and hair. I was scarcely more successful than in my bath at the farmhouse and when I stepped out and wiped the condensation from the mirror above the towel rail, it was a drowned woman's face which stared back at me.

I was only dimly aware of the sound of the flat's door being knocked. I turned that way and saw that the bathroom door was not quite closed, Hutcher appearing in the gap as he hurried to answer the knock. He noticed the gap, glanced through it. I let him see as much as he had an eye for.

The front door suffered a further rap. He turned away. I heard him open the flat's door, heard D.S Galbraith speaking from the other side and then stepping in. I eased the door closed and dried and dressed myself.

Twenty Six

A trip to the station meant a journey to Glasgow's southern fringes. Again, I travelled in the Hutchers' car, the police car now leading the way. At first, neither of the Hutchers said a word to me.

"So what do I tell them?" I finally asked Hutcher.

"They're the police," he said. "You can't lie to them, obviously. That doesn't mean you need to cough up any more of the truth than they ask for. About anything Abby might have done. Or said. Or written."

"Rick...." Amelia cautioned.

"I'm reminding her of her rights," he retorted. "My daughter would be proud of me. - You said you're not sure what happened up at that pool, it all happened so fast, you were confused, not certain it wasn't all an accident? Fine. Tell them that. If they take your word for it, the matter's settled. If not, well, see how much more of the truth they need and serve it up in the appropriate quantity. When you see they're happy, shut your mouth. As a businessman, I know it's the simplest line that sells the product."

"What about the suicide note?"

He looked sharply round at me.

"I think we all owe Abby a better deal than letting a few vague scribblings, which could have meant anything, stand as her last testament. Don't you?"

"What about the shop?" I ventured.

"The shop?" Amelia queried.

"I'm not to mention that business with the shop? I mean, your plans for having one name less on the sign outside?"

"It wasn't like that!" Amelia cried. "Not exactly..."

"Look," said Hutcher, "Abby loved that shop. The last

thing she'd want now would be gossip and allegations scaring the customers away. She'd want Amelia to be free to expand that business, to make it more of a success than ever. Success is down to having more good publicity than bad. Quite a few people stand to benefit should our plans for that business enjoy that kind of success. You understand?"

"I think so," I said.

Slight though it was, Amelia's sigh reached me above the expensive purr of the car's engine.

Soon we pulled up in front of the station. It felt cold and dank in there too, the gleam of the overhead fluorescents off the scuffed linoleum floors chilly-bright as those slabs they dump the corpses on. I supposed Abby was being stripped and laid out at that very moment.

I was told to sit by the reception desk, Hutcher and Amelia at either side of me, neither saying much nor meeting my eye. Long minutes dragged by. Then the door to the street opened, a familiar figure casting me a smile so reassuring and affectionate as to be, in there, as incongruous as the landing of a flying saucer.

"Hi," said Laura, with a further 'Hi' to her parents, her smile punctuated by wide-eyed twinges of a graver sentiment. She told us to wait, then engaged in mumbled conversation with the polis behind the desk before turning and crossing to me, pulling a pack of cigarettes from her handbag.

"They're predictably strict in here," she said, "about smoking in a public place. Mind joining me for a stroll around the car park?"

"I don't smoke," I told her.

"You can smoke passively, can't you? I'm told it's almost as good."

I consented, and we wandered the puddled tarmac. She asked me for my version of whatever had happened; I told her the story I had told her parents, a little more polished now, with the same careful hesitation between making it all sound like a tragic accident and conceding the culpability of the woman I had loved. Just to sell it all the harder, I threw in the titbit about Laura's parents having taken custody of a crucial piece of

120

evidence, the better to shield the dead woman's reputation, while keeping their own reputations spotless with regard to business practice. Laura's professional composure suffered a momentary derailment. She took a draw on her cigarette.

"Abby was one of the family, almost, family quarrels notwithstanding," she said. "And we're a family fond of pulling up the drawbridge and burying family secrets deep. A bad habit. - Come on, let's straighten matters out before they get any more twisted."

She strode ahead of me into the building. Even as I pushed through the glass door, I saw her discreetly confronting her mother and father, looming over them until Amelia reached into her bag and drew out a folded scrap of paper. Laura snatched it, indicating that I should follow as she moved towards the front desk.

I gave my statement in a small room whose plain furnishings and narrow white walls pressed on the spirit like those of a padded cell. D.S. Galbraith presided, my words captured on paper and tape, nailing me into a strategy as improvised as any other lunatic's fit of inspiration.

"… so, eventually she gave up slapping me around the balcony, practically marched me out to the car, drove me up to that field with the pool, saying all the way she was sick of what she took for betrayal, talking about suicide, attempts she'd made at it in the past. The Hutchers just told me about a thing last year. With her previous girlfriend. -- Is it true, Laura? -- A suicide attempt. One she'd dragged the girlfriend into. You'll need to look into that yourselves. Anyhow, she told me she was ready to kill herself. Then and there. Said it was finished. We were finished. Like she… she needed. And I deserved. That was how she put it. She was so angry.

"Then she started the car, up above that pool, sent it skidding downhill, then… then over… over that… I don't remember much of the rest of what happened down there, in that… that water. I fought to get free. I'm not sure I didn't… didn't fight against her. She was crazy down there, as the water started pouring in, grabbing me, clawing at me, screaming that we had to die together. How I got out, I'm not even sure. But I didn't see her after that."

I resisted the temptation to fake tears: I suspected a certain numbness would be psychologically more convincing. "You've... you've seen her?" I asked the D.S. She nodded. "How did she look?"

"Drowned. It's a fairly uniform look. The post mortem will take a while in a case like this. There were abrasions although we can't be sure yet whether or not those were incurred in the impact with the water or through her own attempts at escape. Or, yes, fighting you. There'll have to be an inquest to settle all this. An inquest, at the very least."

"You'd know more about that than me."

"I'm sure there'll be no problem for Melinda in attending any such inquest," said Laura. "But meanwhile, she's had a trying and traumatic day, so given that we've talked our way from one end of the matter to the other, I think we might call it a night, yes?" Already she was encouraging me out of my chair.

"There's just one more thing...." said D.S Galbraith. "One more for the time being, anyway."

"Yes?" I asked.

"You essentially admitted the truth of the accusation that you'd been unfaithful."

"I did, yes, I suppose."

"Who were you unfaithful *with*?"

Before I had begun to think of an answer, Laura had butted in. "Excuse me," she said. "Is my client under arrest?"

"Of course not," the D.S replied.

"Then she doesn't have to answer any questions she doesn't want to, least of all zingers like that, which are of questionable relevance to the matter at hand."

"I'm within my rights to ask," Galbraith said, "She's within her rights to tell me, or not, as she sees fit. - It's up to you, Ms. Carido."

"Should it prove relevant," I said, rising, " I won't hesitate to tell the inquest."

"Until then," said Laura, steering me out, "you'll excuse us if we don't distract you from your police work by indulging your taste for irrelevant gossip."

"The inquest may take a few weeks to prepare," said Galbraith. "Meanwhile, please, don't go booking your return flight to Mexico."

"This is my home," I told her. "I'll be around a while yet."

"See you about, then," she said.

I walked away, confident of the bureaucratic slowness of that cop's less hot-blooded brand of justice: by the time any inquest took place, my vengeance would be complete and Melinda Carido would be dead and gone.

Twenty Seven

Luke opened the Hutchers' front door as we stepped up the path from the driveway, casting me the beginnings of a smile before withdrawing it behind a decently solemn countenance.

His mother begged him to put the kettle on. Hutcher said he would show me out to the cottage, this clearly being the little building I had noticed at the rear of the garden on the night I had stationed myself there. But Amelia intervened, saying he should attend to the tea and that Luke could easily slip on a pair of shoes and take me the length of the garden. "Happy to," Luke replied.

As we stepped through the glass doors of the rear extension and started across the grass, Luke wavered between a show of disinterest plainly intended for any parental eyes that might follow us and sidelong glancings courting an intimacy to which I, exhausted, failed to respond.

We reached the cottage, a little toytown version of a house, single-storied, hidden amid the bushes by the garden's rear corner. "It was designed as a sort of, you know, granny flat," Luke said, unlocking the front door. "But Granny emigrated to Madeira for her asthma, so here it stands: empty, except for when Mum or Dad have a guest too many at one of their not-so-wild parties."

He opened the door onto what I saw, as Luke switched on the light, was a living room small enough for even such sparse furnishings as it boasted to make it seem cramped, the main features being a couch with a murky pattern of outsized flowers, a small portable TV atop a nest of tables and a low bookcase packed with timeworn whodunnits, spy novels, middlebrow romances and piles of gardening and housekeeping magazines.

The place smelled musty, unaired.

"The couch folds down for a bed," said Luke, "Here, I'll show you." Pulling the cushions off the couch, he raised, unfolded and rattled flat its metal inner frame, the mechanism groaning. "The bedding's here," he continued, opening a cupboard and lifting down bed linen. He dumped it on the bed, then began spreading it out and fixing it in place.

"Leave it, Luke," I told him.

He looked up, almost pathetic in his keenness to help.

"I'm just trying to -..."

"Leave it."

"Making the bed doesn't make up, I know, for the mess I've got you into."

"That *you've* got me into?"

"I know it's my fault," he said. "What happened today."

"You think so?"

"Her seeing you like that. I've heard what she tried to do to you, what she managed to do to herself. I'm sorry. So sorry, for all the difference that makes."

"Have you told anyone what happened between us?"

"Hardly."

"Then we're accomplices in crime, if crime it was."

"I can keep a secret. If you think it should be kept."

I stared at his boyish, floppy-fringed face, his expression of trust, of sheer devotion. I turned away, drew shut the curtains of the room's single window, stepped back towards him and then let myself collapse, weeping, into his embrace, which fastened around me with as much strength as any grown man could have bestowed. I soaked his shoulders in tears, half drowning amid their reek of useless regret, regret at Abby's death and *yours* too, the urge to further vengeance tangling itself with the thought of my having gone too far already.

I heard the door click open. Luke loosened his embrace without withdrawing it entirely. I turned my head, blinking moisture from eyes that must have looked red as open wounds. Luke's father stood on the doorstep, a steaming mug in his hand.

"I, um, brought your tea," he said, stepping into the room,

125

setting the mug on top of the bookcase.

"Thank you," I said, stepping clear of Luke, wiping my eyes with my hand. "I... I'll drink it here, if you don't mind, and then turn in. I feel right now I could sleep the rest of the year away."

"I don't doubt it," Hutcher nodded. "Come on, Luke."

He gestured his son into following him. At the door, I saw Hutcher give his son's back a fond pat. "Good lad," I heard him mutter. Equally distinct was the way Luke wriggled aside from that touch, striding towards the house ahead of his father. Hutcher cast me a strained smile and quietly closed the door.

I did not drink the tea. I could smell the sugar they had piled in it and felt more at home with bitterness. I switched off the light, sat on the half-made bed and watched the darkness around me paint its dismal pictures. Eventually, I stripped and wriggled beneath the duvet of the unmade bed, letting blackness flood me all over again, colder than ever. Abby's drowning face bobbed up behind my eyelids as soon as they closed.

I woke from the sudden depth of sleep that had seized me. The night ticked like a beetle in the wall. I had no idea how far adrift I was within it, the blackness of the room unbroken for a moment, before I saw one particular tall and slender blackness shift closer against the general obscurity. The night's chill froze harder in my bones as I wondered if this wasn't Abby, fresh from the pool's depths, slithered there to drag me back with her, her ragged fingers all silt and skeleton.

I fumbled to the bedside lamp, clicked it on. Luke stood over me in jeans and T-shirt. "I sneaked across," he said. "Couldn't bear thinking of you lying here alone and cold and... well, like, scared, I suppose. Scared of your own thoughts."

I pulled back a flap of the duvet.

"Come and help me with the 'alone and cold' part," I murmured.

He stripped off his T-shirt and jeans. He wore nothing underneath. He slid his nakedness, still cold from his scamper across the garden, tight against me. I drew the duvet around us, wrapped myself about him, warming his flesh even as he lessened, somewhat, the shiver in my soul.

126

We did not make love - did not *fuck*, rather, given that there seemed more love in the nothing, the nothing-but-holding, we did for the remainder of the night than I had permitted myself in any of our previous couplings. Soon I slept.

Twenty Eight

I was wakened by a rap on the door. Rising, I tried to alert Luke. As slow to wake as any teenager, he grunted and curled himself deeper under the duvet. I dressed and opened the door by the merest crack. Luke's father stood outside.

"I hope this isn't going to ruin your breakfast," he said, "But Abby's sister's here."

I followed him into the house, where Amelia's solemn countenance was made to seem welcoming by comparison with the broad scowl of a woman, grey-haired and black-eyed, who sat with her at the breakfast table.

"This is Morag," Amelia began. "We phoned her last night."

"You'll be the girlfriend," Morag noted, looking me over as if I were some street-corner prostitute who had wandered into a Free Church Presbytery. She was an elder sister, plainly, and from the look of things older still beyond her years, her dour respectability throwing the very mild rebelliousness of Abby's lesbianism into striking context.

She said nothing more while I was served with breakfast, then invited me to take a walk with her around the garden. No sooner were the extension's glass doors slid shut at our back than she launched into a declaration of her intention to sell Abby's flat.

"We already have a potential buyer," Morag said, walking down the garden, expecting me to keep pace with her. "My assumption is you're the sort who travels through life with the lightest possible baggage. Good. Then you can be out of there by tomorrow."

"If forced, yes."

"I'm prepared to incentivise you, if that's what you'd

128

prefer." She tugged a long fat envelope from a pocket of her thick overcoat. "This ought to be incentive enough."

She wagged the package in her hand with heavy suggestiveness, but made no attempt to hand it over; I made no attempt to take it.

"However," she continued, glancing over her shoulder at the house as we walked on, "It's not just an incentive for you to move out. It's also an incentive for you to keep quiet where keeping quiet would be the option that best honoured my sister's memory."

"Keeping quiet in front of whom, exactly?"

"The press, for example - who might make Heaven knows what kind of sleazy story out of whatever hold it was you had over her. We've been here before, those of us who loved her, as I expect you're aware."

"Sweet little Sally. Yes, I heard."

"You and the readership of the Daily Record, too. If she succeeded with you where she failed with that other girl, half-succeeded at least, then one can imagine how many more newspapers might be interested, how much bigger the headlines."

"Heaven forbid."

She stopped, faced me.

"My sister had many problems in her life," she said. "You were only the latest in a long line of them. But she's at peace now. She came from a Christian family, though that might be hard for you to imagine, given your relationship with her. We have strong beliefs about... suicide. So I speak for us all when I tell you we'd like as little posthumous upset as possible over her strayings from the path in life we'd have had her follow. As far as that's possible, with this carnival of an inquest we're to be put through."

"A carnival of an inquest in which I'm to be star turn on the stand. What are you suggesting I say and not-say when I'm up there?"

"I leave that to your conscience. Just remember how much you owe my sister, what a poor return on her investment in you it would be if you dragged her name through the dirt. Our father is poorly. I don't want him going to his grave thinking the worst of his daughter, or worse than he does already. In essence, I want you, and all the trouble you inspired, to disappear and never return. As quickly as possible."

"Give me the money," I said, holding out my hand, "And I'll show you the kind of disappearing act I'm capable of."

The fixed scowl settling deeper into her doughy features, Morag handed the envelope over. I tossed it into the garden pond next to us. The weight of its contents sank it in an instant. Morag's look of disdainful superiority suffered a matchingly swift plunge.

"There," I said. "Gone. Perhaps the goldfish'll appreciate your bribe more than I do. It won't be the first bit of green sludge they've chewed on down there. Honestly, all these respectable folk hereabouts encouraging me to keep 'mum' with the forces of the law... Heaven forbid word should get around about *that*."

"I loved my sister!" Morag cried, fat tears popping up on her fat face.

"Sister, you didn't love her like I loved her. Which was from the cunt up. Don't kid yourself someone who never saw her come could know what lay in her heart. She used to soak me through, if you're curious. It felt like swimming upstream. So don't you worry about my financial well-being. If I'm stuck for petty cash, I've just the strokes for diving in that pond and rescuing a quid or two. Meanwhile, I'll clear out of the flat this afternoon. It was a fuck and a romance I was after with her, not bricks and mortar. You're welcome to as much of the latter as you can turn a profit on."

And I did clear out, within a matter of hours, speeded through the move by my discomfort over being back on my own in Abby's flat, every corner in the place given a wide berth for fear I should find her ghost waiting at the far side. When I finally took my leave of the place, all I had worth taking stuffed in a large rucksack and a couple of suitcases, it was to confront two police cars drawing up in the car park, D.S Galbraith climbing from the passenger seat of the foremost of them.

"We're here to have a look around your friend's flat," she

said, showing me a smile of commiseration I wasn't sure I could trust. "Her sister gave us a set of keys."

"Well, I've moved out. So it's none of my business what you get up to in there. Unless, maybe, you want to check over my luggage, too?"

"Your luggage isn't currently under investigation, Ms. Carido," she said, "So unless you insist…"

"My luggage is heavy. If you don't mind, the sooner I lug it home, the better."

"Home?"

"With the Hutchers. They've found me a place at the foot of their garden."

"I knew you were staying there. I didn't realise it counted already as 'home'."

"Home enough. Until I move on."

"Well, like I told you, don't move on too fast. There may be need for a more detailed conversation in the weeks ahead. We did, I hope you don't mind, already check you out with our colleagues in Mexico."

"How enterprising of you."

"I hope we can justify the phone bill. You have a clean record with the police over there."

"Tell me something I don't know."

"The only time you seem to have caused them any trouble was three years back, when you got yourself lost in the jungle. You and a girlfriend, plus your husband. Oh, you never mentioned there was a *Mr.* Carido."

"Enrico was a bit of a drifter. Like I was at the time. We drifted into marriage, on a whim. And then, a few months later, into the jungle with the same kind of carelessness."

"It took you a couple of weeks to find your way out and a few weeks more, I understand, for the authorities to track down the other two. Not much of them left. Just bones. And not all of those correct and present."

"The jungle is full of greedy mouths."

"The other girl was a bit of a drifter, as well, I hear. Rootless. But we do know she was Scottish, too."

"Expatriates tend to gravitate to one another, the world

131

over. She was a good friend to me. The shock of losing them both set me on the straight and narrow, at least as far as my drama studies were concerned."

"Yeah, you've built an impressive CV in that field. Drama. Acting."

"I see it as a deeper matter than that."

"Oh really?"

"I see it as the uncovering of human truth. The laying bare of the human heart."

"Well... I'm just a polis. What do I know about aesthetics?"

"Come to one of my classes."

"What, to be stripped bare?"

"Even a polis must have something soft and pink underneath."

She dipped her eyes awkwardly. I swear I saw her blush.

"You're a fascinating woman, Ms.Carido," she said, raising her gaze again. "I haven't begun to get the measure of you."

"I'll be around a while yet, don't worry. Check me out anytime you like. Meanwhile, I have all this stuff to lumber, so I'd better get on."

"Give you a lift, if you'd like?"

"It's the Mearns. People would talk. But thanks, anyway. You're sweet."

"I'm not sweet. I'm a polis."

"You're sweet all the same. Don't let the job grind it out of you."

I stepped onward, pecking a little kiss onto her cheek as I went by. I heard her gasp her surprise, the male cops at her back exchanging furtive schoolboy smirks.

At the far end of the car park, I paused, glancing back as Galbraith and the officers with her made their way through the lobby door. I drew from my pocket the ragged, faded clipping that had tipped me off, a year before, as to Abby's problems coping with heartbreak, the Daily Record article about her attempt to kill herself and Sally which I had stumbled on by chance and which had make me think, way back when I was

still dithering over the details of my plan, th
business partner might be worth drawing i'
I crumpled the article, dropped it
drain by the pavement's edge. It made a .
very provincial scandal - and was easily kickeu .
darkness and water below. I walked on, hating mysc..
more.

Twenty Nine

I woke in the night to hear Luke outside, trying my door. Even after I had regained full consciousness, I hesitated over letting him in. By the time I opted to risk it, the rattling on the door-knob had ceased and I caught, through the door's pebbled glass panel, the briefest glimpse of a dark blotch flitting towards the house.

I unlocked the door, took a step into the night's coolness, looking towards the main house but seeing nothing until the faint glint from a shift in one of the extension's sliding glass doors caught my eye. Amid the shadows thereabouts, one slender obscurity disengaged itself, slinking into the house and sliding the door closed at its back. I stood there wondering if it had been Luke at all.

Then the light in his bedroom came on behind its curtains upstairs and I smiled at the thought of the warmth and comfort that room and its bed might offer on a night so cold. I scampered across the grass on my bare feet, tried the door I had seen slid open. It was unlocked. I accepted what I took for an open invitation, slipping inside.

Within, the house lay silent amid its neatly ordered shadows. A clock ticked. I crept from the extension into the body of the house. It was warm there, the furnishings flaunting their expensiveness through the obscurity. I moved to the foot of the stairs. But what I heard was movement on the ground floor.

The sound - a light thump of something hard against something soft, followed by what could almost have been the snort of some snouted animal - came from the far end of the hallway. Three doors stood there, all closed, one leading to Hutcher's office, its neighbour to a little sitting room the family called 'the den', with the door to the kitchen at the other side of the wall's angle. I inched forward, tensed for whatever sound would come next.

At first there seemed no sound at all, but as I crept deeper into the shadows, I became aware of a whole sequence of sounds: tiny, busy sounds of no distinct character other than their restlessness, like the click and scratch of a rat behind a skirting board, these sounds underscored by a steadier rasp of low breathings I was hard pressed to identify as human. What was unmistakeable was that all these sounds were coming from Hutcher's office.

I drew closer to that door. It had a keyhole, the better to protect whatever dull files Hutcher stashed in there; I lowered my eye to it, peeking through. At first I saw only blackness, until a second blackness flitted across the first, highlighted by some thread of paleness like skin glimpsed between different layers of black clothing. There was a momentary snatch of what might have been breathy laughter or an animal snort, but which, as it sounded a second time, suggested a voice squawking detached syllables over a walkie talkie or pocket tranny.

Then silence reasserted itself, save for that low unnatural breathing and a couple more clicks and shallow creaks, these followed by a soft but distinct sound of cloth brushing wood, suggestive of swift movement towards the door. I caught a busier flicker of blackness on the keyhole's far side.

I rose, darted to the next door along, opening it and hurrying through, clicking it shut even as I heard the office door opening. Haste meant I had been noisier in the move than I hoped, so I pressed my back to the wall alongside the door and moved not another inch. On the door's far side, silence returned. Slowly that strange, snouted - and increasingly familiar - breathing became audible again. Before me, the den ticked its clock, huddled its warmth about its cosy furnishings. The click of the door opening splintered that calm.

The door's inward swing was towards the patch of wall against which I stood, leaving me in the one spot in the room out of sight to the figure now crossing the threshold. I could see nothing as yet of that figure, but it carried the husky, tinny breathing in with it. A shadowy movement on the room's far side drew my attention to the circular mirror which hung there. Upon its slightly convex surface, the entering figure stood dimly reflected, confirming the suspicion the sound of its breathing had already stirred: namely that I had seen the figure before, in the garden outside at a similarly profound hour of the night, the black insectoid head, with its broad glinting eyes and tubed mouth, nothing more, and certainly nothing less, sinister than a first or second world war gas mask.

The figure inched onward, the two great glass eye-discs scanning the room. My hand crept to the small table on the other side of me to the door. My fingers wrapped themselves around the stem of a tall glass vase standing there. The figure retreated from the room, drew the door closed.

I listened as the breathing sound receded into silence, and then listened to that silence for a good couple of minutes before making any further move. Even when I did move, I carried the vase with me, easing the door open and inching back into the hall. Its darknesses lay hushed, unstirred. I turned back to the office door, listened at it, peered through its keyhole. No movement within declared itself. I opened the door.

Yes, all was still in there, still and dark. I groped for the light, switched it on. My eye latched upon the naked and legless body tied to the lamp atop the desk. The shade of the lamp had been removed and dumped on the floor, the better to display what I saw, stepping closer, was an old-fashioned Action Man doll, wire wound around it several times to hold it there, the pulling off of the legs leaving black sockets at the sexless crotch. The wire had been extended towards a chair in front of the desk, wound around the back of this and then stretched to a knotting upon another chair at the desk's far corner. Nearing the desk, I bumped a hip against the wire's horizontal stretch and the doll's head jerked slightly, a voice springing from the stubble-headed, scar-cheeked face in those tinny tones I had earlier thought might come from a walkie-talkie. "*No man left behind - no man left behind -...*" it squawked.

I caught a single harsh rasp of breath, just at my back. I spun around. The gas-masked figure made a lurch for me, swinging overhead a weighty metal torch. But my own swing

136

was quicker, smashing the vase across the mask's rubber and metal. This could inflict no wound, but knocked my attacker into sufficient mis-step for the torch to flap down well clear of me. I shoved the stump of jagged glass left in my hand into the black-clad flesh at the top of the torch-wielding arm, the figure retorting by clamping its free hand, black-gloved, across my throat, pushing me backward against the wire, the chairs to which this was attached dragged askew while the Action Man stuttered repetitions of his robotized sentence. Shoved onto my back across the top of the desk, I lost my grip on the broken vase. It dropped, smashing, against the desk's edge, the fragments tumbling to the floor. The torch was swung high above my head.

I groped at the figure's crotch, clutched hard. This had less than the desired effect, given that I palpably had my hands on a woman. But I wriggled just enough, as the torch swung down, for it to crack the desk's glass top to one side of my head. I grabbed the arm to prevent it rising again. The fabric of the figure's black hooded sweatshirt ripped downward from the point where I had stabbed the broken vase, exposing an arm with a tattooed pattern of thorns wound around it from top to bottom, the thorns sprouting pink roses.

The figure distracted by this, I pushed it into a backward stumble. It made a fresh rush at me but I was already on my feet and grabbing the shadeless lamp, smacking it so hard into the side of the mask that both the bulb and one of the glass eyeholes exploded. The figure reeled away, clutching a hand across that broken eyehole, blood glittering amid the shards. It stumbled into one of the wired-up chairs, bringing both of them crashing down, this whipping the lamp to which the wire was attached from my hand.

Sounds began reaching us from upstairs, the wakened Hutchers calling to one another. My attacker tilted the masked head that way, disentangled herself from the wire and made a run for the door, the wounded eye resulting in a half-blind thump against the wall to one side of the doorway, this followed by a second attempt which carried her into the hallway, where the upstairs light had come on. Bare feet began thumping down

137

the stairs, accompanied by a yell from Hutcher of "You! Stop there!"

I made my own dash after the figure, which raced out into the extension, slid open the door and hurled itself onward across the rear lawn. As I reached the opening in the glass the figure had left, Hutcher blundered against me, pushing me out of the way and hurrying a few steps across the lawn, dressed in black silk pyjamas and an unfastened paisley-pattern robe which flapped at his back. Then, facing the fact that the intruder had evaporated amid the shadows at the garden's far end, he strode back inside, passing me with still less heed than he had shown me on the way out.

I followed him as he marched back along the hall, heading for his office. Amelia stood on the bottom stair in a white nightgown and an unfastened dressing gown of her own, her stare taking fuller cognizance of my presence, the skimpiness of my own nightgown's black lace possibly uppermost in her mind. "Someone tried my door," I honestly recounted. "I went to look and saw someone creep in here. He... he attacked me, ran...."

"Damn it!" cried her husband from his office. I continued that way, reaching the threshold to see him stood within, his back to me as he tore aside the wire fixing the rigged doll to the lampstand, releasing further sputtered repetitions of its recorded message. He cradled the legless toy in his palm for a moment before smacking it against the edge of the desk, knocking the head from the body, the monotonous message terminated with a tiny robotoid belch.

"Luke!" he yelled, turning. His gaze fixed its fierceness my way for an instant, then shifted past me. I made a turn of my own and saw Luke loitering around the foot of the stairs in T-shirt and shorts, trying to look sleepier than I suspected he was.

"You alright?" asked Hutcher. It took me a moment to realise he was talking to me. "Melinda?" he said as I turned. "Are you alright?"

"Yes," I replied.

"We're safe now, I think. You maybe ought to get back to bed."

138

"I'm okay."

"All the same...."

His gaze seemed intolerant of further discussion. I nodded, made my way back out into the night, neither Luke nor his mother keen to meet my eye. Stepping across the lawn, pained by the chill after the warmth of the house, I saw a rectangle of light abruptly cast across the grass to one side of me. I looked back, saw this light came from the kitchen window. On the other side of the glass, Luke was filling the kettle. His father stepped up to him, shouting something I could not make out beyond a dull glassy resonance.

Then Hutcher swung a hand, giving his son's head a clout that sent the kettle flying, spewing its mercifully cold water. Amelia appeared, shouting at her husband. He shouted back and gave his son a second clout, this time knocking the boy below my line of view. I did not see him rise. I remembered a scene played out in my drama class by Hutcher's granddaughter. "I've seen how it is," I recalled Emily saying as I walked on towards the garden's far end.

Thirty

My next wakening came by way of a mobile phone's trill. Eyes opening on a silvery smear of dawn across my ceiling, I groped around the bed, seeking the source of the sound. But already it had been cut off, replaced by Hutcher's voice somewhere outside my window. I scrambled from bed, crawling to the window sill and teasing a slit between the curtains a little wider, revealing the man himself, dressed, standing with his back to me ten feet or so away across the lawn in the still pallid light. His words were pitched too low for me to make them all out but as I tilted my ear towards the glass and the swell of his rage set him swivelling this way and that, I caught his gist.

"Yes, damn it, yes, the usual! No, no, nine, the bloody bank doesn't open till nine! One day, listen, one day soon, you … Never mind! Yes, yes, like before! See you there!"

I drew my head back, let the curtain slip closed as he turned my way. When I heard his grassy tread moving on, I reopened the slit, saw him walking towards the far end of this bottom corner of the garden, approaching the greenhouse which stood there. I realised that the object he carried in his left hand was the mutilated doll from the night before.

He slid back the greenhouse door, stepped inside, fumbled about within and then started back the way he had come. Just before closing the curtain, I noted that the doll was gone from his hand.

After hearing the extension door slide shut at his back, I dressed and sneaked out to the greenhouse. There, stuffed beneath shelves of tomato plants and beds of parsley and cress, I located and dragged out a small, sagging cardboard box. Opening its flaps, I found it full of dolls similar to the one I had seen already, that doll lying on top. They lay there like heaped

140

corpses from some genocide in a toy department: all of them action figures, many of them old fashioned Action Men such as I could recall you playing with as a kid, a generic variety to their super-macho short hair-do's, the set of their lantern jaws. Yet all of them that I could see had suffered the removal of their legs. I closed the box and shoved it back where I found it.

I enjoyed a wordless breakfast with Amelia, who made a point of jumping up from the table when I entered and finishing her corn flakes awkwardly propped against the worktop, after which she wriggled out of the room altogether, leaving me free to be at what I knew - from the address on a statement propped atop the bread bin - to be Hutcher's bank well before nine o'clock.

I positioned myself behind the scuffed plastic shell of the bus stop across the road from the Broom shops, reckoning Hutcher the sort of man who hadn't acknowledged the existence of bus stops since seizing his first teenage set of car keys. At five to nine, as the bank began opening its outer doors, his Mercedes sped up, just in time to lose the sole available parking space to an elderly lady in a much dinkier car. Blaring his horn and yelling out his window, he accelerated around to the car park at the rear of the row of shops, where I could not see him, reappearing a minute or two later at a brisk stride and disappearing inside the bank.

A longer batch of minutes went by, until I began to wonder if he hadn't spotted me and talked his way out though the rear exit. But then he stepped back into sight, complete with a small record shop bag I had not seen him carry on his way in. He took the briefest glance around, then marched to the near corner of the block of shops, disappearing around it. I moved swiftly forward, expecting to see him turn towards the car park. Instead, he continued on up the road, the far end of which, past a playing fields on the left and a row of houses on the right, was dominated by the wooded hill atop which were clustered the secondary school, the grandest of the local churches and the single tower which constituted Mearns Castle. The comparative emptiness of the street meant I had to keep well back, availing myself of the corners of a few immaculately trimmed hedges, but it wasn't hard to see where he was headed.

To one side of the broad, open path up to the school lay a more secluded path winding into dense trees, only a tiny rusted gate at its near end indicating its being there at all. Hutcher stepped through this and, after one last look over his shoulder, almost catching me out as I ducked behind a Volvo in a driveway, continued into the trees. I waited until he was out of sight and then followed.

The woodland lay at the foot of a steep rock-face topped by castle and church, the latter the grander building, a great drum-shaped lump of white-walled modernist architecture which leant its base out over the top of the rock-face like a crash-landed UFO. I had lost sight of Hutcher, so I hastened behind a broad tree trunk while making a fuller scan of my surroundings.

It was, however, my hearing which alerted me to his whereabouts, a rattling of small stones down the rock-face shifting my attention towards its summit, where Hutcher could be seen scrambling up the narrow path I was nostalgically charmed to see still traversed the rock, recalling my days at the school nearby, the ledge above the ideal spot to get the hang of nicotine or be felt-up by a clumsy-fingered boy. Upon the ledge lay a cave-like hollow above the summit of the rock and below the church's elevated base. Hutcher struggled into this, the tightness of the gap forcing him to hunch low as he passed again out of my line of view.

It was a matter of seconds before he reappeared and began descending, no more successful in avoiding the snaggings of the bushes sprouting from the rock-face than I had been years before. As he completed his descent, at a point not far from where I stood, I noted that he no longer carried the bag. With another glance around, to evade which I pressed myself tighter against the side of the tree-trunk invisible to him, he started back the way he had come.

I remained where I was until I had seen him pass from sight, then stepped around the tree-trunk, scanning and listening intently to the bird-chirping woodland calm all around me. I wondered whether I ought to clamber up and investigate what

142

he had left on the ledge or sit tight and see who turned up to claim it. This question was immediately resolved by the sound of a motorbike growling to a halt on the opposite side of the woodland to that at which Hutcher had exited. I ducked back under cover, lying flat behind a fallen and moss-shrouded trunk. Within a minute of the engine being silenced, I saw a figure approach through the trees in black leathers and a motorcycle helmet, the visor down. I thought I recognised, in the swift movement of those slender limbs, my attacker of the previous night.

She, if she it was, began a brisk clamber of the path to the top of the rock-face, passing out of sight as Hutcher had done. It was as the figure reappeared that I heard a snap of undergrowth at my back, followed by the clamp of a masculine hand across my mouth. A face pressed close at the side of my head, smelling of expensive after-shave.

"Don't move, please..." Hutcher whispered. "Whatever you're doing here, it would be a shame to get caught in the crossfire."

He settled next to me, his hand still on my mouth. Above, the helmeted figure had begun descending, carrying the small polythene bag. Hutcher fumbled around the far pocket of his jacket, his free hand returning to my line of view clutching an automatic pistol. Leaning across the fallen trunk, he took aim at the figure as it turned its back on us and began walking towards the area where the motorbike had been heard to stop. I tried wriggling free of Hutcher's grasp. He stared me hard in the face for a second, then slid his hand away, cupping it beneath his gun hand to steady his aim.

"Easier with two hands, anyway," he muttered.

The figure was nearing the area where it would pass from sight. I supposed I ought to say something to discourage Hutcher from breaking the relevant commandment, but I was no great fan of the commandment in question and, anyhow, I didn't see why I should talk him out of digging a grave deep enough to fit him alongside his target.

"With that helmet on," I suggested, "You'd better put it in the spine."

He looked round at me again, grinned, then faced ahead, making a final adjustment to his aim. Just as the figure was about to disappear, he smothered his grin and squeezed the trigger. The firing pin clicked, discharging no bullet. The helmeted figure was swallowed by the most distant foliage. Hutcher drew the gun back, regaining something of his grin, albeit with the bitterness in it brought forward.

"If you're with them," he said, "I'd have thought you'd at least have shouted a warning."

"I'm not with them," I replied. "Who the hell *are* they?"

On the far side of the trees, the motorbike could be heard revving up. Hutcher raised himself from the ground.

"Or maybe you knew the gun wasn't loaded?" he suggested.

"On account, you mean," I queried, also rising, "of being brilliant enough to calculate the weight and make a comparison with what it says in the manual?"

"Or maybe just from foreknowledge of what a sweet, peaceable man I am."

The unseen bike could be heard speeding away as he stuffed the gun in his jacket pocket.

"That kind of man wouldn't be carrying a gun in the first place," I said.

"This kind of man might use it next time."

"Maybe you shouldn't go encouraging that other kind of person, by way of whatever you put in that bag."

"You're in a nosy mood this morning."

"Whatever private business is being enacted here, it almost got my head smashed like a ripe turnip last night. I've a right, I think, to be nosy."

"You followed me?"

"I was at the shops for a paper. Saw you striding up the road, heading here. I didn't take you for a churchgoer, certainly not the kind who'd be scurrying up the cliff at quarter past nine on a weekday morning."

"You've got me sussed. Or so it would seem."

"I'm sure there's more to you than I've worked out already."

144

"You're damn right."

"Share the rest with me if you like. I have a shoulder shaped for crying on."

"I'm not the kind of man who does much crying."

"Let me guess: you get other people crying first."

"Maybe no one out there's been man enough to push me to it yet."

"From the looks of things, someone out there's trying awful hard."

"Trying and failing. None of this is anything I can't get on top of. With or without the gun. I can rely on you, I hope, not to mention this to my family. The gun, I mean."

"How much do they know about the rest of it?"

"Too much, but not all."

"I wondered, specifically, how much Luke knew."

"What would make you wonder that?"

"Last night... on my way back to bed, I couldn't help but notice you getting angry with him."

He dipped his head, a scarlet blush suggesting itself amid the leafy shadows. "I love my son," he said, looking up. "Enough for it to hurt. With pain, it's always a temptation to share it around a little. If I got carried away, I'll apologise, but to him, not you."

"Then your pain over this and your pain over him... they're related?"

"My pain is related to someone outside my family thinking they can muscle in on our private space," he stated. "You wouldn't be trying your own hand at any such thing, would you?"

"Only out of concern for you. For you all. You've made me feel like one of the family in a couple of days flat. Why shouldn't I be concerned about something someone might be putting you through?"

He stared at me a moment longer, then gave the most guarded of nods.

"Your concern," he said, "is duly noted. Meanwhile, I'm late for work. Excuse me."

"I wouldn't have thought a man like you had to punch a

clock."

"I don't. But I have to keep the damn clock wound."

"What corner of the empire are we constructing today?"

"I'm not building an empire. Just homes. Homes where people can live secure, safe from threat."

He turned away, but took no more than a couple of steps before turning back towards me, his face glowing with a kind of carnivorous pride. "Come on," he said, "Let me show you the kind of defences I build for the decent folk of this world, against such scum as might lurk nearby." With a sidelong nod of his head, he strode back down towards the street, leaving it to me to keep up.

Thirty One

He sped his car along the Mearns' quiet streets as if he
owned the whole damn suburb and reserved for himself the
right to flout its speed restrictions. I couldn't deny, sat in his
passenger seat, the buzz there was to his blunt command of the
world about him. I supposed there was some childish version of
that command about him even back in the days when *you* knew
him. I was beginning to understand how the whole tragic mess
came about in the first place.

Our brief journey ended at an edge of the suburb where
there had been no suburb when I was a kid, only an expanse of
muddy fields with a few mangy horses grazing in them. Now
the far extent of the road was dominated, behind a tall iron
fence, by a building site, houses under construction studding its
muddy, much-churned ground. As we drove onto the site, a
massive sign declared that this was LANDORIA and that most
of the units were already sold: the starting price quoted on the
board made it clear these houses were pitched so top-of-the-
range I was surprised they weren't advertised as coming with
their own private sun attached, should the one the rest of us use
prove too weak and downmarket.

Indeed, as the car slowed and bumped its way up the
muddy track already partway to becoming a cul-de-sac road, the
houses at either side of us asserted, even half-finished, an
elegance and scale more suggestive of mediterranean villas than
of the Glaswegian commuter belt. Around and within the shells
of the houses workmen hammered, plastered, scaled
scaffolding, loaded cement mixers, hefted planks, as well as
glancing across at their gaffer and the woman in his passenger
seat so plainly not Mrs. Hutcher, exchanging the odd sidelong
grin with one another as they did so.

Hutcher drove on towards the furthermost, and most finished-looking, of the houses. Drawing to a stop outside this, he lifted a couple of hard hats from the boot of his car and handed me one. Someone by the next house along gave me a wolf whistle. Hutcher scowled in the general direction. "Into the house," he told me.

Its structural completeness meant this house had been temporarily deserted by the workmen while they brought the others to the same mark, yet as he escorted me inside I saw the interior stood utterly blank, its walls and ceiling of undecorated white plaster, the marble and pine of its flooring immaculately laid but still misted with dust and tumbleweeded with crumplings of discarded polythene, the windows similarly whitened with dust where they were not mere gaps covered with fluttering sheets of that same translucent material. And in the absence of any furnishings, the spaces through which he led me seemed still more outsized than was the intention, the echo of our footfalls making the place sound like a house haunted well ahead of schedule.

At the far end, he led me up the few short steps to a sort of mezzanine with a great broad window, its glass installed but still with scraps of tape clinging here and there and the pale fingerprints of glaziers everywhere. Outside lay a grandiose patio, complete with a swimming pool fit for Beverly Hills. The pool was unfilled, the terracotta paving stones littered with fallen leaves and builder's equipment, the wall at the back looking out onto a very Scottish hillock, wind-ruffled and covered in gorse bushes and crowned with a single contorted tree. I pictured future Newton Mearns summers spent around that pool, the loungers glancing over the wall and feeling the power of one's money to perfect the world exposed in all its limitations.

"You see?" said Hutcher. "Here's what I do. I make homes that stand secure against the shoddiness elsewhere. I'm Mearns born and bred, but I've kicked around enough to know how lowdown and nasty life can be elsewhere. Even here, the cruddiness can creep in at the edges. So I make places where people make lives that keep that cruddiness at a comfortable distance. Houses and lives where people feel safe. It's a vocation, almost."

"Look of this place," I ventured, "a customer'd have to be dragging a fat wallet to reap the benefit of that vocation of yours."

"There's a rough justice to the world. People end up where they belong. The sort who can afford a place like this are the sort you can trust not to abuse the privilege. As opposed to that other sort out there, such as we glimpsed this morning and last night, nothing better to do in their poverty of mind than prey on those busy enriching the world, weaseling around their ankles, striving to drag the high and decent to their own depth of squalor.

"The life I've made for myself here... well, I didn't start out a pauper - had a Dad like the Dad I am: a grafter, a builder, no-nonsense - but I've still had a fight on my hands, as with any attempt to make the world better. Driven by a faith in this place, the Mearns that is, and all I think it means. Which is more than just pebble-dash and crazy paving, good housekeeping and lawns like bowling greens, plus Scotland's last hint of a Tory vote.

"No... the point, the meaning, of the Mearns is that within twenty minutes of all those very different things that Glasgow means, you've got... decency, security, neighbourliness, civilised values. Mutual respect. Space to breathe. A hint of nature without being up to your knees in cow-dung. Safety, above all else. If there ever was to be a paradise on earth, a paradise that earthly men could actually live in, it would look like the Mearns. That's not the most romantic idea, I know, it would put the wind up your average utopian socialist, but after all, who'd be at home in a utopia, other than the tyrant cracking his whip and calling it that? The idea behind the Mearns, on the other hand, is just make-do and can-do and cosy and boring and compromised enough to form a solid foundation in real-world dirt. As this... not-quite-empire of mine has proved."

"Except you're not secure here yourself, on the basis of last night and this morning."

"No. Suddenly I'm not."

"You've had break-ins before?"

"Not break-ins. Sometimes the messages even came care of the post office."

"Have all of them been Action Man shaped?"

"You don't know?"

"How would I know?"

"You'd know if you were anything to do with this."

"I told you, I'm not."

"If you *were* anything to do with this, you'd hardly tell me the truth."

"Then what can I do but ask you to trust me?"

"This morning, I'm not in a trusting mood."

"You've trusted me with your philosophy of life."

"I wanted you to know what I stand for. That I'm not just some patsy fit for kicking around. That I'm a man with a passion. A man who cares about what's his. Which makes me a dangerous man to anyone who wanders along and interferes with it. You wandered along. From where? Wound up under my roof. Just like that maniac last night."

"I'm the one that maniac tried to kill."

"I only have your word for that. And then this morning - you hiding in the bushes while I...."

"While you what? Made a pay-off? I assume you're being blackmailed."

"Patently."

"Over what?"

"Over none of your business."

"Maybe I can help."

"Yes... You've been such a help already, to me and mine."

"I've tried, certainly."

"Brought my son out of his shell, it seems. My grand-daughter too."

"I'm a good teacher. Damn good. Come to one of my classes. I might even help you to express yourself."

"I've never needed help in that direction."

"I was teasing."

"Yes," he said. "You are, aren't you?"

He had taken a step closer, caressing a thick-fingered hand through my hair with what felt like deliberate clumsiness. I shrugged his touch aside, inched a step back.

"Am I?"

"The question is... which game is this tease part of? Theirs, or...."

He raised his hand for a second caress. I smacked it aside.

"I'm not here to play games," I told him.

"What are you here for, then? I mean, on top of what you've packed in already... from stripping me to my bollocks to seeing your girlfriend drown."

"That's just the stuff you know about."

"Fill me in, why don't you, on what I've missed."

"I don't give away anything for free. Not even the truth."

"Quote me a price, then. Standing here, you shouldn't doubt my cash flow."

"I don't doubt any of your powers. But you shouldn't doubt mine."

"So tantalising to think what those powers might be."

He made another reach for me. This time I slapped his hand aside so hard the sound of the impact rang the building's hollow length. He scowled like a bear with its paw caught in a trap.

"The power, for starters," I said, "to see through your shiny armour. Clean through to the bones beneath."

"What does that mean?"

"You don't know what bones are? Those things the dead leave behind?"

"Huh?"

"Think, big man... What bones have you got hidden away? Buried in your past?"

"Wait, wait... what are you talking about?"

"Nothing springs to mind? Maybe if you try remembering the luscious and youthful flesh that once clothed the bones in question."

He seized me by both arms, shook me so hard I felt my own bones rattle like marbles in a bag. "*What do you know?!!!!*" he screamed.

"You," I said, when the shaking had been stilled just enough to permit an answer. "You're what I know. Better than your own family knows you, I suspect, when it comes to certain moments of your past."

"Get out of my house!" he yelled, hurling me from him. I landed at full length across the hard floor. "My *home*, I mean! I want you out of it - straight away!"

I raised myself, dusted myself down, looked him in the eye.

"Are you sure that's what you want?" I asked him.

"Of course it's what I bloody want!"

"I'd give that a little more thought if I were you."

His rage suffered a sudden retreat.

"What exactly should I be thinking about?" he murmured.

"About the goodbye I might say to your family - not to mention your friends, your neighbours, your business partners and potential customers. They're none of them, I take it, acquainted with every last detail of your earlier career as a master of men? Indeed, with a daughter who's a criminal lawyer, the inconvenience might be hard to keep out of a courtroom. She might feel a sense of professional duty in the matter."

"You want money too, I suppose," he breathed. "How much?"

"Your money?" I half-laughed. "It'd stink too rank for wiping my arse. You can't buy your way out of what you deserve, not with me."

"What is it you want, then? A pound of flesh?"

"There's more flesh than that on the scale's other side. The flesh in question… the whole weight of a life was in it."

"Is that what you want?" he asked, glancing to the interior's far end, where the front door lay. "My life?"

"Kill you? Your punishment would be done in five minutes flat. The scale calls for more than that."

"And who are you to punish me? What do you know and how do you know it?"

"Cast your memory far enough back and you might just find me, staring out of the shadows of a summer day long ago."

He stared at me without speaking, his frown swelling with

a thought that widened his eyes as if it were a blade driven through his brain. Moisture crept into those eyes as he took another step towards me, caressing my cheek, far more tenderly this time.

"Please..." he said, "...we must talk. We must... must help one another understand...."

I slapped his hand aside, still harder than before.

"I'll see you at the dinner table. We can talk it over there, if you like. Between the main course and your wife's apple pie. Maybe the rest of your family can pitch in an idea or two."

The tears which had threatened his eyes froze where they hung.

"I won't have all this - *this!* - " he did little more than whisper, "-stolen from me, not on any grounds, by any body. I've buried what I've buried, built a life upon it. Built it to stand and last, past any fucking around from a termite like you. You fuck with me, I'll crush you flat."

"I'm fucking already," I said. "And know how weak you stand."

"Quiet!" he yelled, grabbing me by both arms and driving me against the wall, thumping me back and forth against it, as if to crack my skull against the plaster. "I won't, I... I *won't* - !"

"Y'okay there, boss?" came a call from the foot of the steps. Hutcher looked over his shoulder. One of the builders was staring up at us. "Okay? Boss?" he repeated. Hutcher let go of me.

"Yes... yes...." he muttered. "Okay."

I pushed myself from the wall, collected my helmet from the floor, popped it on my head. "Yes," I said, "We're fine, aren't we? - Thanks for the tour, anyway. I'll see you at the house for dinner. Won't I?"

"Yes," Hutcher said.

"I almost feel like part of the family," I chirped, making my way towards the builder. "A big happy family. Nice feeling. Long may it continue. Toodle-oo."

Hutcher watched me go, leaning against that back wall as if requiring its support. I broadened my smile, just for show, and strolled out.

Thirty Two

Yet I had fucked everything up: I knew that for certain as I strode away, careless of the stares and whistles I stirred from the onlooking builders. Standing there in such intimacy with the man, the monstrosity, that had screwed its disease, its gonorrhea, clean through everything I had ever loved, the temptation to strip naked the conflict between us had been too great.

I doubted he'd have the nerve to eject me from his house anytime soon, not after my threat to expose him; all the same, his eye would be tight on me from now on, which meant the most important move might need to be made even sooner than I had planned. But that was okay: more than ever, I felt capable of murder; and besides, on reaching the house, I found fate - or even the Aztec Gods - on my side.

I had crossed from the main house, upon finding it empty, to my cottage. This proved unlocked, the bed within occupied by Luke, who lay atop it in jeans, T-shirt and baseball boots. He was scanning a book of photographs I had brought with me from Mexico.

"What you doing here, Goldilocks?" I asked him.

"Reading," he said, giving me the most casual of glances. "Looking at the pictures, anyway. What's this it's written in? Spanish?"

"*Si*," I replied.

"It's all to do with Aztecs, huh?"

"Smart boy. What do you make of them?"

"Pretty mean-looking, some of these statues and masks. *A re* they masks?"

"They're masks."

I sat next to him on the bed, sliding my hand along his

154

inside leg, from knee to thigh.

"What does the writing say?"

"It's about sacrifice, mostly."

"Blood sacrifice, going by these hieroglyphic things."

"The blood was just for starters. The heart used to get ripped out while the victims were still kicking. Oh, the entrails too. Slap a fellow's entrails down on the floor and you'll find them full of messages."

"Messages from who?"

"The Gods, dummy." I began teasing down his fly. "They were very devout people."

"They sound pretty crazy."

"They understood the world better than us. Understood there are Gods and the Gods are more like jungle beasts than dour old father figures floating among the clouds. They understood Gods like that need feeding." My hand slid inside his opened fly, capturing his cock. "I've been to those temples of theirs. All these centuries later you can still see the bloodstains on the stones." I drew his cock free, caressing it to its fullest length.

He went on browsing the pictures. I glanced at the page he had reached. "Oh… that…" I said. "That's about the festival of Tezcatlipoca." The page in question did not actually concern that, but he wasn't to know.

"Tex who?" he asked.

"Tezcatlipoca," I repeated. "Don't go making a joke out of his name. He might be here right now, listening. He was, is, the Aztec God of darkness, night, discord, war, deceit. And of the north, which makes him the likeliest Aztec God to be lurking hereabouts. 'The Lord Of The Burning Mirror', they called him, because in his dark glass he could see clean through the abyss of men's hearts and the secrets they hid there."

I tore the book from his hands, tossed it aside. Springing onto my knees on the bed, I caught Luke's legs, dragged him flat, crawling myself above and astride him. "And," I continued, "knowing those secrets, he could come at humanity from all sorts of unpredictable directions. The main shape he took was that of the jaguar."

I threw myself flat atop him, reaching under the bed and drawing out the stuffed jaguar paw. I rose to a sitting position upon my knees, still astride him, raking the hooked claws softly downward across his white T-shirt, the gesture still not quite soft enough to avoid one claw catching on the cotton, ripping a thin hole. He flinched; I tugged the paw free, turned it the other way round, latching the claws under the T-shirt's bottom edge, using it now to draw the fabric upward, baring his torso. As I finished pushing the T-shirt's crumple as far as it would go, at a point just above his nipples, he seized the wrist of the hand with which I held the paw.

"I don't want to get hurt this time," he said with boyish solemnity.

"Try telling me so I'll believe you," I said, yanking my hand free and softly raking the claws down the smooth and hairless skin of his chest.

"I believe I love you, but there *are* limits."

"Fewer of them than you've been brought up to believe. Ask the Aztecs."

"I don't know any."

"You know me."

"You're too young and cute to be one of them."

"You're younger and cuter still and I know how the Aztecs treasured beauty like yours. Oh, they were sacrificing people non-stop, waterfalls of blood down the steps of their temples, hearts and guts piled into hillocks. Most of those killed were just cattle to the slaughter. But once a year, on Tezcatlipoca's own festival, they selected a singularly beautiful young man from the tribe and for the next year he was treated like a living God, worshipped everywhere he went. Then, when the next year's festival came round, he was led back to the temple, dressed as the living embodiment of Tezcatlipoca himself. And then…"

"They killed him?" Luke asked.

"What greater honour could they do his beauty than a beautiful death?"

"He still wound up dead."

"Luke, sweetheart, here's a fact of life Mummy and

Daddy maybe haven't got round to sharing with you: we all do."

"It might be nicer to die old, sat on some veranda in the sunset, seventy, eighty years to look back on."

"Yeah. Buried in wrinkles, piss a fluorescent yellow seeping from your catheter, puddling the floor beneath your wheelchair, brain dribbling out your ears and nose. Believe an older woman, Luke: you'll never be as magnificent again as you are right now."

"Then amn't I lucky the Aztecs are extinct?"

"The dead never quite go away, Luke. That's why all those ancient religions felt such a need to placate them. With blood, for starters."

I dug the jaguar's claw a fraction deeper, drawing shallow tracks of scarlet moistness from his pale skin. He yelped, pushing the claw aside and rolling me onto my back, planting himself atop me, the paw now seized by his own hand and positioned against my cheek.

"Maybe, today, it's my turn to do the hurting," he suggested, striving to chisel that soft androgynous face macho mean. I laughed and tickled him. He writhed off me, shrieking a giggle as he rolled from the bed and thumped onto the floor. I sprung to the bed's edge, recapturing the paw and then straightening up to loom above him, a giddiness gathering in my heart at the thought that this might just be my moment: that - My God! - within five, ten, minutes I might well have ripped him wide, gutted him, frozen his beauty and destroyed it in the same instant.

I made a playful cat snarl, swung the paw with no attempt at contact. Luke wriggled upright, giggling still, grabbed a chair, holding it with its legs my way, as if he were a lion tamer. I slunk off the bed and began stalking him, jabbing with the paw. He freed a hand from the chair just long enough to work his dick back into his trousers. As he fussed with the zip, I swiped with the claws, catching the bar between two of the chair legs and tearing the chair from his grasp. As it clattered down, I threw myself against him in a kiss which he instantly reciprocated, this broken only when he pushed me inches away, my careless purchase on the paw having dug its sharp ends into the small of his back. He took hold of it, eased it down.

"Haven't we got claws enough of our own?" he suggested.

I threw the paw aside, flexing my fingers feline taut and using them to rake the girlish-soft flesh of his cheeks. "You bet," I agreed, "Now why don't we both get naked and in that bed and see whose claws are sharpest?"

"I've got a better idea," he replied. "This time of day we've got the whole place to ourselves. Why don't we smuggle a wee bit of outrage into the big house? Fuck on the kitchen floor, the living room couch, the stairs, the…."

"Mummy and Daddy's bed," I suggested.

He pushed me back. It was hard to see where, in his response, the dividing line fell between titillation and discomfort. "You really are a corrupting influence, aren't you?" he frowned.

I resumed my feline pose. "I'm the Catwoman, Boy Wonder, and I won't rest till I've raped you for the forces of evil!"

I darted after him. He twisted by me, laughing, and sprinted for the door. I chased him across the lawn, outrunning any impulse on my part to run in the opposite direction until the Mearns, and my boy's place at its heart, had been lost to sight.

Thirty Three

Inside the main house, our chase continued. In and out of the tickety-boo rooms we zipped and play-acted, laughed and snarled. Glimpsing his swerve up the stairs, I made a moment's discreet retreat from the fun to collect, from a drawer in the kitchen, the sharpest knife I could find. A sob broke past my laughter; I stifled it, tugging up my skirt at the right hip and sliding the blade between my stocking top and the skin of my leg. Draping the skirt over it and hastening on, I felt the blade-tip give my skin a shallow jab with each fresh step, but that was fine: I needed to feel the violence-to-be take on just that tangible, irresistible pulse.

I climbed the stairs, mind darting ahead to the swiftness of the escape I'd have to make when the deed was done. I half-amused myself with a vision of myself stood at the Mearns Road bus stop in less than an hour's time, crusted with blood beneath a change of clothes, riding out of the Mearns as discreetly as I'd rode in, my role of Melinda Carido discarded as thoroughly as the bones of the real Melinda, back in that Mexican jungle, my new self reaching Glasgow airport, fake passport and all, in time for the first flight in the general direction of South America. I pictured Scotland disappearing below the clouds through the window, thought of my bare feet sinking, within a single day's time, into the warm sand of some distant shore, the sky above and sea before me blue as Luke's destruction would be red.

And then I wondered if this wasn't sheerest madness seizing me, wonder turning to worry as to how little hope there actually was of my getting away with such a thing. I had spent so long plotting the broad outline of my plan, while avoiding more than the most fanciful envisioning of the atrocity itself; I

159

think I had assumed that fate or the Aztec Gods or your ghost would deliver the appropriate moment on their own initiative, and that my hate and love would improvise a route to that moment's far side. And here I was, racing through that moment as swift as my legs would carry me; yet every step brought a cautioning jab sharper than those from the knife in my stocking: was it possible to do such a thing, was it conceivable to do something else entirely: to surrender my warring heart to tenderness, even?

I reached the top of the stairs. This portion of the house had remained unknown to me until then, the fact that the Hutchers enjoyed the luxury of a downstairs toilet leaving me without even the excuse of climbing the stairs for a pee. The landing was as spacious and tastefully furnished as I expected, its several doors all neatly closed, only one, at the far end, having its panelled whiteness disturbed by ornament, this in the form of a small poster blu-tacked to the wood, depicting an engraving of Mozart, the black and white image having been coloured with a psychedelic array of felt pen hues, the words DO NOT DISTURB OR TIDY! GENIUS THRIVES ON CHAOS! scribbled above and below in red marker pen.

I tapped the door. "You there, Amadeus?" I cooed through the panelling. No answer came. I opened the door.

It was a teenage boy's bedroom, little different from my memory of yours in its careless heapings and scatterings and near-carpeting with pop-culture detritus: rock magazines and CDs, Sci Fi and Fantasy books and comics, computer games and DVDs of special effectsy blockbusters, the tamer sorts of lad mags with their cover shots of girls who might have been bred in a test tube to fit the pubescent male imagination. The only thing missing was the teenage boy himself, the rumples of his unmade bed bare of the body I sought.

The wall above the bed was covered in photographs and posters from movies and rock concerts. One of them, in the centre of the wall, drew my attention, this the crudest, most home-made of the posters. On bright yellow paper, it advertised a gig by The Bleeding Hearts, a large and smudgy monochrome photograph in the poster's centre depicting the band themselves:

160

a group of three boys trying their damnedest to look like young men on the edge, plus a slender young woman of strikingly androgynous appearance. One of the boys was Luke, but it was that young woman who had drawn my attention - or, more precisely, the dense tattoos woven around both the arms in which she held her drumsticks.

A familiar hand fixed itself across my eyes from behind, still more familiar lips half-murmuring, half-kissing at my ear. "Not here," they said. "Fucking in that squeaky little single bed of mine. You're right. Let's really be a scandal."

I felt Luke's teeth nip the lobe of my ear. A second later he was gone. I turned to see him darting across the landing, naked but for a semi-transparent silk scarf with a paisley pattern of curling greens and blues - his mother's, doubtless - which he had knotted about his waist like the loincloth of *un tres chic Tarzan*. I gave chase, although the knife-point was jabbing my leg close to real soreness, my stocking dampening with blood at that spot.

He had scurried through a door halfway along the landing, leaving it open at his back. I followed him through into a more spacious bedroom, this as dazzlingly tidy as the previous one had been disordered. The great double bed dominating the centre of the room had its pale duvet so neatly made it was like a sheet of plastic, the mirrors fronting the walk-in wardrobes along both side walls so free of blemish, of crack or smudge, that it seemed impossible to imagine their reflecting, still less the bed's embracing, the messy throes of conjugal intercourse. Luke, indeed, had turned to face me at the side of the bed, suddenly deprived of his naughty boy's enthusiasm for the despoiling of this tabernacle.

I stepped forward, caught hold of the knotted end of that silly loincloth and whipped it off him, liberating a surge to fullest strength at his loins. I pushed him across the bed on his back. "We… we have to be careful…." he smiled and trembled.

"No," I said, almost shocked by how solemn I sounded. "It's time, I think, to be bolder than ever." I wound the scarf into a tight band and tied it around his head as a blindfold. His hands made the feeblest of attempts to stop me. "Trust me,

161

please," I told him. "I love you, Luke. Do you love me?" He gave a cautious nod. "Love is trust to the edge of nothingness. We can go there, you and I, if we're unafraid. And we're not afraid, are we? Not of loving one another, of being naked with one another, way beyond the rules of family etiquette, of clean sheets and all other civilised bullshit. We're beyond all that, don't you think?"

He gave another little nod. "I think," he mumbled.

"Then just lie there," I said, rising from the bed, "While I get naked myself."

"Now you're talking," he smiled.

"And it's important that we talk first, Luke. I want you to understand. That I love you, yes, but also that I loved someone else once." His smile dwindled. "No, lie still... You remind me of him. He was a little younger than you, but not by much. Just as beautiful. And he fell in love. Oh, not with me. But by God he fell."

I had stripped to my stockings and shoes, moving more carefully as I detached the knife from its hiding place. I saw that the break to my skin and stain to my stocking were very minor: I'd live. With the knife in my right hand, I used the left to slip off the remainder of my clothing. I supposed nakedness convenient for a murderess, saving one's outfit from bloodstains; I had read that this was how Lizzie Borden got away with it and supposed her the best role model a woman in my situation could have.

"But sometimes," I said, approaching the bed again, "The person you love isn't worthy of it. This lover led him on, spun a line, dragged him deeper and deeper into the feeling - or was the feeling shared, I wonder, on the other side as well? For a time at least? Which would make the betrayal still worse when the betrayal came. Because it came like a bomb going off in a birthday cake."

Through the bedroom window, we caught the sound of a car pulling into the street, a sound which on this road, where hours might go by between the cruising past of individual vehicles, caught both our attentions with the impatient growl of its engine. When, a second later, we heard the car's wheels

162

crackle up the gravel driveway, it was only the press of my free hand upon Luke's chest that kept him from leaping off the bed.

"Fuck-!" Luke cried, "It's my Dad!" Even as I pushed him back down, he was attempting to untie his blindfold.

"Wait - wait!" I insisted, fighting his hands aside, having to fix my free hand across his face to ensure the scarf stayed in place. "I want you, I need you, to hear."

Below, the car stopped, one of its doors opening, closing.

"The boy was betrayed," I continued, even as steps began scrunching towards the front doorstep. "Humiliated. And not privately. No. This was made a show for a whole suburb's worth of nasty young minds. They were on him like beasts, hounding him to death."

A key turned in the front door. Luke made a fresh attempt at sitting up. I fixed my grip upon his throat, forcing him back down. I set the knife's sheerest tip at the lower edge of the bone between his nipples. A single bubble of blood swelled around the knife-point.

"He died in - listen! - black water, dark and cold, that same water Abby drowned in. And his murderer walked away and conquered the world, this tiny corner of it, anyway. The murdered boy left a sister, younger than he was even, young enough for the horror of it to warp her in the bud, to canker her whole life. You know that sister, Luke. And you know the murderer too - ...."

He had caught hold of my choking arm with both his hands and now succeeded in wrenching my grasp aside, struggling up and tearing the scarf from his eyes. The knife remained poised to thump through his breastbone, but he was blind to it and numb to its pinch, as surely as he had been deaf to all I had attempted to say.

Elbowing me aside, he sped to the far corner of the room, muttering "Fuck - Fuck - Fuck...!" as he fumbled his clothes over a sagging erection. I remained kneeling on the bed, tears in my eyes and knife ready, waiting for him to turn and see me properly, thereby leaving me no choice but to stab him dead - and to hell with the fact that I'd have to fight my way out of that house, with no hope of fighting very far. I honestly hadn't thought of prison as a serious prospect until that moment - and now I did, I realised I hardly cared.

But then the sound of Laura's voice reached us from the hallway below, calling her brother's name. Luke froze, only fractionally relieved, and then dashed out, still without seeing what I meant him to see. I lowered the knife. He popped his head back round the door, glancing my way. "Get dressed, but... but stay in here!" he said in a harsh whisper, but still it was clear he barely saw me. He drew his head back and closed the door. I heard his bare feet thumping down the stairs.

Thirty Four

Still naked, I crept onto the landing, squatting behind the rail overlooking the hallway below, watching Luke reach the foot of the stairs. His sister called his name again, although I could see no more of her than a faint shadow across the carpet cast from the direction of the extension.

"I'm here - I'm here!" he called, passing out of sight in the same direction. "What's the hassle?"

"The hassle?" I heard Laura say. "You're a world of hassle, baby-bro."

"Hassle how?"

"Well, for starters, I've just had Mum in my office."

"Your office?"

"Yeah, I know, she's got a coffee shop to run, but the coffee shop must be running itself, 'cause there she was, in among the crack addict mums and low grade gangsters, talking about someone breaking in here, about blackmail, about Dad flying off the handle and about how she found a receipt for a gun in his overcoat pocket. Which sounds like hassle indeed. What the Hell is going on?"

"Not all this hassle can be laid at my door alone, don't you think?"

"Which means what? Duncan, you mean? Is that it? Is it him, Luke? Is it?!"

"Well, it can't just be him. He'd hardly be fit for breaking and entering. Certainly wasn't last time we saw him. Was he?"

"Then who else?"

"I have my suspicions."

"Then spit 'em out! Someone else from the band? Luke -?!"

"Shush!"

"Don't shush me! Dad's not here, is he?"

"The mood he's in, we'd know it if he was."

"Well, I can't help but sympathise, bull in a china shop though he might be."

"It's your fault, Laura, at least as much as it's mine."

"Okay, okay, shut the fuck up and let's concentrate on how we get this mess sorted out. How do I get in touch with him?"

"In touch with who?"

"In touch with who-do-you-think! Don't you reckon it's time we negotiated our way out of this?"

"I don't know where he is."

"What about that posh place his Mum and Dad moved to?"

"It's all shut up. I've checked it out myself, believe me."

"What about the girl?"

"What girl?"

"Lydia, the tattooed drummer. Frankie or Frannie, or whatever her name was. She was pretty mean and agile. Where was it she kept the neighbours awake? Some estate out by Cowcaddens, was it? Wasn't it? Luke? Where, Luke?"

"I don't know where she is now."

"Where was she when you last knew?"

"I... I don't know, I... I tried to find out but...."

"But?"

"I took your Goddamned fucking advice, Laura! Your advice not to stir things up any more, however much I found out. How did I know letters and phone calls and doctored DC comics dumped in the garden were going to turn into breaking and entering and murder attempts on the godamn lodger?"

"That scrapbook you used to keep, your little chronicle of that pipsqueak band out to conquer the world, there's nothing in there that might help me?"

"The scrapbook went in the bin the same time as the band did."

"Oh yeah? The one piece of evidence you had of your life amounting to something and you junked it? I don't believe that, Luke!"

"Listen - shush! Shush!"

166

"You listen! You're the world to me, baby brother, in spite of all the bullshit. I'm here to fight your corner, whether you care for the gesture or not."

"I'm not looking for a lawyer."

"A lawyer? You need a fucking saviour!"

Their argument continued, but I didn't catch the details of this, for I had hastened along the landing to Luke's room, where I scanned the general chaos for anything that might resemble a scrapbook. I had just begun a move towards the room's over-stuffed bookcase when I heard two pairs of feet making a swift climb of the stairs, Luke and Laura's still argumentative voices ascending with them.

"This can't be allowed to go any further, Luke," Laura was declaring. "If you're not up to confronting them, then leave it to me. All I'm asking is that you point me in the right direction."

Looking around for a hiding place, I glanced to the wardrobe, but would sooner have been dragged naked through the streets than be caught making such a cliché of myself. No: my sense of humour was sharp enough for a fresh turn to the screw I was fixing in the Hutcher coffin.

"Listen - Laura!" I could hear Luke protesting, "Let's... let's just go back downstairs and... and talk...."

"No!" insisted his sister, audibly right outside the bedroom door. "Let's stop talking and start sorting things ou -..."

I heard her throw open the bedroom door, caught and relished the sound of her sentence's last word sticking in her throat. Snuggled in Luke's bed, I turned my head on the pillow and faked a slow wakening. "Luke... sweetheart...?" I mumbled, having to choke hard on a snort of laughter when I saw their shared stupefaction. I drew the duvet up around my breasts, the gesture intended to stress, more than conceal, my nakedness.

"Oh... hi...." I said to Laura, "I... I was just... well, you know. Having a nap."

I was looking forward to seeing the jaw of that polished lawyer's face dent the floorboards, but what I actually beheld was the cut through her of some profounder shock, the determined expression with which she had entered slipping into not being much of an expression at all, her widening gaze seeming to recede into the depths of some deep wound, one not entirely fresh. Then came a somewhat strained smile and a breath of laughter.

"Yes..." she sighed, "...he's worn you out, I'm sure." She turned to Luke. "We'll sort out what I was talking about later," she told him. "I'll leave you two to whatever you need leaving to."

She turned swiftly back along the landing. Luke watched her until she reached the head of the stairs and then pushed the door closed. "What the fuck are you playing at?" he demanded.

I whipped the duvet off myself and rose. "What's the matter?" I said. "Your big sis seems quite tolerant. I'll bet she wouldn't even mind if we finished off up here while she puts the kettle on."

I seized his zipper. He wrenched my hand aside.

"Why don't you get dressed?" he suggested. "Then *you* can go down and have a cuppa with her. I'd be a wee bit stuck for words right now."

"Fair enough," I said. "When a boy's as beautiful as you, he can safely leave all the talking to the ladies around him."

I gave him a chaste peck on the lips and stepped along the hall to his parents' bedroom. Swiftly dressed, the knife slid into my other stocking, I stepped back onto the landing, where I caught sight of Luke through his bedroom door as he stood with his back to me, his head tilting this way and that as he surveyed the room's far side. Balanced in one hand was an outsized and tatty volume, its pages stuffed with inserted material like the layers in an overpacked sandwich: the very image of a scrapbook fattened by boyish enthusiasms. I saw him open a guitar case propped upright against the wall. He tilted forward the electric guitar within, sliding the scrapbook behind the body of the instrument.

As he fastened the case, I slipped back into the bedroom, busying myself with the restoration of order to the parental bed, so that when Luke came peering through the doorway a moment later, he could not have guessed how recently our positions had

168

been reversed.

"What the fuck are you playing at?" he whispered.

"It's okay," I suggested. "Your sister strikes me as pretty cool. Someone who can keep a secret."

He stared at me without speaking and I lamented, fondly, the fact that I hadn't killed him ten minutes before: the outrage upon his features threatened to age him terribly. Much more drift in the same direction and he wouldn't be worth murdering. He strode off down the stairs and I waited a minute or so before returning to his bedroom to take hold of the scrapbook.

The swift flick which was all I had time for didn't take long to confirm the volume as being a scrapbook of Luke's band, photos showing rehearsals and sweaty, haphazardly-lit performances in cramped venues - some of the shots juxtaposing rock-star attitudes with posh school uniforms - alongside home-made posters for those performances. I noted the tall, short-haired girl with the tattooed arms blurring away at her drum-kit, she herself free of school uniform throughout, plus Luke's front-line rapport with his bassist, a young man of roughly the same age, handsome enough with his spiked blonde hair and a jaunty tilt to his faux-NHS specs, but no match in looks for his lead singer.

Two thirds of the way through the pages, the photos ran out, just after a page of shots showing some drunken party. One picture showed Luke and his blonde bassist arm in arm as they puckered up and blew the camera a kiss past the top of their Grolsch bottles. Just below was a photo of the drummer-girl posing topless with her tongue sticking out, establishing that those tattooed thorns wound around her belly and chest, only two circles left clear around her flat, boyish breasts. Below this was a shot of the bassist dancing with a woman in an incongruously smart business suit, their arms wrapped around one another. The woman was averting her face into her partner's shoulder, but it was plain this was Laura, just as an onlooking smudge in the background revealed itself, as I tilted the page more fully into the light, as being Luke, his obscured expression hinting at either extreme drunkenness or some reserve regarding the coupling in the foreground.

Beyond this page lay nothing but blank sheets. I was flicking through them when Laura called from below, asking if I wanted a cup of tea. I fumbled the book back towards its hiding place. As I did so, something slipped free that had been shoved, unattached, in at the rear of the book.

It fluttered to the carpet. I picked it up. It was a sheet of white paper, folded in four. Setting the scrapbook aside, I opened it out. Printed on its far side was another photo, the image's fuzziness suggesting something shot with a mobile phone and then loaded onto a computer. The photo showed a gaunt blur of black-clad figure I had to stare at intently to be sure it was that of the drummer-girl. She was pushing a hunched and aged-looking figure in a wheelchair along a grey and rain-slicked street, this second figure with a hood around its features. At the right end of the image a great tatty poster was stuck to the wall past which they were hurrying. Only the left end of whatever was printed on the poster in great gaudy letters had been caught within the photo's frame.

BAR
BIG
ANT
SAL

…it read. Scribbled in pen on the white margin just beneath the photo were the words, in what seemed to be Luke's hand: **"Near their place-"** and a date about two months before. I slipped the sheet back inside the scrapbook, the scrapbook back inside the guitar case and then hastened downstairs for my cuppa.

Thirty Five

Laura had it ready for me in the kitchen. On my way through, I spotted Luke in the extension, standing and staring out at the garden. He glanced my way, but only for a second, his expression remote. Laura greeted me more accommodatingly, the melancholy set to her features as she turned my way swiftly replaced by a smile so broad it threatened to crack the sheen of her cheeks. She strode across, seizing me in a hug so sisterly as to be slightly embarrassing. "I should kill you," she muttered fondly.

"Squeeze me a little harder," I said, "And you might just manage it."

"Sorry," she said, releasing me. "Still reeling from the shock. Glad of something to cling to. Not that I didn't suspect what you were up to."

"Oh, really?"

"The day of the *fete*. You were a little unguarded in your praise of your star pupil."

"I can see why they pay you so much money to be a lawyer."

"I make an even better sister than a lawyer. And I do that for free."

"Is that a warning?"

"I don't think so," she said, motioning me to a seat at the kitchen table and passing me my mug of tea. "But you may have to allow me another little moment or two while I work out what the hell I *do* think. Suspicion is one thing, seeing you there... you really are a disgrace to your profession and an outrage to common decency, aren't you?" She smiled as she made this latter comment.

"He's over the age of consent, isn't he? I am as well, in

171

case you were wondering."

"They say an older woman can be the best thing to happen a young man. So long as she's not just taking advantage."

"He was the seducer more than the seduced. I did what I could to resist. These things aren't exactly in the teacher's rule book. But that brother of yours... well, he charmed the rules clean out of my heart. Seized me when my guard was weakest, took me like I was the virgin and he was the one who'd been a few times round the block. He'll tell you different, obviously."

Tears began to suggest themselves above the dwindling good humour at her lips. "You bitch. You fucking child-molesting bitch. I'm sorry. I think you're fantastic, gorgeous, sort of, just the right thing for him, maybe. Maybe. That kid deserves a whole world of love. You'd better give him it, or I don't know what I'll do to you."

"Oh, I love him alright," I told her. "Worth his weight in cuddles and kisses."

"Glad to hear you say so. You might shift some of the burden of worrying about him off my hands."

"To be any use in that regard, I'd have to know what specifically you're worried about."

"His self-imposed isolation, for starters. I suppose you've already dealt with that. Plus...."

"Plus?"

"Plus all the things which isolated him in the first place. Which weren't his fault alone. Wrong decisions were made all along the line, by all involved. And even now, I'm not sure which decisions were most wrong and which were almost right. We've... we've shielded him too much, maybe, from temptations and dangers. And that had dangers of its own. It's time we all buried our mistakes and walked away."

"Can't you clarify those mistakes?" I asked. "So I don't repeat them myself?"

"You strike me," she said, "as the kind of lover who'll make no one's mistakes but her own. More power to you, I say. You two look like you'll have fun making them."

"What about last night?" I pressed.

"Last night?"

"You've heard about what happened?"

"Assuming you're not referring to the crap night on the telly, I take it that's a reference to the break in?"

"My skull was the thing that came closest to a break."

"I heard about that too. You're okay?"

"Fighting fit, as you see. But next time someone takes a swing at me, I'd appreciate knowing where the swing's coming from. Is the aggro in question, tell me, tied up with this family's mistakes?"

"Luke hasn't….?"

"Hasn't what?"

"…said anything?"

"This is to do with Luke? Luke specifically?"

"It's to do with all of us. But, yes… Luke might just be the core of the problem."

"How?"

"On account, more than anything, of his great big loving heart."

"Go on, sis," I heard at my back. "Tell her about my heart."

We both looked to the doorway. Luke stood there.

"On second thoughts," said Laura, sloshing the remainder of her tea down the sink, "You're the one sharing a bed with her. Why don't you tell her anything that needs telling? Meanwhile, I can't devote all day to the gothic novel I call my family. Believe it or not, there are even more desperate characters waiting for me at the office. - You gonna be through with screwing your teacher in time to pick Emily up from school?"

"We're done screwing for today," said Luke.

"Then I'll see you tonight," she said, stepping past Luke and pecking him a kiss on the cheek before casting me a sidelong glance and moving on. Luke lingered where he stood, keeping his eyes fixed my way, saying nothing until we heard Laura close the front door at her back.

I rose, stepped towards him. "You sure we're done screwing?" I asked. "Seems like we've got away with it so far. Why don't we see how much further we can go?"

His hands fixed around my throat. No sooner had I felt his thumbs on my windpipe than I was several backward steps across the room, the base of my spine thumping against the worktop. It was only then that I realised how thoroughly the passage of breath to my lungs had been arrested, a great airless silence wedging in my skull, his beautiful face bloating and purpling and blackening across my misting gaze.

And then the pressure dropped aside, and so did he. He collapsed to his knees, pressing his head against my belly, which heaved as I gulped back breath, and I heard him, past my gasps and coughs, weep with a child's wild needfulness, his hand straying so close to the knife concealed beneath my skirt that I expected him to cut his hand at any moment. "I'm sorry, so... so... I... I don't know why... why..." I heard him mutter, "I... I just... I don't know who I am sometimes.... I *do* know I'm... I'm nothing without you to hold on to. Worse... worse than nothing. So... so please...."

His tears washed his words away. I caressed the hair at the top of his head, wondering if it wouldn't be a mercy to cut his throat right there. He spasmed back from me and onto his feet, a harsh rigidity suddenly shoring itself up upon those teary features.

"I'm going upstairs," he said. "To my own room. To lie down. And be alone. I feel the need, suddenly. For both our sakes."

He turned away and I heard his steps thump up the stairs, his bedroom door slamming at his back.

Thirty Six

He declined to reappear in time for that evening's drama class. Without my star pupil, things were a little flat-footed, but towards the end of my session with the older kids there was one unforeseen dividend.

Our final round of improvisations was built around the idea of status: in each of the performing couples one participant was to enjoy a position of dominance over the other, the situations the kids devised to illustrate this ranging from a hammed-up adventure on a pirate ship to an impressively gritty portrayal of the tough end of drug peddling. But the one which resonated with me most deeply was a prosaic scene involving a haggle between vendor and buyer at a market stall. Molly, playing the former, got a laugh with a line about how the customer, if he wanted genuine Christian Dior, *"should'a dragged his arse to Harvey Nick's, no' the bloody Barras!"*

It was only after I had said goodbye to the kids and was locking up that this latter reference to Glasgow's great weekend street market connected with something seen earlier that day. Returning home - and wasn't it piquant to find the Hutcher homestead defined as such in my mind? - I passed through the main house, tracing a murmur of polite chatter to the living room, where I found Rick and Amelia entertaining a couple from their golf club: Tilly and Hector, no less, both middle-aged and smoothly upholstered in pastel shades, their smug pleasantness making me wonder if they didn't have 'Newton Mearns' stamped through them like 'Blackpool' through a stick of rock.

I said I wasn't stopping when Amelia, plainly reluctantly, offered me a glass of the wine they were working their way through. "I just popped my head in," I explained, "to tell Rick

175

about something that came up in one of the improvisations tonight."

The man himself, facing me from an armchair at the far side of the room, had said nothing to me thus far but his eyes had locked upon me the moment I entered, the '*mein host*' witticisms with which he had been lording it over the conversation now wilted on his lips.

"We were doing a little haunted house routine," I lied, "And one of the kids said he'd read about an old builder's custom of burying the body of a sacrificed child under the foundations of a new building. It was supposed to bring good luck to the building and all who lived in it. Just a shame, I suppose, if you were the poor murdered kid stuffed beneath all those prosperous footsteps. I think the Aztecs did something like that too. What d'you reckon, Rick? That's not the way you do things in the Hutcher empire, I take it?"

"Oh heaven forfend," chortled Hector. "Richard's places are erected on the corpses of a few overworked plasterers and plumbers, maybe, but otherwise he's only lethal when it comes to a wage demand. Eh, Rick?"

Hutcher didn't answer, didn't laugh, his eyes fixed on me with all the amusement of a fox strangling in a farmer's snare, his eyes slowly swelling in a face reddening and drawing waxy taut across its bones.

"Look at that -" Hector teased, "- He's getting into character for his big speech at the weekend, cutting the tape on the new estate. He's going to tell the assembled workers they're having their wages docked on account of squeaky floorboards!"

"Rick, could you -?" Amelia began, as alert as I was to this paralysis of her husband's *bonhomie*.

Whatever she was asking him to do, it didn't get done, for his next move was to bolt from his seat and march the length of the room, pushing me clear as he strode into the hall. "Rick - !" Amelia called, only to shudder the latter consonant back down her throat, forcing a smile towards their guests which spoke her helplessness still more loudly than the preceding outburst.

"My goodness, is Rick okay?" I asked the three of them, Hector and Tilly shifting awkward glances from myself to

176

Amelia to the drinks in their hands.

"I'll go and check," I said, leaving them to their companionable silence. A short way along the hall, through the marginally ajar doorway of the downstairs bathroom, I caught the sound of a single guttural sob. I eased the door wider on the sight of Hutcher standing by the sink, cold water running into it, both his hands clamping the sink's edge while he stared, redder of face than ever, at his reflection in the mirror above. Not yet aware of my presence, I heard him mutter something that sounded like the words "*dead man...*" It was only after he dipped his head, splashing water in a face already dampened with tears, that he sensed my gaze.

Raising his streaming face, he stared at me with an expression that would have been easy to mistake for some dumbstruck plea for forgiveness. But then a familiar fire sprung up in those dampened embers as he stepped my way.

"I know who you are," he said in a gruff whisper. "And I can haunt you at least as hard as you can haunt me. Take my word for it."

Then he shut the door between us.

Thirty Seven

The Barras, Glasgow's weekend street market, stretched itself across so many streets and alleys of the city's east end, so many market halls, outdoor stalls and hole-in-the-wall shopfronts, that my search of its windings took some while. Just as in my childhood, it seemed to yield no clear geography but rather, like a maze, to keep twisting itself into new and bewildering formations with every turn one took.

Each of these twistings displayed stalls heaped with the drab and the extraordinary: knock-off designer clobber and garish shell-suits, mouldering piles of second hand rags punctuated by the shabby grandeur of ancient fur coats; banners and strips for the city's warring football teams close by plaster figurines of saints and Madonnas and pit-bull dogs; racks of kitsch cards for confirmations and condolences juxtaposed with old Connie Francis LPs, Elvis memorabilia and cellophane wrapped pornography ranging from contemporary tat to saucy Edwardian postcards and sideburned 70s softcore. In a yard between two of the buildings, a butcher on a podium was barking the cuts he offered through a microphone as if he were a muezzin enumerating the thousand names of God, while below him pirate DVDs were being hawked from a trestle table, Hollywood's glamorous ad campaigns reduced on their covers to bleary black and white photocopies.

I passed a stall offering nylon wigs for women, each on a plastic head so perfectly poised between the utterly fake and creepily life-like as to suggest severed heads in some back alley of Revolutionary Paris. The stall beyond offered gilded figurines of IRA hunger strikers for the terminally nostalgic, this adjoining another stall boasting an array of mock-marble headstones graced with inscriptions such as *MISS YOU*

KAYLEIGH - A WEE LASSIE WITH A BIG HEART and *ON YE GO BIG MAN - FIRST ROUND IN HEAVEN IS YOURS*. And everywhere hung the scent of frying onions, the old school Scottish square sausage still going strong at the fast food stalls.

But I had been weaving my way through all this for a good hour before a straying into an alleyway confronted me with at least the first part of what I had come looking for. Just to be sure, I stepped back into the doorway from which I had emerged. As I did so, the tattered poster on the wall at the alley's far side, declaring the proximity of

BARRAS
BIGGEST EVER
ANTIQUES
SALE!!!!

…had its message reduced, by the intervening door frame, to the more familiar announcement of

BAR
BIG
ANT
SAL

I stepped back out into the alley, this merely one more pointer on my quest. Indeed, the large doorway adjacent to the sign was sealed by a rusty shutter and I had to proceed further along the alley before finding an open entrance into a building hunched as low and shabby as the stalls outside.

Entering, I passed a stall displaying a wallful of paintings in a crude Glasgow-expressionist style, their subjects ranging from street scenes - in which the city's buildings were impastoed into resembling mushrooms blossoming in a damp cupboard - to portraits of celebrities such as Sinatra, Robbie Williams and Wee Jimmy Johnstone, the familiar features variously shrunk, swollen or skewed to the brink of recognisability. In a corner below sat an old man in a flat cap and thick spectacles, his gaunt and worn-out features tallying sufficiently with what I took for a little cluster of self-portraits to suggest he might be the artist himself, inspiration perpetually lured away from the sublime by the face he saw in the bathroom mirror every morning.

179

Moving onward along an interior like a broad white-washed tunnel, I found the centre of the floor crowded with antique furniture. Weaving my way past everything from a goggle-eye rocking horse to a stuffed swordfish and a tribe of African fetish dolls bristling with stuck-in arrows, I found an archway opening from the chamber's far end into another, slightly smaller area, this mostly taken up with further antiques stalls, although I passed a curtained booth in which a tarot reader in an cabbalistic headscarf sat looking bored.

It was another arch at the rear corner of this second area which fixed my attention, the words **NEVER FORGET** painted in mock art nouveau around the top of the arch, images of super heroes and movie stars from Bogart to Rambo daubed below. I stepped to the arch, looking through at tables, shelves and walls jam-packed with pop culture hand-me-downs, from ancient comic books in cellophane sleeves to models of Thunderbirds, wind-up robots and posters for Hollywood melodramas of the 1940s.

Plus dolls. These were everywhere: Victorian china dolls done up in dense crumples of dusty fabric, their soiled and cracked faces and staring eyes offering all the welcome of a cryptful of revenants; action figures based on characters from Star Wars and Batman comics and old monster movies; as well as a wealth of the soldier-boy dolls I had seen summoned to action in someone's nocturnal campaign against the Hutchers.

Stepping through the arch, I took the place for empty until a muffled snort drew my attention towards the shadows at one side of the arch. There, amid a thicket of Victorian dolls' eyes, a pair of human eyes squinted through thick glasses. The figure sitting there, male and tall and lanky, a black beany cap pulled down to the top of the glasses, a scarf heaped high around the chin, seemed simultaneously boyish and ancient, the pale sliver of face left showing and the awkward lie of the limbs upon their seat suggesting the corrosions of age, complete with tartan rug across the knees, even while the Spider-Man T-shirt beneath his denim jacket and a certain shy intensity in his gaze spurred thoughts of youth at its geekiest and gawkiest. It was a moment before I grasped that he sat in a wheelchair.

"You've got some interesting stuff here," I observed. He made no reply.

At the rear of the recess in which I stood another arch, partitioned by a beaded curtain, opened onto a further chamber still. I rattled my way through. This was a tight little space lit only by such illumination as filtered through the curtain, but I could see that it was stuffed with war memorabilia: medals in glass cases, model planes and tanks, mean-looking but presumably deactivated guns, even a couple of mannikins dressed in full uniform, one of them done up as a First World War German soldier, complete with spiked helmet, and the other as a British squaddie from the Second World War, a gas mask strapped on beneath the tin helmet.

I detected muffled voices from the curtain's far side: two of them, one male and the other female. I inched closer to the curtain, squinting past the coloured beads. What I saw was the figure in the wheelchair being leaned over by a tall thin woman in black top and leather jacket, short leather skirt, tights patterned with an aggressively red tartan and pink Doc Marten boots, her black hair cropped close against her skull. The man in the wheelchair weakly extended a finger my way, at which the young woman straightened up and turned her head, allowing me to see the white muslin patch taped across her furthermost eye.

I pushed back the curtain. The woman turned, ran. I ran after her. The man in the wheelchair attempted to skew his wheelchair across my path. I tripped past him, rocking him momentarily onto one wheel while I sped on.

Already the girl was out of sight, but as I swerved within sight of the exit onto the alley, I caught sight of her again and she spotted me, which prompted us both into a sprint towards a wider space of open ground where a caravan hawked hot dogs and yet more fried onions, just across from a stall where an amplified hard sell was being given to toy dogs mechanised to wag their tails, do backward somersaults and yap disco hits of yesteryear.

My quarry darted into one of the larger market halls. I followed, briefly losing her again before spotting her running along the aisle between two rows of stalls, this one aisle away from that in which I stood. I hurried up my aisle, keeping a parallel course.

The commentary from some football match was crackling at full volume from several stall holders' radios and I had to struggle past a group of kids in Rangers tracksuits who were giving a seller of Celtic gear a hard time, before I caught sight of the girl opening a door in the rear corner of the hall. She disappeared into the shadows on the door's other side.

Approaching the door, I discreetly purloined a large spanner from a tool stall, its owner busy fiddling with his radio to improve reception of the football match while haranguing the scrawny kid assisting him over an earlier retuning to "yon fuckin' hip-hop shite!" I concealed the spanner against the inner side of my forearm and eased open the door, ignoring the sheet of paper sellotaped to it saying: 'DO NOT ENTER'.

I stepped into a small lobby with a floor of warped linoleum, its yellow walls blotched with fungus and coursing with damp. In one corner lay a thickly packed black bin bag, a stuffed stag's head protruding some way above its top edge, one antler missing, the other chipped and cracked, its left eye staring glassily across at me, ends of straw protruding from the ragged socket where the other eye had been. A couple of doors opened off the lobby, one marked with a stick-on man in a suit to signify a Gents toilet, the other door sending the complementary message, its symbolic lady in a twin set. The door of the gents toilet was slightly ajar, exuding a mouldering odour and a variety of echoing drips.

I advanced on the door. "Listen…" I called. "…I just want to talk. We have a mutual interest in the Hutcher family. And I think we maybe ought to see if we can't come to an arrangement over the whole thing."

I pushed open the door. The full odour of decaying sanitation surged to meet me. At the far side of the room, a small window of fogged glass let in daylight, this curdling as it fell about the cracked and mould-spotted mirrors above a row of three broken sinks filled to overflowing with drippings from their rusty taps.

On the near side of the sinks, three urinals hung on the

wall, their china yellowed and reeking, while the facing wall offered three cubicles of gun-metal grey, one with its door hanging wide at a skew-whiff angle, another with its door absent entirely, these two offering views of seatless toilet bowls choked with dark fluid and crumplings of vaguely-defined matter. The door of the third cubicle was shut. I gave it a gentle push. It did not yield.

I crept into the adjoining cubicle, stepping up onto the thin rim of the seatless bowl, raising myself toward a hold on the top of the partition between the cubicles. As I did so I heard a scuffling from the other side. I raised my head, looking over the partition so swiftly that I became careless of the purchase of my feet on the scum-slicked china.

One foot slipped, began a plunge into the bowl. It was only by clamping both hands to the partition's upper edge that I kept myself from falling entirely, this entailing my dropping the spanner, which clanged on the floor. No sooner had the heel of my boot splashed into the choked water than I began dragging myself upright again, looking over the partition in time to spot my quarry unbolting and dragging wide the door of that other cubicle.

I leapt down, grabbed the spanner and chased her as she ran for the door into the lobby, As she reached it, I hurled the spanner. Its weight smacked into her shoulder, sending her stumbling sideways. I hurled myself against her, knocking both of us against the wall of the lobby. We reeled around, grabbing untidily at one another and falling together through the door of the ladies toilet.

The linoleum floor on which we landed was deeply puddled in its warpings. I landed atop the girl, pushing her flat on her back and pinning her there while I commanded her to "Listen-!" She writhed beneath me until she could tear an arm free, smacking its fist across my face and then rolling out from under me, kicking me aside. Then it was she who was pushing me flat, sitting astride me as her hands latched around my throat, thumping - and splashing - the back of my head against the floor.

"Who the fuck d'you think you are?" she cried. "Musclin'

183

in on what's fuck-all your business? What are you, anyhow? Their fuckin' security guard? Fuck you all, whatever you are!"

She had dipped her head close to mine, spitting that last sentence in my face. I rammed a thumb into the thin wad of muslin taped across her injured eye. The fierce angular beauty of her face convulsed as she squealed her pain. I pushed her off me, scrambled upright and ran for the lobby, reaching for the spot where the spanner had fallen.

No sooner had my fingertips brushed the implement than she was screaming into me from behind, both of us knocked against the wall and slipping to the ground, close by the stag's head, our hands fighting for control of the weapon.

A couple of times the spanner was dropped and then recaptured before I succeeded in gaining a firmer grasp, only to feel her teeth digging into the back of my hand. It was my turn to squeal as I dropped the tool. She seized it, scrambling to her feet and then swinging it high and bringing it down.

I darted my head to the side. The spanner smashed through the stag's scalp, yellow straw erupting from the divot torn in the threadbare fur. I wriggled away across the floor as she advanced on me again.

"I'll send you home to the Hutchers in a box, you nosy fuckin' cow!" she snorted. "To let them know how hard we are on their fuckin' case!"

She began a fresh swing. I kicked the soles of both my boots into her right knee. She cried out, stumbling forward even as she swung, crashing down at my side. I drove myself upward, ran for the door out into the market hall. I had seized the handle and begun pulling it open, gaining a glimpse of the prosaic bustle so close at hand, before a fresh swing of the spanner forced me to leap back, the door clunking shut, the tool's hooked end scraping paint off the woodwork.

"Listen," I said retreating towards the Gents toilet, "Whoever you are, whatever you're up to, we'd be better off talking, you and I."

"Talkin' about what?" she retorted, following me through the doorway. "About the beauty young Luke brings to the world? You've been fuckin' his cute wee bod, I know, till his bones squeak. We've had a eye on you since you first flung your knickers his way. That's a big part of the role I play in the game, you see. A pair of eyes for him. Until you took a smack at one of them."

"A pair of eyes for who?"

"Don't play-act being stupid, you smart fuckin' cow! You know about us, we know about you. And I know I'm takin' you down before you deprive me of another eye!"

She swung the spanner at my head. I dodged sideways, against one of the broken, overflowing sinks. She swung again. I dodged the other way. The spanner smashed the cracked mirror above the sink, shards dropping noisily from the wall.

I backed away as she advanced once more, only to realise I was wedging myself in a corner, my back against a vertical pipe. She swung the spanner again. I ducked, heard it crack the pipe's rusty metal. This was followed by a squeal of loose bolts and a shrill jetting of cold water from the joint the blow had shattered, the bulk of its force hitting my opponent in her face, sending her reeling backwards. I hurled myself against her, knocking her off her feet, the spanner clattering to the floor.

Falling, we hurtled inside one of the doorless cubicles. She landed in an sprawl across the toilet bowl, face-down, and I, thumping against her back, grabbed the rear of her head, driving her face into the foul water with which the bowl all but overbrimmed.

She wriggled and kicked, but I kept her face submerged, stinking water being splashed and sputtered over the bowl's rim. Her hands flailed around until the right hand caught the handle for flushing the toilet. I smiled at the thought of how a handhold like that was likelier to worsen than improve her predicament.

The next thing I knew, a tug of her hand had wrenched the handle clear of its socket on the cistern. I had barely registered this before the handle's metal thumped into my forehead just above the eyebrow, knocking me back just far enough for my captive to rear up from the toilet bowl, bellowing a mouthful of filthy water, spinning about to smack a second blow with the handle across the centre of my face, knocking me to the floor.

Landing with a snort of blood from my bleeding nostrils, I

saw her tower above me, grabbing both my ankles and then dragging me across the wet floor in the direction of the sinks. She reached down, grabbed me at the shoulders, dragged upright my still-stunned form, knotted herself a grip amid the curls at the back of my head and then drove me towards the greyish water choking one of the sinks.

My head was driven down into that water, held there as tightly as I had submerged hers. I did my best to hold my breath but as she jostled my head up and down in the clammy fluid, it was not long before my mouth was jolted open, a flood of foul liquid shooting up my throat and nostrils.

I sputtered, retched, but she kept my head pressed down and within seconds it was a blacker flood still I felt surging the channels of my mind. And it smelled like the silt in the pool where you died.

Thirty Eight

And then I felt myself released - plunging, weightless, through a liquid void thicker, colder than the waters of either pool or blocked sink. I settled at the bottom of that murk with a boneless jolt, lying there some while before a voice floated down my way, saying something to someone else about my being dead.

I opened my eyes. Whiteness broke upon the blackness. I sputtered up a throatful of water. The sound of the sputtering seemed to reach me across a vast distance, like the echo of a door slamming at the far end of some empty cathedral. But it was no cathedral that swam into focus, only the same wreck of a Gents toilet, as seen from its floor, my face towards the line of cubicles.

Yet the light upon them now was brighter, if chillier, like a reflection of sunlight off snow. And in the doorless cubicle directly facing me, *you* stood, or floated rather, for your bare and dripping feet hung a good six inches above the ground.

I tried to raise my head. You were smiling down at me as you floated there, naked in all your white and bony beauty, the whole of you streaming and beaded with water, scraps of dark pool-weed snarled around you here and there.

Someone behind me was saying something about someone being alive, asking what to do, quibbling over the answer, finally saying "Yes... yes..." and "...yes..." again, before telling whoever she spoke to something about a van and being "There!" in a few minutes; oh, and the listener was to start shutting something up straightaway. Then the radiance of your image grew too bright for looking at, burning through my gaze until a fresh blackness flared around me.

This blackness smelled of oil and felt hard and metallic

beneath me. It rattled me about in its grasp, squealing and squeaking to make me think of being stuck in some rusty metal coffin the rats were swarming around, trying to work out the best way of gnawing through. I forced open my eyes and their hungry stares swam into focus, closer still than I had imagined.

My eyes started wide, my head rising sharply as I shook focus into my gaze. At the same moment, I realised that something was tied across my mouth, gagging me, and that I was likewise bound around the ankles and wrists, the latter fixed behind my back.

It was not the eyes of rats which surrounded me but those of dolls, the same dolls and action figures I had seen on the market stall, now packed untidily into open-topped cardboard boxes, the creaking movements of the metallic interior in which I found myself sending shudders through them to suggest a restless animation.

Looking around, I realised I was in the back of something like a transit van, the van in motion along what sounded to be a busy road, a couple of blarings of the horn suggesting impatience up front. Looking that way, I faced the inner wall of the compartment in which I lay. There was a small window let into this and through the greasy glass, I saw a pair of spectacled eyes staring down at me. But as soon as my own eyes had made contact with them, their owner turned away out of my line of view. I tried to wriggle up into a sitting position, but my bindings made this awkward and the struggle only quickened my feelings of weakness and nausea, so I lay still and let myself be carried wherever my captors had in mind.

Before long, I must have sagged back out of consciousness, for I suddenly found myself starting awake to the sound and vibration of the van crunching over gravel. A box of dolls fell over, spilling its inhabitants around and across me. Then the van stopped, its engine left running. I heard a door up front open and looked to the little window, but saw nothing more through it. I did, however, hear swift steps on gravel and then a metallic rattle very like that of a garage door being swung up and open, this followed by returning footsteps, the slight vibration of someone climbing into the van, and then a

188

slamming of the door and an urging of the vehicle forward.

The crunch of gravel under the wheels gave way to a brief sensation of movement across smoother ground before the van juddered to another stop, the engine switched off this time. I heard muffled voices up front, first from the cab of the van and then from what I took for the interior of the garage, these accompanied by openings and slammings of the van's front doors, by some more delicate fumblings and clatterings of metal and then by what was distinctly a single pair of steps moving across the garage floor and the gravel outside, this accompanied by what I assumed was the roll and slight squeak of a wheelchair.

I wriggled towards the rear door, raising my bound feet to kick at its handle in a hope against hope that it might prove unlocked; the hope proved unfounded. I rolled onto my side, shaking and stretching as best I could at the bindings around my wrists. I was spared further useless exertions by the swift return of the footsteps on the gravel, this followed by the rattling of a key in the van's rear door. Both halves of the door flew wide, the tall girl I had fought at the Barras standing there, little more than a silhouette against a background of night.

I kicked at her. She dodged clear, catching my ankles and dragging me clear of the van. I landed agonisingly hard, especially with my arms trapped beneath me, on the garage's stone floor. Then, as swiftly, I was dragged from the garage floor onto the gravel outside, a pause for a rattling down and locking of the garage door swiftly followed by my being dragged onward around the side of the garage and towards a grand sandstone villa.

As my weight became difficult and noisy to drag across such a rough surface, my legs were let go. Instead, my captor darted to my side, turned me over and yanked me onto my feet, one hand on the scruff of my neck and the other on the bindings at my wrist. I was pushed into a swift run towards the house and then swerved towards its rear corner, noting, as I was turned the other way, a grassy slope descending in front of the villa, the gravel driveway curling across this towards a gateway in a high wall, the road beyond untroubled by traffic and with a tight little cluster of woodland on its far side. Every window of the villa itself seemed shuttered, but this was as much stock of my surroundings as I was able to take before being shoved through a door at the rear of the house.

I landed across a smoothly tiled floor in a darkened room, close by a pair of wheels that swivelled my way. "Take her down," a male voice said, incongruously soft in its tone and suggestive, also, of some impediment to the projection of the words, like a fat lip or a cleft palate. "And don't be *too* rough."

"No," I heard the woman say as she tugged me upright. "Just rough enough."

Bustled past cardboard boxes overflowing with the sort of odds and ends they sold on the stall, I was shoved on across a broad hallway and through a spacious living room, the furniture giving ghostly hints of its splendour through white dust-sheets.

At the far end of this room, I was forced along a short passage and through a doorway into a darkness suffused, a little further on, with murky moonlight. Abruptly, the floor disappeared beneath me as I was hurled into emptiness, my plunge terminated by a thump and a slide at full length across a floor of smoothly varnished wood, this at a lower level to that on which I had stood a moment before.

Coming to a stop, several fresh bruises making their presence felt, I raised my head, noting the line of tall windows which comprised one wall of the place, an expanse of garden bordered by a high wall lying beyond. The moonlight through these windows glinted off the surface of a substantial indoor swimming pool just beyond the point at which I had come to rest, pale blue ripples of light reflected off the water shimmering around the remainder of a large games room, complete with a pool table, weightlifting gear, ping-pong table and drum kit.

I became conscious of a ruddier light creeping in around those bluish glints. Looking back towards the doorway, I saw a cluster of candle-flames being wheeled in, held aloft by the figure in the wheelchair, the dancing glow revealing not only the short flight of steps from the top of which I had been pushed, but also a ramp alongside, down which the chair was advancing with a low electric hum, the tall girl descending the steps at a matching pace.

"Excuse the candles," that gentle and somehow disjointed male voice requested, "But we're not really here, you see, so we don't like to be too obvious about having lights on." His face, still bordered by hat and scarf, floated in amber tints amid the faint heat-haze off the candles. Even so, I was certain by now I recognised him.

Reaching the floor of the games room, he brought the wheelchair to a stop just short of my feet, extending the branched candelabra so its glow fell more fully across me. The girl crossed to the wall, pushing a button that set curtains closing across those floor-length windows, after which she settled herself on one arm of the wheelchair, draping an arm around its occupant's shoulders, pulling off his beanie cap and planting a kiss on the top of a head patchily covered with blonde stubble, and also with irregular dark lines I took for partially-healed stitchings.

"Well, well," said the man, looking me over, "So our sweet little Luke found himself a sexy older woman."

"Yeah," said the girl. "One with quite a kick on her. Fuckin' bitch almost killed me. Which is why I'd be keen to kill her right this minute if you'll only give me the say-so."

"First things first," her companion insisted. "I want to know what game she's playing, with us *and* them. Get that thing out of her mouth."

With a reluctant smirk, the girl rose, stepping to my side and sinking to one knee, drawing a flick-knife from her leather jacket and springing its blade upright. Catching my gag where it lay across my cheek, she began sawing through the fabric. The binding snapped and she dragged it away, revealing it, while I coughed myself a breath, as the pair of tartan tights I had noticed the girl was no longer wearing.

"It's a pretty mouth, certainly," the girl sneered. "If she won't use it like we tell her, we can always smack it a brighter shade of lipstick."

She ran a thumb along my lower lip in a rough caress. I shifted my head clear.

"You're acting awful coy for someone who's been

profaning Lukey-boy's virgin innocence like we've seen you do," the young man commented.

"I didn't realise I had an audience," I replied, my voice only huskily regained.

"It wasn't you we were out to keep an eye on," he said, pulling the scarf looser about his features, revealing more fully a strange asymmetry to his smile.

"No," I said, "I'd worked out it was Luke and his family you were focused on. Luke, especially. I've seen you both, in photos he had. You were in a band with him."

"We have a real detective on our hands here, Fran," he said.

"Yeah," grinned Fran. "Miss Marple crossed with Wonder Woman. Crossed with Emmanuelle. Or so she must think."

"I think you," I said to the young man, "might just be the friend of his I heard about. You were cosied up at some fancy private school, formed your band there. Only there was a falling out between you, or so a passing breeze whispered in my ear."

A harsh breath escaped the strangely rigid set of his jaw.

"Your breeze is well-informed," he said. "We... fell out and then some, Luke and me. From a considerable height."

"What was it over?" I asked. "The best rhyme for 'baby' or a bruise too many on the rugger field?"

"I'll fuckin' bruise you, you smart-mouthed cow!" yelled Fran, lunging to her feet and kicking me in the belly. "You're in no fuckin' position to talk down to us!"

"Fran!" yelled the young man. "That's enough!"

"She's got too close already," Fran retorted. "We both know what needs doing with her. So we can do what we like in the meantime."

"I told you, we haven't decided what we're doing yet," he insisted. "Not beyond getting straight what she's up to, with us and with Luke and his family."

"Face facts, Duncan-!" she snapped.

"No one's had to face the facts harder than yours truly!" he replied. "Which earns me the right to say when and where the shit gets shovelled back! So park your arse until I say so!"

As she settled reluctantly back on the arm of the

wheelchair, he faced me again. "I'm sorry," he said. "Violence isn't what we're about. In spite of how it might look. - Frannie, untie her hands and feet."

"You're kidding!" Fran protested.

"We're not thugs, Fran! Maybe... who knows... she's in need of our protection, not our bullying. Let her go. She doesn't look fit for putting up a fight. Not against you, Frannie-sweet."

Fran rose, flicked the knife-blade up again.

"She'd be stupid to try," declared Fran. Kneeling again, she rolled me onto my front, cutting my bindings with scant concern for the jabs she gave the surrounding skin. As she drew the tetherings away, I rolled back, shifting my legs and arms to more comfortable positions with an arthritic slowness born of severe pins and needles.

"Sit her down, Fran," Duncan suggested. "There, by the pool."

Fran grabbed me, dragging me upright, drawing me to the poolside, then dumping me across a canopied couch which stood there. Duncan wheeled himself across, holding the candelabra.

"Sit yourself comfortably," he said. "We've a story to share with you. A love story... for all the mess it made of me."

He shifted the candelabra alongside his face, parting the shadows from his features. And I saw that his face - still recognisable as that boy's face in the band photos - had been aged far ahead of time by the lengthy curving indentations of scars that had never fully healed, his left eye half-closed with one of them, that rigid lower jaw looking more than ever like some plastic imitation glued on as a replacement for the real one.

He saw me wince at the sight of him and winced himself, tears beading eyes that seemed the most aged part of him. He lowered the candles and began his story, as if to distract us both from the embarrassment.

Thirty Nine

"Luke and me, yeah, we were at school together. Not Frannie. Frannie's much too common. And with the wrong set of genitals. Very posh boy's school, it was. Strictly for the sons and heirs of the south side's high and mighty.

"Me and Luke hit it off, straightaway. Well, you know Luke. How could a person not be... charmed? Besides, we were a couple of soulful guitar strummers in a class of rugger buggers, wannabe tycoons and general upper class mediocrities. He'd read Yeats, I'd read Lorca: no one else there ever looked at a poem when there wasn't an exam due. It was natural we hit it off.

"Soon we were dreaming rock-star daydreams, strumming and scribbling songs every free moment. He had a way with a flashy riff, I could stab your heart with a sardonic love lyric. A band seemed the obvious next step. So Fran came aboard, courtesy of an advert in the NME, alongside a keyboard player from East Kilbride with clumsy fingers but a down-payment made on the hardware. And things went well. Oh, fame and fortune's phone number proved surprisingly elusive, but we had a blast all the same, advancing from gym hall jam sessions to real gigs in the backrooms of pubs we were too young to buy a drink in, that same transit van you were shoved in tootling around the M8, broadcasting the message of what hot up-and-comers we were.

"Trouble was, our little band, like any decent beat combo, was bound together with all kinds of emotional tensions. Those love songs I was scribbling, sat so close to my songwriting partner the hairs on our arms tickled one another when we hit a good line and those hairs stood up... well, I wasn't *just* rehashing the cliches. Or at least feeling those cliches for real for the first time. True love, as all those other songs put it. Love for who? Who do you think?

"Of course, I've no illusions about Luke. Not now, anyway. Oh, he's beautiful. So beautiful it hurts. But when you're that beautiful, beautiful's usually all you add up to. That kind of beauty's like a cancer. It eats away anything else you might be, claims the whole of you. A nothing, that's what you are when you're seriously beautiful. A nothing sucking down every something that comes your way, never letting it go again.

"Maybe I knew that even then, but I leapt in deep, anyhow. I loved the bastard so, silently at first, not knowing which way he might swing should I let a word or a touch slip from cover. But little by little, what with the everyday intimacies of the low budget end of the rock star life, it became easy enough to offer the odd hint, the hints soon shifting helluva close to a grasp on the fruit I'd forbidden myself.

"And Luke... he seemed to be playing along. What did that mean, I wondered? Feelings to match mine, or just him fooling around, as young men sometimes do, usually to prove they could never have any such feelings for real? And then there were the moments when he wasn't playful at all. When that sunny glare of his shaded towards the dark side of the moon. Still, we danced in the light more often than the shadow. Until one day it got a wee touch too bright. And we both got burned.

"It was just before our final exams. They give you days at home to study. So, of course, Luke and I spent most of those days snug in that cottage at the foot of their garden, strumming away at songs and dreams, leaving the textbooks to gather dust in the corner.

"One of those days - a rainy Tuesday morning, I recall - I arrived to find him alone in the main house, having his breakfast. I was hot for getting to work, but he was in one of his middle-range sullen moods, stirring his muesli and not saying much. So I lost my temper, in a fooling around kind of way, poured his muesli over his head. That woke him up, roused him to a food fight, the two of us leaping around that spotless Hutcher kitchen, hurling marmalade, yoghurt, you name it, at one another. The fight turned into a chase around that big back garden of theirs, him dressed in just T-shirt and shorts, plus an open robe flapping every which way. And it was wet and muddy and he slid and crashed down on top of me, straddling me in one of the flower beds, pinning me there.

"He must have felt how hard I'd got, 'cause next thing I knew he was sliding his hand over the crotch of my jeans. 'Don't worry', he grinned, 'I understand. I'm artistic too. Too much to say 'no' to sudden inspirations.'

"He kissed me. Just on the forehead. And then he leapt off me, running for the cottage, disappearing inside. I followed him, you fuckin' bet I did, found his robe and T-shirt and shorts on the floor of the living room, heard the shower come on in the bathroom. I was frightened, sort of, very. I wasn't inexperienced, not totally. Precocious, even, where the love of my fellow men was concerned. But all that was just fooling around. Luke... Luke was something else.

"I stepped into the bathroom. He was in the shower already, his nakedness a pinky shimmer behind that pebbled glass screen. I stripped off my own clothes, stepped in behind him. He turned, looked surprised. Was he surprised? Well, maybe. All the same the first touch was his. A tentative touch, a caress of my chest. I shifted things on a bit, fixed a great lip-chewing kiss on him. He pulled back, we started soaping, washing one another. He got hard soon enough, hard as I was. But when I tried kissing him again, he slipped by me, out into the main room.

"I followed, found him laid across the bed, trickled over by the shadows from the rain on the window. I settled alongside him and we stroked one another and he said he was scared and I said '*You're* scared?' and suggested we just hold one another until the scariness sorted itself out, one way or the other. And so we did, the rain on the window ticking the time out slowly. Was he gay, did he have that in him? Who the fuck knows or cares? Labels are something you take off with your clothes.

"But the clothed world caught up with us that morning. It came pinstriped, no less, in the form of his Dad, who must have popped home from one of his innumerable building sites, found the mess we'd made of his designer kitchen, then come searching for us. He stepped right in and saw us there, looming over the

196

bed like the Stone Guest. Mozart, you know? Or is it Pushkin?

"I saw him first. That face of his. If he'd been Caravaggio, he might have seen the beauty in what was laid out there. But a ramrod-straight suburban tyrant, that's all he was, is. And all the hate the super-straight world of the Mearns has for anything, anyone, playing by rules they wouldn't accept down the golf club... that's all I saw in Rick Hutcher's eyes.

"Then Luke, who had settled into a doze, woke, saw where my eyes were fixed, looked that same way himself. He leapt off the bed, fumbling the floor for his boxer shorts, dragging them on so quick he got both legs stuck in one leg-hole, had to totter back, trying again as his Dad advanced.

"Just as Daddy dear got close, raising a hand that looked set to smack the head from his shoulders, Luke darted out the door, still just in his boxers, a terror naked in him that was more than just the fear of a clout. He was still a kid, after all, and even a hard-hearted father is a God to his child. A beating off a parent's metaphysical, don't you think? It's the tablets from the mount thumping you. And Luke's Dad thumped him that day. By Christ, it looked like he had it in him to murder the kid....

"I missed the first part of the beating, busy grabbing my jeans and T-shirt. By the time I was half-dressed and running after them into the garden, Luke's dad was already full steam into an assault an S.S guard would have tipped his cap to. Just slaps, but hard slaps, to the head mostly, hard enough to keep putting Luke down, down in the mud the rain was churning the lawn into.

"Luke kept taking it and getting up and every time he got up his father clouted him back down. Luke could probably have put up a decent fight if he'd tried. But he didn't. A child was all he could be beneath those particular blows. His father's child.

"Before long, he was spattered all over with mud, soaked by the rain, seeming far more naked in those saturated boxers than he'd been lying with me. The worst kind of naked. I think there were tears mixed in among all that mud and rain and purple swelling on his beautiful face. His father was yelling at him, something about... it was strange... about a ghost... Can you imagine? Some... some curse getting hold of his son, his not allowing it ... something about someone coming between them, someone more of a threat than yours truly, stood there zipping his zipper. At least the bits where he accused his kid of being a filthy little pervert were easier to follow.

"Well, Luke *was* filthy by that point. And if anything was going to get the neighbours' curtains twitching and their tongues clucking, it was the commotion the master of the house was making. He seemed to realise that, because he stopped, just as Luke did a belly flop in one of the flower beds, the paternal eye glaring around the windows of the houses overlooking the garden, catching sight - so did I - of at least one prim suburban face ducking behind a prim suburban curtain.

"He grabbed Luke under the arm, hauled him up, started dragging him towards the house. But that was when Luke found it in himself to fight back, elbowing his Dad aside with such force that it was the King of the castle who almost got laid flat among the Azaleas. Suddenly it was Luke with a face on him that looked set to lay the other bastard dead.

"He turned aside from that feeling, if it was the feeling I took it for, started marching towards me, me who'd stood and watched and done nothing, no better excuse than having been paralysed by the sheer squalid grimness of the thing. As he drew nearer, I reached out to him. He pushed me away too.

"The father was staring at us. I stared back, that stare struggling to tell him what an animal he was. He strode off towards the house. I shifted back into the cottage, went to the bathroom to finish dressing. Luke was taking another turn in the shower, soaping all that dirt off. I took another good look at him but didn't touch, not this time. The look he cast me told me not to - as if, at that point, I needed telling. But it didn't say 'don't *look*'. Quite the opposite, I thought. But I'd seen enough for one day, so I finished dressing and made my exit over the back fence. I could climb that thing as fit as you back in those days.

"The next day we had an exam, but Luke wasn't there. The school contacted his parents, but they didn't know where he was either. Outside, afterward, as I dragged home the thought of how all these distractions had helped me fuck up the test, a car pulled in at my side. In it was his sister Laura. She asked me to go for a drive with her."

Forty

"Word had reached her of Luke's no-show. She wanted me to help her track him down, so we drove around the few places in the Mearns a young man might hang around to think deep thoughts. Finding no trace of him, sister Laura came over all liberal, telling me it was okay with her if Luke and I were lovers. I looked out the window to hide my smile.

"Fact is, Laura was a friendly girl. She'd flirted with me a fair few times during the band's climb to fame. Was I giving the wrong signals? Was I giving the right ones, but she was overlooking them, too busy getting vicariously close to the cute little brother whose own bod was, of course, out of bounds? Or maybe trying to see if she couldn't rescue him, in some conniving way, from the temptations I offered? Or maybe teasing out his gift for jealousy, just for the fun of it? I'm an only child, sibling games are closed rituals to me. You got a sister, a brother?"

I told him to go on.

"Well, anyhow, evening caught up with us and we still hadn't caught up with our boy. Laura offered me dinner, drove me to her place. Ever been there? No? It's a big fancy place past Uplawmoor, right out in the countryside. Her kid was with her parents, so we had the place to ourselves. She rustled up a mean pasta, popped open a bottle of red wine, sat down and ate and chatted with me like I was some hunky blind date, not just an overgrown schoolboy. She talked about her and Luke, how close they'd always been, how she'd made a lifelong job of shielding him from his father's temper and his mother's frosty disapproval.

"She got a wee bit drunk, started coming onto me, or so it seemed, shifting our chin wag from the dinner table to the couch, asking me how long a kid like me'd known he was gay, and how sure of the fact someone so young could be. I flirted back. There was a kind of fun to it, given how certain I was of nothing actually happening. Then she made a joke out of how strange it felt sharing a couch and a second bottle of wine with someone still in school uniform. She said to come upstairs with her, telling me she'd sort me out something a wee bit more informal, taking my hand to make sure I came with her.

"It was, you guessed it, the bedroom she led me to, throwing open a corner of her wardrobe where she kept a few odds and ends from her ex-husband, things to have handy - she said - should the prick get caught in the rain on one of the infrequent weekends he came to take their kid for a walk round Rouken Glen park. She picked out a cashmere sweater, a pair of chinos, told me to get into them, then laid herself across the foot of the bed, watching me.

"I said I wasn't used to doing a striptease when there was a lady present. She replied that she wasn't a lady, she was a big sister and she thought it was her duty to check out just who and what her baby brother was risking propriety for. So, I don't know why... the cheap thrill of a situation so strange, the way that teasing manner made her seem more like Luke than ever... but I began stripping off and when I was down to my underwear I saw from her stare and her smile that she wanted me to strip that off too. So that's just what I did. What the hell? - I thought: I'd always been a bit of a poser, keen to promote reverence for the male form.

"And reverent's how she looked. She told me to lie next to her on the bed, naked, caressed me, asked me if I was certain women weren't my thing. 'Luke's my thing', I told her, 'and I'm not letting him go'. She smiled, produced a tobacco tin of premium-grade coke from under her bed, introduced me to that pleasure, previously out of my price range. And while we buzzed like kids introducing one another to the facts of life, she started telling me... things about... about her and Luke. Oh... innocent things. By any legal definition, anyway. But stuff about... well, let's just say, she talked like a kindred spirit where Luke was concerned. She got me roused, in a way that would normally lie beyond a woman's power.

"So, drunk and buzzing and dreamy, we slid, caress by caress, mental image by mental image, into making love. A threesome, sort of, given that it was the phantom of our darling boy we were really fucking between us. She kept her eyes tight shut, betrayed a tear or two, seemed to breathe his name, or did my ears deceive me, as we finished off about a minute and a half later. We slept after that, still tangled up with one another, her naked as me by that point.

"I can't speak for her dreams, but mine, there, were so vivid I could almost feel Luke in the room. And then I woke with a start, because I realised he was in the room for real. He was standing against the mirrored door of the walk-in wardrobe, staring at us like he'd been staring for some while, a brilliant, scruffy shadow in the moonlight. My move stirred Laura awake. She wriggled clear of me, tugging the bedclothes around herself, like Eve the day God checked up on her taste in fruit.

"You - what?" Luke quietly said, stepping forward. "You tried to molest me, now you've - what? - raped my sister? Raped my fucking sister! You stood by and saw Dad drag me through the dirt for *your* perversions and now turn round and fuck AIDS into my fucking sister? How the fuck am I supposed to keep my head straight with the directions I'm being pulled in? How am I supposed to make sense of this world unless I slap it back?!'

"That's when his first slap came, just as I was scrambling off the bed. It was a clout his father would have envied, knocking me off my feet. I struggled up, did my best to fight back, but there was a madness in him beyond anything I'd had to put up with from him before, as if that sweet face of his had been strung across the mug of some demon in a Kabuki play. A few poundings later, he was slamming me against the window sill, the latest clout keeping me passive just long enough for him to fumble the window open. Then he had a hold on me around the middle, forcing me through the window head first. It was only when I heard Laura screaming that my ringing head caught up with the danger I was in.

"I struggled, but the upshot of that was to loosen his grip, which sent me slipping, upside down, through the opening even faster than he had in mind. I heard Laura scream again, closer this time, then felt two sets of hands fumbling about me as I hung there, too petrified to make any move of my own

"Then I heard a great rough sob that could only have been Luke's, felt the fiercest fumbling yet of those two sets of hands, someone's nails tearing into my leg, after which I was slipping free, falling, the moonlit patio below swelling to meet me. As I hit the paving slabs, the moonlight exploded. Blue, white, scarlet, purple, black. A black with my screaming bones buried within it.

"For a moment, just a moment, moonlight seeped back in, all smeared out of focus but letting me see the crazy jumble of my own body, the blackness of my blood everywhere. Beyond, I saw a figure blur into view around the corner of the house, drawing near and then stopping short, stifling a scream. I supposed it was Laura, but the blackness smothered me again before I could be sure.

"Someone was crying in that darkness. I thought at first it was me, except every muscle in me felt too sore to shift a tear. The blackness slid aside and I saw a figure towering over me, a hundred feet high, an unfastened bathrobe flapping about her nakedness. And when she spoke, she said the single word 'Luke....'

"And then Luke was alongside her. I couldn't make out his expression as anything more than a dark blot, but the way he stood suggested exhaustion, defeat. She tugged him round to face her, kissed him, locking her arms around him.

"And then she was pushing him aside, shouting something, I don't know what. Then the blackness drowned me again, a thousand tints of agony stirred up in it. The blackness didn't bob me up again till I woke in hospital."

Forty One

Duncan stuffed the cigarette which Fran had lit for him into the clench of his reconstructed jaw, coughing sorely on the first draw. I could see more distinctly than ever how the woundings and repairs to his features had aged him: he was just a kid after all, no older than Luke, a sweet suburban boy ejected overnight into a world of pain and injustice and bloody-minded plotting. I would have felt sorry for him were I not currently a prisoner of his grudge against the world.

"You woke in hospital," I suggested, "With a hell of a story to tell."

"By the time I woke up," he said, his features tensing uglier still, "The Hutchers had told their own story. To my own parents, most importantly. Hutcher senior taking command of the telling. The story of how I'd abused Laura's hospitality by bringing class A drugs into her home - my folks already prejudiced against me on that count, thanks to my being suspended over ownership of one measly Ecstasy tablet a year before. The fact that the police, guess what, had found Laura's cocaine stash in my schoolbag not helping matters. The story of how I'd raped Laura and been caught in the act by Luke, getting in a cocaine-maddened fight with him, only to fall out the window as much through my own drug-induced mania as his honest self defence. I had a whole new reason to curse my own skill in keeping my homosexuality a secret from those closest to me.

"My first thought was to tell the truth, or scribble it down, at least, given that my jaw was hung together like a birdcage a pterodactyl had fought its way out of. Then I thought of what I'd be up against, dragging the Hutchers into court, the Hutchers with their smart lawyer daughter and their genetically modified version of events, not to mention their money and charm, the latter of which I'd be the last to deny. I wondered if I wouldn't be booking my ticket to some young offenders shithole on a rape and drugs charge. Just the place for an artistically inclined suburban homosexual to feel at home.

"Then my parents pitched in with an extra complication: the pay-off they'd just taken from Hutcher. My Dad's an architect, you see, not a very successful one at the time. But now Hutcher had offered him a long-term contract as pet architect for the Hutcher empire. 'How could they say no?' my Dad asked rhetorically. On the back of the sudden cash flow, they traded in our old house in the Mearns, the one they were struggling to pay the mortgage on, for this dream palace here. Except now things are going so well, my folks are in Slovakia for the next six months while Dad oversees Hutcher's expansion into the holiday homes market.

"But what really sealed the deal on my silence was the night Luke came to visit me. All that Hutcher money was paying for me to have a room to myself in a private hospital. So when Luke sneaked in, right at the close of visiting time, he had me all to himself.

"And this was the Luke I'd swooned for right from the start: so tender, unguarded, in his apology that if I could have shifted a muscle, I'd have clutched and comforted him as if he'd come off worst. He told me he didn't understand what he'd done anymore than I did, but was ready to spend his life making up for it. He talked of the fresh start we were going to give the band, how we were going to finish school soon as we could, go professional, knock the world dead. He apologised for that last turn of phrase, smiling sweetly.

"Then, when he was sure things out in the corridor had settled for the night, he stripped naked, climbed into the bed, snuggled next to me. He didn't dare touch me. There wasn't a scrap of me that mightn't have cracked like spun glass and I was hardly in a position to touch him, but we lay there, anyway. And the beauty of him - that beauty I'd barely escaped from with my life - fixed its teeth in my flesh all over again.

"I still love him. I'll make that plain. I may be locked in a cold war with him and his family, but I don't love him any less, even as I do what I can to gnaw on the foundations of his happy home. Passion, reverence even, hardly precludes profanity, violence, cold fury.

"And by the time I got out of hospital, cold fury *et cetera* was heaped high in my heart. Because Luke, guess what, didn't keep his promises. I haven't even seen the bastard since, other than in photos Frannie's taken. He'd got himself expelled, meanwhile, from school. The word is some other kid made an insinuation about our relationship. Luke denied it, said something or other dismissive of this crippled faggot, got in a fight over the point, this culminating in his punching flat a teacher who tried to intervene. Two broken jaws in the space of three weeks. Maybe he notches them on his bedpost.

"Then I got this fake replacement for my own jawbone, regained the power of speech by way of it. First thing I did with that power was to fall out with my parents over the compromises they'd made. Not sure what to do, I slid into a depression deep enough to drown the Titanic. Fran here rescued me, helped me escape my parents house."

"I had a squat going," Fran chipped in. "Hardly fancy as this place, but homey enough. Dunc got back the knack of being alive, helped me start up the stall. Together we made just enough money to be able to say 'no' to the bribes his parents were offering, in the form of hand-outs of Hutcher money."

"Then I got word my folks were being seconded to Hutcher's overseas jamboree," Duncan went on. "So we crept in here soon as they were gone, made a squat out of this place. My parents don't know we're here, which is why we're so low-profile about the fact. Any neighbours who do glimpse us must assume the son and heir's here on Mummy and Daddy's say-so. But it's a secluded neighbourhood, too posh for people to go tapping on one another's doors for cups of sugar."

"So if we wind up killing you," Fran winked, "We could stuff you nice and cosy under the floorboards, at least until Duncan's Mum and Dad get back, and who'd be any the wiser?"

"You'd go to all that fuss," I asked, "just to protect your

little blackmail scheme? You won't take Hutcher money off your parents, but you'll take it off the man himself by way of fun and games with Action Men and Superboy comics?"

"Its not about money!" Duncan snarled, so hard I could see it hurt the tetherings of his face. "I'd tell you what we do with his precious bank-notes, but you might find the details a touch coarse. We take his money because money's the meaning of life to a man like that, the thing it hurts most to be bested over. And hurting him, them, that whole family... that's what matters. It's a game - no more, no less. A game we don't intend to lose."

"Which is why we're not in a mood to let you interfere with it," Fran stated.

"Hurting you is beside the point," Duncan said, more gently. "I'd much rather you took this as a warning about the family you're mixed up in. Please, take that warning and stop messing with us. With us and them. Go, lose yourself, far away. Counting yourself lucky to have survived both ends of the equation."

"Otherwise..." Fran began.

"Shhh!" Duncan told her. "You think you've got a sweet thing going with Luke? So had I. See where it left me."

"I love him," I said. "And I have to stand by him, whatever he's done or not done."

"Not done?" Duncan cried, hunching in the chair as if trying to leap out of it. "How many of my scars do you want to see? How deeply do you want your face rubbed in them? That streak of dark in him... it's downright psychopathic! How long before someone toys with his tender heart enough to get murdered in return? Mightn't you be that someone?"

"I love him," I said, "I trust him."

"Oh, spare us the Mills and Boon!" Fran snarled, rearing to her full height. "You know what, Dunc? I reckon there's more to Anna Karenina here than honest cradle-snatching. The way she tracked us down, the fight she put up, it showed more talent for that sort of thing than you'd credit a love-struck drama teacher with. So is that truly all you are?"

"It seemed enough," I said, "to justify finding out who the

206

hell you were and what the hell you're up to."

"Gee," mocked Fran, "Maybe it *is* true love, after all. Mutual, is it?"

"Fran..." Duncan cautioned.

"I mean, does Lukey-boy ache as fierce for you? Would he wriggle out on as thin a limb as you're on here, just to fight the good fight on *your* behalf?"

"Fran - please...." Duncan muttered.

"Why don't we test young Luke's devotion?" she asked him. "I have an idea for our next wee message to the Hutcher household. A photo display of Luke's true beloved here, candidly laid-out as your wounds in our last edition of 'Superboy'."

She grabbed me, wrenched me to my feet, threw me to the other end of the room, where I landed in a slide at full length on the varnished floorboards, just short of the snooker table. Fran wheeled Duncan around to face in the same direction before stepping to a hook on the wall and lifting down a classy-looking camera hung there by its strap.

"Go on," she told Duncan, tossing the camera onto his lap, "Think of Luke's gorgeous mop of hair prickling when he sees these shots. - Okay, sweetheart: strip."

I took hold of the nearmost leg of the snooker table, began pulling myself towards a sitting position, noting the red ball lying at the bottom of the net below the nearmost pocket. "What...?" I asked.

Fran lifted down a snooker cue from a rack on the wall. "Get yourself naked, your ladyship. C'mon, it's for Luke. You haven't been shy in the past about getting your kit off for his benefit. - Go on!"

Holding the cue like a weapon, she jabbed me in the shoulder with its tip. I rose to my feet, knowing they had left me no choice but to do what I was about to do. As Fran flipped the cue around in her hands, holding it by its pointed end and raising the blunt end like a club, I began pulling off my jacket.

"And when you've taken whatever porno shots you have in mind," I said, dumping the jacket across the near corner of the pool table, "What happens to me?"

207

"You…" Duncan began uncertainly.

"You need to disappear," Fran interrupted. "One way or another."

"Fran…" Duncan quietly implored.

"It's the only way!" Fran retorted. "She can either be a good cradle-snatcher and go and lose herself or we can give her a helping hand. Which, to me, looks like the safer option."

"True, Fran," I suggested. "We all three know there's too much risk for you in just letting me walk away. Isn't that so, Duncan?" That pain-bleached face of his blanched paler still. "What option have you got but to kill me?" I said.

"Shut up and strip!" Fran demanded.

"*Killing*, Duncan…" I continued, "…that's a big leap beyond anything you've got up to so far. Are you up to it?"

"Just get your fuckin' clothes off!" Fran growled.

"What about you, Fran?" I said, pulling off my sweater. "You've played a rough game so far, but killing someone's no game."

"I can do what needs doing, believe me," she said.

"I don't believe it, Fran. You're acting tough but you're shaking like an amateur." I set the sweater down by the pocket at the table's corner. "And I, Franny-sweet…" I said, slipping my hand into the pocket, grasping the ball hanging below, "…am no amateur."

I yanked out the ball, hurled it at her skull. Its weight cracked her forehead, amid a spray of blood-spots. As she tottered, I grabbed the near end of the cue, yanking her forward. She tripped over her own feet, her head suffering a second crack against the table's edge.

She dropped to the floor, rolling onto her back. I raised the snooker cue high, waited a second to let her fluttering eye get some focus on me, then brought the heavy end down. I heard Duncan call out, but the thump of wood through bone choked his voice dry, leaving him sitting in silence while I brought it down again and again until it broke, after which I finished off the job with one of the bar bells from the weightlifting rig. She was more delicate than one would have thought and didn't take much killing.

Forty Two

Spattered with the mess I had made of Fran's head, I must have looked quite a sight to Duncky-boy as I turned his way, for after a further second of goggling at me as if I were some Hydra that had reared out of the ground, he raised that stupid camera to his eye and took a shot of me, the flash flaring. I seized the thinner half of the snapped cue, driving its pointed end through the camera's outsized lens, whipping the camera from his hands and sending it crashing to the floor.

He reversed the chair with its electric control, turning to face the ramp to the doorway. He started to wheel himself in that direction, but I hurried alongside, shoving the cue between the spokes of the nearmost wheel. The chair upended, throwing him to the floor. Even as he raised his head, I was pulling the cue free, thumping his head back down with the blunt end.

By the time he woke, I had bound his arms and legs to the chair, using Fran's tights and cute little Batgirl panties among other odds and ends. With the chair still on its side, I had taken hold of its wheels and was dragging it in the direction of the pool when I saw his head raise and shake itself, squinting through his cracked glasses.

"Fran...?" he muttered.

"Dead," I told him. "Now shut up and lie still."

He twisted his neck to look across at me.

"What...? Wh... what...?" was the best he could come up with to say.

"Dead. Like you, sonny boy, in a minute or two. So no point making a fuss."

He strained his head the other way, caught sight of Fran. "Oh fuck... fuuucccckkkk....!" he whimpered.

"You see now," I said, "how out of your depth you both

were fucking with me? With *me*? Revenge - that's what you were after the Hutchers for? Revenge for a broken heart and having your puny mug bounced off a patio slab? Revenge in the form of fun and games with Action Men and Hutcher's small change? Don't make me laugh. There's serious revenge happening hereabouts and you and Frannie were getting under its feet. You can have too many cunts in a kitchen and my cunt outranks yours, sonny boy. Make do with the consolation that my vengeance is going to cost them more than a table-lamp or a scratched desk-top."

"Your... veng'nce? F'r'what...?" he asked.

I had dragged him to the edge of the pool and now stood upright, feeling downright Amazonian with Fran's blood drying on my half-naked chest.

"For never you mind," I said. "Just take it as read. The Hutchers have done worse still than they did to you. One victim didn't live to fight another day, not even from a wheelchair. It was that person I loved and love now, not Luke. Luke? A means to an end. Someone to hurt as a way of hurting someone else. He'll be dead too, soon. I'll mash him up bloodier than Frannie there. You don't need to know why. Just accept that there are fiercer degrees of love and hate than you've ever felt. Which is why you're there and I'm here. Except you're not even *there* anymore."

I gave the chair a push, sending him and it plunging over the edge. He let out a breathy yelp of "*Luke-!*" in the instant before he hit the water. Sinking shut him up, the chair's weight carrying him swiftly down, the metal frame making a ghostly clunk as it settled, on its back, on the pool's bottom.

I stood and watched him drown, but there wasn't much to see, his body so securely tethered that he made little movement beyond a swaying of his head that soon fixed itself into an upward stare my way. He had lost his specs on the way down, so I doubt I was more than the murkiest candlelit smudge to him, 20,000 leagues above. It was a shame, of course: he seemed a decent enough young man, hating nowhere hate wasn't deserved, possibly even as talented as he himself implied. But, let's face it, he was never going to top the charts

210

with a face like that and wheels where his legs should be, so maybe it was a mercy I was drowning his rock star dreams alongside the rest of him.

Air bubbles started to escape him. Then, suddenly, one of his arms was free. It flapped upward, seeming to reach my way, but without even the strength to point an accusing finger, the face below dissolving amid a fiercer uprush of bubbles.

The bubbles didn't take long to reach the surface, nor to pop when they got there; after that, there were no more bubbles. Duncan stared up from the foot of the pool with that fake jawbone sagged wide, resembling some doll carelessly dropped on a playground slab. But still that arm hung raised, doubtless just driftwood in the water's buoyancy but not a thing a murderess would want to stare at indefinitely, so I turned away and went upstairs to run myself a bath.

Lying in it, the bathroom a classy marbled affair with plenty to offer in the way of bath salts and shampoo, I pondered the problems and opportunities raised by my run-in with Fran and Dunc. I supposed that if I left the house still passing for empty, their bodies might remain undiscovered for a few days at least. But this meant I would have to be well clear of the country, 'Melinda Carido' buried at my back, by the time those few days were up. Which meant the time for the killing that really mattered was close at hand.

But that was no problem; indeed, what I had learned that evening inspired me now with the thought of a much richer murder than the one I had had in mind thus far. That tendency to violent temper in both father and son, the son's proneness to murderous jealousy, the father's rabid intolerance of sexual transgression in his boy... *"By Christ, it looked like he had it in him to murder the kid..."* Dunc had said of Papa Hutcher; and of Luke: *"that streak of dark in him... it's downright psychopathic! How long before someone toys with his tender heart enough to get murdered in return?"* Well, it would have been a crime against life's proferring of such gifts not to make the most of those. It was all so perfect, like a nudge from fate, an intervention from the Aztec Gods... the plotting of a vengeful ghost, even. *Yours?* Justice, of the poetic sort at least, suddenly seemed a real possibility in the world.

Climbing out of the bath, I searched the walk-in wardrobe of the adjoining bedroom, wherein I located a pair of D & G ladies jeans to replace my own cheaper pair, crusted with spray from Fran's brains, plus a swanky pair of suede boots. Before putting these on, I went back down to the basement, dragging Fran to the pool and dumping her in, weighed down with an exercise bike which I tied to her legs.

She sank swiftly, billowing a last curdle of blood from her bludgeoned head, settling close by Duncan, who still waved that arm my way. I suddenly thought, as the ooze of Fran's blood drifted across his blindly staring features, that at any moment that bloody cloud would clear and it would be *your* face staring up at me, chiding me for doing such a thing in your name; either that or goading me to the next spill of blood faster than I dared move.

I blew out the last of the candles and quit the house, a short walk along the neighbouring streets revealing my location as Pollokshields, still on the south side of Glasgow. From there, a couple of bus trips saw me back in Newton Mearns in time for some supper.

Forty Three

All seemed calm in the Hutcher home when I arrived. Amelia was in the kitchen, icing a carrot cake and a coffee cake. Caught up in this, she looked almost rapturous, like a girl having her first shot at baking cookies for her dolls. And then she spotted me in the doorway and her rapture crumbled.

I asked her where Luke and his father were. She said, voice drying at the back of her throat, that Luke was in his room and his Dad...

"...well, he's in the study but he's... he's not...."

"Not?"

"Not to be disturbed. His speech, for tomorrow... the company barbecue at the new development. I'm... these cakes... I like to make a contribution."

"You're a very devoted wife," I suggested.

"Yes!" she blurted. "Yes... I am, I... I...."

"You're not happy about my being here, are you?" I said, stepping towards her.

"I..." She tried backing away, but the corner formed by the worktops at her back allowed little room for manoeuvre. "I... I cared for Abby, so...."

"So?"

"She wouldn't, I'm sure, want us to just... just...."

"Cast me out into the night? For that I'm grateful. When the time comes for me to go, I'll give you all one heck of a parting gift."

"When... when do you... think you might...?"

"Go? Soon. Very soon."

"When?"

"As soon as my responsibilities here allow."

"What... what re-...."

She turned sharply away, strode from me to the kitchen's opposite corner, stood with her back to me, arms crossed tight upon her chest.

"I… I know about you and Rick," she said.

"You do?"

"You're not the first, you know. Hardly. I've known what he's like since the early days. That callous streak in him."

"Callous?"

"You don't make a success out of life like Rick has without a certain… ruthlessness. Right from the start, there have been other women. And, Heaven knows, we married young." She turned to face me. I suppressed my smile. "I've tried not to make a fuss. I've got so much out of being his wife. You see it all around you. I'm not some love-struck girl. Not the girl I was when I first fell for him. I wasn't that girl by the time I married him. I know what matters in marriage is the unromantic stuff: the roof over your head, financial security, children you can afford to take care of and educate, can offer a decent future. Freedom from worry about all these things. I've had as much of that as Rick's money can buy. And it can buy a lot. Set on the other half of the scale a few fumblings around with silly girls, here today, paid off tomorrow… well, why should I feel threatened by that? But you… you're the first he's had the nerve to install at the bottom of the garden. You *are* his lover, aren't you?"

"I'm… I'm not sure that isn't too romantic a term," I said, seizing my opportunity.

That frail little face of hers toughened its expression.

"Well, I'll defer to your experience in the matter."

"The first time he approached me…" I went on.

"I don't need to hear the details."

"…in the steam room at the health club…."

"Please!"

"…it was… well, very nearly rape, the way he stripped that bathing suit off me, took me then and there, where anyone could have walked in. But you must know yourself how… how masterful, how charming, how… how uncompromising he can be, how helpless a woman is in the grip of a man as brilliant as

214

that. Some of the things he's done with me, Amelia - they're disgusting, I know...."

"I don't want to hear!" she whined, twisting away as I stepped close enough to make her imagine his scent clinging to me.

"...but I have to confess," I continued, "he's got me hooked on him, the bastard. Like a drug injected into my heart. I know, one day, he'll kick me into the street like some fifteen quid tart who knew when to swallow. But in the meantime I'm, well... a prisoner in his arms."

"Oh God," she gasped, facing me, "Did Abby find out... was that why...?"

I gave my head a shame-burdened nod. She closed her eyes, clamped a hand across her mouth. After a moment, she lowered her hand, opened her eyes, their grey hue almost brilliant with tears.

"Right from the start," she said, "I had to fight to catch his eye, get myself involved in... well, things I'd rather not have been involved in."

"Such as?"

"Such as never you mind. But I... I did what I needed to and, doing so, *thought* my way around him as none of those other girls could. And won him from all of them. Won him and kept him, getting pregnant with Laura at the cost of my own shot at university. I lost so many battles, but I knew I'd won the war. It's always been a relief to him, I think, that I've seen past his charm. Sparing him the effort of putting it through its somersaults when he comes home and puts his feet up. We've been like... like criminals all along, cosy together knowing the worst about one another. Except, when you get complacent about the worst in a loved one, it's a shock when it gets worse still. Still... I made my choice long ago. What's to do beyond making do? I'm so good at that."

She had stepped back to the kitchen table, fussing with the cakes, when her husband appeared in the doorway at her back, his reading glasses halfway down his nose, a pen behind his ear and an A4 notepad stuffed under his arm. It was me his eyes fastened on.

"Gossiping in the kitchen?" he said. "You really have lowered the tone hereabouts, haven't you?"

"She's hardly done it alone, has she?" declared his wife, with a soft-edged snarl. Ignoring this, he stepped closer to me, lifting off his glasses.

"What happened to your face?" he said.

I raised a defensive hand towards the various minor bruisings and cuts I had received from Frannie. "Don't you know, Rick?" I asked.

He cradled my face roughly in his broad hand, tilting it further into the light, a frown taking hold of his own features. "Know?" he said.

"Look, please, Rick," I went on. "Not here, not in front of your wife...."

He deepened his frown, uncertain of the point I was making.

"Yes, please, Rick!" Amelia cried. "Not in front of me, for God's sake!"

He dropped his hand from my face, took a quizzical step towards his wife. She slipped her hand under the outsized carrot cake, flinging the whole thing Hutcher's way. But her aim lacked the slapstick precision required and the cake's iced surface impacted its white smear upon his right shoulder, the impeccably moist sponge collapsing into fragments and tumbling to the floor.

Amelia stumbled back against the table, venting a single note of shrill laughter. "Don't fret," she said. "In my line of work there's always another cake."

Stony-faced, Hutcher did what he could to brush the icing from his shoulder. This sent a second spasm of laughter through Amelia. He responded by taking a single step forward and slapping her so hard she stumbled half the kitchen's width, only kept upright by a collision with the worktop.

For a moment, we none of us made any further move, Hutcher looking as startled by this assault as myself or its victim. Then, with the surreality only a couple truly, grimly, made for one another could rise to, he resumed brushing the icing from his shoulder while she collected a dust pan and

216

brush, squatting while she began sweeping up the lumps of fallen cake, muttering about how pressed for time she'd be in terms of baking a replacement, he mumbling in his turn about how there was no need, the caterers being perfectly reliable.

But then, with half the crumbs still unswept, she paused, stood and threw dust-pan and brush to the floor, scattering the mess still further. "I know, you see," she told her husband. "She told me all about this... this *thing* between you and her."

"Thing?" he breathed. "What thing? What did she tell you?"

"My God, Rick... rape, she says, as good as. Was it you who put those bruises on her face? But then, I've known you too well and too long to be surprised by anything you might do. Haven't I?"

She swerved past him. He tried to catch her arm, but didn't try very hard and she was swiftly through the doorway. Hutcher faced me, saying nothing for a moment. Then he shifted to the door and quietly closed it.

"What have you told her?" he said, moving towards me.

"She seems to have got some idea in her head about your having installed me here as your spare time squeeze. She seemed ready enough to believe such things of you. It was difficult not to be tempted into pushing my luck."

"You've pushed your luck way too far, I reckon."

"That's rich, coming from a man who's got away with as much as you have, and for so long."

Hate flared so intensely in his features that I thought he might strike me still harder than he had hit his wife. But then that fire in him flickered from red to palest blue, burning inward rather than outward, inducing a single shudder.

"Look..." he said, "...You want money? How much?"

"You haven't enough, Rick."

"I have a lot."

"It's used toilet paper to me. And I doubt I'd care for the smell."

"What can I offer you, then?"

"You could try an apology."

He paused and then said, simply: "I apologise."

"That won't do," I told him.

"You said - "

"You didn't, on the day in question, do and say all you said and did in *private*, did you? You made a public spectacle out of the matter."

"I... I did a terrible thing," he said, "But... but I did it a long time ago and there's nothing now I can...."

While he fumbled for the next word, we caught the sound of a car starting its engine in the driveway. Hutcher hurried into the hall. I followed, catching up as he stood on the doorstep, looking out at his wife's car as it sped off along the road. After the sound of its engine and the red pocks of its tail lights had been swallowed by the night, he lingered on the doorstep and then stepped back inside, closing the door.

"Is this what you want?" he asked. "To tear my family apart?"

"The question I have to ask myself is... what would Alec want?"

The utterance of your name, for so long too sacred for speaking, sent a tremor through my spirit even as I saw it shake his, as if I had invoked your ghost and you had set a hand upon both of us.

Hutcher made the tiniest sidelong tilt of his head. "The living room," he said. "Let's have a drink."

Forty Four

"Melinda Carido..." he said, pouring me a brandy as substantial as the one he had poured for himself, "Did you make that name up or acquire it on your travels?"

"My secrets aren't the ones on trial here," I replied.

"The travels themselves, Mexico and all that," he pondered, handing me my glass, "did they take place, or have you been spying on us over the garden fence for the last five years?"

"Five years spying wasn't required. I knew what I needed to know a long time ago."

"A really good spy wouldn't blow her cover like you've done."

"I'm not a spy. Matters here are more personal than that. It's important to have you know who I am, what and who I'm here on account of."

"Alec's baby sister," he sighed, settling in an armchair opposite me. "I remember you now."

"Cute, wasn't I?"

"More cute now than ever. What was your first name again? Something sweet like -"

"You've poisoned enough of my past between those lips. Wrap them round my real name and I'll smack it clear."

"I don't recall you playing so rough back in the old days."

"Who roughened me up but you?"

"I never touched you."

"You murdered my brother. That counts as touching."

He spasmed to his feet, brandy sloshing over the rim of his glass.

"I didn't -..."

"We both know what you did."

He settled back into his seat.

"Like I say, I didn't...." he began, his gaze losing itself amid the threads of the carpet.

"There's nothing you could say," I stated, "that would make you any less of a monster. I wonder if there's anything you could *do* that would settle the debt you owe me - me and the ghost of my family. Other than maybe drowning yourself in that pool."

He blanched, as if fearing I was about to drag him there that instant. "That... that's not an option," he protested, his tone weak enough to make me wonder if he hadn't pondered that very course of action himself once or twice over the years.

"No," I replied. "Too quick a get-out for you. Unless there's a Hell. There probably is for men like you, but I don't like gambling when it's less than a sure thing. - No, the most sensible option is to have you stand up in public, O Pillar Of The Community, and confess your crime. That shindig at your new development tomorrow would fit the bill nicely."

"No!" he snarled, slamming down his glass and returning to his feet. "No way! Anyway, it... it wasn't a crime. Not as such. It was just... just...."

"What? Fun and games? A roundabout way of saying 'I love-'"

"It was what it was!" he yelled, before continuing in a pained whisper: "And there's nothing can be done about it now. What I did back then was shameful, rotten, I don't deny, but what did it amount to beyond a misunderstanding and a... a cruel and immature game that got seriously out of hand, as happens with children's games?"

"It was a more grown-up game than that, surely?" I suggested. "After Alec was dredged out of that pool, I raided his room for keepsakes. Found your letters to him. I have them with me."

"What?"

"I've read them so many times in the years since, memorised the crucial passages. As in '*Ready to live dangerously, super-hero? I am.*"

"Stop it," he said.

"'Let's sneak away from suburban boredom, run wild while we can.'"

"Stop it," he repeated.

"'Up by the old pool past the Trenchard farm - that wild enough for you?'"

"Stop it."

"'We can skinny dip, if you've the nerve. Guess what -?'"

"Stop."

"'I think I have. I think suddenly I'm sick of being scared of what might be waiting to happen between you and me."

"Please…."

"Got this heart of mine set, believe me, on making up for any cruel words I might have said, any wrong impression I might have given.'"

"Don't."

"'Maybe a kiss would make it all better?'"

"Please!"

"'Maybe it's best if I just wind up here saying meet me at the pool and we'll see there -'"

"No!"

"'- what plunge we have it in us to take together, my golden Al-… "

"Stop!"

He leapt from his chair, crossed the room in what seemed a single step and clamped a hand across my mouth. I smiled my eyes up at him, then licked the palm of his hand. The blood drained from his stare, tears welling to fill the gap. And I could see, as if I were an X-ray slicing to his skeleton, the boy I was after, hidden for so long behind the grown man's armour. That boy was frightened, nakedly so; I wondered if this fear was a fresh sensation after years of assuming he'd got away with his crime, or if the terror had been there all along, nagging at his every moment of triumph, warning him of the inevitability of a comeuppance like this.

"Destroying me…" he barely more than whispered, "…destroying all I have… that's the only thing that would satisfy you, isn't it?" He had slid his hand from my mouth, taking a couple of shaky backward steps.

221

"It would satisfy me to see the truth put out there," I told him. "It can do what it likes with you once it's been set free."

"I won't allow this!" he declared.

I took a swig from my brandy, set it aside and then stood. "What you going to do?" I queried. "Kill me too?"

I saw a savage humour flicker in his wounded features and felt my own twinge of fear, for this was the boy in him too, surely: that boy malicious enough to have laughed my brother into the grave.

"Isn't *that* a temptation?" he muttered. "I'm sure I could find a foundation stone to plant you under, some wet cement to sink you in."

"What sinks one day, bobs up another. Isn't one ghost on your conscience burden enough? Or - My God - are you so cold-hearted you're blind to his ghost, his ghost that I've seen every day since? His ghost that's here between us now, naked and dripping, looking you in the eye and saying -"

"I don't want to hear!" he screamed, grabbing me, hurling me to the far end of the room, where my fall brought a small table laden with showy ornaments crashing down alongside me.

"You think you can drag me down, humiliate me, haul me through the streets of the Mearns in shame, destroy all I've built," he snorted. "But, guess what, I'm no stupid kid now, but a man taller in the world than a gnat like you can take down. Do your worst: I'll crush you before you've so much as raised a bruise on me."

"Your armour's pierced already, big man," I said, dragging myself from the floor. "I'm through to the pinkest meat you've got."

"What does that mean?" he asked.

Above us, a door flapped open, closed, followed by a swift trot of feet down the stairs.

"There we go - I've got a friend in high places. More than a friend, to be frank."

"What does that mean?"

"Your son and heir's a gorgeous hunk of young manhood. And I'm a woman mature enough to know what a young man wants and needs. Better than he knows himself. And still young enough to make the fullest use of that knowledge."

"What?" he snapped, striding across to grab me again, shaking me too hard for answering him to have been a practicable option. "What?!!!"

I glimpsed a figure in the doorway. Hutcher, seeing this shift of my attention, stilled his assault, looking round, then pushing me from him.

"Isn't it the teenager who's supposed to make too much noise around bedtime?" Luke mused, warily.

Forty Five

"Luke…" his father began.

"What exactly was he doing to you?" Luke asked me.

"What's she been doing to you, that's the question!" his father interrupted.

"He forced me to tell him, Luke," I sighed. "Beat it out of me. You see?"

I made sure Luke got a clear look at the bruises and cuts on my face. He strode up to me, caressed my features far more tenderly than his father had done.

"Now wait a minute - !" Hutcher intervened.

"No, you wait a minute!" Luke yelled. "What the hell have you done to her?"

"He… he was coming onto me, Luke…" I stuttered.

"What?"

"Oh, for heaven's - !" Hutcher snorted.

"You shut up!" Luke cried. "Now, tell me…."

"He was coming on strong, Luke. I resisted. Then he…."

Hutcher gave a grunt of humourless laughter.

"Shut up!" Luke insisted.

"…well, that's when he started getting rough. I said I'd call for you if he didn't stop… 'Luke? What's it got to do with him?' - he demanded. And that… that's when he forced me to tell him about… about us, Luke. And that's when he got seriously rough. He told me… he… he said things about you, Luke."

"Such as what?"

"Luke…" his father began.

"SHUT UP!" Luke screamed. He faced me again. "Go on," he said.

"He… he said he… he knew things about you that… that

224

made you loving me a ridiculous idea, made the idea of you being... being man enough a joke, said he'd... had to step in before to set your love-life straight and wouldn't think twice about doing it again. Even if he had to beat the sense into you hard as he was about to beat me. Thank God you came down, Luke."

I threw myself against him, pressing my face to his shoulder, faking a few sobs. He closed his arms around me.

"Luke-..." his father said, "...everything she's told you is just -..."

"Just what, Dad? Inconceivable? That you'd come on to an attractive woman like an alpha male gorilla with an itchy crotch? That you could get violent when someone didn't do things your way? That you'd promise the same kind of violence for me? What's not to believe?"

"And am I to believe her," Hutcher countered, "when she tells me she's seduced you?"

"Seduction's what creeps like you do. This... her and me... this is a thing you never heard of - called 'love'."

Even I was a little taken aback by this, but it was Hutcher who did the snorting. "Love?" he retorted.

"Well, I had to find it somewhere!" Luke snapped. "Come on, Melinda. Why don't we get up to bed?"

I raised my head, looked him in the eye, his boyish face suddenly that of a man indeed, the sort of man whose strength of devotion I'd given up looking for years before. Killing him abruptly struck me as an absurd thing to do.

"Not to any bed under any roof of mine!" Hutcher declared.

Luke, an arm around my shoulders, began steering me towards the door. "It's two against one," he told his father, "And you're looking a little past it for laying down the law."

"Luke..." he said in a more placatory tone, shifting himself between us and the doorway.

"You could try hitting me, Dad," Luke said. "But time's gone by since your last slap. Reckon I'm old enough now to thump you harder than you can thump me. And that you're too old to get up quickly from the thump I'd give you. Now... out of the way."

"Luke..."

"Out of the way!"

His father shifted, very slowly, out of the doorway. Luke and I continued into the hall. I smiled at Hutcher almost fondly as we went by.

It was only as we were heading towards the stairs that I began to feel how Luke was shaking. I think he sensed as keenly as I did that his father was following us, although the paternal step was all but silent upon those plush carpets and the paternal voice hushed until we were on the lowermost steps.

"Luke, please, don't...." was what he finally said, and then, as we climbed higher, "I... I know who she is, Luke, I...! - N... never mind who she is, but... but *I* know! We can't trust her - any of us! Luke! Luke! For this whole family's sake - don't! Luke!"

And then, when we were almost at the top of the stairs, we heard him charging up after us. Luke froze at my side, his heart thumping its rhythm through both his ribs and mine.

But his father halted several steps below us, with another, feebler, repetition of "Luke...please... don't....", to which Luke responded by resuming our ascent.

"No... Not my son... You can't have my son!" he screamed. "Not my son!"

We continued on. At the top of the stairs, I looked back. Hutcher was glowering at us from halfway up, but as my eyes fixed on him, I raised a cautioning finger to my lips and saw Hutcher drop his gaze, turning away and slumping to a sitting position, his back to us.

Then I let Luke carry me to his bedroom, where he sat me down on the end of his bed, kissed me lightly on the brow and then returned to the door, closing it softly, leaning his back against it and looking my way through the moonlight.

"The important thing," Luke whispered, "is what he imagines."

He stood there, silent, for what seemed hours, his shadowed face fixed in my direction, for all that I could not be sure I existed for him, at that moment, as anything other than a

226

well-placed nought or cross in this game with his father, who remained likewise silent, however near or far from the door's other side.

At last, Luke shifted towards the bed, pushed me flat across it, stripped me naked and fucked me every way he pleased, still silent as he pushed me from position to position, until he loosed his youthful heat about the mouth of my womb and wept for a moment, before sliding aside and lying still and, to all outward appearances, sleeping.

I twined my nakedness around the foetal curl of his, immersing myself in that silence with which I had drowned the Hutcher household. Before long, I had settled into a sleep calm and dreamless beyond anything I had experienced in all the years since Rick Hutcher stripped you from my life.

I woke, once, at some unguessable hour of the night, hearing the voice of Luke's father from what must have been the same spot on the stairs where I had seen him last, the utterance beginning as a few gruff, unintelligible whimperings, as if he had fallen asleep and was now starting from a nightmare.

And then those gruntings, just for a second, gained the shape of a single word before his voice fell silent again and I heard him stumbling up and along to his own bedroom. It was *your* name, Alec, I heard him call.

Forty Six

The next sound I heard, waking to pale morning light and a spatter of raindrops on the far side of the closed curtains, was that of an engine starting up in the driveway below. I rose, drew back the curtain, looked down upon Hutcher's Mercedes as it reversed into the road and drove swiftly away.

"Was that Dad...?" I heard Luke mutter, sticky-lipped. I turned to him, nodded. He stretched his lanky magnificence upon the bed, yawned, scratched his balls and then suddenly took on a look of the most unbecoming seriousness.

"We didn't just dream all that last night, did we?" he enquired.

"Did you dream being my big strong protector? No. All that was for real."

He sat up straight as I began pulling on my clothes. "So where do we go from here?" he asked, a child's anxious face appearing atop that manly nakedness.

"We run away like lovers," I told him. "That ought to be obvious."

"Where? And when exactly?"

"Soon as poss. And wherever the mood takes us."

"I... I hadn't thought about leaving home. Not... not seriously... "

"We'll make ourselves a whole new home, one that's ours and ours alone. Weave it from my cunt and your cum, how about it?"

"Can we afford the mortgage?" he queried.

"We've already made a down payment, don't you think? Meanwhile, we have a bolthole, don't forget."

"We do?"

"Yeah. That old farmhouse, opposite the golf course."

"You want to stay *there*?"

"I want to meet you there, certainly. This afternoon, after I've seen to a few other things I have to take care of."

"It's weird and creepy and downright dangerous in there. I nearly got my neck broken last time, don't forget."

"It wasn't all bad in there, I recall."

"At best, it was a place for fucking in, not living in."

"So we'll fuck. And then we'll move on. So be there. Two o' clock, let's say. I'll ring you on your mobile to confirm."

"Should I pack a case?"

"That's up to you. Where I'm taking you, you're not going to have a whole lot of need for clothes."

"A nudist colony?"

"The Garden of Eden. Watch out for snakes."

"I might just uncoil a snake of my own," he said, toying with his cock.

"Bring it along this afternoon and it can corrupt me all over again."

"It's willing to corrupt you this morning, if you like."

"I have places to be. And breakfast to grab before I get there."

"What places?"

"Your Dad's big bash at that new development of his, for starters. Assuming he's still in the mood to be master of ceremonies."

Luke started from bed, dragging on his clothes. "You're going there?" he asked.

"I'll let him know I don't bear him any hard feelings. Wanna come?"

"You're kidding."

"Yeah, maybe I am. We wouldn't want to put him off on his big day, would we?"

Fully dressed, I set off downstairs. Luke hurried after me, still struggling into his clothes. "Wait, I... I don't think it's a good idea for you... for you to...."

I had stopped by the kitchen doorway. Luke, catching up with me while tugging on his T-shirt, wriggled his head through the collar only to halt abruptly, having seen, like me, his mother standing in the conservatory. She had plainly just emerged from the garden, wet of hair and flushed of complexion in a waxed jacket, jeans and wellingtons.

"Mum…" said Luke, "…Hi… Wondered where you'd got to."

"I've been tidying up," she said, reddened eyes fixed on me. "In the cottage. Your stuff is out there."

I stepped her way, looked through the extension's glass doors to see my rucksack and suitcases, packed to the point of overflowing, propped against a stuffed black bin bag in front of the cottage. When I looked around at Amelia again, she shivered back a step, as if fearful I might bite her.

"You're going," she said. "This morning."

"I'm going right now," I smiled. "I'll pick up that stuff later - Give you a buzz, Luke."

I waved to my boy and then collected my coat. I left and never returned, and for all I know those things of Melinda Carido's still lie on that lawn, moss creeping over the bags, the rain forming small puddles amid the wrinklings of the rucksack and bin bag, autumn leaves garlanding them. For Melinda Carido is dead: deader than she was to begin with.

Forty Seven

I grabbed a late breakfast up at the Mearns Cross shopping centre and then wandered through the drizzle to Rick's new estate, observing from the far side of the street the settings-up for the mid-day festivities, a broad patch of grass facing the grandest houses now dominated by the inflating battlements of a bouncy castle, an open-fronted marquee being erected next to this. In front of the very grandest house, a banner was being erected over a podium in the centre of the still-unlevelled *cul de sac* road, the banner reading: LANDORIA - A NEW HIGHPOINT FOR HUTCHER HOMES, the canvas on which this was printed already dampened and sagging.

Soon tables were set up and a buffet laid out within the great marquee and by lunchtime a sizeable crowd had gathered to shelter within from the stubborn drizzle. The shindig was open to all well-behaved comers, so I had no trouble slipping in; I succeeded, however, in keeping myself all-but-invisible while grabbing a glass of sparkling wine and a cracker heaped with crayfish. The dress-code was plainly smart-casual, those assembled ranging from figures previously seen thereabouts in helmets and overalls to the sort of blue-rinsed *grand dames*, ugly-pretty horsey types and well-trimmed golf club stalwarts whom one could be sure had never dirtied an overall in their lives.

Hutcher himself was moving amongst them, shaking hands, patting backs, swigging on the sparkling wine, making apologetic gestures towards the heavens, generally smiling and greeting as if nothing troubled the foundations of his authority and nothing ever could. Amelia had returned, dutifully, to her husband's side, changed from her wellies into a neat little trouser suit and doing as much as her spouse to spread the word of Hutcher prosperity. I suppose only I could spot the tense little twitches which punctuated her smiling encounters.

Laura had showed up, too, with little Emily. I was watching her discreetly caution her father over his seizure of another glass of wine when Emily happened to look around, spotting me. A finger to my lips kept her quiet, a half-smile on that solemn little face suggesting relief at the thought of a drama game amid all this grown-up dullness. I eased myself a little further away.

Before long a break in the clouds and a single noncommittal ray of sunlight saw Hutcher giving instructions to a few groundlings, swigging back his latest glass of wine and then summoning those around him out to the vicinity of the podium, where within seconds the Emerson, Lake & Palmer version of 'Fanfare For The Common Man' was belting from the PA system.

Already, with the brightening of the weather, a number of people had wandered out from under the marquee to stroll among the new houses, the most complete of which had been opened to general view, even the bouncy castle belatedly wobbling its towers under childish invasion. The adults began congregating at the foot of the podium as Hutcher made a showy sprint up onto it. He accepted a mild round of applause as if it were a Nobel Prize and then signalled for the music to be turned down, thumping the microphone to test it was working.

"Ladies and gentlemen," he declared "Neighbours, prospective customers, the simply curious and, of course, those of you who helped me build this step beyond in state of the art living... let me welcome you to the - almost! - completed Landoria, a place that dreams can call 'home'!

"You know, in this business, no one's more aware than I am that one isn't simply trading in bricks and mortar. No - it's dreams indeed. Dreams and families, fresh starts in life and secure retirements, healthy places for childhoods to blossom, rewards for those with the gumption to earn a decent living for themselves and those they love.

"And here at Landoria, it'll be a safe living too. We all read the papers. We all know it's a tough world: decent, hard-working people so often threatened by those too busy preying

232

on others to earn themselves homes like these. That's why the final stage to this project will see state of the art security installed, keeping Landorians safe from all those dangers which, even in a place like the Mearns, can upset the lives of decent folk. Life in Landoria... well, it's not going to be paradise - we build our homes in the real world, for better or worse - but it's going to be the best living the earth of the Mearns can hold.

"And if I'm motivated by an ideal, a ideal of the sort of life that might be lived in these homes of mine, it's because I go home at night - schedule allowing! - to a home of my own, a *family*, where...."

I had discreetly weaved a path from the rear of his audience towards the front and it was now, as I found a position immediately below his podium, that my friendly smile caught his eye.

"Um... wh... where..." he resumed, wrenching his gaze from me, "...where... where one can... can rely on... I mean... Family! Family, it matters, so... um, so I'd like to say, pay, eh, eh, tribute to my wife for her... Amy, for her... her support, my whole family in fact... My daughter's there - Laura! - Top of the league lawyer. Might come in handy some day! And my beautiful grand-daughter Emily. Grand-daughter! Makes me feel old. Old. Like I say... Family! It matters! Family... Matters! Matters...."

He stared down at me again.

"I know what counts," he continued. "What... what counts is... is standing strong by what matters, as in... values! Family! The things one builds with one's own hands! Not... not letting anything... anything...!"

Again, his eyes took in the broader gathering.

"I'm not, you know I'm not, always the... Well, I can be a tough guy, a driven man, a getter-of-the-job done. But don't think-! Don't think for a moment I'm not... I mean... It's not beyond the bounds of possibility that... that slanders might be made... now and then... against me - and the things I've done - and the things I've built, but... but know this - !"

It was becoming clear our master of ceremonies had swigged too freely at his own free bubbly, this coupling, no doubt, with the pressures inherent in such a grand project to render his oratory somewhat overheated; either that or maybe his prompt cards had become jumbled or had their ink set running by the preceding rain. At any rate, his wife - good egg - was by now ascending the podium to be at his side.

I, however, muse of this one-man drama, had plainly fired him too sorely with the urge to state his case before the trap flipped open beneath his feet, so that as Amelia tried to take his hand, he shrugged aside the gesture, inching to the podium's brink.

"I know, I... I've known...." He swayed slightly. I saw his wife make a pathetic little catch at the tail of his jacket. "...I know what matters, at the end of the day. I've... I've known..." Again his eyes were fixed on me. "...Beauty, I've known. I... God. God. The ugliness of it all."

He swayed forward, reaching for the microphone on its stand but only succeeding in knocking the whole thing over, those of us below having to jerk clear as it hit the ground, discharging an electronic squeal through the PA system. Hutcher looked from the mike to me and then past the top of my head, unnerving even me with the sudden fixity which seized his features. It was at this point I'm certain I heard him mutter the words "Alec... you got here at last...."

I looked round, expecting to see you smiling from the far edge of the crowd. But either you weren't there or his murderer's eye could see with a clarity denied a loving sister; and if that were true, then I hated him more than ever.

It was only vaguely that I caught the clatter of his feet down the steps of the podium; it took his pushing past me to draw my attention to his lurching run from the scene. I caught his arm. He looked round, face red as an open wound.

"You know where I live," I did little more than mouth. "Meet me there at three o'clock." I held up three fingers, making sure he got the message.

He pulled free of my grip so violently that he almost overbalanced before running on, bulldozing a route through the remainder of the crowd, apologies muttered to a few of them that only made him sound still more unhinged: "S-sorry, I... do, do finish off that buffet, I... I just have to... I thought I saw - I

234

did see… It's okay, I'll catch up - catch up! I'm okay… okay… busy man, you know. Busy man!"

His car was parked by the half-finished pavement past the rear of the crowd. He climbed in, reversing it with reckless speed towards the road beyond, almost running over a few of his guests, spraying several more with the mud his wheels threw up and all but drowning his wife's cry of "*Richard*!"

As his car sped out of view, I began a brisk departure of my own, only to find my path cut off by the appearance, directly in front of me, of Laura. I cast her an affectionate smile, all the more affectionate on account of my new knowledge of her part in the Hutcher saga, and then attempted to walk by. She caught my arm.

"What's happening with Dad?" she demanded.

"Your Dad's the one to ask, surely?" I said.

"Mum says she's evicted you. She has you down for a malign influence. She hasn't yet spelled out why, not to me, anyway."

"You're a top rank lawyer, according to your Dad," I said. "If you can't get an answer out of her, then who can?"

"Is it just to do with your fucking my brother? Or have you taken even more of a liberty than that?"

"That must be liberty enough, I'm sure, to set *you* on edge."

"What does that mean?"

"You have a positive passion, I hear, for prying into your brother's affairs. To the point of incriminating yourself."

She squeezed my arm tighter.

"What have you heard?"

I yanked her hand away.

"I wouldn't go playing the strong arm of the law, Laura, not with me. I know too much about your deviances from the strict letter of sisterly behaviour."

"I… I don't know what…" she muttered, blanching as the first fat drops of returning rain hit her face.

"I hope you sound more convincing in court, Laura. Otherwise, it could affect your career advancement."

I walked on. On my way out of the estate, I rang Luke's mobile. "Get to the farmhouse now," I told him. "Now as in *now*!"

Forty Eight

I wound my way swiftly to the farmhouse, breaking into a run as soon as I was clear of those streets upon streets of whited sepulchres they called a suburb. When the familiar, lonely huddling of wind-blown buildings came into view, I paused, pondering an avoidance of that turn in the road, followed by a sprinting over the brow of the hill and down towards Eaglesham, where I could catch a bus for Glasgow, and then catch another bus for the airport and be far above the clouds in a matter of two or three hours.

But as the wind and intensifying rain swept across me, I saw, all of a sudden, how closely my old home's outline resembled the time-gutted temples of the Aztecs, Tezcatlipoca himself seeming to vent his jaguar growl amid the intervening wilderness of rough grass, and I realised I could not run from what was sacred and inevitable, from that alone which could knot up the chaos of my life, giving it a meaning of which I could count myself master.

So I took that turn in the road and hurried on. And as I crept inside the old place, my every previous moment within fleshed itself forth from the damp woodwork, like those shades in Greek myth which drink blood to grow solid. Mum and Dad were everywhere: the memory of their scent, their smiles, their moodinesses, their trivial arguments, their reconciliations, Dad's crass jokes, Mum's backyard profundities, their matter-of-fact passion for our protection, their weight of sorrow when Hutcher's hand stole their son away, a sorrow crushing them slowly, inch by inch, both of them too crushed by life already to rouse a scream, that wounded silence between them sorer than any teary outcry.

I saw, yet again, the sagged mess Dad made of himself

that day out in the byre, the cowshed selected for his suicide - we always assumed - on account of his not wanting to make any such bloody mess in Mum's nice, tidy home. Yet it was the smell, still more than the sight, of his blood and brain cow-shat up that metal partition which forced itself upon me more fiercely than on any of the ten thousand previous occasions I'd recalled it. Likewise, Mum's slow dissolution into her own living ghost - each year of the horror's aftermath rendering her still more transparent, until the white walls of the loony bin absorbed her entirely - fixed its chill through me with sorer bite than ever before.

I checked the cupboard beneath the sink: the little rucksack I had concealed there on the day of my return remained intact, everything I would need for my onward journey secure within, from the faked passport in my next faked name to hair dye and the new bikini which would be just the thing on the volcanic sand of that distant, lonely beach where I planned to do nothing for a very long time. It was as I shoved the rucksack back out of sight, after the extra precaution of slipping the passport into the back pocket of my jeans, that a creak from above and a tickle of falling plaster dust alerted me to my not being alone in the house.

Sliding the cupboard door closed again, I proceeded to the foot of the stairs, called up them.

"Luke?"

I received no answer and heard no further movement until an echoing flurry of what I took for pigeon wings sounded from one of the rooms above. I began creeping up the steps, skin tingling at the thought of Luke's proximity and the thought, too, of the sight I might shortly be able to confront his father with, of the conflagration I reckoned I had it in me to force upon their already inflammable relationship. Ah, the poverty of my initial ambition: merely to commit murder by my own hand, some low budget version of an Aztec heart-ripping. This would be so much better: seeing the Hutcher clan tear its *own* heart out. Whether it was the father's heart or the son's that came off worst hardly mattered to me.

"Luke?" I called again at the top of the stairs. Again my

call went unanswered, but as I scanned the landing's length, finishing by looking towards the door of my old room, I felt a shadow fall across my back in the murky light, the faint, tense breathing of a watching presence filtering past innumerable rainy drips through the holes in the roof.

I turned, and as I turned I heard a scuffling movement by the doorway of your old room; completing my turn, I saw no one there. "Hide and seek, Luke?" I asked, stepping that way. "Haven't we played this game already?"

Except I couldn't be sure it *was* Luke and as I slowly, carefully rounded the edge of that doorway and stepped within, the gloom seemed pregnant with possible forms, living and dead. "Luke…?" I muttered, for the sake of wishful thinking.

A hand fixed itself across the lower half of my face, dragging me back, a matching hand latching itself between my legs, pulling me onto my tip-toes. Hutcher senior's voice hooked itself at my ear.

"One of the many lessons I've learned in my long business career," he said, "is always get to the meeting well ahead of schedule!"

He let go of me. I lost my footing, dropping to my hands and knees before struggling up to face him. He stepped forward, looking a good deal more composed than I had seen him twenty minutes before, quite at home - one might almost have said - amid the greenish shadows. I tensed, ready for a further assault but he wandered by me, stroking a hand along the mouldy wallpaper as he approached the ivy-choked window.

"The times I spent here," he mused. "Wet afternoons in the school holidays, hot Saturday mornings when your parents were at market. We used to climb, Alec and me, onto the corrugated roof of the shed round the back, strip off, sunbathe. On the brightest days, you could see all the way to the Campsie Fells, Ben Lomond even. It was a whole other world to me, this place. Rough and tumble, smelling of…." - he laughed to himself. - "…nature." He faced my way. "It's criminal I haven't popped back, not once in all these years. I'm a member across the road, you know. Handicap of two and hell-bent on that big *numero uno*. Out on the fairways, I couldn't help but notice the old place. Occasionally, I'd drop a stroke or two on the holes with the clearest view."

"Guilt?" I suggested.

"Oh yes," he said. "Guilt, obviously. Not quite the guilt *you'd* have me feel, but guilt all the same. The last thing I wanted was for your brother to kill himself."

"You killed him."

"I did no such thing. I played a joke on him that got out of hand. That was naïve and childishly cruel on my part and, like I say, I've never quite forgiven myself, but youthful stupidity and murder are hardly the same thing."

"He loved you. You tore his heart out. Fed it to your pals. What sort of life was he supposed to lead after that?"

"He made his own decision. The young give and take a lot of cruelties. Most of us take the worst of them in our stride and get on with growing up, knowing nothing in our lives will ever be so tough again. Why the hell couldn't he? Is it my fault he couldn't?"

"You raped him, you pig out of hell, gang-raped him. That's hardly part of the standard ups and downs of being young."

"It wasn't… wasn't like that!"

"He had a fucking branch shoved up his arse. In what way is that not rape?"

"What would you know about that?" he asked.

"I know what I saw."

"Saw?"

"I was there."

"No you weren't."

"Look in these eyes of mine. You'll see it reflected there still."

"I didn't see you."

"But you *never* really saw me. A little squit of a thing I was, a whole ten years younger. Even when you and Alec fooled around here, you lost sight of me among the ponies on the wallpaper. And that day, out there by the pool, having followed you in my anxiety over my brother's mood, I was able to hide in the gorse bushes on the slope above, unseen by any of you big kids, my little lips and teeth biting on that gorse to stifle my screams."

"I do remember you," he said. "Not that day, but other days. Your hair wasn't black, not then. Red... wasn't it?"

"Red," I confirmed. "Red is still my colour."

"A cute wee thing, I recall. Big dark eyes. Those haven't changed."

"What now? Coming onto me? Then what? You'll rape *me*? Discard me? Bury me?"

"I didn't rape - !"

"You raped us all! Alec, my parents, me - shoved your thorny shaft through all our hearts. Do you know what happened to this family?"

"Of course I bloody know! You don't think it's haunted my every step in the world since that day? Tainted every positive thing I've done?"

"With what? The fear of getting caught, you selfish cunt?"

"The fear of that and... so much more besides."

"The thought of Hell, maybe? Don't kid me, you Godless fuck."

"Hell... well, it's just a word. There are feelings, places your feelings can take you, that no words can ever capture. I've been to one or two of those places. The dead were there and wouldn't let me go. Life all around me, jumping through every hoop I held up, rolling over to have its tummy tickled, shitting gold when I clicked my fingers and still... still the dead had me, grey and cold. I looked in my family's eyes and your family floated between me and them like a mist. A freezing mist, freezing the love I might have felt... *should* have felt for... for my own... my own. That's Hell! Hell-nor-am-I-out-of-it.

"And I tried, by God, to claw my way up and out. All the good I've done, houses built, lives secured, money earned, lavished on those I love... in my heart I knew, and in their eyes I saw, how futile a gesture it all was. Did I kill your brother? I certainly killed myself. And all for a stupid boyish joke, long ago, on a day in the summer holidays when there was a little too much time to kill."

I had glimpsed a sheen of tears thickening upon his cheeks

while he spoke. Now sobbings shook him, forcing a clamp of his hand across his eyes.

"You want sympathy, a shoulder to cry on?" I said. "That's what families are for. I knew all about it when I still had one of my own. Admit to yours what you've admitted to me and see the hug they give you. Why... one or other of them might squeeze the breath clean out of you."

Abruptly his hand was lowered from a face firm in the set of its features. "I've thought of a more practical solution," he said. "Solid businessman that I am."

He reached to the inside pocket of his overcoat. I hoped-against-hope for the sight of a cheque book I might laugh at. But it was a gun he produced, the same handgun I had seen him draw in the woods beneath the castle. He took aim. I turned, ran, threw myself towards the doorway, diving through the air at full length.

I heard the gun go off, felt a thump the length of my right calf and saw, amid the blur the leap made of my view ahead, one of the wooden struts of the rail overlooking the stairs burst into splinters halfway down. I hit the floor, landing on my front, my upper half on the landing, my lower still in the bedroom, a sharper pain razoring across my calf, accompanied by the hot, sticky sensation of my beginning to bleed.

The next thing I heard and felt was the pounding of Hutcher's feet across the floorboards, followed by his sliding to one knee at my side and turning me onto my back. My next sensation was that of the gun's warm barrel being pressed to my temple. Hutcher was all smiles now.

"Sorry about that," he said. "That wasn't terribly practical, not with a golf course on the other side of the road. Even this weather, there's a few hookers and slicers out there with their hoods up. I'll make sure the next shot is nice and quiet. Muffled. There must be something lying around here I can use. Your throat or your cunt, maybe."

"You think you're such a big man you can get away with killing me?"

"I'm a big enough man to try," he said. "When you've achieved as much in your life as I have, new challenges can put fresh spring in a man's stride. And you've been nothing if not a challenge. Stimulating, even. My high school chum's baby sis blossomed into a captivating little Venus fly trap. Almost worth a bitten finger or two. Maybe I *should* have raped you. Or worked my way into your pants some more charming way. This..." He roughly caressed his free hand through my curls, "...this dye-job, which I presume it is... does it go all the way? Fore and aft? I mean, if I had got into your pants mightn't I have spotted the ruse? How scrupulous a spy were you?"

His hand made a spidery leap from my hair to the buttons of my jeans, tugging unfastened the top one. My own hands tried to fight his aside. He screwed the gun barrel tighter against my temple.

"It's a wee bit late for coming over all coy," he snorted. "The man with the gun against your head says 'you've fucked with us long enough, now take your share of the punishment'." His hand worked loose the other buttons of my fly.

"You get off having power over other people, don't you?" I said.

"It's the very essence of getting off, I've found," he said. "Even that day with your brother.... Oh, don't get me wrong, I regret with all my heart the damage done. But on that day, in that moment, there was... oh, here's the deepest source of the guilt, the horror... in that moment, the power of the thing, the sheer power over another bastard's nakedness... it felt like Heaven exploding in my head.

"And all those thousand-million times I've thought of it since then, I've felt, yes, all the shame I told you of, but also... also... the ghost of that delight shrieking through me. I regret it all. I regret fuck-all. Has, Jesus, any other moment made me feel like that? All my other conquests, they were palest shadows of that moment, however much they fattened my wallet. I suppose you're right. I *was* a murderer that day. And I've missed being a murderer ever since. So here we are, murder and I. Reunited. I'm prepared to find it sweeter than ever, if needs be."

I heard the rough scrape of what I took for a footstep below. He seemed too busy squeezing the gun barrel against my skull to have noticed.

242

"You want to see my cunt, big man?" I whispered. "Rape me? Murder me? Claim one last scalp from this family? What can I do to stop you?" I pushed my jeans and panties halfway down my thighs, at cost of an intensified sting of pain from my bullet-scraped leg, the fabric of my jeans having glued itself to the blood.

He frowned at my sudden submission, then stole a glance at what I was letting him see. A fresh jolt of tears hit him as he roved his gaze the length of me. "Beauty runs in your damned yokel family, obviously," he sputtered. "Such... beauty.... - Christ, it's enough to kill a man." He withdrew the gun from my temple, pressing it against his own and shutting tight his streaming eyes.

I was going to whisper him into the simple squeeze which was all that separated me from the end of my quest when we were both distracted by a swift stumble of feet up the dust-heaped stairs. We both glanced that way. "...Alec?" Hutcher whimpered, opening his eyes and lowering the gun. "Luke?" I cried.

Luke it was, materialising at the top of the stairs amid a cloud of the dust he had disturbed.

I tugged my jeans up, tilting my body towards him. "Luke - Luke - he tried to - !" I cried, feeling Hutcher's free hand catch hold of me at the hip. "Luke - please!" Hutcher pleaded.

"I'm listening," Luke said, climbing the last step and moving towards us.

Forty Nine

" - rape me, Luke," I said, "He tried to -..."

"Shut up!" cried Hutcher, starting to his feet, aiming the gun down at me. "Or by Christ, I'll -!"

"No!" Luke yelled. "You'll give me that gun."

"Luke..." his father pleaded, the barrel still vaguely aimed my way.

"The gun!" he cried. "Give me it!"

Hutcher looked at me as I dragged myself towards a sitting position against the wooden rail, then extended his gun arm Luke's way, swivelling the weapon around his trigger finger, so that the inverted handle, rather than the barrel, was toward his son. Luke took the gun, weighed it in his hand.

"What you doing with this, Dad?" he said.

"Protecting our family."

"Against her?"

"Yes. Against her."

"What danger's she to us?"

"She...."

"Go on, Rick," I said, dragging myself to my feet. "Tell him."

"Yes, Dad," said Luke. "Tell me."

"I... I don't exactly know what she had in mind for us, not at the end of it all, but -..."

"Justice, Luke," I interrupted, "That's what I'm here for."

"Justice? Justice over what?"

"Over a crime your father committed."

"Luke, that's - " Hutcher began, but then stopped, arrested - it seemed - by the intensity of gaze his son had fixed upon him. That gaze then fixed on me, my teeth gritting as my wounded leg took its share of my weight. Luke caught my shoulder with his free hand, tilting me so my back was to him

244

and he could see the wound. He let go of me, eyes fixing tighter than ever upon his father.

"You shot her?" he asked.

"Yes," Hutcher said.

"Come on," Luke said, curling his free arm around my shoulders and steering me towards your old room. His eyes remained on his father for our first couple of steps. He had barely looked away when Hutcher stepped after us, setting a hand on his son's shoulder on the other side to that at which I leaned. "Luke...-" Hutcher began.

Luke swung back with his gun hand, smacking the weapon into his father's jaw, knocking him away from us. Luke guided me on into the room. "Here," he said, steering me around until my back was against one of the side walls, "Sit down. I'll see what I can do."

With his aid, I slid down to sit at the foot of the wall. Perhaps I exaggerated the pain of what was no more than a messy graze: it was sweet to have a little T.L.C amid the blood and dust of the arena. While he examined my leg, I caught the scrape of Hutcher's footfall upon the threshold. I looked that way to see him hovering there, the half light just enough for me to see that the area above his mouth was streaked with blood. Luke glanced that way too.

"Give me your tie," Luke said.

"My what?"

Luke rose, marched across, caught his father's smart silk tie with his free hand, tugging on it in what must have been an attempt to unknot and slide it off but which had the initial effect of drawing the knot strangling-tight. Hutcher strove to fight off the one-handed assault and somewhere in the thick of their struggle, the knot came loose, the tie wrenched away in Luke's hand. Hutcher made a reach for it. Luke shoved the barrel of the gun against his father's chest.

"You'd threaten me with that?" Hutcher asked.

Luke lowered the gun. "I haven't heard your story yet," he said, turning away.

He crossed back to me, kneeling and laying the gun on the floor, using the tie to knot a tourniquet just beneath the knee of my wounded leg. "I saw this done in a Vietnam movie," he told me with a smile.

"Did the character in the movie live?" I asked.

"Yeah. He lost the leg, but he was only a bit-part actor, not a star like you. - Does that hurt?"

"Oohh... Just enough," I smiled.

"Now listen - !" his Dad said.

"We *are* listening, Rick," I said, "All ears for that story you need to tell your son. The story of the crime you committed, back when you were even younger than Luke is now. The crime which made this moment here inevitable, however many years it took us to reach it."

"What was your crime, Dad?" Luke asked.

"Luke... Luke, I...." his father murmured.

"The crime, Dad!" Luke screamed. "What was it?"

"A... a boy... died. Drowned himself. In that... that pool where Abby died. It was... it was a long time ago."

"Your father drove him to it," I said.

"I did not-!" Hutcher began, before falling silent for a second. "Yes... yes of course I did," he resumed.

"Drove him to it how?" Luke asked.

"The boy, I... I think he loved me," Hutcher sighed.

"I know he loved you," I said. "He was my brother, Luke. My beautiful, loving big brother. We lived here. In this house, long ago."

Luke stared at me and in the half-light I saw the most muffled tremor of shock segue into more tenderness towards me than I could comfortably bear.

"And that's why you came here?" he asked. "That's why you..." - and then I saw that tenderness fix into something harder-edged, more guarded. "You and me, you and my family, that's how this all came about?"

"She's a poisonous whore, Luke," his father threw in, "She -"

"No one asked you!" Luke yelled. "What I want from you is the details of what happened with you and her brother. Now!" His father sighed, leaned his back against the wall. "He..."

"Alec, his name was," I said.

"Alec..." Hutcher acknowledged. "He was an okay kid.

246

We... we were at school together. Alright guy to hang out with, so long as you weren't in the mood for kicking a ball or heavy breathing in some girl's ear. The bookish, artistic type, that was Alec. Good for a laugh, in his own quiet way."

"He had a guitar, Luke," I said. "Liked writing songs. Just like you. God knows what he might have made of himself. If he'd lived."

"We got friendly, sort of," Hutcher continued. "But not as friendly, plainly, as he was looking for. He was, well you know - my God, you must know! - just that little bit too 'artistic'. You get me?"

"Artistic how, Dad?" Luke said.

"How the Hell do you think?"

"What? Queer, maybe? Limp-wristed? Effeminate? Sensitive? Crap at rugby? Overly good at writing poetry? What, Dad, what?!"

"I suppose it was a sickness he had," I suggested. "A mental imbalance. I don't mean being homosexual, I mean getting all homosexual over a straight-down-the-line maggot like your father."

"You're right about the 'straight' bit," Hutcher asserted. "So you'll understand that when someone I looked at as just a casual mate started crooning over me like a fucking Pet Shop Boy, I reckoned enough was enough. And came up with what seemed an amusing way to send the message."

"You have a father, Luke," I said, "Who finds murder amusing."

"It wasn't meant to be murder!" Hutcher yelled. "It *wasn't* murder! It was just... just a laugh, a game. Like teenage boys have been playing at one another's expense since time began."

"What did you do, Dad?"

"What? Well, I... I faked returning the kid's affections, tricked him into a meeting with me up at that pool in the middle of nowhere."

"I have your father's letter, Luke," I said. "I found it stuffed under a floorboard in this house, years later."

"He doesn't need to see that!" Hutcher snapped. "All that matters is that the kid -"

"Alec," I interjected.

"The kid! The... the kid, Alec, he... he followed me up there. Hot, hot summer holiday afternoon, the kind you never know again when you're an adult. It was on the promise, a promise I'd made of, of a... a skinny dip, just him and me - that plus whatever offer of lovestruck fondlings he read between the lines of my letter."

"The promises weren't exclusively between the lines, you bastard," I pointed out.

"I don't recall every last word of a scribble I passed on decades ago!"

"But you recall what came of it," I said. "So tell the boy."

"I... well, I met him there. And then I... well, I dared him to strip off and dive in ahead of me. He... he wanted to fool around first, up on the bank. I... I had to go along with it, Luke. Just to... just to keep the joke going."

"What did you do, Dad? Kiss him?"

"No, no, yes -....Yes. Just... just... disgusting stuff, but I... I knew I could laugh it off afterwards if I just saw the whole gag through. Then, suddenly, he couldn't wait to get naked. He stood before me and... and stripped off in what seemed a second or two, as if... as if his nakedness just burned through those thin summer clothes. And there he was... naked before me. That shade of sunlight suited him, I can't deny."

"He was beautiful, Luke," I said. "Beautiful like you. The sun paused as it passed over him."

"Not that there wasn't something feminine, poncy, in the way he stood there, making that full-armed cock sticking out of him more than a little disgusting," Hutcher continued. "Unnatural. Like one of those Roman hermaphrodites. It came as a relief when he took himself out of my eyeline by plunging into that pool.

"Then as now, it was a bit of a murky pit, but sunlight bright as that had the trick of making it gleam like molten gold. Even the dung-bugs buzzing around shone like diamonds. Fuck, son... there's me chattering like a poof. - Anyway, he swam into the middle of the pool, called for me to join him. Jesus... he looked like he was backstroking the clouds of Heaven."

248

"So you made a Hell for him," I said.

"You're damned right. The sight of him there, the memory of those… those kisses he'd forced me to share… well, 'righteous anger' wouldn't do justice to what I felt. So I called to the top of the bluff, where all my mates were waiting. My proper mates, the ones not slavvering to suck my dick. They leapt out of hiding, giving our boy below a shock. They started lobbing stones his way, splashing them into the water, shouting all the things… well, all the things you'd expect kids to shout at a moment like that.

"I started too, lobbed the biggest rocks of all. Well, I had a point to prove, hadn't I? The others had seen me in that little waterside fumble: I had to show how fake that had all been. So I showed it loud and clear, shouted to the blue heavens how disgusting I found him, how worthy he was of the treatment he was getting. Doesn't… doesn't mean I believed it. Not all of it. But one wouldn't want to be on the receiving end of that kind of treatment oneself. When some of the stones hit him, after all, I felt it in my own bones.

"Eventually, he fought and splashed and half-drowned his way to the bank. The bank where the whole crowd of us were gathered by that point. It was his clothes he was after. I snatched them up before he could reach them, threw them to…."

He sighed, dropped his head, voiced something like a sob.

"To?" Luke asked.

It was only slowly that he raised his head.

"Your Mum was there, Luke. Tagging along at the tail end of our crowd. Plain little thing. Not my sort, not at the time. I'd barely noticed her until that day. I suppose the things she did that day were an attempt to catch my attention. By the end of that day, they had. We never told you why we married so young. It wasn't just her getting pregnant with your sister. I knew that day I'd never share with another woman what I'd just shared with her. It seemed a good idea to keep her close. I'm sure she thought the same. Criminals and their complicities, Luke… what bonds can match those?"

"What did you do… together?" Luke asked.

"Well, poor Alec, he…he struggled after those clothes,

but… but Amy took care of their being passed on, on, further and further out of reach. How naked he looked, glinting with water, smeared with mud, trickling with blood. The beauty and horror of it, all mixed up in my mind and my eye. I tried to simplify things in my head, shouting myself and the others into the roughest treatment yet."

"How rough?" Luke said.

"You don't need to know every last detail," his father replied.

"Every last detail! I want to know!"

"I'll tell you, Luke," I said. "I was there also. Just a little squit of a thing, much younger than all those teenagers. But sister enough to my great big angel of a brother to have sensed, earlier that day, something's having been set up with him, for better or worse. Maybe I was even a bit jealous of the hold I'd seen your father take over him. So I followed him up there. Unseen by any of them, I hid among the bushes overlooking the pool."

"And you did nothing?" Luke asked.

"I'm doing something now, amn't I? At the time… well, I felt so tiny, isolated, and they… his gang… they were like animals … a pack of wolves on a lamb. They beat, kicked him, forced him down. One of them got some cow-shit from the field above, forced it into his mouth. Queers, you know… they love the taste of shit, no?"

"I knew by then," Hutcher said, "the joke had gone too far. So I… I had to keep getting louder and nastier, just to drown that thought out before it put me the wrong side of the divide between victimisers and victim. Oh, I was a monster to him that day. But I won't take the blame for everything. My little gang - once I had them fired up, they showed their own initiative. The… the worst bit was… was nothing to do with me, not on my say-so, anyhow."

"It was all on your say-so!" I protested.

"The… the thing itself yes, but that… that business with the… the…."

"What? What, Dad?"

"One of them got a branch, a branch thick with thorns…" I began.

250

"Nick Turnbull, it was - not me!"

"Yes," I said. "Nicholas Turnbull. He shoved that branch up my brother's virgin rectum. While your father held him in a head-lock."

"H...- Headlock and all, I was... I was looking the other way! I didn't see every detail...."

"You must have heard him scream," I said. "I heard."

"I... Yes. Yes, I heard," he said.

"Wee Nicky Turnbull..." I mused, "...he died, didn't he?"

"What?" responded Hutcher. "Eh... yes. Yes. A... a couple of years ago. We didn't really keep in touch."

"It was in London he died," I said. "Wasn't it?"

Hutcher's attention fixed more intently upon me. "Yes," he said. "It even made the local paper here. Some kind of assault."

"He was mugged. And gang-raped. And thrown in the Thames to drown. Headline stuff, seeing how high in the world Wee Nicky had climbed. Didn't stop him sinking, all the same."

"What had that to do with you?" Hutcher asked.

"Well, I didn't rape him," I said. "I don't have a penis. As you probably noticed when you tried to rape me yourself."

"I reckon you could seduce anyone into anything. And if seduction didn't work, there's always money. - My God, Luke, we have to get out of here. I think... I think she's here to kill me."

"You're the killer," I said. "You didn't even have the decency to pull that thing out of Alec when you were done. Just left him there in the mud at the side of the pool."

"I had to get away. The way he... looked up at me, the scream he cast my way past those shit-caked lips, that scream that made no sound, no sound but... but this sound that's been rattling round my skull ever since... I had to get away from that look in his eyes...."

"But you whispered something to him before you went. Didn't you? I saw you leaning over him."

"Yes..."

"What did you say? 'Hurry up and die'?"

"No."

"What, then?"

"I... I said... said I was... sorry. Said it was just... just a laugh. And I said... Oh, I don't know. I don't know where it came from."

"What?" Luke asked.

"Nothing."

"What did you say?" Luke pressed.

"I said...."

"What?"

"I said he... he was the most beautiful thing I'd ever seen...."

"You bastard," I all but wept, "You greedy fucking cannibal."

"Listen! Listen!" he protested. "I... I don't know... like I say, I... I don't know where it came from. It was just... It was true! I mean, I... I knew I'd never see anything again as... as... as brilliant as he'd been that day, stripping off, standing there like... It was like Ancient Greece, where some God would spring from a thicket, pole-axe a mortal with its perfection... the sight of him leaping in that water, splashing the droplets high in the sunlight, even... even crying there in the mud, shit-smeared, thorned-through, leaking blood... I still knew I'd never again see something, someone, as... And I never did. And I never have. I never will."

"And you walked away," I said.

"It was a hot day. We were tired out. We walked down to the shopping centre at Mearns Cross. There was a good ice cream parlour there in those days. And we were all thirsty."

"I went down to him Luke," I said. "My big brother. 'Big Bwuwwa', I used to say when I was very young. He didn't notice I was there until the tears flooding my face dripped onto his cheek. He was barely alive, even then. I don't know how wounded your father had actually left him, physically I mean. But his soul, I could see as he looked up at me, lay gutted like a fish. And his worst horror, I realised, was for me, of all people, to see him there like that. He whimpered for me to go. So I ran. I suppose he drowned himself not long after."

"And you told what you'd seen?" Luke asked.

"Not at first," I replied. "I didn't, couldn't, say anything at first, not after the news came through of him being found, a

252

whole day after the police had started searching. I worried, mite that I was, about getting the blame for leaving him there and saying nothing. But then, finally, in words hard to find for someone so young, I did tell. My poor Mum and Dad... I think the shock when they heard was partly shock at the thought of quiet, humble farming folk like them having to pit themselves against the power the Hutcher family had hereabouts even then. But they went for it. Your family and the families of all those other kids were suddenly the subject of a police inquiry. Looked like we might have our day in court.

"Then, one evening, the Hutchers' lawyer turns up, plumps his well-upholstered arse at our kitchen table and states his case. Which is that there's no way your father and the others are going to be held guilty of anything more than adolescent bullying, Alec's death plainly self-inflicted, his client's son verifiably enjoying a milk shake at the time of death. Furthermore, they had letters and testimony from your father establishing that Alec had been homosexual - as regards which the world was less liberal in those days - and that he had, on several occasions, attempted to sexually molest your straight-as-an-arrow Papa, the worst attempt having come on the afternoon in question, as the other kids would testify, this prompting, and largely justifying, young Richard's defence of his masculine honour. An over-enthusiastic defence, perhaps, but understandable, in those days, when a gay boy was on the prowl. And a bit of detective work had established Alec as having made a few tentative trips to a gay bar in the city centre, his visits to the swamp of sin which was the gents toilet doubtless explaining any rectal damage on the corpse.

"My parents... You have to understand, they were old-fashioned even in that era, Renfrewshire farming stock you could trace back to the days when there was no Newton Mearns, just fields and farms and not much need for a mind-set more advanced than the medieval. The revelation that their son might have been a pervert was on a par with finding out he'd sold his soul to Satan at the crossroads. Not a thing they were keen to publicise.

"Then, the cruncher. Your Grandfather's people had done their homework. They knew all about the financial problems my parents were having with the farm. The fat lawyer had a settlement to offer: precisely calculated as just enough to keep my Dad out of a debtor's court and a For Sale sign out of our front garden. So, like so many before and since, they took the Hutcher shilling. And the whole matter was buried still deeper than my brother's dripping carcass. The culprits had to suffer a spot of gossip for a short while, but we were an insignificant family, on the outermost fringes of the Mearns. No one cared. Everyone cared, on the other hand, about keeping right side of the Hutchers. Think of the dinner party invites! The passport to the *fondue* circuit!

"But the money might as well have crumbled to ash as soon as it was handed over. Everything on the farm rotted in my father's grasp. My Mum, never talkative to begin with, gave up talking altogether. She'd sit at the kitchen table where the deal was made, staring at the dust thickening in the air. I think they blamed one another for taking the cash. She blamed harder than he did, so he was the one who stumbled into the foulest end of the cow-shed a year and a half later and shotgunned his brains up the wall.

"After that, Mum's silence deepened until she drowned in it. They took her away, to one of the places you take people like that. Only the look in her eyes complained. I was sent to be brought up by my Gran, way out on the coast at Troon. The house... well, you see what happened to the house. The whole matter was forgotten as far as the Mearns was concerned. Wilfully forgotten.

"But I remembered. Every now and then, over the years, I'd make the trip back here, wander the streets. No one recognised me. The first thing I did when I got my driving licence was to run off the road that guy who smeared the cow shit, way out in the countryside by Uplawmoor. Maybe your Dad recalls that fatal accident.

"And I'd come back *here*. And I'd call to my brother's ghost, to the ghosts of all I'd known and lost. And the ghosts answered, telling me what to do. I ended up running from what they demanded, running for a long time. Finally, in Mexico, an Aztec God or two impressed on me the importance of carrying a sacred duty to its conclusion. So here I am, Luke... concluding."

254

Fifty

"Her name's not Melinda Carido," said Hutcher, "It's -..."

"Isn't it the lies *you've* been telling that are the real issue here?" snapped Luke, standing, stepping towards him.

"Luke, this is all the ancient past," said Hutcher. "Nothing to do with you."

"But you caught *me* showing love in a way you didn't approve of and damn near killed *me!*"

"And maybe, now, you understand why I did that."

"Understand?"

"Understand that when I found out what that boy was perverting you towards, it was like the whole thing happening all over again, like that was how his ghost... Alec's... had chosen to haunt me. Through you. Making you do things like that, that aren't in your nature. Like a curse recurring in the next generation. Oh, I know that's superstitious crap, but I was a guilty man - superstition comes as part of the deal. There's a joke for *you*, little sister. What if your revenge is redundant, what if your brother's phantom got here first, fucked up our lives months ago? What's the point of any of this if Alec's already had his last laugh?"

Luke found an answer quicker than I did. "So you'd sooner believe in ghosts and curses than in your son's having honest feelings you don't happen to agree with?"

"Maybe," he said, "when my son has given up his squalid little secret passion for this lying whore, he'll be in a position to lecture me about honesty."

"Here's some honesty!" Luke cried.

He slapped his father across the face, sending Hutcher lurching sideways. As Hutcher's head swung upright again, I could see, even in the gloom, that his face was scarlet with more than blood and Luke's palm-print. Yet he strung a tight leash upon his anger, saying to his son, in a voice straining so for calm that the tone kept cracking at the back of his throat: "Look, son, I love you. If I've hurt you - and I know I have - you must understand that even my most wrong-headed actions have come from an attempt to protect you. And all that has nothing to do with any of *this*."

Luke slapped his father again: same hand, same cheek, same jolt to his father's stance. "It all has to do with your being an intolerant bastard out to crush anything you can't control or make a profit from. You love me, Dad? You think you can claim ownership of *that* word, when you're down on other people's love like a fox on a hen's neck?"

"Squalid teenage poofter crushes are not -"

Luke slapped his Dad again.

"*- are not love, Luke!*" his father said, seizing his son's slapping hand by the wrist. "And nor is this slut's little scheme of vengeance. Love? Love is you and me and Laura and Emily and your Mum, plus that thing between us which makes us a family, holds us strong against outsiders who'd worm in on what we've got. Once upon a time, yes, I protected myself from her pervert brother. More recently, I protected you from your band-mate's limp-wristed strummings on your zipper. Now I'm here to rescue you from whatever *she's* been plotting. In none of these acts of defence have I been over-subtle. That's not my nature. But when I do a thing it gets done, done to the advantage of me and mine and God rot all the rest. You've benefited from that all your life. You're benefiting now. If only you'd realise."

Luke tugged his hand free of his father's grip.

"You'll stifle the life out of me with that protection of yours," he said. "Or will if I let you. Except I won't. Her and me, Dad, I've decided, we're going far from here, far from you, fast as we can. We might send you a postcard. But then again maybe not. We might be too busy, making up a future that buries the past. The past you made, Dad."

Hutcher glanced over his son's shoulder, allowing himself a harsh little smile.

"Looks to me," he said, "Like your sweetheart has

256

alternative plans for both our futures."

Luke turned. Anything but stupid, if I do say so myself, it was a good minute since I'd picked up the gun Luke had left on the floor next to me, my aiming of it at Luke's father entailing my aiming it at Luke, too, immediately in front of him.

"So the question would seem to be, Luke," Hutcher continued, "How far does her lust for revenge extend? Is it just me she wants to destroy, or my whole family? If she's a good enough shot, she might, at this range, take us both out with a single bullet. What's it to be, Medea? Is the father enough, or are you out to bathe in the blood of his offspring too?"

"Luke," I said, "Be a dear and step aside."

Luke remained where he was. "We don't need that kind of hassle," he said. "Let's just leave him and walk away. You can lean on me if that leg's a problem."

"You're his property, Luke. The most precious he's got. You think he'll let me walk away with something of his so valuable? He's *Mister* Property! I'm of a mind to see my scores settled here and now, so I really *can* walk away."

"*I* can walk away?" Luke queried. "You do mean 'we', don't you?"

"I don't think she's the commitment type, son," Hutcher said. "But maybe… if you begged her… on your knees!"

He pushed Luke towards me, so that Luke did indeed drop to his knees, bumping into my gun arm and knocking it sideways, Luke's weight toppling on top of me. The next thing I knew, Hutcher had darted forward, grabbing my gun hand with both his own hands, pinning it to the floor and stomping his right foot on top of my forearm to hold it there. I struggled to keep a hold on the weapon but he tore it from me, staggering backwards and taking aim my way.

"Luke… get away from her," he said.

"Dad…?" Luke said, easing himself back from me. "Don't…."

"Don't?" his father replied. "I don't know what else to do, son. I won't give up what's mine, whether it be my blood or my family or all that I've built. I had my moments of idiocy as a boy. As a man, I've more than made up for them. Half of what stands in this suburb was built by me. And I built it well, built it like I built myself: to not be brought down by some termite in the basement. So please, son, stand aside."

"No," Luke said, rising. "She's driven me half-crazy, too. But I've come to enjoy the feeling. So I'm telling you... put the gun down. Or I'll take it off you."

"You're what... threatening me, son?"

"You think you're the only person in the family who can bully another human being?" Luke replied, inching closer. "For a long time, you were. But I've done a lot of growing up these last few weeks. So let's see who's the bigger bastard now!"

Luke seized his father's gun hand with both his own hands, his father's free hand trying to tear Luke aside by the scruff of his neck, this rapidly developing into a stumbling, circling, crab-stepped struggle, which sent them lurching towards the door for the landing. I forced myself up, limping after them as they reeled across the landing, colliding with the wooden rail that overlooked the stairs. I heard its fastenings groan, the rail to either side of them undulating like a stiff curtain in a breeze, dust billowing around them.

The gun stabbed upward into the air, the confusion of hands around it making it impossible to judge who had the firmer grip. Then the weapon was tugged downward and I lost sight of it. The roar of a shot sounded, accompanied by a white flaring amid their entangled legs, an indrawn howl accompanying the shot's echo.

As I reached the doorway, the figures staggered apart, Luke remaining against the rail, the gun exhaling smokily in his hand, his father bumping backward into the wall, features contorting and flooding with sweat. It was only as he began a rapid, limping backing away that I noticed the bloody rag his left foot had been blasted to within its sleek Italian shoe.

"Luke..." Hutcher sputtered. His son glanced to the weapon in his hand as if wondering how it had got there. "Give me that, you stupid bloody...!" his father demanded, lunging forward on his good leg. Luke's bewilderment was shunted aside by a furious howl, with which he almost drowned the din of the gun's going off again, this shot smacking blood from the

258

thigh above his father's wounded foot. The fury dropped from Luke's features as abruptly as it had taken hold, replaced once more by boyish confusion. His father thumped back against the wall and began a mixture of slide and stagger towards the far end of the landing.

I stepped to Luke's side. "Kill him, Luke," I said.

Luke turned to me, plainly shocked by how close he had come to doing so already. "You've gone this far," I said. "Now there's only two ways out. Number one is that you call it a day here and submit to the hardest beating you've taken yet, a beating he'll subcontract to the law on the grounds of attempted murder. You heard: piss-poor, gutless, failed, *attempted* murder. Or you finish this like a man and we make the getaway I've got all planned. Kill him, Luke. And never take a beating again."

Luke glared from the gun to me and then to his father. He raised the gun, took aim at his father's heart. "No, L-...!" Hutcher called: I could hear mortal dread in the swell and fall of his words; it was the sweetest music imaginable.

Luke lowered the gun. I snatched it from him, urged myself after Hutcher on my wounded leg, taking aim of my own. Hutcher turned, hastening his limp through the doorway nearest him, which happened to be that of my old room. I followed him through - Luke yelling for me to wait - in time to see Hutcher discover for himself the hole through the floorboards which Luke's fall had put there a few days before.

Hutcher had stumbled to its brink and now tottered around, facing back my way. Oh, bliss it was to see him register how trapped he was. And then, sweetening the moment still further, there came the sound of a slow cracking through the shelf of ragged wood upon which he stood.

Suddenly Luke was at my side, grabbing my gun hand, wrestling the weapon back into his own grasp. His father twitched forward. "Wait!" Luke yelled, aiming the gun in the same direction as I had done. His father halted.

"I... I just..." Luke stammered, gun hand trembling, "I... I don't know who I am... who you are, anymore... what to do... what I *can* do... where... where I can go...."

"You can put that gun down, son, help me out of here, and

we can put all this…" Hutcher said, indicating the wounds that were making him strain to remain upright. "… behind us, and… and then we…."

"And then what, Rick?" I said. "You'll report me to the police, maybe? That would just make more of a mess of your life, given what I'd tell them. Face it, Big Man, you're on your last legs."

"Give me the gun, son," he said, reaching his son's way while fixing his eyes on me.

"You can't just walk away from all that happened here, surely?" I said. "If you can turn your back on the crime, what about the beauty?"

"What…?" he muttered.

"You admitted yourself there were sweet moments between you and Alec. Beautiful moments, intimate moments. Right here at this house, remember? Remember?!"

With a groan, Hutcher dropped to his knees, the redistribution of his weight sending a still harsher cracking sound through the floorboards, which could be seen to indent and tilt slightly beneath him.

"His ghost's here," I went on. "I've felt him near me every time I've come here. Can't you, Rick? After all the intimacy of murdering him… can't you?"

"No!" he cried, attempting to force himself up onto his feet, the effort sending the sorest cracking yet through the floorboards. He froze, the floor indenting further beneath him.

"No!" Luke yelled, casting the gun aside, darting forward. Even as he did so, the floor beneath his father gave way entirely, Hutcher casting us a glance of - I like to think - more than physical terror an instant before disappearing amid the dying house's dragon belch of dust and whirling splinters.

Luke ran past the edge of the murky cloud, past the point where one could have a hope of distinguishing floor from hole. And even as I hobbled after him, catching his arm on the edge of the widened drop, I asked myself why I hadn't just let him run on and plunge on top of his father, setting myself wholly free.

But I didn't, and so we stood coughing and choking on

that uprush of dust, looking down at nothing but the ghostliest wisp of the destruction below, until one of Luke's sputterings became the gruffest of sobs, my own next cough cut off by the clamping of both his hands around my throat.

He drove me backward across the room, thumped me against the wall and then swung me back around, pushing me through the dust-cloud and laying me flat on my back, the rear of my head dipping past a splintered edge into empty space, his face paling and eyes reddening with the thickening of the dust upon them.

Yet as abruptly as his grip had attached itself, it now relaxed. He shrank from me, stumbling to the doorway. I coughed myself some air and followed. My toe hit the gun.

Fifty One

Luke stomped down the rubble-heaped steps so fast he lost his footing, sliding the rest of the way on his back-side amid a further cloud of dust. Pursuing him through it, with a few slips of my own, I caught up with him as he stood beneath the hole in the kitchen ceiling, looking down at the hole in its floor, through which only a curling of dust in the cellar's black air could be seen. A single muffled cough filtered up though the murk.

"The cellar-!" Luke called, turning to me. "How do you get down to it?" I indicated the far corner. He dashed that way, yelling "Where? - Where?!" I limped after him, one hand pointing towards the door of mud-dark wood, the other passing him the gun.

"Kill him, Luke," I said gently. "The law'll hold you guilty already for those two shots you've put in him. Get it over with. Set yourself free."

He took the gun, studied it, pressed its barrel into my belly.

"You won't. You can't," I said, looking him in the eye. "Not to me."

He looked down at the gun again, removed it from my stomach and then wrestled open the cellar door's rusted hinges. I followed him down the skeletal, groaning stairs, two or three steps missing entirely, this necessitating a cling to the wobbling banister.

Our descent from the final step landed our feet ankle deep in black water lightened by a scum of pale grey dust. From the far end of the cellar's obscurity came a belated flutter of tumbling scraps of floor and ceiling, as well as the lowest, most broken of groans. As we began wading that way, our feet and legs jostled a tangle of half-submerged objects, their identity unclear even to me.

Luke stumbled across one of these with such force that his top half was thrown forward, hands thumping down to hold him upright with a grasp on the curved lid of what my own eyes, adjusting to a darkness broken only by tricklings of fading daylight through the gaps in the ceiling and down the steps at our back, recognised as an old wooden trunk in which Mum once stored nick-nacks from her wedding day. Recalling the use it had been put to subsequently, I elbowed Luke out of the way, flipped it open. reached inside, pulling out the topmost of the folded newspapers within, its texture akin to crumbling snakeskin, its odour a thick brownish-yellow in the blackness.

"Papers," I said. "Old newspapers. It started with my Mum keeping those few that mentioned Alec's death. Then any paper reporting your father's climb to success: snippets in the local Advertiser about his triumphs on the rugby field, his 'Business Graduate of The Year' award at Edinburgh Uni, his marriage to your Mum, his..."

Luke snatched the newspaper from me, stuffing the gun in the waistband of his jeans while he rolled the paper into a tight cylinder, pulling out a cigarette lighter and, although the mouldering pulp was reluctant to catch light, setting fire to the end, creating a crude torch.

As a flicker of greenish flame blossomed into a fuller, ruddier hue, I saw scraps of my childhood come fluttering out of the dark like dusty-winged moths. My old doll Ainsley sat on the edge of a crate, staring through a veil of thickest cobweb. A cardboard box plump with your old DC comics lay half-drowned by my feet, 'Swamp Thing' and 'The Batman Family' uppermost. A beach ball I could recall you and I kicking around the beach at Scarborough floated nearby. Dad's fishing gear still hung, rusting, from hooks on the near wall, Mum's old sewing machine stranded on a listing table.

Luke had waded ahead, following the faint sounds from the cellar's far end. I caught up with him just as a great sprawled shape fell within reach of the torch's flame. It lay upon the flooded floor like some grotesquely bloated water lily but was no more nor less than Hutcher sprawled on his back, limbs broken, across a jagged bed of splintered crates, crushed boxes and ceiling fragments. One of the boxes was an old toy box, its sodden seams burst by the impact, our old dolls and ray guns and rubber tarantulas, our gonks and superheroes, spilled into the black water around him, bobbing there and looking no more or less broken than he was.

Hutcher looked ancient as an excavated pharaoh, what with the crusting of dust, the spatterings of blood and filthy water, with which his fall had mantled him. He was plainly too pained to move any part of him by anything more than hair's breadth - save for his eyes, dust-reddened against his dust-paled face, these tilting our way as we stood over him.

"Dad..." Luke breathed, sounding like the tiniest, most hapless child for having seen his mighty father brought so low.
Hutcher's eyes struggled to focus, the lips below twitching towards speech. Rainy drippings into the water around him mocked his struggle against silence. "Who?...Who?...Who?" he finally said.

Luke shoved his torch into my hand and sank to one knee at his father's side, albeit without daring to touch that human wreckage.

"Me, Dad," he said.

"Dad?" Hutcher echoed, as if the meaning of the term escaped him.

"Luke!" Luke said.

"Luke...? - Luke...!" He tried to raise an arm to catch hold of his son, but the gesture hurt too much to be carried through. "I..." he mumbled, licking more life into his drying lips, "...I don't want to...die... here... not *here*... not...."

"You won't!" said Luke. "You... you're injured but you're not... We'll get an ambulance. You'll be fine..."

A fond smile twitched the wounded features. "Luke..." Hutcher said again, making another failed attempt to raise his arm.

"It's not Luke," I said. He kept his eyes on his son but the face around them contorted into a frown. "Can't you see, Richard?" I went on. "It's Alec."

"Shut your mouth!" snarled Luke.

"His ghost," I pressed, "Waiting for you here by the shore

264

of the pool. The pool where you drowned him. Remember?"

"That's not true, Dad!" Luke insisted. His father was forcing through a raising of his arm, for all that one could almost feel the grind of the fissured bones in one's own marrow. His hand, shaking as sorely as his lungs could be heard to wheeze, touched Luke's cheek.

"Ahhh... Alec...?" he asked.

"No, Dad!" said Luke, seizing that hand, his tenderness doubling his father's pain.

"Yes, Rick," I continued. "It's Alec. Remember? The sweet times that long summer holiday, the cruelty with which you ended it, ended him?"

"Yes, I..." Hutcher breathed.

"No, Dad...!"

"Oh, Alec," Hutcher said, commanding his head to rise on a neck all but broken. "I lied my whole life... Walked tall... on top of it all...."

"Dad...."

"...But I had... don't you see, don't you think... the odd... honest... moment with... you... Didn't I? Oh yes..." The ghost of a smile haunted his features. "You... you lay there... naked and I... whispered... in your ear...."

"Dad!"

Luke gathered his father up in the tightest of embraces. We learned later, by way of the inquest, that one of Hutcher's ribs, broken at the rear, had its jagged end wedged against his lung: poor loving Luke now urged that end deep into the tissue. All we knew at the time was that his father reacted to the embrace with a strangled wheeze, a bubbling and streaming of blackest blood from his lips and nostrils, a flickering and then a blinding-over of his staring eyes, a sagging back of his head, a single shudder the length of his body, and then a stillness more inanimate than that of the derelict toys floating around him.

A second of utter silence followed, if one discounts those drips from the ceiling. The crude torch I held had burned its way down to my hand: feeling the flames start work on my skin, I cast it aside. It dropped into the water, doused with a hiss. A few crimson scraps that had flaked from the torch's main body floated in the air, glowing, for a few seconds before devouring themselves, consigning us to a darkness like a glance over a ledge in my bottomless soul, for in that moment of triumph a horror at my actions, that dark and that deep, seized me.

Luke sobbed; it was the raw agony of the sound which set my horror in stone. But I had, on my long road to that moment, uprooted and shoved aside so many other twinges of weakness, of self-defeating conscience and impractical love, that this - even this - I found I could elbow from my path.

"It's over, Luke," I said. "I'm going. Just remember... there was justice in it."

I started wading away, steering myself towards that ghost of light draped around the cellar steps. When I heard, at my back, the soft splash of Hutcher's body being settled and then the harsher splash of Luke's rising, I thought of running, but the distance between myself and the steps was too cluttered for me to get far without tripping, so I continued on at the same careful pace.

"Stop!" he called. "If you don't...."

"If I don't?" I asked.

"I've still got the gun, remember."

I stopped. "But not the light to fire it by," I said.

"A few shots this way and that, I'm bound to hit something."

"Do you have the heart for that, Luke?"

"The heart?!! After what you've just done?"

"Wasn't it you who put those bullets in him? Who crushed the life out of him a moment ago?"

"You know what I mean!"

I took an onward step. "We both know how guilty we are," I said. "And how much more guilty he was."

"Stop, I said!"

The gun roared twice, paralysing me, white flarings flooding the darkness for the briefest instant. I waited for my body to tell me where one or both of those bullets had buried themselves. But I found myself struck by nothing more than the tang of gunsmoke in the air.

Then I heard the splashings, stumblings and splashings-on of Luke's approach. I began as swift a movement towards the

266

steps, but before I had the chance to so much as bump the first of the obstacles in my path, I felt Luke thump against me from behind, knocking both of us from our feet, splashing us down amid the filthy liquid and its flotsam.

I landed on my back with him atop me. He clamped his hand across my face, driving my head underwater. I did my best to hold my breath; just as the first throatful of stagnant liquid broke past my frail defences, I found myself dragged upright, choking, sputtering, retching, to be fixed in an embrace, blind kisses bullying my face. I heard him weeping, saying "I... I should... should... kill you... You've killed me. Killed me, goddamnit! I loved you... loved you so... Oh... oh Christ, I... I love you now. Crazy, insane, so... crazy ... it all has to stop. Now... now!"

I struggled against him, wriggling myself upright, floundering clear of him only to feel myself caught anew and wrestled through the darkness, colliding with the wall, with objects fixed there which felt slender and jagged, diaphanous and weighty. Luke dragged me downward, a tangle of those objects pulled down on top of us as we tumbled back into the water, delayed recognition of them as Dad's odds and ends of fishing gear catching up with me even as Luke cupped both my cheeks in hands that felt equally ready to crush my skull or deliver me to his kiss. My right hand, submerged, seemed to have an object thrust into it through the shallow water, as if from another hand whose fingers brushed mine for a second and one second only.

"We... monsters... That's how we've wound up, you and me..." whimpered the darkness above me, "...Monsters scrambling in the dark. It has to end, you and me. A disease, we are, needing burning out of a corpse. Crying shame. I so loved being sick with you."

"Let me go, Luke," I said, the hand I had free gently encouraging his hands aside as I began to rise. "What's between me and you, my family and yours, is something no bullet, no policeman, no wider world, not even your own Mum and sister, can ever drag down or up to their own level of reasoning. It's monstrous, you bet. But monstrosities make their own rules. And this monster's claiming her right to disappear into the mist."

I was on my feet by this point, only to feel him floundering after me, gaining a blind grip on my left arm. "No..." he said, "You can't leave me, not after..."

"You can't come, Luke. Be grateful for that."

"You said I could..."

"And now I say you can't."

"Why? Why?! Because I've done what you needed me to do and now I'm discarded?"

"Because I love you. Too much to look you in the face ever again."

"If you love me, then... then why wasn't that enough to save us, all of us, from... from all this?"

"Nothing would have been enough."

"Oh yeah, you're a real Aztec. Like one of those masks in that book of yours. Set in stone, you're so bloodthirsty."

"Yes, Luke. Set in stone."

"So why am I not dead? Huh? That thing you told me... the young man treated like a god... That's what I was to you, wasn't I?"

"A god? Not quite. But you *were* cute."

"And still here. I thought the gilded youth was supposed to get his heart torn out. I mean, not just figuratively."

"Your Dad's heart was easier, Luke. Smaller and harder, for an easier grip."

"Grip this!" he demanded, dragging my left hand up, shoving it into a clumsy thump on the bone of his chest. "Go on, my days of gilded youth are finished now. Cut me wide, get the agony over with."

I disentangled my hand from his grasp.

"That's what I came here to do, Luke," I said. "Trouble is you were the real teacher. Showed me I'm no Aztec, not where you're concerned. Won me round to the heresy that beauty like yours is better left to get on with life as best it can, far from lunatics like me."

I attempted an onward step. He blundered his way into a grasp further up my left arm. "No-...!" he began, only to be interrupted by footsteps thumping the floorboards above our heads.

Fifty Two

"S'anybody in here?" a voice called across the kitchen, a
genteel Newton Mearns lilt to its feigning of gruff masculinity.
There followed a muttering of two or three voices, the words
indistinct, a further creak of steps across the kitchen floor and
then a flicker of torchlight through the gaps between the
floorboards above our heads, the glintings too irregular to
suggest any attempt at peering down our way.

But these sideswipes of light were enough to tease angles
and curves of Luke's face and shoulders from the darkness. That
was a shame for, blanched by the pale glintings, he struck me as
suddenly aged and withered, stripped of his beauty - barely
worth the effort, one might have reckoned.

The intruders above could be heard arguing about what
they had heard: whether it was gun shots, and if it was did it
make sense to be checking it out themselves, as opposed to
getting straight on the mobile to the police? Or was it all a false
alarm and should they be getting back to their golf before the
bloody course flooded? Then a new set of steps came thumping
in, knocking dust down around us, a voice declaring that the
speaker had caught sight of Rick Hutcher's Mercedes tucked
away at the bottom of the lane and did anyone know what that
was all about?

"Okay, okay," someone said, "It's nothing, I bet you, but
get on the phone to the police, anyhow!" Another voice
bellowed the length and depth and height of the house, declaring
that if anyone was in there who wasn't supposed to be there,
then "You'd better show yourselves because the police - the
polis! - they're on their way! Pronto!"

The torch-glints had deserted Luke's face for a moment,
but now they caught at his features again, just as he was in the

269

act of looking upward, hesitantly parting his lips, his tongue-tip licking moisture into them. I touched a finger of my free hand to those lips, sealing them. He looked at me and I felt a shudder deeper within me than the damp and cold of that cellar could reach. The thought of Mexico, its heat and colour, its distance from the Mearns, shimmered before me. Wishing I had never thought of revenge, I turned, took the first cold, wet step back towards the warmth and brilliance of my second and truer home.

We caught the sound of a car crunching up the gravel outside the house, so swift in its approach I reckon we all, above and below, thought it set to collide with the front wall. The intruders above yelled their trepidation, Luke fixing a fresh grip on my arm, the right this time, and pulling me back a step, as if expecting the vehicle to come crashing through the cellar's ceiling.

The wheels skidded to a halt just short of the kitchen wall and, with the engine left running, there followed the sound of one of the car's doors swinging open, a pair of light, swift feet hurrying back and forth outside, Luke's name called again and again in what distinctly, even with a ceiling and a wall in the way, was his sister's voice. I felt Luke's hand begin to slip from my arm: the very thing I had wanted a moment before, although suddenly it felt like an abandonment.

The voices and footsteps already inside hurried towards Laura's, directions for entry being shouted, these followed by a clatter of kick-ass heels on the floorboards above. Luke's hand had, by now, let go my arm entirely. As his sister alternated shouts of "Luke!" and "Dad!", I turned to my partner in darkness and, with the straying flits of torchbeam again glancing across his features, saw something very like hope flicker about his blood-spotted pallor, hope of something to live for on the far side of this brutal moment, hope of arms that might embrace and forgive him, guide him to some fresh beginning: a sister's arms.

I saw that hope twitch his lips apart, preparatory to a call her way, a watery step threatening to carry him past me. Brother and sister, they lay adrift, at my hand, in the widest, deepest lake of Hell, but still had one another to cling to - which meant

270

they had a hell of a lot more than I had known since their family murdered *you*, Alec. Which struck me as a crime.

As he took another onward step, I caught Luke's arm with my free hand. He glanced my way, the next downward flit of torchlight rendering his expression only murkily visible. But I detected there impatience with an obstacle to his own selfish happiness. He was still a child, after all, and who knew more than I did about the callousness of children?

His sister called his name again. I saw him draw the breath for calling back. And I decided I'd witnessed one injustice too many.

I swung my right hand. The object it held - which I only now realised was the short, broad knife Dad used on his fishing trips, some of them to that pool where his son would later drown - sank its hooked end in the side of Luke's neck, as if some spirit with sharper eyes than mine for the dark were guiding my hand. The brightest flit yet of torchlight from above caught a renewed blossoming of Luke's beauty, courtesy of the gasp convulsing his features, a blossom of blood shaking its petals from his severed artery.

He raised a hand towards the spurtings. The white hand was instantly, impotently, gloved in the blood's darkness, bouncing the black fluid back across features twitching and quaking, the black centres of his eyes swelling as he grasped how dead he was. His whole body began to shudder, to sway; I struggled to drag the knife's end free, spatters of blood soaking my own hand, beading my own face, hotter still than my tears. Luke's legs spasmed from under him, dragging us into a shared fall. I landed on top, his wound and the knife's end disappearing underwater, only the upper portions of his face remaining unsubmerged, the rent in his artery blowing bubbles through the murk's surface.

We lay there, close-pressed as lovers, while the intruders above blundered around, oblivious, the sister's callings of "Luke...? Luke...?" sounding like an echo of the silent horror filling my own skull. Luke's arms rose around me, feeling less like those of someone fighting off his killer than those of a lover indeed, a little shaky and shy over his partner's maturer ardour

271

but matchingly sincere. I loved you, Luke, more than even murder could say.

Ripping the knife free, I clamped my hand across your face, pushing it under. Your hands spasmed into fighting me, feebly, for a moment, until your arms sank at either side of me. And as the last black bubble from your dying popped, the thought swelled in my mind of how much finer a revenge I might have won had I let you live, loving me, stolen you away, wafted you off with me to wilder, warmer places. We might have lived naked in some jungle, chewing scarlet fruit and sending postcards declaring our perversities to your Mum and Dad back home: fiery life my vengeance, not cold and watery death.

But it was a little late for a notion like that and so I rose and retreated from the mess I had made, knowing whatever was best in me drowned deeper there than Luke or his father.

Fifty Three

I took with me the gun, my departing caress of Luke's corpse having located it within his waistband. I crept up the cellar steps and gazed the length of the kitchen to where three figures stood looking through the hole in the floor beneath which Hutcher lay, muttering their confusion as to what the hell the beam of the torch one of them held had settled on. Two of them, including the torch-bearer, were male: golf-club types in saturated cagouls and waterproof trousers, the other being Laura. I think she recognised first what they were looking at: recognised and then refused to recognise, striding on into the hallway and calling up the stairs for her brother and father.

I began to back away towards the exit at my end of the kitchen. My feet could not help giving the rubble on the floor a discreet scraping, but I think it was less this than some profounder alertness on Laura's part that saw her turning my way.

Her expression, to the extent that I could make it out in what was, at best, a half-light, seemed less one of shock or outrage, however ghastly and blood-soaked I must have looked, than of a cautious bewilderment, followed by a shudder the length of her. I wondered if she hadn't mistaken me for a ghost, which of course, in a way, I was. And like a ghost of the most portentous sort, I pointed towards the doorway for the cellar stairs.

Grabbing the torch from the man at her side, she started walking my way, turning that white glare upon me. I shielded my eyes with a hand still dripping blood and continued backing off. Past the glare, I thought I could see comprehension sap the blood from her features; we enjoyed, I suppose, a mutual understanding in that moment such as few people can share

273

without killing one another. It was a little intense, even for a killer like me and so I turned and moved off at a swift limp.

Exiting through the adjoining byre, I heard Laura's steps accelerating across the kitchen and tensed myself for her catching up with me. But her steps veered towards the cellar and I relaxed somewhat, if only in resignation over how deep a horror I had directed her to.

Stepping out into the chilly, rainy breeze, I saw how dark the clouds above the golf course had grown, night swashing ahead of time over the crumbling shore of the wet afternoon. I had, of course, had to abandon the rucksack under the sink; even with the faked passport in the back pocket of my jeans, I wondered how far I thought I could get, and this even before I noticed the plump figure blocking the short stretch of weed-sprouting ground between myself and the road.

The figure had its back to me, the hood of its grey waterproof poncho up, the tail of that voluminous garment flapping in the wind. The figure had a finger pressed in one ear, a mobile phone held against the other, words barked into the phone reaching me on the breeze as, on a whim, I aimed the gun at the back of the figure's head.

"…That's right! Gunshots! Yes!" the figure was saying. "We were just finishing a round of golf and we heard… well, I don't know, but I reckon it ought to be checked out, and by someone other than us poor bastards! The Mearns may be the Mearns, but where's safe these days? I'm telling you -…."

Sensing me a few steps behind, the figure turned, a gust of wind blowing the hood off his head, exposing the balding combed-over pate and well-fed features of Hector, the Hutchers' house guest a few nights before. He registered my preparedness to blow his brains in the general direction of the 18th. hole by extending his mobile my way. "Here - !" he said. "Take it, please! It's a Nokia! Latest model!"

And then I saw him recognise me, his features inching towards a smile, only to draw back from it, as if in presentiment of all he was about to discover.

"What…" he sputtered past the rain on his face, "…what are you doing here?"

I lowered the gun. There was something sacred, I concluded, in horror such as I had wrought; I opted not to profane it with the spilling of blood as trivial as his.

"I live here," I said.

Fifty Four

Yet, when the first echoes of Laura's cries from the cellar reached me, I felt a renewed urge to get far away as fast as I could. I staggered forward. Hector caught my gun arm, only to jump back so nervously that for a second I couldn't be sure I hadn't shot him. Reassuring myself that I wouldn't have failed to notice the bang or smell the mess the bullet would have made of his blubber, I limped on, only to stop halfway across the narrow road, halfway to the bushes that would have helped conceal my escape, having caught the clatter of Laura's swift ascent from the basement.

I turned, looked back towards the house. Yelling "She's got a gun - a gunnnn!!!", Hector hurled himself face down in the tall grass before the boarded up windows. Laura lurched into view, bedraggled and bone-white, the torch abandoned below in the dark. She hastened my way. I raised the gun. She halted. I hurled the gun towards her. It landed on the ground just short of her. She stared at it a second, before picking it up and aiming it my way.

I took a step back, readying myself for whatever she had it in herself to do. This, I thought, might be my masterstroke: to die, like you Alec, at a Hutcher's hand, my ghost united with yours in the grounds of our old home, our enemies squandering the chance to be innocent victims this time round. Such an idea hadn't occurred to me two seconds before, but now it seemed the conclusion I should have been working towards all along.

As the wind across the golf course kissed roughly at the back of my neck, I looked up and away from Laura's struggle to master the trigger, taking in the windows of the house's top floor. As the gun went off, I blinked hard and when my eyes reopened I thought, looking through the upward drift of

276

gunsmoke, that the boards had disappeared from my own window. There, in the dark behind the glassless frame, stood *you*, Alec, looking down at me with a sadness I assumed, at first, was sadness over my reckless abandonment of life. But then, as I shivered in the redoubled grasp of the damp afternoon, I realised it was a further postponement of our reunion you sorrowed over.

I looked down. Laura still held the smouldering gun, its barrel aimed at the ground alongside her, a similarly smouldering mess of splintered stone at the spot she had wasted the bullet on. Hector was rising from the grass, inching towards Laura's gun hand, his golfing companions cautiously emerging from the house. Laura looked at me, the churning sorrow and fury upon her face now setting to a wind-gnawed hardness, very like that of the haunted house at her back.

Hector and co. approached me, curving about me the little line they formed so as to block any route of escape, rain-swept faces scowling at my villainy without any of them finding the nerve to lay a hand on me. The one to my right gestured to Hector, who crossed back to Laura, encouraging her towards the house. She nodded and turned with him, his arm slipping around her shoulders. It was only as they neared the entrance that she began screaming and had to be all but wrestled inside.

"Right, come on," the fellow who had sent Hector off said without meeting my eyes, a tilt of his head indicating the golf club, "Let's sit and wait for the police somewhere out of this rain."

"I'm not," I explained, "A member of your fucking golf club," and limped back towards the house. They meekly followed. My God: what a terrible, inexplicable creature I must have struck them as. My God: what a terrible, inexplicable creature I am.

Fifty Five

By the time I had ascended into the kitchen, Laura had conveniently been shifted towards some nook at the far end of the hallway, for although I could not see her, her screams - in effect, a single scream splintered into a hundred pieces by the recapturings of breath it demanded - kept stabbing at me from that quarter, until one half-feared the house might collapse with the racket.

It came as a perverse relief, therefore, when police sirens began hastening their own cacophony up the road outside. DS Galbraith - whose name I had suggested to my captors when they made a second call - arrived amid a flood of flashing blue light, surveying me with unmistakeable anxiety over how it was going to look, in both the station canteen and the media, when word got around of how signally she'd failed to detect my murderous tendencies. "You and me are overdue for an intimate conversation," she said, after returning from the cellar. "Tragically overdue."

"If I have anything to say," I shrugged, "I'll say it where the world can hear."

"The world's out that door," she sighed. "Let's go."

She and a brick shithouse of a constable were steering me out into what was by now very definitely night when another, instantly familiar, car screeched to a stop at the road's far side, Amelia climbing out. Seeing me, she shivered, began to sag at the knees, then clung to the car's door frame while she straightened herself up. DS Galbraith gestured to a WPC, who hastened Amelia's way. Amelia wriggled past her, advancing on those wobbly legs to confront me with the stare a cavewoman might have shown a solar eclipse: wonderment stirred in with her horror.

278

"Who are you?" she whispered.

"Someone who knows who *you* are," I quietly replied. "Or were. Which is bad enough."

She caught my shoulders, giving me a pathetic little shake even as Galbraith and the uniformed officers tried to ease us apart.

"*Who are you?*" she asked again.

"I'm a summer's day," I said, "Come back to haunt you on a rainy evening. You remember, Amelia, the sunny days of your childhood? One of them at least? What about that day you signed your unborn child over to a future like this, using another young man's blood for ink?"

Her hands slid from me. I could see the memories bubbling, nice and slow, up through the floorboards of her spick-and-span mind. The police led me by her. Her attack, a couple of seconds later, caught me by surprise, her clawed hands sinking so deep into my shoulder that when the cops dragged us apart, the sleeve of my coat was ripped half away. She began screaming, a couple of male constables hauling her aside, that immaculately coiffed and made-up face shaking itself into a chaos like a raw wound overspilling its bandages.

Behind the back seat window of Amelia's car's, Emily stared out, features chalk-white against the darkness of the car's interior, the glass in front of her nose and mouth misting with condensation to make something ghostly of her stare, her expression a silent outcry of rage at my betrayal. I and my drama classes had encouraged Emily clear of silence and shyness and now into silence she was shrinking back, this fresh silence a thousand leagues deeper.

They put me, tender-hearted things, into the back of an ambulance, the paramedics encouraging me to lie down while they cut away the denim around my wounded calf. Just as D.S Galbraith was climbing in and reaching back to pull the doors closed, I heard a muffled cry from outside and then saw Emily, escaped from Amelia's car, running up and stopping just on the other side of the remaining gap. And the look she fixed my way told me that if and when I got out of prison, this child would be waiting for me, this child the same age as I was when I saw *you* killed. She'd be a woman by then, a woman like me, woman enough to work up a vengeance as terrible as my own. There was, I saw in that little face and vast stare, no escape for me.

Her grandmother appeared, drew her away. Galbraith slammed the doors and the ambulance sped off with a snarl of farmyard gravel. I lay back, knowing I was going nowhere that Emily's stare wouldn't haunt me.

Fifty Six

Lying there, my drugged gaze wandering through the window alongside, I marvelled at the way the warm and homely light behind the windows of the tickety-boo housefronts seemed to banish, to shrink to nothing, the wetness and wildness of the night: this, after all, was the optical illusion Newton Mearns was built around.

I had always loved the place, don't get me wrong; and for all my eagerness to tell my story in court, for all my fancy of the sheer weight of scandal and revelation burying the Mearns as the rainforests once engulfed the cities of the Aztecs, I couldn't find it in my heart to wish the place wholly destroyed. It was one vast lie, that suburb, but it was a charming one, the lie I had grown up with. Hadn't it helped make me the charming liar I was?

I recalled that matchingly rainy morning when I made my return, sat on the 44 bus, dreaming of being the murderess I now was. I had accomplished so much, yet had to ask myself if it was nearly enough. Hadn't I, after all, come back not merely to seek vengeance for your death, Alec, but to somehow dredge you yourself, my sense of you, further out of that void of dissolving memories in which Hutcher had sunk you? Hadn't I run this race in expectation of finding you waiting to embrace me on the finishing line, the most substantial of phantoms?

But there I was, resplendent in my war-wounds on that triumphant evening, and you suddenly felt further away than ever. And now I didn't even have Luke. It was very cold without him. I loved him, I suppose, as much as I love you, Alec. That love was the most monstrous of my crimes. It persecutes me still.

I closed my eyes, tried to picture sunlight on boyish skin.

But only an image of black beads of water pressing on a sunken car window - or was it black bubblings from a cut in a submerged throat? - solidified for me, so I opened my eyes again and saw that we had left Newton Mearns behind and were almost at the city boundary, my only true home now lost for good.

It's for you, Alec, I've written all this down, (an Aztec curse, of course, on any other nosy bastard who reads it) in the hope that the shedding of ink might conjure you where blood has failed. And still your ghost deserts me, as it has ever since my crime was completed. When I saw that ghost before, was it just a fantasy? Was Hutcher right? Had your ghost been and gone and passed on its curse long before I got there: passing it on by filling that kid with a love innocent as yours, all those years before? Making my own vengeance - so corrupting and destructive of love - a waste of time and life, my own as much as theirs? What spectre have I been chasing that dumps me in the dark of this cell, so lonely?

Won't you swim to me through your blackness while I swim to you through mine? Somewhere between life and death we must surely, finally, reach one another. Have faith, Alec: I'm a murderess. I know that borderline well.

Lightning Source UK Ltd.
Milton Keynes UK
171602UK00001B/10/P